Praise for *Murky Overhead*

"*Murky Overhead* reminded me of so many memories of growing up on Munjoy Hill. It actually made me feel better about myself. Mike Connolly could not have done a better job in capturing the spirit of those times, and I found that his words agreed with the long-held thoughts of my own mind."

~ Joseph E. Brennan, former two-term Maine Governor and
a longtime resident of Portland's Munjoy Hill

"This book goes deep into the lives and into the hearts of Irish emigrants in Portland, Maine, at the turn of the 20th Century. It resonates with me, as my own family experienced many of the same triumphs and difficulties as the family depicted in this true-to-life historical novel. My father, John Walsh, emigrated from the area of Callowfeenish, on the far west coast of Connemara, the same area from where one of the main characters in this book, Coley Folan, left for America. My mother is from the neighboring area of Ros Muc. These stories of emigrants' courage and heartache are central to the story of America."

~ Martin J. Walsh, Secretary of Labor for the United States
and former Mayor of Boston

"Michael Connolly is a renowned historian of the Irish in Maine, who has worked extensively with the Maine Irish Heritage Center to research and communicate the experience of the generations of Irish immigrants who settled in Portland and elsewhere in Maine. In *Murky Overhead*, he combines historical fiction with meticulous research to bring to life in vivid detail the hopes, struggles and dreams of those Irish who made their homes in this 'next parish west of Galway.'

~ Laoise Moore, Consul General of Ireland for New England

"Coley Folan and Mary Joyce could be the ancestors of millions of Irish Americans. While the author has set *Murky Overhead* in the genre of historical fiction, this story of emigration from the rural west of Ireland, and from the Gaelic-speaking communities, encapsulates the reality of leaving a poverty-stricken land in the 19th Century and survival on a lowly rung in America. The focus is on Portland, Maine, but the story can be related to any city where the Irish made a home in the United States."

~ Máirtín Ó Catháin, Chairman of the
Center, Carna, County Galway, Ire

"As a longtime colleague of Michael Connolly's, and also a descendant of Irish immigrants, I am delighted to find in *Murky Overhead* the historian meet the novelist. Having studied extensively the story of Irish longshoremen on Portland's docks, Professor Connolly has brought that history alive with deeply engaging characters facing the challenges of building a new life in a new world."

> ~ Edward J. Rielly, Professor Emeritus of Saint Joseph's College (Maine) and author, among many other books, of *Baseball: An Encyclopedia of Popular Culture* and *Legends of American Indian Resistance*

"Connolly enriches a familiar plot with a thorough knowledge and empathy for the Irish, a people he knows, loves, and respects. Readers will gain valuable insight regarding the cultures, history, and politics of both Connemara and Portland, as well as becoming aware of the Irish words and phrases, mythology, and stories Connolly liberally sprinkles throughout. The native Irish immigrants were a tough and tender people, and he captures their transformation from poverty-stricken immigrants to American citizens with grace, humor, admiration, and love. Connolly loves his people and readers will, too."

> ~ Morgan Callan Rogers, author of *Red Ruby Heart in a Cold Blue Sea* and *Written on My Heart*

"*Murky Overhead* resonates with the rich speech, known in Irish as the *blas*, that the people of Connemara, and particularly those from *Cois Fharraige* and *Cárna*, brought with them to Portland's dockside neighborhoods mere generations ago. The music, wisdom, and wit of the Irish come alive effortlessly in Michael Connolly's downeast historical fiction."

> ~ Brian Frykenberg, New England and the Irish Language Oral History Project, *Cumann na Gaeilge i mBoston*.

Murky Overhead

A novel by

Michael C. Connolly

TOWER
PUBLISHING

The book can be ordered through Tower Publishing:
via our website: www.TowerPub.com (direct link: https://tinyurl.com/Murky-Overhead)
or on www.Amazon.com
or by calling Tower Publishing directly at 1-800-969-8693

Cover designed by: Rebecca Blaesing, Design & Branding

Cover illustration: *Precautious Dawn* (detail), oil on canvas, 2020
used with permission from the artist, Holly E. Gilfillan Ready

ISBN-13: 978-1-7355660-6-1

PRINTED IN THE UNITED STATES OF AMERICA

10 9 8 7 6 5 4 3 2   1

DEDICATION

To all immigrants everywhere – may your roads be made easy.
(*Go n-éirígh an bóthar libh*)

To my kind and gentle Irish relatives who helped my Irishness come alive,
especially Babe Folan of Callowfeenish and Babe Greene of Mynish.

And in particular, to two kindred souls who spent their lifetimes
preserving and promoting Gaelic culture:
Claire J. McAleese Foley (nee Ward) and Dr. Kenneth E. Nilsen.

Is glas iad no cnoic i bhfad uainn.
(Faraway hills are green)

Table of Contents

Part I Morning – "At the Dawning of the Day"

Sea Smoke   3

Mother of Pearl   18

Marcusin's Dog   37

Murky Overhead   57

The World's a Bubble   74

Why Women Sin   96

Part II Afternoon – "Let the Echoes Ring"

Strange Bedfellows   115

Coxey's Army   130

Between a Rock and a Hard Place   142

Broken Irish   153

Never be Dull Again   163

In the Land of the Blind   175

Part III Evening – "The Wealth of Nature"

Solidarity Forever   195

Every Child is a Blessing   209

The Great Commoner   222

A Labor of Love   234

Homeward Bound   242

Between the Dark and the Daylight   259

Preface

Murky Overhead is a work of historical fiction that tells the story of a day in the life of a typical Irish-American working-class family, the Folans. It follows them on the streets and docks of their new American home in maritime Portland, Maine, at the turn of the 20th century.

While Coleman (Coley) shovels coal for the longshore union, his wife Mary, who is nearly full-term with their 10th child, does her best to keep the family going. Challenges abound. Coley has suffered from periodic bouts of binge drinking that have put the well-being of him and the family at risk. But presently, he is "on the wagon" and working – for the moment, at least. Mary is the stalwart rock that manages to hold things together despite the current and every-growing number of hurdles her family faces.

They both must take on each new day one at a time. The labor is taking its toll, and it remains to be seen if Mary's eternal optimism will be enough to get them through. Some days the prospects of the Folans appear to be murky, at best.

Part I ~ Morning

"At the Dawning of the Day"

"And the larks they sang melodious at the dawning of the day."

~ Popular sea-inspired love ballad

Chapter 1

Sea Smoke

"The man who has experienced shipwreck
shudders even at a calm sea."

– Ovid

... hills are green. Hills covered in green, many shades of green, both summer
and winter. How many shades? It is green all year round in Ireland, not like in
Portland. Where am I now, in America or in Galway? Am I asleep or awake?
If I'm dreaming, where does the dream end and the real world begin?
Why can't I sleep and dream just a wee bit longer?

These and other thoughts danced on and off in the mind of a man caught between wake and sleep, between warm and cold, between his old and new homes. Why did it have to be so – couldn't he simply let this pleasant dream go on just a little longer? Sadly, the green was fading and was now being replaced by a contrasting vision of a cold, bleak, icy-white reality that was his home in Portland in the midst of a harsh Maine winter.

This pleasant reminiscence of Ireland was overtaken by a dream not nearly as sanguine. It all seemed so real. Somewhere in the depths of Coleman Folan's consciousness there was an intense confrontation playing out that involved the most serious of consequences. This frightening threat to the very survival of his family appeared to be clearer and more ominous by the moment.

"No, this must be a bad dream – this can't really be happening..."

"I'm afraid it's not a dream, Coley. As you know we've been down this road before. Do you recall the last time that you were away from work for several weeks? You put your gang at a severe disadvantage! It occurred at a very busy time for us all."

"Yes, but my gang boss hired one of the youngsters to take my place. It was all taken care of, or so I thought."

"Well, it was sorted out temporarily. You'll remember, I'm sure, that you made a promise to me as the walking boss that you'd stay off the drink, at least

3

during the busy winter season longshore – do you remember promising that, Coley?"

"I do, and I've done my very best..."

"Unfortunately, your best was simply not good enough, at least not this time. The union has covered for you far too often, and we're getting into real trouble with the shipping agents. They are now threatening to re-open their contract with the Portland Longshoremen's Benevolent Society [PLSBS] unless we fire any members who have missed work on more than two occasions due to the drink – and as you know, you're not the only one."

"But I thought the PLSBS would protect me..."

"We've tried, but at some point you have to take responsibility for your own actions. We have to look out for the good of the union as a whole, not just for you even though you are one of our Charter Members. And we've bent over backwards already on your behalf, two or three times at least."

"But what about my family and what am I to do about my Mary? You know that she's expecting again any day now, and this will be our ninth child, not counting poor William, God rest his soul. How am I supposed to pay the rent and feed my family? How am I to buy coal for them? It's Christly frigid outside! I signed the Society's original Charter back in 1880, you know, even if only with my X."

"Well, Coley, you might have thought more about your family before going off on this latest drinking binge. You promised me that you'd stay 'on the wagon,' but now you've let us all down once again."

"But how will I provide for my family, you've not told me that, and how on earth can I even begin to tell this to Mary?"

"You'd best go see Father Draine at the Cathedral – perhaps he might be able to provide some sort of assistance to your family."

"This must be just a bad dream – this can't really be happening to me... It must be a dream... Can this really be happening?"

Coleman Folan slowly and reluctantly awoke to the cold darkness of his sparsely furnished bedroom. He had partially shaken off what must have been a bad dream – he had them at times. Yes, it was just another of his bad dreams, like so many that crowded out the happier dreams of earlier times in Ireland. In some ways he felt relieved to awaken and put it aside, but his stomach was still in knots because this particular dream always seemed so very real, a recurring nightmare that struck at his very core. It always stung and pained him greatly.

In the distance, Coleman could hear the mournful, lonely droning of the fog horn at Portland Head which told him that it could be yet another inclement day of work on the docks. He would likely be confronted either by the mysterious sea smoke, an eerie swirling kind of harbor fog present only on the most bitterly cold days of the year, or more likely the omnipresent light blowing snow that regularly lessened the visibility here and all along the Maine coast.

The midwinter weather had been atrocious lately. The crews of incoming ships were all very much relieved merely to have reached land safely. A local newspaper had recently reported on winter's travail: "The North Atlantic is a gay old bird at this season of the year and the steamer people say the season is a terror."

An officer of a ship that had only recently arrived in Portland reportedly remarked graphically to one of the local longshoremen, 'We made practically a submarine passage.' When another local attempted to encourage him with the prospect of improved weather by the time of his departure, the officer, an educated man, knowingly responded, 'The man who has experienced shipwreck shudders even at a calm sea.'

Coleman was reminded of the ferocious storms of the previous winter, one of which had claimed the passenger vessel *Portland* with the loss of over one hundred souls. A local newspaper confirmed his memory of that event, "The storm of Monday was a terror, only second to the great storms of last year." The article compared conditions lately with those at the time of the loss of the *Portland* when "the entire New England coast was lined with wreckage."

Regardless of the weather, Coleman soon arose in the dark and prepared for another long day of work unloading coal near the Randall and McAllister dock. The most recently arrived steamer had deposited over 3,000 tons of coal. Local business concerns felt that with winter now officially one month along, or nearly one-third complete, their stock of coal would be sufficient. With such frigid temperatures at this time of the year, however, it would only take one or two unexpected reversals to change matters in an instant – to say nothing of the fate of the poor sailors who delivered this crucial product and faced these threats directly on the open seas, the menacing and unpredictable ocean highway.

Today, Coleman would work again on the coal steamer *Avona* that had arrived the previous day from Louisburg, Nova Scotia. He was pleased that the labor of unloading this ship would give both him and his gang steady work for the next few days at least. The *Avona* carried 3,677 tons of coal for the Maine Central Railroad as well as 250 tons of bunker coal. Its voyage had not been pleasant, and the newspapers reported, "She came in iced to the bridge and showing in every possible way the evidence of a hard pounding."

It was a Wednesday, the last day of January in the year 1900. Coleman thought this would be a day not unlike most other days in his life and the lives of his fellow Irish longshoremen. They were now living in a very different environment, no longer that of Ireland but now under the changed sky of Portland, Maine. These few moments between his waking and rising were Coleman's own. He would often pleasantly reminisce about the circumstances that had brought him to his present condition.

~ ~ ~

Coley, as he was known to his family and friends, was now forty-one, some twenty years removed from when he had left the tiny townland of Callowfeenish (*Calibhfuinse*) along the Atlantic shore of County Galway, Ireland. There were many reasons why he and thousands like him had already or would soon emigrate from that region of south Connemara known locally as *Iorras Aithneach,* or from the coastal areas nearer to Galway City known locally as *Cois Fharraige* (Beside the Sea). As a ubiquitous agricultural laborer and the son of poor, landless parents, Coleman had few prospects for success in Ireland. America seemed to him like a safety valve, or almost more like a distant magnet attracting thousands like him to its shores.

Armed with the knowledge that his sister Catherine, known by all as Caita, would stay behind in Callowfeenish to care for their parents, Coley felt both prepared and justified in leaving on this self-imposed exile from all that he knew and loved. Widespread crop failure again began threatening Ireland just the year before in 1879. Fearing the possibility of yet another devastating famine such as that which had decimated the western regions of Ireland just one generation earlier, he and countless other hundreds of thousands had ventured off in search of their mythical *Tír na n-Óir* (Country of Gold) in far-off America.

Along with friends from the parish of Ballinahinch, Coley set off in the spring of 1880, first by donkey cart and foot to Galway City, nearly fifty miles away, and from there by train to Cork. A Cunard liner awaited them at the harbor of Cobh, then known as Queenstown. This represented his first experience with both of these modern modes of transportation. Soon aboard a steamship, they were all bidding farewell, most of them tearfully, to Saint Colman's Church steeple, one of the last images of their homeland. Almost before they were emotionally ready, they were steaming toward Boston or Pennsylvania, or some other strange sounding place in America.

Coley was happy to be on a steamer. He had heard of the long, difficult passages to America by the older sailing ships, but by now the steamer could make the voyage in about two weeks, less than half the time required for the even more arduous earlier crossings that were entirely dependent upon the presence, direction, and velocity of the wind.

As if he was already a seasoned traveler, Coley declared to a good friend from his local parish, 'Sure, the steamer is the only way to travel.' And now feeling quite full of himself, he proceeded to loudly proclaim to anyone within hearing range of his broken English, always colorfully influenced by his own native Irish language, 'Don't I feel like I'm being lifted on the wings of good fortune!' And so he was.

In addition to the many reasons pushing him to leave Callowfeenish and Ireland, there were also numerous attractions drawing him and many of his closest friends to America. Letters from earlier Irish emigrants who had settled in Maine had indicated that, despite its severe winters and the occasional unfriendly attitude of some native Yankees, America could at least offer the opportunity of work. A laborer's earnings here were much greater than anything Coley could have hoped for in Ireland, but every bit of that was needed, as good steady wages were necessary to pay for the relatively costly clothing, food, heat, and especially rents.

Oh, if only to own your own home in America! Well, that would remain a dream to be fulfilled by their children or grandchildren – providing that they, like him, would be hard-working, frugal, healthy, and lucky. It was indeed true that, as in the old Irish saying, '*Talamh gan cios o'n bhliain seo amach*' (Land without taxes from this year out) was a dream on both sides of the Atlantic!

By 1900, the depression of the early 1890s in America was finally ending and modest prosperity seemed to be returning, even to the working poor, or so it was being reported. The contrast between the Old World and the New could hardly have been more stark. Portland, Maine, was his destination. Coley's uncle and several other friends and relatives from south Connemara had already successfully found work there on the Grand Trunk, Maine Central, Boston and Maine, or Portland and Rochester Railroads.

Some found construction work on one of the numerous downtown building sites, a few of which now had work gangs with Irish bosses. One or two of these large construction companies were even managed by Irish owners only one generation removed from poverty in the Old Country – imagine what Ireland might have looked like, he often thought, if only these workers could have labored for improvements there! What a fantastic development, and what an opportunity this presented to unskilled Irish male laborers like himself.

Single Irish women were numerous in Portland, and often found labor as domestic workers in the Falmouth Hotel, or other similar settings, such as the homes of the wealthy Yankee families living along its beautiful, albeit socially inaccessible, Western and Eastern Promenades. But Coley's more realistic and scaled-down dream was to find work as a longshoreman along Portland's waterfront. From the many letters mailed from Portland back to relatives in Callowfeenish, he had heard that the Irish dominated the local docks and that wages were good from steady work, at least during the frigid winter months. Other types of manual work such as construction could be found in the otherwise quiet shipping season during the summer months and into the early fall.

One recent immigrant had written to his family in Ireland that there was also plenty of Irish spoken by Portland's longshore workers, and that anyone from Callowfeenish would feel right at home here. Another wrote about the abundance of work and the large number of Irish being hired. He colorfully claimed, 'There would be one thousand sure. It would look like Holy Name Sunday up at Saint Dominic's! O, jeepers, the place would be packed.'

Coley always regretted not staying longer in Boston after his ship first arrived, for he had never been back in the twenty years since. From what he had seen in the harbor alone, he knew that Boston was by far the largest city he'd yet visited. Of course, Coley had only been to Clifden in far western County Galway a few times for tools. He had never even been to the city of Galway, except just that once while in transit to the steamer that would take him to America.

Upon passing a simple medical check at immigration control in Boston, and assuring the officials there that he was not completely without financial resources (only partially true), Coley quickly proceeded to an adjacent dock where he was told by a friendly Irish dockhand that the *Bay State*, one of the nightly mail boats belonging to the Portland Steamship Company, would later be sailing directly for Portland. The trip would cost $1.00, but he was not yet familiar enough with American money to relate that amount to the British Pound Sterling, about which he had only the most cursory familiarity in any case. He was about to spend his first American dollar! The dockhand himself had only arrived from Galway six months earlier and had already landed a steady job here in Boston. Coley marveled that the stories he had heard about America seemed true. In his own native language he was informed, 'You can travel to Portland aboard the *Governor Dingley* or the *Bay State*. These ships will arrive in Portland at the Franklin Wharf and return to Boston, one or the other, every evening at seven o'clock.'

Coley later discovered that in 1880 for the value of $1.00 a person could buy a pair of ladies' walking shoes or men's strap shoes which could be seen displayed in the glass window of the W.P. Goss Company then located on the ground floor of the Falmouth Hotel at 212 Middle Street in Portland's downtown. Coffee was then selling for 15 cents a pound, and a boy's all-wool suit could be had for between $6.00 and $7.00.

By the turn of the twentieth century and after living in America for twenty years, Coley knew that this same $1.00 would represent about half a day's union wages. Most of Portland's labor unions by this time averaged a pay scale of between $1.75 and $3.50 for a ten-hour day. He thought that he was doing quite well. But by now there were several mouths to feed in the Folan family, and somehow all the money that Coley earned, and then some, was sorely needed for daily expenses.

He still smiled when he remembered his arrival into Portland. How much Maine's rocky coastline had reminded him of the shoreline of his native Connemara! The natural and well-protected harbor of Portland looked remarkably similar to harbors in Galway, such as Roundstone or Kilkerrin, or even the larger Queenstown in County Cork from which he had only recently departed. The islands of Casco Bay reminded him fondly of Mynish, Feenish or even the more remote Furnace, Dinish, or *Inis Bearacháin* back home.

Before the *Bay State* was firmly secured at Portland's Franklin Wharf, someone had already notified Coley's uncle of his imminent arrival, and his uncle was there to greet him at the pier with a smile. What a difference that had made to Coleman!

Within a week he was working as a longshoreman in a gang that included his uncle and several others from south Connemara, all of whom were Irish speakers like himself. Someone had told him once that Galway had the highest number of Irish speakers in the whole of Ireland, and that the local newspapers reported that this amounted to about seventy percent of the total population. But that seemed low to Coley because everyone he knew at home, with the exception of a few government workers who periodically ventured out from Clifden or Galway City, spoke Irish.

The Galway men were among the last to give up the Irish (Gaelic) language, even here in Portland. There were still a few who could speak no English at all, but they seemed to somehow get along just fine as long as they remained within the Irish neighborhoods. One such person had recently returned to Carna after nearly two years in America, and Coley was told by one who knew this man well, almost boastfully, 'Even then he had hardly a single word of English on him!'

While this made Coley feel at home and comfortable to be among his own kind, he instinctively knew that in order to "get ahead" in Portland, sooner or later he and especially his children would have to succumb to this new language and many of America's other peculiar cultural customs and styles. This eventually became even more apparent in later years after his marriage and especially after the arrival of children, now numbering eight.

Coley also worried about whether the Irish language would survive in Portland at all. His children seemed to prefer to speak English to each other and especially amongst their closest school friends. Coley had once queried his sympathetic wife, 'Would Portland, Maine, be the place where our priceless heritage would finally be lost?' Only John, his eldest, had a smattering of the Gaelic language, the beloved and musical verse that had been spoken by countless generations of Folans well into the distant past.

~ ~ ~

All of these many thoughts and concerns seemed to slowly recede as the smell of bacon frying on the stove in the kitchen below coaxed Coley away from his dream state. Gently repositioning the youngest child, Michael – called Míchilín – on the pillow, Coley swiftly dressed himself in layers of cotton and wool. He had learned to anticipate the bitter cold of a late January day along Portland's waterfront. Looking outside he could see some small bits of blowing snow, and the frost inside his bedroom window told him that the temperature had again taken a downward turn.

The temperature extremes in Portland were much greater than in Ireland. Here they averaged about twenty degrees in the winter and seventy degrees in mid-summer. Roughly ten to twenty days annually in the winter had subzero readings, and then there were also those rare but dreaded ninety degree days in the summer. Both of these extremes were severe challenges to these Irish immigrants, but particularly the stifling summer heat.

What a change from Galway! Coley still had not completely adjusted to these extremes in weather in the twenty years he'd been living in Portland. Ireland's weather was much more temperate, usually varying only about twenty degrees throughout the year, ranging from about forty degrees in the winter to about sixty degrees in the summer. 'Everything in moderation,' the local Yankees here were quite fond of saying, which prompted Coley to once ask his best friend Joe Loftus, 'So why is this not true of their blasted weather?'

Coleman's wife, Mary Josephine Folan, having first stoked the fire, had his breakfast ready by the time he arrived in the kitchen. On most days Coley would quickly devour his morning meal, put on his final layer of clothing, kiss his wife, and then whisper a short prayer for both of them and for the protection of their children throughout each new day. Finally, he would summon up the courage to walk the short distance over to the Randall and McAllister Wharf just off Commercial Street. Work started for Coley and his gang at seven o'clock each morning. Whenever he walked to and from work, he felt comfortable in knowing how many longshoremen lived in that same waterfront district of Portland. He knew of no Irish longshoremen who didn't live either in the east or the west end of the city, the Cathedral parish or the Saint Dominic's parish, respectively.

Coleman eventually learned that it would have been very difficult to live elsewhere. For one thing, how would one get to work and back home each day unless you could walk? For another, the rents always seemed to be much cheaper the closer you were to the docks. He had often heard his wife proclaim, 'The rents downtown are entirely too dear, and we'd hardly know anyone there!'

And, finally, he believed that the Irish were not always welcomed outside of their own well-defined neighborhoods. So it seemed to Coley that he could make a virtue of a necessity. In any case, this was really not much of a stretch of the truth as he always maintained that he chose to live amongst his own. Coley wanted it to be his choice.

The Folan's rented tenement on the corner of Fore and Franklin Streets, at the foot of Munjoy Hill, was in the very heart of what had long been Portland's east end

Irish neighborhood. It was similar in many ways to Portland's other Irish enclave that spiraled out from Gorham's Corner in the west end of the city. These ten Folans crowded into five rooms, and the lack of space dictated that four of the younger children had to share one large bed. As tough a neighborhood as it was in 1900, it could hardly compare with reports of this same area just fifty years earlier.

Along Fore Street between Franklin and India, and nearly adjacent to where the Folans now resided, there had previously existed the infamous "Sebastopol" block. This area had been described in the mid-1850s as "a nest of rum shops and Irish habitations," and was even labeled by the noted Portland writer John Neal as "the Gomorrah of Portland." Ownership of this block had changed hands several times since just before the Civil War, and then in 1857 it was sold by Daniel Woodman Jr. to a Portland physician, Horatio G. Newton. This was obviously not a solid investment because the mortgage was foreclosed one year later by Moses Gould to whom it had been assigned. Gould was a developer of industry in the Back Bay area of the city and of housing on Portland's east end Munjoy Hill. He owned the entire parcel as late as 1872, just before Coley arrived to take up residence here and start his family.

The name "Sebastopol" came from the famous fortress Sevastopol in the Russian Crimea. Thus, it had obviously given its name to yet another fortress, this one being a crowded refuge for Portland's desperately poor Irish working class. Providing cheap housing for poor immigrants was an obvious challenge in a city like Portland where apartments were already scarce and the demand increasing almost daily. Such concentration of poverty often led to problems such as overcrowding, crime, abuse of alcohol, and even prostitution. Sebastopol over the years would see all of these urban blights, and more. Another tough neighborhood by the turn of the twentieth century was "The Bight," also located nearby at the base of Munjoy Hill near the intersection of Mountfort and Fore.

From the east end of Portland at the base of Munjoy Hill to Gorham's Corner in the west end, and along most of the smaller streets intersecting Fore Street such as Vine, Deer, and Chatham, the concentration of Irish and other first-generation immigrant families was intense. This was a run-down and exhausted neighborhood. Most of the Irish inhabitants, it seemed to Coley, were like himself from one of four regions of his own County Galway: *Cois Fharraige*, Connemara, *Calibhfuinse* (Callowfeenish), or Cornamona.

Although these regions in Galway were in relatively close proximity to each other, with none of these even much more than twenty or thirty miles apart, there was a tremendous sense of rivalry both in Ireland and now in Portland between the immigrants from each of these particular regions. A priest at the Cathedral had once told Coleman that the Irish were a parochial people wherever they lived. Coley, not knowing the meaning of "parochial," wasn't sure whether this was meant as a compliment or a criticism, but he dutifully had nodded in full agreement nonetheless.

Most of Coleman's fellow workers had not been born in America, but most were by now planning to stay here permanently. This was certainly true of his closest Irish friends. At least two-thirds of the Portland longshoremen had been born outside of America. Although he had heard of some foreign-born Portlanders returning to their places of birth, he had not heard of any Irish doing so. They liked the security of work here and the comfort of being in a familiar Irish neighborhood. With the Irish, when they came they stayed. Portland was now their home. Coley had more than once proclaimed, 'Portland will be the home of our children and, please God, of any of our future grandchildren. It's not Galway, but it's still a fine place to call home!'

The more Coleman worked the more he found that dock work was the domain of foreign-born, mainly Irish, laborers. In the city as a whole Yankees certainly predominated, especially in business and politics, but the waterfront was a different story. There the Irish were clearly in control. Coleman was typical in the manner in which he had taken out "Citizen Papers" to begin the process of naturalization as soon as he was eligible to do so. His unfortunate pronunciation of this important word made it sound more like "shitizen." Mary had instructed her children for their own good never to laugh at this slip of the tongue. Her husband was generally quite even-tempered, but he did not abide being challenged or ridiculed, especially within his own family. Mary was never quite sure whether this was a male or an Irish trait – or both.

Coleman and his fellow Irish longshoremen were encouraged by local Democratic ward captains to become naturalized as quickly as possible, and thereafter to actively support Democratic candidates at the local, state, and national levels. Although by 1900 no Irish politician had as yet broken the Yankee stranglehold on Portland's mayoralty, familiar surnames such as Driscoll or Milliken could be found among Portland's nine aldermen. Additionally, surnames such as Connellan, Griffin, Kavanough, McLaughlin, and Murphy were prominent among Portland's twenty-seven city councilors. The system in effect in Portland at the turn of the twentieth century consisted of a mayor, nine aldermen (one per ward), and twenty-seven councilors (three per ward).

The process of becoming naturalized and gaining the power of the vote, with the friendly assistance of an Irish-American ward boss, was more easily achieved in Portland than was the process of becoming fully accepted by the native Yankee elites. But that acceptance too, or so Coleman believed, would also come in God's own good time. He and his friends wasted little time in becoming Irish Americans – they chose to stay in Portland and to make the best of it.

Some of Coley's friends, especially when they had "too much drink taken," would wax poetic about "the old country" and speak in exaggerated nationalistic terms of England forcing the unwilling Irish to be exiled to the four corners of the globe. However, few if any ever voluntarily went back to live in Ireland, although the opportunity was certainly there for some to do so. Most of their wishful thinking now would be focused more practically on future generations. In that context, 1900 in America certainly had it all over Ireland as far as opportunity was concerned. At least this seemed to be true in Coley's humble opinion.

Of Coley's closest friends who were born in Ireland, almost all lived along or directly adjacent to the Portland waterfront. He had only recently learned that some of their children were starting to move away from the old neighborhoods even though their parents nearly always chose to stay put. These parents were comfortable to live where they were known by their own first names. Out of necessity, most of their older children, as with Coley's own, also lived at home as it often took their combined earnings to maintain any large household. Of those who married and moved out of the family home, most seemed to stay within the Irish neighborhoods, as these seemed to be the only places with affordable rents.

Coley had recently noticed that some of the younger and more affluent American-born, second-generation "corner boys," "native borns," "narrow backs," or "*amadáin* (fools)," as they were jokingly called, were apparently spreading their wings and choosing to live further up Munjoy Hill, or further west of Gorham's Corner, or in a few cases even on the west end of Congress Street. Although this demonstrated the type of freedom seemingly to be desired by the Portland Irish – a chance to live wherever they chose – Coley and his wife feared that this could also mean the beginning of the dissolution of the traditional Irish neighborhood.

The first generation Irish, represented by Coleman and Mary, viewed this development with a mixture of confusion, pride, jealousy, and concern. Although they instinctively knew that their dreams of success and acceptance would not be fully realized until their children, the second-generation Irish, were able to branch out in terms of labor and place of residence, they simultaneously worried about what this "success" would mean for the Portland with which they had become familiar and to which they had become accustomed. Their children would be moving from someplace familiar, but would their new homes be in a true neighborhood, and would these be recognizable as such?

Coley, for his part, did not want any of his sons to follow him onto the docks as a longshoreman. He was proud of his work, but he expected much more for his children. The opportunity for them to become educated, to grow and prosper, was perhaps the major reason that he and countless others had chosen to come to America. Yet among his fellow longshoremen, several of their sons had already followed in their fathers' footsteps, at least for a time.

If schooling or ventures into small business were not immediately successful, dock work was a relatively predictable and somewhat secure temporary opportunity, especially during the busy winter shipping season. Often these young sons or nephews would follow their fathers or uncles in a steady work gang that could guarantee them a solid income through at least that season. This was one way in which the Irish presence on the docks of Portland had been preserved, even in these later years when Italians, Poles, and other immigrants were beginning to compete for work alongshore.

Coley had an easy time managing his boys. His daughters, however, continued to baffle him. Mamie, the second born, had recently informed her parents that she preferred to be called by the surname Foley rather than Folan or the Irish *Ní Chualáin*. This was the kind of thing that nearly always drove Coleman to distraction. He informed Mamie in no uncertain terms that if Folan was a good enough Irish name for her father and mother it was certainly good enough for her. He would not accept the Americanization of his family name. Coley insisted to Mamie that she was born a Folan and would keep that name until she married a good Irish Catholic boy, and that she could then take her husband's name, if he'd have her. Mamie argued strenuously, however, that several of her friends had slightly changed or Americanized their family surnames, such as Winnie Conley and Dervla Waters. As with most children of that age, Mamie wanted to know of her father, 'Why do I have to be the only old-fashioned one?'

Mamie was too independent for Coley, and there were often rows between them over his paternal authority in the house. This was confusing to Coley; and such behavior marked a significant change from family life in Galway where young daughters were usually seen but not heard, and always obedient. The next four children after Mamie were all enrolled in the public schools, leaving only Margaret (Peg) and little Michael (Míchilín) still at home with their mother during the day.

Mary had given up her domestic work as soon as there were three children at home. She supplemented the family income by running a small "restaurant" in the dining room of their apartment, mostly to serve young unmarried longshoremen at dinner time, the mid-day meal. The Portland Irish had always referred to their three meals as breakfast, dinner and supper.

Coley had suggested to Mary a year or so before, 'It makes sense since you are cookin' for ten already for nothin', why not cook for a few more and make some money from it?'

Mary's response was as direct as ever, 'Yes, but who'll be doing the extra cookin', lovie, and who'll be buying the extra leg of lamb, and with what fortune?'

There was nary a good answer from Coley to these practical queries from his wife, but nonetheless Mary, as usual, had complied and several hungry and expectant longshoremen now descended upon her every work day at noon.

For Coleman, the winter work shift both began and ended in the dark. This was the busiest time of the year for longshore work. On one day alone in the previous month, December 23, 1899, a total of four transatlantic steamships had all cleared Portland harbor. Now with a huge new grain elevator near the Grand Trunk terminal there was often a large supply of Canadian grain waiting to be transshipped to Europe during these months when the St. Lawrence River remained frozen. Since the mid-nineteenth century Canadian exports were transported from Montreal to Portland, and this closest ice-free harbor subsequently earned the nickname "Canada's winter port."

Working in the hold of a ship, either with coal or grain, it was only possible to see the light of day for one brief hour at dinnertime. For the past several weeks there had been overtime work available – too much, perhaps. Coley's regular work gang had been working steadily on colliers, the wooden coastal schooners that brought coal from Virginia to the merchants operating out of Portland, such as the Pocahontas Company, the A.R. Wright Company, William H. Dugan and Sons, and the Randall and McAllister Company.

The coal would then be redistributed from Portland throughout northern New England, and especially to the massive paper-making factories along several of Maine and New Hampshire's rivers. Coal also went to the railroads for steam transportation, and, of course, for the heating of homes. Home stoves locally would usually start with wood before shifting to coal for the long winter nights. Anthracite was preferred when it could be afforded. Usually the cheaper but smokier bituminous was burned, however, as that was all that one could afford. The Folans burned mainly bituminous.

Thus, one could gauge the affluence or relative poverty of any given household by the color and quality of the smoke that emerged from their chimneys. Sometimes Coleman provided this coal "compliments," he would say, of the stevedoring companies. This was unorthodox surely, and probably unethical to boot. But for the Folan family, coal for heat was undeniably a necessity. At the end of the day and with a growing family of ten to care for, no one in Portland had ever denied that Coleman was a good provider.

~ ~ ~

"*Dia dhuit ar maidín, a Mháire* (God be with you this morning, Mary)," Coley called out to his wife, his lovie as he always called her. They were about to begin yet another day of challenge and opportunity. Would it be a day like many others? And then quite out of character, yet presciently, Coley added, "I wonder if this day will be much."

Chapter 2

Mother of Pearl

"Buy hyacinths to feed thy soul."

– from the *Sanskrit*

Abalone… Mother of pearl… Such exotic-sounding names
ran through Mary's mind, but they hardly seemed exaggerated.
Abalone – what a beautiful yet appropriate sound for such a lovely object…

Mary was daydreaming. Together with her nightly ritual of searching for restful sleep, these early morning hours were Mary's only times to be alone. She cherished being alone with her thoughts, and along with this came some degree of peace and rare stillness. Each morning, almost ritualistically, she would make her first cup of tea, wrap herself warmly in her Galway shawl, and sit in the parlor quietly admiring her one and only sole possession. It was a piece of art, a reverse painting done directly on glass in a beautifully ornate wooden frame. It had cost her a pretty penny, more than she should have spent and more than she would have otherwise allowed herself to spend under normal circumstances. But now, at times like this when she could be alone in the brief moments of an early morning stillness, Mary felt that her one and only extravagance had been repaid time and again and that she had truly gotten value for her money.

Mary's eldest son, John, the scholar in the family, had once shared with her a poem that his class had learned when they were grammar students at the North School near the base of Munjoy Hill. Mary loved that Johnny always seemed to enjoy learning and reciting poems. To Coley, however, this was a waste of time. 'A poem has no practical value, and it's no way to bring money into the house,' an opinion that Coley had emphatically claimed more than once.

But this particular poem had impressed both mother and son, even though it was neither old Irish nor old English for that matter. 'It's from something called Sanskrit,' Johnny explained to his incredulous mother. 'Whatever that means when you're at home,' Mary uttered when she first heard the name of this ancient language – it remained a total mystery.

Johnny told his mother that his teacher, a Miss Florence Vose, was an old Yankee spinster. She loved music and poetry and taught both of these in a way that made her students love them too. What a gift to give to these immigrant children! She always treated each of them as if they were her own. This dedicated molder of young minds had learned many tricks and educational techniques over her many years and she was able to employ them clandestinely to earn the devotion and respect of those in her care. Miss Vose told her eager young scholars, 'This poem has been translated into English from an ancient language of India, but it still speaks to me over hundreds of years and thousands of miles.' Miss Vose called this a "universal truth."

'At least it came from another British colony, like Ireland,' Coleman had stated when he first heard it recited, 'but I'll be damned if I have any idea what these curious words about some silly flowers actually mean.' And he had been in no mood to even try! 'It's only a poem, and a strange one at that. My children should be taught good sensible poems about real Irish heroes like *Fionn MacCumhaill* or *Diamaid agus Grainne*.'

When Mary asked her husband why he must see everything through Irish eyes, Coley had innocently replied, 'Sure, aren't they the only two eyes I have?' He then winked playfully in the general direction of his amused children as if to imply what a silly question their mommy had just asked him.

Coley always seemed ready with a simple answer, even for Mary's most serious questions. She seldom accepted his simplistic take on things, particularly on such important matters. But the children, on the other hand, thought of their *Daide* (Father) as being nothing short of brilliant, especially for his quick wit and ready replies. Johnny realized that his parents simply demonstrated their gifts of wit and wisdom in very different ways. Who was to say which style was superior?

Johnny told Mary that this short poem was one of his favorites, and that he would remember it forever, even though it was neither by Longfellow, Portland's own famous bard, nor from the Bible. These were the two most common sources for verse then being taught in Portland's public schools. Johnny, in turn, had passed on his love of English-language poetry to his mother. Although unable to read or write in English, Mary had an abiding love for all types of words – their sounds, their meanings, and their orderliness.

Even though English was a learned language for Mary, and Irish would always be her first tongue, she had carried from Ireland an abiding love for verse and oral expression. Mary memorized this poem from the Sanskrit on the spot, coached along by her Johnny who had to decipher one or two unusual bits of vocabulary for her, just as they had been equally lovingly deciphered for him earlier.

Miss Vose would often enhance these poems with a personal meaning in her class – what a gift she possessed, and how freely she shared this gift with her lucky young scholars. Ever since, Mary had often murmured the short verse to herself, almost like a mantra. It had a deeply personal meaning for her, coming as it did from her eldest. Now that she understood the precise meaning of each of these individual words, her enjoyment only heightened, especially now as she regarded her own glorious piece of art on the wall:

> *If of thy mortal goods thou art bereft,*
> *And to thy humble store two loaves alone to thee are left;*
> *Sell one, and with the dole*
> *Buy hyacinths to feed thy soul.*

"Yes, those Indians had got it just right," Mary intoned quietly to herself.

She liked this feeling so much that she repeated the poem again, much to her delight. To Mary it meant that even in a new country she was able to buy, with her own money, a piece of art to soothe and nourish her soul, even though it might have put a strain on the family budget for the next several weeks. The food that her family would eat, the three meals a day as represented by the "loaves" in the poem, was long gone, but the painting remained and was a constant in her life that had a deeply personal meaning to her.

To Mary this painting represented her hyacinths, flowers that neither faded nor ever needed the nourishment of water, but which still gave both comfort and strength to her body and soul as she began each day. She wondered sometimes what kind of a scholar she might have been if ever she had been given the chance. Caring for her children came first, but even so Mary envied the little ones for their wonderful opportunity to learn.

"I would have mastered poetry at the very least," she now boasted to her reverse painting, her silent but attentive audience of one.

From the moment she'd first laid eyes on this exquisitely framed painting it reminded Mary of Mynish (*Muighinis*), her island home off the western coast of County Galway, Ireland. The colors were just right – the verdant greens in rich and multiple shades, the mountains in the background just like Connemara's Twelve Pins, and the house constructed of native stone and situated beside the sea, in Irish literally "at the foot of the sea (*cois fharraige*)," as they would have said at home.

The children, especially the youngest, often asked their mother to tell them again and again the story behind the picture. Even after hearing it dozens of times, they persisted, 'Tell us the story again, Máma. Tell us how you swimmed all the way from Ireland,' they exaggerated, as their mother always did in her grand telling of the now familiar story. On those evenings when she didn't feel up to repeating the story yet again, Mary would make them laugh with doggerel verse or scraps of nonsense.

As her ritualistic telling of the familiar story unfolded, the elegant painting with its mother of pearl luminescence became a sort of talisman for the Folans in America. Mary's reverse painting had by now transcended into the tangible and visible image that connected the New with the Old. Mary told the revered tale with such conviction and strength that even her eldest children sometimes wondered if it wasn't actually true. Mary's story would always follow the same familiar framework.

'This was our family's home in Galway over many generations. One night, after all were asleep, I slowly crawled through the hole at the base of the stone wall, crept quietly to the edge of the sea, swam out to the Galway hooker in the bay, and sailed all the way over to Amerikay.'

This represented the bare bones of the story, but it could be embellished to any degree necessary for any occasion – and wasn't Mary just the natural story-teller to deliver the tale with the grace and energy that it so richly deserved? In reality, the true story of Mary Joyce's emigration was far less romantic and more fraught with difficulty.

Mary's own mother, Norah Lee, had married a William Joyce from the nearby island of *Inis Bearacháin*. After the birth of a few children, including Mary, William had died. Norah shocked the sensibilities of this strictly religious and traditional community by courting Dan Mulkern and then marrying again well before the proscribed mourning period had been thoroughly completed. Norah had further stunned many back home by "dancing at the crossroads" within a few months of William's death. Norah's reasoning for this unusual behavior was simple and succinct, 'Sure, how's a single woman to get by in this world on her own? And anyways didn't my William always love to see me dance?'

As shocked as her family and friends might have been at Norah's unorthodox behavior, no one had a ready answer for her troubling question about survival. Therefore, no one was surprised when just a few years later, in June of 1883, Norah and her second husband, Dan, also sailed to Portland, Maine, in order to join her daughters, Bridget Joyce and Mary, who were both already established here. By this time, Mary had only recently married Coleman, just one month earlier in May of 1883, with her sister, Bridget, serving as a witness.

Mary's eloquent and romantic story behind the reverse painting, regardless of its veracity, was a thrilling account, and it was illustrated there for all to see – the truth of the story revealed through the artist's brush! Mary, like her resourceful mother, Norah, had clearly taken control of her own life. Although she loved her Irish family dearly, and her mother especially so, Mary knew that her own future and fortune could only be made on the other side of the Atlantic in what was often called at home "the next parish west of Galway." And now here she was in the Diocese of Portland, state of Maine, almost literally the next American parish west of Galway.

'But Máma,' one of the children would invariably ask, 'why did you leave such a beautiful place and such a big house? It's much bigger than our own place here!'

And don't children have a knack of cutting through to the truth and thereby exposing the weakness of any myth? This represented, of course, the weak link in Mary's story. The massive house in the painting was indeed elegant. In appearance it was almost like a castle. Actually painted from behind and directly onto the glass itself, backwards, by an artist using a mirror to correct the image for his own eyes – a reverse painting it was called.

This family treasure now seemed to be a metaphor for how their lives had been utterly changed since their arrival from Ireland. Much had been gained, but much had also been lost. Who was to tally the equation?

'What is the truest way of understanding our new lives here in Portland,' Mary had often asked her husband, 'Or the lives of those dear to us that we have both painfully left behind?' This seemed like another of Mary's questions without a ready answer.

The stone structure depicted in her dear painting seemed both immense and romantic, with lovely stained-glass windows consisting of in-laid mother of pearl. This rare and mysterious substance seemed to generate a warm light that appeared to originate from within the building itself. In this characteristic it was similar to Ireland's famous illuminated manuscripts such as the *Book of Kells*. The substantial building even had an ivy-covered tower.

'Why," the children would persist in asking, 'did you leave such a beautiful place? Do they ever have winter over there? Are we ever to go back?'

'Why, indeed?' Mary often put that very question to herself. Coley, as always, supplied the simple answer, 'Your Máma left Ireland to get her pot of gold in America – and that, of course, was meself!'

The children loved this predictably boastful response from their Daide. Mary, however, kept her thoughts on this subject, and indeed many other things, well to herself. But she never conveyed even one instant of doubt to her family that she dearly loved her Coley, her lovie, and the beloved father of their children.

The oldest in the family, of course, knew that Mary's story was at best a pure exaggeration. The painted building appeared more like an elegant castle, and well they knew that their mother's family, the Joyces, was surely not to the manor born, at least not the Joyces of Portland! Had she sacrificed all of this, including such a lovely home in Ireland, in order to raise a large family in this country? Was it for their sake alone that she left all of this, together with her family, behind? Or as they suspected, had the Joyces come from poor peasant stock like most of their Irish neighbors, especially those now living along Fore and Franklin Streets at the foot of the busy, noisy, hardscrabble waterfront of Portland, Maine? How could anyone ever truly know?

'There's no harm in your asking,' she would often explain. 'Not every woman is born a queen, and not every home is a castle, as the saying goes, except in one's dreams – and sure what's the harm in dreamin'?'

Slowly moving back to reality again, Mary would often try to stay in this restful, blissful, contemplative reverie at least until she heard the sound of Coley stirring above. He was about to descend the hall stairs for his hearty breakfast. She knew that this would be only the beginning. After Coley left for work, there would be a nearly endless procession of little feet into the warm kitchen: John (Johnny) sixteen, and Mary Magdalen (Mamie) fourteen, the two eldest; followed next by Thomas (Tom) twelve, Joseph (Joe) ten, Agnes eight, Katherine (Kitty) six, Margaret Theresa (Peg) four; and finally there was Michael Francis

(Míchilín) two, the baby of the family, at least for the time being.

Mary and Coleman's children were all born healthy, *buíochas le Día* (thanks be to God), except for poor William. Named after his maternal grandfather, William had been born third in line between Mamie and Tom, but unfortunately he had died in infancy. He had been named for Mary's own father who had died in Ireland. The Folans grieved the loss of this baby, but they also knew that many of their neighbors had lost more than one child. So they prayed for William's soul, counted their blessings, and then, with courage and hope, moved on to serve those remaining to the best of their ability.

But of course, now there was also Míchilín, the cudeen (*cuidín*, the "little portion") or the baby of the family, and the troubling and mysterious problem he was experiencing with his leg. Although he was born healthy, during the summer of his second year he had cried about a sudden and strange numbness in his spine which seemed to slowly radiate down his leg. Mary tried rubbing and massaging it, and she even applied rubbing alcohol, but nothing seemed to help. A doctor was finally called for. Due to the expense, this was done only in extreme emergencies. The diagnosis was at first undetermined.

Some sick immigrant children were cared for by the municipality, but the Folans were reticent to apply for any kind of assistance as it appeared to them to be an admission of failure or weakness. It was eventually discovered that Michael suffered from what was formally called infantile paralysis or poliomyelitis (polio). Although polio was widespread in America, sometimes affecting even the children of wealthy families, it was still a very confusing malady to the Folan family. Among the Irish, as with other similar physical imperfections, they fatalistically blamed themselves as being responsible for this failure. For years afterwards this malady was simply referred to as Michael's "bad leg" or "bad knee," especially within their circle of friends. He would heal eventually, or so they all hoped, *le cúnamh Dé* (God willing).

'Probably,' the doctor had once stated in front of his young patient and some of his shocked siblings, 'your Michael will never again walk normally.' But Mary sternly warned the doctor to never again say that in front of her child, and what was more, 'At least the *creatúr bocht* (poor creature) will always have his brothers and sisters to lean on.'

The doctor was well rebuked by this loving mother, and Míchilín never complained about his lot in life. In any case it wasn't part of the Folan family character to whine or complain about any of their misfortunes. This simply was just not done. Whining would be dealt with swiftly and decisively by both parents together with their older children clearly stating, 'You're not allowed!'

Michael would not be the last of her children, as Mary knew only too well. She was now full term with what would any day now be her tenth child. As she was only thirty-five years of age, she suspected that this new one also might not be her cudeen for long. 'With every child comes a new blessing!' as Bishop Healy had often said at the Cathedral. But Mary quietly protested that the Folans already felt sufficiently blessed.

Once her parish priest asked her, 'Mary, do you love all of your children equally?' She answered with humor and disarming innocence, 'Well, Father, to tell you the truth, I really only know the half of them!'

~ ~ ~

"*Dia dhuit ar maidin, a Mháire* (God be with you this morning, Mary)," Coleman greeted his wife.

He always spoke Irish with his wife at home, and this was the daily greeting so familiar to them both. His townland of *Calibhfuinse* (Callowfeenish) was only three or four miles east of her island of *Muighinis* (Mynish). Both of these were firmly within the Irish-speaking *Gaeltacht* region on the western edge of County Galway. Neither of them could speak much more than an occasional phrase of English when they first had arrived in Portland. Fortunately, they didn't need it immediately as their neighborhood was largely Irish-speaking here, too.

"*Dia 's Mhuire dhuit, a Cholmán* (God and the Blessed Virgin Mary be with you, Coleman)," Mary replied, which was the only proper response to his greeting.

In more formal circumstances this greeting between Irish-speakers could go on indefinitely with each response adding a name from the endless pantheon of Irish saints, beginning, of course, with God and the Virgin Mary, and then with Patrick before next moving on to Brígid, Columcille, Columbanus, Brendan, and so on. It was this kind of endearing and playful linguistic challenge in which the Irish seemed to revel, both at home and now here in Portland. Participants always wanted to see just how far one could tease this out, but always, of course, it had to be done in the proper sequence. It was a test of both their Irish and their memory, but it always represented a pleasant and mutually affirming social exchange.

Both Mary and Coleman liked to add the name of Macdara, a local south

Connemara saint whose festival was celebrated every summer on an island, *Oileán Mhic Dara*, equally close to both *Calibhfuinse* and *Muighinis*. And wasn't it at *Féile Macdara*, the Festival of Macdara on the island bearing his name, that a young Coleman Folan had first tentatively laid eyes on an even younger Mary Joyce?

Local Connemara sailors and fishermen back in Galway still lower their sails upon passing Macdara's Island as a sign of respect. Mary remembered Coley from that feast day, but he always pretended not to have noticed her. Perhaps he thought that she was too young. Coley always maintained that the first time he ever truly saw Mary was while walking along India Street in Portland's east end, and that he was mainly impressed with her command of the Irish language. 'The Irish language, indeed!' she often exclaimed in feigned disgust. When shortly thereafter, however, Coley had boldly asked her to walk out with him to the Promenade, her Irish was even more succinct and painfully clear, 'The first place you'll walk out with me will be down the aisle of the Cathedral!'

Mary had quickly and strongly blushed as soon as these words came out of her mouth, almost without thinking. Was she embarrassed at her own directness with a nearly total stranger, or was it her tacit acknowledgement to Coley and all those within earshot that she might even consider marrying him? Mary herself was not entirely sure if what had just happened was real, but her blush was all too real and readily apparent – this she could clearly sense, and Coley sensed it, too. And so only a few months thereafter they did take that short walk down the Cathedral aisle. Coley's version of their engagement was predictably quite different, of course. The children giggled whenever their father innocently and sincerely maintained, 'I chased your mother until she finally caught me!'

"How are you feeling this morning, lovie?" This was the more affectionate and more secular greeting that Mary yearned to hear each morning. "Lovie" seemed to be the local version of the Irish, *a chuid*, meaning "my little portion." It signified for her that all was well with her husband. Coley's adjustment to Portland had been a bit more difficult than her own. She loved this term of endearment from her Coleman. Their boys often mimicked their Daide in calling their mother, "lovie." That never ceased to both amuse and please her. She would pretend to be annoyed by this juvenile familiarity, but then Mary would often respond in a pretended dismissive fashion, '*Mac an t-athair* (Son of, or just like the father)!'

This was for Mary a very good thing. It meant that the children witnessed the way their father bantered and playfully teased his wife. Maybe someday they would have children of their own or even grandchildren for Mary and Coley, please God. If only they all could first find their own lovies, then they might also tease them in a similar fashion.

It was now nearing time for Coley to depart. "How much coal have we left?" Coley now asked, fearful of the expected answer.

"Only enough for this day, if I'm very careful with it," Mary warned.

She had spoken to Coleman about this nearly constantly over the past weeks, as there were only a few extra pennies in the house account, kept in a jar in the kitchen that was strictly managed by Mary, with which to buy coal. The stevedores, working for the shipping companies, together with the union walking bosses who were responsible for maintaining discipline alongshore, were all watching these men very carefully to dissuade them from pilfering along the coal docks, especially during this harsh winter season.

"I know that only too well, Mary. I'll do what I can today, but if I'm not careful I could be sacked for stealing like poor Joe Burke only last week."

Joe Burke, a neighbor of the Folans, had been warned twice about pilfering coal. But his family was as large as the Folans and his house was even draftier than theirs, with more than one pane of glass missing from several windows. The Burkes didn't dare ask their landlord to address this deficiency as they feared that even if he complied with their request he might well respond by raising their rent as he had once done before. Then last week Joe had been suspended for two full weeks for stealing coal a third time.

Coleman and his fellow longshoremen didn't know exactly how to feel about this. Pilfering was wrong and against their own union's work rules, this was true, but the need was real especially for families like the Burkes. Everyone knew this to be true. The union had briefly considered going out on a job action, a one-day strike to protest Joe's punishment, but few could stand to lose even one day's wages during this difficult and bitter season. It had been brutally cold nearly every day since Christmas.

It might be two months or even longer before the days would lengthen and the desperately cold temperatures might finally begin to moderate. In Galway an ancient poem had more optimistically declared, *"Tar eis La Féile Bhríde"* (After

Saint Brígid's Day, on February the first), that the days would begin to lengthen and spring would formally arrive. On that same day the ancient Celtic calendar marked the beginning of spring, which they called *Imbolg*, meaning "in the belly." This signified the season in Ireland when the farm animals would predictably become pregnant, thus representing a clear sign of renewal and hope.

But here at the far northeastern tip of this country, Coleman's seasonal saying had to be somewhat modified and slightly postponed. He had often maintained, 'Come March the 17th (St. Patrick's Day) the winter's back is broke!' To this Coleman would often playfully add, 'Better the winter's back than me own!'

Coley had hopefully repeated this saying each and every spring since his arrival in Portland. This prediction appeared to Mary and the older members of his family to be more a declaration of faith and hope, appearing now almost in the form of an uttered prayer by their patriarch. Maine winters were hard on everyone.

But even in this, Coley was being optimistic. There could still be plenty of cold weather well into late March, to say nothing of snow, some years going even well into the month of April. Yes, Portland was like Galway in so many ways, but the winter and the summer here were both much more extreme than the climate of Galway, bathed as it was by the moderating Gulf Stream. Coley had once cursed, 'God blast this Arctic current anyways – why don't they send the damned thing back to the Arctic, wherever the hell that is!'

Mary knew well of Coley's dilemma regarding the pilfering of coal. Out of pure exasperation, however, she had once implored of him, 'Christ, you're shoveling the blasted coal all day long for the damned paper mills, and all we're askin' for here is only a few buckets full!' But the look of deep sadness in her husband's eyes had convinced her of the hopelessness that he must have been feeling. How could he provide for his desperate family and simultaneously keep his job? She would be careful never to go to that extreme again with her husband.

It remained, however, one of Mary's many tasks to keep their large and drafty apartment warm through the winter, especially with Michael's crippled leg and a new child on the way. This was certainly not easy when the coal was being quickly depleted, as it nearly was on this bitter day. She could only imagine how Joe's wife, Annie Burke, must have felt.

On more than one occasion Mary had reluctantly sent Johnny and Mamie out to scavenge for kindling wood just to keep the fire burning feebly in their stove.

One time Johnny had taken some wooden planks from a nearby horse stable that had been built years earlier by a fellow Irishman, Sylvanus Lyng. Johnny argued that the fence was already tipping over and was, therefore, of no practical use to the current owner or to any horses for that matter. Mary listened with an amused look on her face, but she disapproved of this line of reasoning and sternly told him so. Her smile returned as she then added, "I fear we may be grooming the first lawyer in the Folan family, but if he proceeds with this line of reasoning he'll soon be arguing his own case!" However reluctantly, Mary burned the precious stable wood all the same.

Coley's breakfast in the winter months always consisted of stirabout, locally called porridge or oatmeal, and always served with something to sweeten it. All of the Folans had a sweet tooth. Coley's favorite sweetener was the brown sugar that was produced right here in Portland at the J.B. Brown Sugar Factory; but honey, molasses or even on rare occasions pure maple syrup would also do quite well. Today he would take an extra helping of brown sugar as the weather over these past few days had been particularly trying.

The previous day, Tuesday, had been especially painful for him. Mary was instinctively aware of this, so she had added a few strips of bacon – rashers as they still called them – to Coley's meal. These were most appreciated and quickly devoured. Even now he almost dreaded leaving home, though he would never openly show any lack of courage to Mary or any of his children, and certainly not to any of his fellow laborers. Mary knew by intuition of Coley's reluctance to leave her and his warm kitchen, and so she now firmly tightened the woolen scarf around his neck and gave him a gentle kiss on his cheek while whispering, "Love keeps the cold out better than a cloak."

This gorgeous phrase was not original to Mary, as Coley would have liked to believe, but rather another gem from Henry Wadsworth Longfellow that their son Johnny had once carried home with him from North School. But now he must go face the day, so go he must, and go he would. Coley and Mary both knew this.

"Don't forget the coal, Coley!" she chuckled, amused at her own often repeated play on words. He was quickly out the door and off into the early morning cold and dark. "What a strange language, this English," Mary now mumbled to herself, as she mused about, "my Coleman, the coal man!"

Mary loved such comical turns of phrases, and there were many more that she knew in Irish. She now had to master these sayings in a second language, but isn't it a true sign of competence in a language when one can tell and also understand puns and jokes? Once a friend had complimented Mary on her beautiful red-tinted hair, only to have her respond, 'Ah, but it was my mother that had the lovely auburn hair,' before adding in reference to Maine's twin cities on the Andro-scoggin River, 'and her Lewiston eyebrows!' Yes, Mary was becoming familiar with this new language.

'There had been a man from Quebec,' Coleman had once told her, 'whose name was Marcel Charboneau.' That surname meant "coal" in French. So in order to sound more like a native Mainer, Charboneau had changed his name to Mark Cole! Coleman felt that this was a shame because he thought that people should be proud of their roots and their family names, and not a weakened Americanized version of them. He liked the ring of the name Charboneau along with other exotic-sounding French names like Rossignol, Buotte, and Bissonette, but especially the melodious Robitaille. He liked the way these names sounded so different from the way they looked on paper, just as Gaelic appeared strange to most English speakers. 'If I ever die,' he once had proclaimed to his amused wife, 'I'll come back as a Frenchman with one of those beautiful names – how would you like to be a Robitaille?'

Mary loved to see him smiling, especially as he was about to leave the house – his face was ever so much brighter when he did smile. It seemed to lift years from his weathered countenance. But today, both Mary and Coleman knew the seriousness of her plea for coal – it was badly needed. He had promised Mary that he would try his level best, and Mary whispered, almost inaudibly to herself, "He always has tried his very best, my lovie."

As soon as Coleman was away, Mary began to rouse the children for their breakfast of oatmeal porridge, similar to the stirabout on which she had been raised. Like her husband, Mary had come from south Connemara. Her family, the Joyces, had originated in Oughterard, but after a death in the family they moved further west to Mynish, an island just off the coast near Carna that was accessible by a series of stone bridges and causeways. Mynish was only about five miles from Coleman's home at the other end of the parish in Callowfeenish, but much closer by boat.

Mary had slightly known of the Folan family in Ireland as they often attended Mass together in Carna. She didn't really know Coleman before their meeting in Portland, however. This could partially be explained because Galway men would traditionally congregate during Mass at the very rear of the church, or sometimes even outside the door, while the women devotedly occupied the front rows. Some speculated that this was to place the men strategically nearer to the pub door, but this separation of genders was nearly always strictly observed, almost as if by dictum.

Mary's voyage to Portland in 1881 at the tender age of seventeen had followed Coleman's by less than one year. Typical of so many young Irish women migrating to America, she had come alone. Her mother would join her two years later. Like Coleman, she also had relatives in this coastal New England city. Mary had come directly from Boston aboard the *Governor Dingley* without so much as an overnight stay in that large and intimidating city.

Mary's first memory of America, after passing through immigration control, was of the short walk over to the Portland boat. During this walk, she saw her first Negro, but pretended not to have noticed. Her curiosity got the best of her, however, and setting down her bags she had turned around to get another look. As she turned, she saw that the old colored man had done exactly the same to get another view of this strangely clad Irish greenhorn, complete with her shawl and knit woolen sweater, and fresh off the wild bogs of Connemara. They gazed for a few moments at each other in embarrassment, but as they perceived the humor in what had just occurred they each had a good laugh at each other and at themselves, considering the comical nature of this incident. It was Mary's first full-throated laugh since tearfully leaving her family behind in Galway. It seemed to Mary a wonderful way to begin her stay in this strange and varied new home of her choice. These two then parted with a smile, a nod of the head, and a slight wave of the hand – each on their own way to God only knew what ends.

It had also seemed ironic to Mary, after she had been in Portland only a short while, that many of the Irish here cared so little for these American residents whose families had originally come from somewhere in Africa, often long before many of the Irish had arrived here. There were so few Negroes, and the anti-black jokes and the suspicion of this group seemed to Mary to be disproportionate and quite unfair and out of place. If, as she had heard, there were fewer than 300 Negroes living in the city, and that would have amounted to less than one percent of Portland's total population, then how could they be seen as a threat to the Irish, or to anyone else for that matter?

Even after Coley explained to her how Portland's "coloreds," as he called them, had controlled the longshore work in Portland in the years before the Irish arrived and how the Portland Longshoremen's Benevolent Society (PLSBS) Bylaws specifically excluded "colored men" from union membership, Mary still failed to understand what the Irish had against this group.

'Don't they have to feed their children like we do?' Mary would ask. 'And isn't the Bishop of Portland, James Augustine Healy, himself partly a Negro, too?'

Coleman had no ready answer for either of these questions, and so Mary determined that she, at least in her own small way, would try to treat these Negroes fairly. To her husband she put the proposition, 'Hadn't the Irish been treated as slaves by the English for hundreds of years?'

Again, Coley had no answer. Rarely did he attempt to analyze things in the same way that his wife did. He had often wondered what made them so different in that regard.

Some of the Irish at the Cathedral had been heard to whisper things like, 'Jasus, the Bishop's a Naygur,' or even worse things about Bishop Healy. 'Where did this hatred come from?' Mary had often asked this of her husband, and of others.

There were few opportunities for interaction, however. Even though their two east end neighborhoods were cheek by jowl, members of Portland's small Negro population usually did not venture into the Irish neighborhood, especially merely for social visits – this just didn't happen!

Mary was aware of other types of discrimination in Portland as well, especially by social class. Most of the Irish were also aware of this, or at least should have been. She was fond of telling her friends the story of her short boat trip from Boston to Portland. She was thoroughly exhausted by her two-week voyage from Ireland. Although the fare to Portland was only $1.00, she had no extra money to pay for an inside cabin. Mary was much relieved upon being directed to an outside deck chair by a helpful official of the Portland Steamship Company. Shortly after settling in, however, a proper looking Yankee lady, only slightly older than she, informed Mary that the official had made a mistake and that she had already reserved that very chair for her own use. Mary quickly sized up the woman and the situation. Almost as though she was somehow already prepared for such a confrontation, Mary then calmly yet firmly stated in her somewhat broken English, 'If the official made a mistake in givin' this chair to me, I'll not be makin' another mistake by givin' it back to you.'

Perhaps Mary had known instinctively that it would take both courage and wit to survive in this new land. She had almost inadvertently thus taken her first small step, or seat as it were, toward survival in this famous "land of liberty." Mary had often proclaimed to her family concerning life in America, 'Tis a wonderful place if you're willing to stand up for yourself!'

To Mary, the Irish community in Portland often seemed like a little bit of Galway, only transferred over to this side of the Atlantic. The Irish, and other groups for that matter, could survive quite nicely in their own ethnic enclaves. Mary, like most of her Irish women friends in Portland, had started work here as a domestic servant. Just having a job made some of the Irish feel that they somehow owned the keys to the city.

Mary recalled a humorous story told by a friend who was an Irish cleaning lady at J. B. Brown's elegant Falmouth Hotel on Middle Street. Late one evening, long after the main doors had been locked, a bedraggled, unkempt, and somewhat boisterous Irishman attempted to gain admission through the hotel lobby. He was, in fact, a distant relative of this friend of Mary's. He was fresh from the bogs of Connemara, and he certainly looked the part, and he was now searching for his relative. But when he was told that he couldn't enter the hotel at that late hour, especially without a room key or a reservation, the brawny Irishman protested indignantly, 'You must let me in. I have every right to be here. I've got a cousin on the scrubbin'.'

Mary worked, as did many of her friends, for one of the wealthy Yankee families located in or near one of Portland's most elegant neighborhoods. Their decorous homes, especially those along the city's Eastern or Western Promenades, were only a short jaunt from the neighborhoods where most of the Irish lived, and yet the social distinctions were enormous. Mary lived with an aunt in the east end when she first arrived in Portland. Almost immediately, she was told by another Irish domestic who was already working there about an available domestic position. She soon discovered that nearly the entire household staff was Irish but that they had an unusually friendly relationship with the owners, a middle-aged doctor and his large family.

Tradition in Portland had ordained that domestic workers could have their afternoons free on Thursdays and Sundays. It was quite common during the summer months to see many young Irishmen and Irishwomen strolling leisurely along the city's Western or Eastern Promenades. These strolls were as much a part of the Irish social calendar as the weekly dances at the Ancient Order of Hibernians

(AOH) Hall located at 491-1/2 Congress Street or the occasional *céili* (Irish dance party) in someone's downstairs kitchen. Many longshoremen could regularly be seen strolling on these afternoons when their shorefront work waned in the summer months. To many an observer, they appeared to be trolling as if for breams or mackerel off the coast of Cape Elizabeth. Several of Coleman's friends had already found Irish wives in this manner.

After noticing Mary Joyce at the Cathedral for several consecutive weeks, Coleman had finally summoned up the courage during one of those Thursday afternoon strolls to ask if he could walk with her. Mary's answer to Coleman was as swift and cagey as the one she had once given to the Yankee lady aboard the *Governor Dingley*. Although she was happy to meet one of her own, and especially one from her very own Carna parish, and an Irish speaker like herself, she instructed Coleman that if he wanted to walk out with her that he would have to quickly solemnize their relationship. The vast majority of the immigrants in Portland around this time, or so it appeared to Mary, would only marry someone from their own native country. This seemed to be an iron-clad tradition and one that was apparently strictly enforced by both family and church.

Following this pattern, and after only a very brief courtship, Coleman Folan and Mary Josephine Joyce were married on May 16, 1883, at the Cathedral of the Immaculate Conception. Better economic opportunity had allowed for greater marriage prospects for the Irish in America than in Ireland, especially after the devastating and recurring crop failures and famines of the nineteenth century.

On top of these natural disasters, there was also the discriminatory and unjust distribution of farmland throughout most of Ireland which could thus support only a small portion of its rapidly growing population. At home, many of the girls went off to Galway City or even further afield, including to Dublin or to cities in England or even America. There they hoped to find work or husbands who could support them and their future families. Many of the men left behind on the farms, especially poor agricultural laborers in the west of Ireland, were forced to remain on the land as celibate bachelors, which led to frustration and often anger.

Mary would soon be giving birth to her tenth child, and at thirty-five could expect to continue having children for another several years. She was not the same young and vivacious *cailín* (colleen, female) who had arrived in Portland nearly twenty years earlier. Even Coleman had noticed how weary and tired his wife sometimes appeared.

~ ~ ~

The two eldest children, Johnny and Mamie, sat down for breakfast, now that their father left for the docks. Johnny had been working part time at a nearby bottling plant, although he was not currently needed during this slow winter season. His parents had assumed he was again attending classes at Portland High School. Mamie, at age fourteen and one-half, was already working nearly full time in a clothing shop. They both contributed most of their meager earnings to the family, but lately Mamie had incurred her father's wrath by insisting that she should be able to keep a slightly larger portion of her weekly pay for her own use. Mary understood this desire on the part of her daughter, but Coley wouldn't hear of it. He said that other neighborhood children all turned their entire earnings over each week to their families and he clearly couldn't understand why Mamie should be any different.

Coley had especially wanted his oldest son to be able to finish school, but at sixteen Johnny's added income was needed now more than ever. Given the part-time nature of his work, the hope was that Johnny could somehow also attend enough classes to enable him to graduate from high school on schedule, maybe with a business diploma. In any case, Coley hoped that if his son could get training and work experience that perhaps one day he could open a small business of his own, such as a corner store or a bar, and thus further help the family financially.

There were by now several examples of successful Irish-owned businesses in Portland for these second-generation children to follow. At the very least, Irish-owned shops could provide employment and job training. The brewing business and the selling of alcohol, both legal and illegal, were other examples of such possible enterprises. The McGlinchy family, originally from County Tyrone in the north of Ireland, had earlier run a bottling house at the base of Munjoy Hill, and they also owned saloons in various parts of the city. The McGlinchys were often just one step ahead of the law, which made them even more popular in Irish eyes. Given the long history of English rule over Ireland, they often admired those who ignored the edicts of authority, a trait that crossed the Atlantic with them. By now this family had already accumulated a significant store of wealth.

Mary instinctively flinched every time alcohol was mentioned, either as a source of employment or as a social custom. She had been against the use of alcohol even as a young child back in Ireland where she had seen its horrendous damage to family and friends. The Irish, she thought, had always had a confused relationship with the *creatúr* (whiskey), *uisce beatha* (the water of life, also whiskey), or *poitín* (moonshine), as the various forms of alcohol were called back home.

Unfortunately, in America things were quite the same. The biggest difference was that here there was more money to buy this cursed liquor. Mary's own husband suffered greatly from excessive consumption, and at times he would seem to be completely under its spell, unable to work or even to communicate. Mary was loath to contemplate anyone in her family, especially her children, being involved in such a harmful and dangerous business.

Publicans in Ireland were often seen as being wealthy and lucky, but Mary knew better. Even those who profited from the sale of drink often suffered in other ways. Children of publicans were often forced to work long hours in the bar from an early age, and a public house was just that – it was public. Where was their privacy? When the owner would address his clients late at night, well after the official closing time, he was probably thinking of his own home and family upstairs as he plaintively cried out, 'Ladies and gents – have youse no homes to go to?'

~ ~ ~

On this new day, Coleman was working and he was sober. Mary was always happy to see him off to work because he was locally renowned as a very hard worker. Once there with his regular gang, he was likely to remain focused on his work and would be largely free from the temptations of booze. Mary had herself a good man, at least when he was "on the wagon." As her Coley was sober on this last day of January, so then was Mary relieved. And for this day at least Mary was grateful that she could now fully concentrate on her many other pressing responsibilities.

Chapter 3

Marcusín's Dog

"Tá Gaeilge go leor ag na buachailli bó"

(The cowboys speak good Irish)

Marcus Gorham's dog was a local legend. He was renowned for his ability to attract female dogs of all descriptions, shapes, and sizes. On this early Wednesday morning, Marcus and a fellow longshoreman, Dara Green, were chatting on the corner of Deer and Fore Streets near the Curtis Spruce Chewing Gum factory before heading to the shape-up on the waterfront. At this very same spot on many summer days the neighborhood children would often gather to retrieve pieces of spruce gum casually tossed to these anticipating street urchins from inside the factory. The practice was not considered a waste of resources, the company insisted, as it was deemed to be a sound business practice to help ensure future dependable customers.

Then, suddenly, a well-coiffed white female poodle with a very fancy jeweled collar happened to wander by. She was instantly smitten by the sight of a scruffy little mongrel which was called Bran and owned by Mark Gorham, better known as Marcusín (little Marcus) by his Irish-speaking neighbors. Bran took his name from the loyal hound of the legendary Irish warrior Fionn MacCumhaill. The two love-smitten canines, an odd couple if ever there was one, gleefully scampered through a hole in a nearby fence in search of privacy.

Shortly thereafter, an elegantly-dressed middle-aged woman arrived breathlessly on the scene. She was not only well attired but also unusually tall, quite portly, and entirely proper in her manner, an unfamiliar sight in this neighborhood, to be sure. Dara winked at Marcus, and in typical Irish fashion he instantly sized her up and with withering brevity quietly proclaimed, "She's beef to the heel, like a Mullingar heifer!"

But at this moment the poor woman was obviously more than a little distracted. Since neither of the men had ever seen her before, they guessed that she must have been a stranger to Munjoy Hill in the east end of the city. She appeared pre-occupied and worried, as though looking for something of value that had been lost. Almost out of sheer desperation, she hesitatingly inquired of the two dockers, "Have either of you gentlemen seen my Daisy? She's a poodle and has uncharacteristically gone off her leash somewhere in this section of the city with which she is totally unacquainted, as am I!"

Her manner and style of speech were thoroughly unfamiliar to both of these longshoremen who wondered if she was from Portland at all. Marcus hesitated as he didn't know whether or not he should be completely honest with this stranger. The truth would certainly not be welcomed news. Therefore, he stammered, collected his thoughts, and haltingly and cautiously began to speak, only to be bluntly interrupted by his friend Dara, who almost gleefully blurted out, "Sorry, Missus, but you see your precious poodle has gone off with Marcusín's dog, and when any pup goes off with Marcusín's dog, you see, they won't be back for quite some time! But you've nothing to fear. For you see, Bran's a brave hound and is very well known in these parts. So you see, Missus, the good news is that your poodle's not really lost at all – it's just seems that she's found a new friend, I'd say."

The look of disbelief and trepidation on the stranger's face quickly turned to shock and despair, whereupon she cried out, "But, gentlemen, as I've already told you, my Daisy is quite innocent and has never been alone in this area of town before!"

"As I've already explained, Missus, Marcusín's dog knows the area backwards and forwards, so you've really nothing to fear. It's a sensitive matter, I'd say. It's just that you can't rush this sort of thing, kind of, if ye folley me?"

Dara then slyly turned toward Marcus with that all-knowing wink that's as good as a nod. And with that, Marcus and Dara quickly bade the flustered stranger a good morning. They were off to the waterfront where they would lustfully sing the praises and thus augment the already stellar reputation of Marcusín's dog – the current and future pride of the Cathedral parish! It was another win for the home team!

As these longshoremen jaunted off towards their work site on Commercial Street, Dara spoke admiringly of Bran in terms comparable to the famous "black and tans," the hunting dogs so revered in many parts of Ireland. Then, in honor of Daisy the poodle, they now sang a familiar Irish courting song, appropriately ending each verse emphatically with, "Maids, when you're young never wed an old man!"

~ ~ ~

Coleman Folan supplied his own work shovel. Hoisted daily upon the shaft of that shovel he proudly carried aloft his shield, a very real badge of honor. The shield was a heavy steel-cast triangular funnel that allowed the coal heavers to more easily slide their flat-edged shovels into the huge piles of coal. Any new recruit to this line of work, even a young, strong, and eager worker, would be at a distinct disadvantage compared with these shield-toting veterans. Their fellow workers considered the coal shovellers to be the waterfront's elite. They often thought that they should be paid on a different wage scale than most other dockworkers, not because of any particular skill involved but rather because of the backbreaking demands of this challenging job.

There had been an earlier effort by these coal shovellers to be paid by volume. The amount requested was only two and one-half cents per ton of coal, or 15 cents per ton for a six-man gang. This request, however, was not accepted by the local stevedores who worked in Portland in the interest of the shipping companies. The regular longshore wages were thirty cents per hour for day work, forty cents for night work, and sixty cents for trimming grain. The latter was considered a skilled job upon which the balance and therefore the safety of the steamships depended. These wages represented about the average for union labor in Portland, but were significantly higher than most other non-skilled, non-union labor wages paid locally. All longshoremen were well aware of this important fact, you could be sure of that!

From the hold of the collier, the coal would be shoveled into buckets which were lowered and raised by steam-operated winches. The bucket would be emptied into the large coal pockets that would either store the coal or dump it directly into horse-drawn carts for local consumption or onto railroad cars for longer distance transport. Railroad cars were used, for example, to transport bulk coal to the S.D. Warren Paper Mill in nearby Westbrook. It was one of the largest paper mills in the world. S.D. Warren was a major importer of coal, wood pulp, china clay, and other bulk goods shipped into Portland by sea or rail. The Maine Central and the Grand Trunk Railroads were also major users of coal, and they each had their own coal pockets at either end of the Portland waterfront.

The work of shoveling coal was backbreaking, "skull-draggin" as Coley often complained. He had been working at this difficult manual labor for twenty years, almost since the day of his arrival in Portland, and it was now taking its toll on his aging body. Coley did not know how much longer he could maintain this challenging work pace in competition with an almost endless supply of eager younger laborers.

Early in 1881, Coleman had been among the charter members of the newly formed dockworkers' union, the Portland Longshoremen's Benevolent Society, simply known by all locally as the PLSBS. In return for an initiation fee, which fluctuated between $5 and $20 in these years, and dues that averaged thirty cents per month, Coleman received the security of somewhat steady work, at least in the winter months, a $5 weekly sick benefit up to a total of $50, if needed, and a $100 death benefit for his wife and family. Longshoremen all hoped that they would never have to collect on those benefits, especially the latter!

In addition, the Society provided a collective bargaining structure, several hundred strong, from which to negotiate for increased wages and improved working conditions along Portland's deepwater wharves. For many years they had maintained the union's independence and even now had continued to resist several entreaties to join with larger nation-wide labor organizations such as the International Longshoremen's Association (ILA) out of New York.

Coleman remembered signing the official union ledger with a mixture of pride and humiliation. The latter was caused by his inability to write his name. This necessitated his request of the union secretary to inscribe "His Mark" around the "X" that Coleman made in the official book. The official PLSBS Charter, with signatures affixed, showed that this was not an uncommon problem. Coley was typical of his fellow longshoremen in this regard. Although all could speak at least some broken English, Coleman estimated that one in five was illiterate.

Perhaps, he imagined, this was caused by the Irish-speaking nature of Portland's Galway-based immigrants and by a general lack of educational opportunities for them back in rural western Ireland prior to their emigration. The ability to read, to write, and to speak in the community's vernacular, in this case English, would have been a definite advantage even for longshore work. It might have eventually enabled a skilled and lucky worker to advance to a less physically strenuous and better paid position alongshore, such as timekeeper or checker.

"Thems with the smarts get them jobs," Coley complained to his good friend, Joe Loftus.

Joe sadly responded, as he was wont to do, "Yes, but that's derogatory wrong!"

For that morning's work, Coley unloaded coal from the steamer *Avona* that had arrived from Nova Scotia the previous day after a difficult journey. One of his fellow workers told him that the ship's problems had not ended when the *Avona* reached the entrance to Portland Harbor. The Portland pilot boat with Captain McDuffee aboard could not pull close enough alongside the *Avona* because of high waves, and the Captain ended up in the frigid waters of Casco Bay after he attempted unsuccessfully to jump from the pilot boat to the rail of the ice-encrusted steamer. Bartley Conley read to Coley's gang from a local newspaper an account of this dangerous episode, "He was rescued with great difficulty, but wet and bruised as he took his place at once in the pilot house and brought the coal steamer in."

Coley then replied to Bartley, "I guess we longshoremen aren't the only mucks working under difficult conditions!" Coley had once heard that some of the Protestants in Portland believed in what they called "total immersion baptism," and he now joked about this to Bartley, "For Captain McDuffee, at least, this unplanned baptism was too much to ask as the sea water isn't exactly inviting in January. This would have tested the faith of any saint!"

When Bartley further described the dangers of working aboard these coastal steamers, Coley reminded him, "That's all true, Bartley, but our own work is no bed of roses either. Don't forget that only a few months ago one of our closest longshore friends slipped on the icy deck of a Liverpool steamer, fell thirty feet into the ship's hold, broke his neck, and died instantly."

All too common episodes of severe accidents and deaths alongshore such as this were easily recalled by many of Coleman's fellow dock hands. The cold, icy, wintry weather contributed to a great increase in the frequency and severity of accidents all along Portland's busy waterfront. There was always a predictably dramatic increase in the number of those receiving union benefits for sickness or injury in the six winter months of November through April as these represented the waterfront's busy season. The most recent PLSBS Sick Committee Report had attested to making $5.00 payments to seven longshoremen: Patrick Bowen (9th week), Michael Whalen (6th week), P.J. Higgins (4th week), George James (3rd week), George Robin (5th week), Charles Carlson (1st week) and Thomas Fitzsimons (1st week). The Sick Committee was authorized to pay sick or injured workers at the rate of $5.00 per week to a maximum of ten weeks. After that they and their families were on their own, or as they might say in Ireland, "severely left alone."

On one day alone earlier this same winter, three longshoremen suffered crushed arms and legs when a pallet carrying baled pulp broke free from the winch. Like Coley, most of his friends carried scars from mishaps suffered on Portland's docks. Small wonder that they needed the union for whatever paltry compensation they could get. There was no one else concerned for the workers' welfare other than their own benevolent society. This was a lesson that Coley had learned the hard way – always look out for yourself. It remained his personal guide.

The normal ten-hour day shift ran from 7 a.m. to 6 p.m. with an hour off for dinner at noon. Five hours of steady work before dinner, and five hours of steady work afterwards, for six or seven days a week, and with few, if any, holidays. That was the norm, at least during the busy winter. During his dinner break, Coley didn't have enough time to walk home, unless he happened to be working at the nearby Grand Trunk wharves.

It was now difficult for him to even check on Mary's condition. He would usually eat his dinner on site and then return to work by one o'clock. If work took him to the western end of the waterfront near the Maine Central Railroad terminal, at least in the summer months when there was no school, Coley and others from the east end would sometimes have their eager children deliver a hot dinner from home in a lunch pail. That was a treat for all concerned, especially for the curious and wide-eyed children. It was believed, however, that some proper Yankees in Portland, referred to locally as "the quality," wanted to discourage the presence of lunch pails from Portland's main commercial district along Congress Street, maintaining that it made the city appear to be too "low-brow."

Mary had seemed a bit more tired than usual this morning, but she convinced her husband that she was doing just fine. Coley had arrived at the head of the Randall and McAllister dock for the twice-daily shape-up just a few minutes before seven. He always had difficulty with time, a common Irish trait. Coley was predictably a little late to almost everything, and this included work, union meetings, Ancient Order of Hibernians meetings, and even Church. Mary had often admonished him, 'Coley, you'll be late to your own funeral!'

Mary urged her husband that the American trait of promptness should replace his easy-going Connemara style. He had never seen a watch until he arrived in

Portland. He had one now, but it was mainly for show. 'What Christly good are they?' he had openly wondered, adding philosophically, 'They only make you rush about. They'll either tell you to speed up or to slow done, for Christ's sake! Who needs to be nagged at by a damned silly little machine anyways?'

Coley was concerned these days about Mary as the new baby was due at almost any time – watch or no watch. Mary had told her lovie that she would have his favorite meal, boiled shoulder of lamb ladled over baked potatoes in their skins, when he returned home for supper that evening shortly after six o'clock. She knew that for some reason Coley was greatly concerned about the union meeting later this evening and she further reasoned that a hearty meal of lamb might calm and fortify him for the tasks at hand.

The shape-up, the method by which work gangs would be picked for each shift, was already under way a little before seven that morning by the time Coley had reached the head of the pier. The sounds of his workplace and of the shape-up were as familiar to him as they would have been foreign to any visitor.

"Average Man? – Here. Blessed Virgin? – Here. Bridget? – Here. Cockaneeney? – Here. Philip go fada? – Here. Cois Fharraige Mike? – Here. Iron Horse? – Here. Lovely Mike? – Here. Dinish? – Here. Mickey from Lynn? – Here. Moose? – Here. Paddy na gCnoic? – Here. President Gorham? – Here. Sir Walter? – Here. Spareribs? – Here. Lamb? – Here." All present and accounted for just barely, in the case of Coley, the "Lamb."

Coley's work gang was thus in place, called out by their gang boss as usual using these nicknames by which they were all well known. Sixteen men were now ready for another day of work unloading coal from the *Avona*. Coley's gang included Pat Green, Michael McDonough, Michael Gorham, Martin McDonough, Philip Foley, Mike Conley, Philip O'Donnell, Michael Mulkern, Joe Loftus, Michael Quarry, Michael Joyce, Pat Joyce, Michael Gorham, Walter Joyce, Patrick Welch, and himself, Coleman Folan.

Each gang member gave their chip to the gang boss. This small round unimposing piece of metal permitted these men to work this ship. The chips were, in turn, given to the checker for payroll purposes. This was yet another shape-up, similar to the many hundreds that Coleman had participated in over the past twenty years. All longshoremen, not only in Portland but along the entire Atlantic and Gulf Coasts, went through a similar ritual twice daily. By this method ships were loaded or unloaded and men were employed to do this strenuous labor.

Coleman and the others knew that some West Coast longshoremen used a different system, but this was what they were familiar with and, with the exception of a few of the younger members, most saw no need for change. The gang would remain the same until the work was complete and the ship, thus loaded or unloaded, was ready to sail. This would be true unless one or more of the gang members became sick or perhaps "fell off the wagon" and was thus unfit to work – if they, to use a local phrase, had become "disguised by drink." In those cases that member would be replaced by one of the many eager younger members of the Society who were waiting patiently for any chance to prove themselves.

Almost every man had a nickname by which he was known. Often even their very best friends might not know their real full names. When the checkers reported to the clerks who were responsible for doing the payroll, they also used these nicknames. Someone once told Coleman that the clerks had a file with all these nicknames listed alphabetically and, supposedly, on one occasion an inexperienced checker had only a list with their real names that hardly anyone recognized. This innocent mistake caused near pandemonium.

'Which Joyce do you mean? Which McDonough? Which Folan? Connolly the long way or Conley the short way? What the hell are you trying to do to us?' These questions rang out until the unsuspecting newcomer rectified his list and all was made right again. There indeed is much to learn from someone's name!

Coleman's name was the "Lamb." He would proudly carry that moniker throughout his lifetime and he would pass it along to his eldest son, Johnny. All of the family, including each and every one of Coley's children, would eventually be known in Portland as the Lambs. Perhaps even into the future.

'Which Folan are you?' was a common question from the older Portland Irish. To such an inquiry as this, there could only be one correct answer – the "Lamb." Johnny and even Mamie had gone through this routine several times already at school and in their jobs, and soon it would be the others' turns. A common response from the questioner, usually an older person, might often be something like, 'Ah, the Lamb! Now I see the resemblance. My people are from Bontraghard, just two or three miles from his birthplace in Callowfeenish. And sure don't I know well your mother, too, from just over on Mynish.'

It was strangely reassuring for the Folan children just to know that they were known. The Irish have an incredible aptitude for remembering family genealogy. They could extend these connections to cousins, nieces, and nephews. It was said that the Irish word for cousin contains the number four, suggesting relationships over four different family surnames, paternal and maternal grandparents, as well as one's own mother and father. Some of these experts could give you all four tracks by which one might be related to any other Irish soul now living here in Portland. The younger members of most of these families seemed to have either little skill or no interest in learning these complex family ties, and thus a wonderfully personal way of making human contact was slowly being lost.

One or two of the very oldest Irish, one in the east end and one in the west end, were commonly spoken of locally as *seanchai* (from the Irish meaning storytellers or keepers of the old cultural history). These *seanchai* were quite remarkable! They wrote nothing down, ever. One, it was said, was himself completely illiterate, yet amazingly he never forgot anyone's family roots or its many branches. Coleman often wondered what would happen if his neighborhood's treasured memories were to die. Who would then remember? Mary fully agreed with her husband and presciently further added, 'When a *seanchi* dies it's like a library burning to the ground – only it is even sadder still because it's your own personal library.'

It was said that when such great spirits as those of these *seanchai* left this Earth it would take a great wind to send them onto the next. Almost unbelievably one of these local *seanchai* had recently died during a Portland hurricane, even though this occurred only rarely as far north as Portland. Most of his contemporaries were not in the least surprised by this remarkable coincidence, and at his wake more than one of them smiled when they spoke of this twist of fate, as if to confirm the old spiritual belief to themselves, by nodding their heads and proclaiming to each other with absolute affirmation, 'It's true. It's true for you!'

The shape-up was the Portland longshoremen's rigorously enforced system, and they stuck to it religiously. Once, a new younger member failed to get hired and had complained vociferously that the system was rigged. Mike Gorham, the walking boss, predictably and sharply berated him in front of all the assembled dockworkers, 'Is it a job or justice you're looking for? For a job you'll need a chip. If it's justice you want, you'll find it in the dictionary!'

The shape-up, of course, favored the older, more experienced workers. It obviously also favored those with relatives. Many gangs had several related McDonoughs, Connollys, or Joyces. It also clearly favored the Irish. After all, hadn't they formed the union some twenty years earlier? And so now many of them reasoned, 'Why wouldn't we look out for our own first?'

Younger members, some of them probably capable of doing twice the work, couldn't understand why an older, weaker man should be given work preference over them. If these newer members had relatives on a gang, however, they might get a spot if a position were ever to open up. If they were strong and capable, and it was agreeable to the other gang members, they might be able to keep the spot, fully aware, of course, that the senior longshoremen would really "put it to them" to test their resilience. If nothing opened up, however, they would simply have to continue to wait for a whole new gang to form during any especially busy time and only hope that they might be included. Getting in, of course, that was the trick!

Coley had once heard an amusing and unique story concerning "getting in" that he personally knew to be true. He had been speaking a few years back during the lunch break alongshore with a young blue-eyed, blond-haired longshoreman from a fairly new gang. Coleman knew his name to be Joyce. Since that was also his wife Mary's family name, he was curious enough to ask the newcomer the standard question, "Which Joyce are you?"

The young longshoremen hesitated, looking confused and even perplexed, and so Coleman tried another avenue by asking, "Is it Recess, Maam Cross, or Cornamona that your Joyces are from?"

Again, no answer was immediately forthcoming from the young longshoreman who continued to look directly at the ground. Finally, after a long and uncomfortable silence, the sheepish newcomer reluctantly confessed.

"It's none of those. My people are Helstroms from Sweden, and that's where I was born, too. Shortly after I arrived in Portland, and when I tried for several weeks with no success to land a job on any gang, I finally decided to pay closer attention to what was happening every morning. One gang was half full of Joyces, so the next morning when I was asked my name by a new gang boss, I simply answered 'Mike Joyce' – and I've been working ever since! So Mike Joyce it is for me, as long as I'm living here and working on the Portland waterfront at least. My children seem to like it, and my wife likes the wages. It's a good name, yes?"

Coley smiled. He liked this kid and his answer was not only true, but clever. His wife's Joyces were originally from Oughterard near the eastern edge of the Twelve Pins. Only later, and following a death in the family, had they migrated further west into Connemara and to the island called Mynish. A few of the Joyces had blue eyes, like Helstrom, so Coley now figured what's the bother?

"*Ná bach leis* (don't bother with it), *is cuma* (no problem)," Coley told his new young friend. "Sure they get all our names mixed up in the immigration station anyways. *ÓConghaile* becomes Connolly or Conley, or even as I once heard, Cornelia. My own *ÓCuláin* first became Folan over there and then Foley over here. You've picked a good name in Joyce – they don't butcher that name much, so stick with it, boyo!"

Sensing that the young Mike Joyce was still not totally convinced that his secret was secure with him, Coley had then added, "You've nothing to fear. Your story is safe with me. Just hold up your end and you'll be fine. And if anyone should ever ask where your Joyces are from, just tell them that you're from 'Joyce's Country,' of course. Then they'll know exactly what you mean and they'll not bother you further."

There were a few other non-Irish laborers working alongshore. Coley generally liked them. Some were Swedes, like Mike Joyce – "squareheads" as some of Coley's friends called them, but not maliciously and seldom directly to their faces. Others were Poles, Italians, or even a few Russian Jews. One of the latter was a real scrapper, and it was known that some of the Irish street-toughs alongshore weren't too kind to him. Coley called him the "Irish Jew." This man whose surname was Warsaw could box with the best of them, and he often taught an unsuspecting Irish braggart a lasting lesson with a solid right uppercut that usually served to inspire instant respect.

Italians were starting to arrive in Portland, although not too many yet, but their numbers seemed to be growing steadily. Many of them found work as freight handlers on the railroad. They would load or off-load the railroad cars, often in close proximity to the Irish longshoremen. But the more lucrative work on the docks and especially on the English steamers, sometimes called "blue water freighters," was and would remain essentially Irish labor, with only a very few notable exceptions.

Portland's small Negro community was the only group that had no presence whatsoever on the waterfront. Coleman had often been told that before the Irish had arrived in force in this city, a small Negro neighborhood at the base of Munjoy Hill had provided much of the poorly paid and unsteady longshore labor. Portland's early maritime commerce largely concerned West Indies molasses. Portland businesses refined both sugar and rum from this natural liquid product. And quite a few of the city's Negro citizens had come to this seaport via the Caribbean trade route. The J.B. Brown sugar refinery was one of the largest in the entire country and the extended family of the original owner had thus become some of Portland's wealthiest and most prominent citizens.

When the famine hit Ireland in the mid-1840s, the Irish were already emigrating in stunningly large numbers and many had made it as far as Portland, Maine. In 1833, a Galway-born Irish Dominican, Father Charles Ffrench, helped build the first Catholic Church in the west end of the city, which he predictably named Saint Dominic's.

In the early 1850s Portland was linked by rail to Montreal via the Grand Trunk Railroad, and the volume of Canadian grain shipped out of this port primarily aboard English steamers increased dramatically. By the time of the Civil War the Irish were well ensconced on the city's docks, largely displacing the much smaller Negro workforce at exactly the same time that this work was becoming more abundant and reliable and, therefore, more lucrative.

Around this same time an informal Portland Longshoremen's Association had formed and they soon struck for higher wages. Their labor was crucial during the Civil War when munitions, canned goods, woolens, and many other vital supplies were being shipped out of Portland to the Union armies. Wages and shipping volume increased. Immigration from Ireland was answering the growing demand for this type of manual labor. The ever-increasing Irish Catholic population in the city's east end was then being served by the new Cathedral of the Immaculate Conception built just after the Great Portland Fire of 1866.

By the early 1880s, just as Coleman and Mary and many others from Galway were about to arrive in Portland, they were already well aware of plentiful jobs available for men along its waterfront. This knowledge came from letters back to Galway from those then living and prospering here. And so in early 1881, Coleman became one of the charter members of the newly-formed Portland Longshoremen's Benevolent Society (PLSBS).

The gangs that he worked on in these early years were almost exclusively Irish speaking. The three main regions of Galway from which most of Portland's Irish originated were all *Gaeltacht*, or Irish-speaking districts. These included *Cois Fharraige*, west of Galway City; the townlands around Carna in south Connemara; and Cornamona, northwest of Galway City. This was at a time when the Irish language was in rapid historic decline in Ireland being pushed further westward by the steady encroachment of English, especially within most Irish cities and towns. All of a sudden, Coleman found himself in what must have seemed like another, albeit much smaller, *Gaeltacht* – only this time on the other side of the Atlantic!

The Irish language was yet another way for the older longshoremen to separate themselves from the younger crowd. Very few of the young "native-borns" or "corner-boys," or the more pejorative "narrow backs," as they were often called, had much skill in the Irish language. It was a convenient way for the older longshoremen to express what they were truly thinking, and in their very own way of speaking, without being ridiculed. The youngsters did have the English, to be sure. But to Coleman and others of his age group, the Irish language was a soothing consolation.

At home Mary, just as most of the other longshore wives, would speak mainly Gaelic to their husbands. Coley yearned for Johnny, or indeed any of his own children, to speak Irish, but he knew by now that this was an unrealistic dream and quite unlikely to ever happen in Portland. 'What use is it to me?' Johnny had once asked his mother.

When Mary related this to Coley he was sad at first, but quickly changed his tune to one part optimism and one part realism as he responded to his wife, 'Maybe he's right, Mary. That boy of ours will be a success in this country, dearie – and the loss of our own language might be the price we'll have to pay for his success.'

~ ~ ~

Coleman's gang continued to tackle the *Avona* throughout the rest of the morning. The poor ship was still caked in ice, and with the weather being what it was, things were not likely to change any time soon. The morning's work was usually the easiest, or so it always seemed, as he and the others in his gang would still be partially warm and somewhat rested.

The story telling would start almost as soon as the first shield plowed through the first pile of coal. His gang was almost like a second family to him. They all knew each other well enough that no one could easily get away with stretching the truth too far, although that never deterred any one of them from boldly trying. That was the test of a true story teller – the ability to spin a tale that was both tantalizing and simultaneously believable – even if totally conjured. Coleman Folan was known in his gang, and well beyond, as being one of the best.

Joe Loftus, known alongshore as "Dinish" from the birthplace of his father, was Coley's best friend in Portland. On this day, Joe's gang was working the very same pier adjacent to Coley's gang.

"Are any of the 99ers working in your hold today, Coley?" Joe shouted over.

"Only Lovely Mike," replied Coley, knowing that the Mulkerns were known by that name as there were so many of them working alongshore. "How many Joyce's are there working down below over by you," Coley yelled back.

Joe, skillfully playing the straight man and knowing that the answer he was meant to give required an odd number, appropriately responded, "Seven," thus setting up Coley's expected reply.

"Well then, have half of them come up on deck!"

No matter how many times these innocent and silly jokes or similar stories were told they always resulted in broad smiles or even raucous laughter if told appropriately. Usually the Irish themselves were the butt of their own jokes, but that was only to be expected. This fact had more than once prompted the "Iron Horse," Phil O'Donnell, to blithely inquire of those present, "What use is there in being Irish unless you're thick?"

Phil had his own unique vocabulary that was spiced with many colorful personal phrases. He referred to arthritis, for example, as "the old man with the whiskers." Phil was also renowned for exaggeration. Such was the case of his famous story of how, during one recent unique and extremely cold spell, the ocean waves had frozen in place. According to Phil's telling of the story, 'Portlanders could then easily skate over to Peaks Island by carefully skipping from the crest of one frozen wave to another.'

On this morning, Phil now proceeded to tell the gang another well-known story of a local Irishman who had stumbled upon a heated argument among a small group of men, none of whom he knew. The Irishman, quickly sized up the situation and the opportunity that it presented, and then earnestly inquired of the angry crowd, "Is this a private fight, or can anyone join in?"

Coley loved these stories and jokes, but Joe Loftus was often much less sanguine about hearing these.

On this occasion Joe protested, "It makes us look unintelligent. My sister ridicules our own parents for speaking in their own style of broken English. She mimics the way they say things like, 'Bring the baby's face up while I wash it.' It's nearly a direct translation of how they would state this in Irish, for Christ's sake. But when my sister ridicules them, it makes them and all of us look like *amadáin* (fools)."

Coley was usually unsure of the reason that his friend was so sensitive to these humorous and harmless stories while he was not. Coley would often try to diffuse the tension by inserting pieces of senseless Irish doggerel, such as, '*Tá Gaeilge go leor ag na buachailli bó* (The cowboys speak good Irish)!'

Sometimes these distractions worked. The one thing upon which all the long-shoremen could agree was that these comical stories about the Irish that were "derogatory wrong," to use Joe's words, could only be told by a fellow Irishman. That was a given. Woe betide any other person who tried to mimic someone from Ireland. In local parlance that would be skating on thin ice and punishment would be swift and sure. Joe had once expressed this sentiment in the words of a popular refrain, 'And I'll not be laughed at anywhere, but highly represented!'

These humorous stories could go on endlessly. It helped to pass the time be-tween the buckets or sling loads being sent down into the hold. A younger longshoreman had once said that the telling of these stories by the Irish gangs was similar to the alleged practice of the Negroes who had formerly done much of the longshore work in Portland. He said that they had worked to the musical beat of their own singing. This may have been correct, but somehow the story didn't strike Coley as appropriate. Coley knew few if any of Portland's Negroes, but he didn't want to be publicly compared to them in any way. Where this feeling came from he simply couldn't say – it wasn't just Coley who held this sentiment, it was shared by many of his fellow Irish laborers.

One of the best loved stories concerned John Brown, the Irish beat patrolman who had only recently arrived from County Galway with a somewhat limited grasp of English. During a mid-summer heat wave, the horse of a Jewish peddler had succumbed to the high temperatures and lack of water and had dropped over dead right in the middle of Cumberland Street, a major thoroughfare. A crowd had instantly gathered. When Officer Brown arrived on the scene to write his report, he surveyed the situation and then addressed the large group of curious mostly Irish spectators by asking, 'Could someone spell for me 'Cumberland Street'?'

Unfortunately, Officer Brown was met with stone silence and blank stares from the assembly of largely illiterate onlookers. After several embarrassing mo-ments that seemed more like an hour with everyone looking down at their feet, Brown then cleverly diffused the embarrassing situation when he declared, 'Well then, some of youse grab hold iv the horse's hind quarters and drag her on over to Oak Street!'

Whether or not the story was actually true didn't really matter. It was the style of relating this incident and its comical message – an unsophisticated Irishman's clever reversal out of a tight situation – rather than the veracity of the story itself – that was the key. Embellishment and exaggeration were essential elements of this art form. A simple or well-known story could be a success only if told in exactly the correct manner. What was essential to story-telling was proper intonation and timing, but also the appropriate degree of surprise and enthusiasm.

Joe Loftus thankfully was once again in a jovial mood. He shared a story about Pat Jennings and swore to the attentive crowd that it was entirely true. Jennings, it seems, while working in another gang had been complaining almost on a daily basis about getting the same sandwich for his lunch. Day in and day out he had exclaimed, with growing exasperation, 'Jesus Christ, tuna again!'

Finally one of his fellow gang members had tired of this repeated episode, and out of pure exasperation he had inquired, 'Pat, for Christ's sake, why don't you ask your Bridie to make you another kind of sandwich?'

Pat, defiantly and seemingly annoyed at this impertinent intrusion, proudly proclaimed to all present, 'What the hell do you mean? I makes me own sangwiches!'

Sometimes these stories could take a more serious turn. Michael McDonough, "The Blessed Virgin," remarked that his wife had read in the previous day's newspaper that the SS *California* had safely passed by Inistrahull on its journey from Portland to Liverpool. "Thank God Almighty!" the cry rose in near unison from these two gangs. They had all witnessed that steamer cautiously creep out of Portland harbor a couple of weeks earlier, dangerously listing to one side. The stevedores had not allowed the longshoremen sufficient time to properly trim the large load of grain in its holds.

McDonough added the exclamation point, "And they can thank their lucky stars that they didn't hit any rough seas on their crossing!"

Mike "Moose" Joyce then seriously proclaimed as if speaking for them all, "And they surely benefitted from all of our prayers over these past two weeks, no doubt!"

Following along on this more serious trend, Coley then asked if anyone had witnessed the collapse of the huge water reservoir on the top of Munjoy Hill about six years earlier. Mike Gorham, one of the older gang members, replied that much of his family lived on Munjoy Hill at that time. Gorham then said that of the four people who had died in this disaster, two were friends of his family. He next related details of the story, which he had committed to memory, to the two attentive work gangs.

"The entire northeastern corner of the reservoir suddenly failed at around 5:30 a.m. on the morning of August 6, 1893. People were still sleeping in their beds. This sent a huge wave of millions of gallons of water onto their homes located beneath the reservoir, crushing them like tiny wooden boxes and also crushing many of the poor occupants inside. Four died instantly, and many more were seriously injured on that day."

"But that's not the worst way to die, I suppose," affirmed Coley who then added, "not that there's too many good ways to go, except in your sleep. You all remember the case of Jimmy Connolly who died twice in the fire on the wharf a few summers back? He was burned alive by a fire and then drowned too when his poor body fell into the harbor. I'd like to know one thing – did he feel the pain of both of those deaths? Do you suppose it makes a difference how a person dies?"

Hearing no replies to his serious inquiries and seeing the blank expressions on the faces of the gang members at this far too philosophical question, Coley then wisely decided to change the subject quickly by asking, "Speaking of Munjoy Hill – is it true, do you suppose, what they say about the 'Thirteen Club' at the Saint Lawrence Church up there?"

His friend Joe was first to respond, "I'd say it's true entirely. There they are, thirteen of the richest and most powerful men in Portland, and all of them in the one same Protestant church that was built entirely of stone just three years ago up there on the top of the Hill. And aren't they making decisions, wouldn't you think, that will mainly benefit themselves? And these same decisions are being made, I'd venture to say, without as much as a thought for the likes of any of us!"

Joe and all the Loftuses were known to have a suspicious nature. This was especially true if they thought they were being slighted in any way. Joe continued to hold these views very firmly, and some of them were passed on through his family. He next pointed to another example of the perceived mistreatment of the Irish locally which involved the specific location of the three Catholic churches in Portland.

"The newest one, Sacred Heart, is over there on the corner of Mellen and Sherman, not exactly your central arteries in Portland. And look at the Cathedral itself, looking meekly out over Cumberland Street with only its bare arse facing onto Congress Street, the most important street in the city! And that's not even to mention good ol' Saint Dom's whose large wooden doors open onto Gray Street rather than the busier and more elegant State Street. Now tell me, do youse all think that these things are just coincidences?"

As much as Coley admired his friend Joe Loftus, he could not buy into this pessimistic belief that here in Portland there might be a substantial number of people staying up day and night conspiring to keep the Irish and all Catholics in their place.

Coley then rebuffed Joe's assertions and more optimistically maintained, "Our people have come a long way since arriving here in Portland, and we're treated better by the Yankees here than by the English back in our own country, I'd say. Give them their Thirteen Club and their churches on Congress Street – I'll take our AOH and Hibernian Knights, the Knights of Columbus, and our own PLSBS. For Christ's sake, we already have our own three large beautiful churches here, to say nothing of Mother Petronilla and the Sisters of Mercy up on Free Street, and also out there near Stevens Avenue at Saint Joseph's Home Chapel!"

Coleman Lee from Mountfort Street, who was also in Joe's gang and a relative to Coley's wife Mary, then shouted over in Coley's support, "And don't forget we've got Alderman Joseph Connolly and Florence Driscoll."

At this point, and predictably, Pat Green chimed in, as he was wont to do, "The average man would say we've done quite well for ourselves. And don't forget Councillors Lindsay Griffin, Ed Murphy, Martin Kelley, and George Kavanough."

Pat Green was known to start most sentences with that phrase, "the average man," as it seemed to give him the aura of being well read and widely informed. An admirer, who was impressed by the breadth of Pat's knowledge, once asked if he was a well-travelled person. Pat had proudly responded in the affirmative, and then added, "Oh, yes indeed, I've travelled extensively... in Portland." These latter two words, however, had been spoken almost inaudibly.

Another of the older men in Joe's gang was Joe Burke who was usually uninterested in politics either on the local or the national level, but he then interjected, "Don't be walking all over the Eastern Prom and back to Gorham's Corner." This was his perennial way of saying, "Get to the point." This caused the entire group to laugh as they knew all too well that Joe Burke only wanted to hear more of the humorous stories that he so loved. Burke then deftly took the spotlight off himself with another of his well-known phrases, "Tell me this and tell me no more…"

It was young Martin Flaherty, surprisingly, who answered the call with a new story, one never heard before, at least by this crowd. It was young Flaherty's first attempt at telling a story, and he had waited patiently for this opportunity. He appropriately started by acknowledging that the story had come down from his father who had been born in Bontroughard in County Galway, quite close to Coley's Callowfeenish. Flaherty proceeded cautiously with his tale.

"It seems that there was a cat who had tried for many years to catch the same mouse only to be outsmarted each and every time by the clever little fella. It was quite embarrassing to the cat, as it was known that catching mice was the chief function of any self-respecting cat that was worth its salt. And besides hadn't he caught hundreds of these little creatures over the years? But this particular mouse had him banjaxed, and his confidence was badly shaken. Until one day when the cat was outside and the mouse took the opportunity to start snooping around an open cask of porter. And didn't the poor fella fall into the booze! He swam around for hours on end, unable to recover until he was nearly exhausted. Being a good Catholic mouse, he had even started saying his final prayers when after some time, who should appear but his arch-rival, Mr. Cat himself. The cat couldn't believe his good fortune! He carefully considered how he should play out this winning hand as there were many options open to him, all of them good. As he pondered this lucky twist of fate, the poor mouse, by now very nearly wasted, cried out to him in desperation, 'Take me from this cask and I promise I'll not try to escape.'

"The cat, no fool himself and clearly not wanting to give up his advantage, then asked, 'But, how do I know I can trust you?' To this question the little mouse, now quite the pitiful creature entirely, meekly and pathetically replied, 'I give you my solemn word as a good Catholic mouse. I'm yours to do with whatever you will. You've finally won.'

"The cat then confidently lifted the mouse out of the cask of porter and carefully set him on the floor, whereupon it quickly dashed toward a small hole in the nearby wall. From the safety of the hole the mouse then looked out on the bewildered and entirely flummoxed poor cat that wailed, 'But you gave me your solemn word, so you did…'

"To this the self-satisfied little mouse then quite matter-of-factly replied, in all seriousness and with an absolutely straight face, 'Never trust anyone who is on the booze!'"

Chapter 4

Murky Overhead

"But when the snow is snowin' and it's murky overhead,
Sure, it's nice to get up in the morning but it's better to stay in bed."

– Popular Irish ditty

Between the dark and the daylight, the silence and the commotion, the sleeping and the waking, there were few and all too brief moments for Mary to be alone. The winter nights were not only bitterly cold but oh so very long. Mary never had to worry about rousing Coley or the eldest two children, and the youngest two could lounge in bed, but the middle four aspiring scholars were quite another matter altogether.

Tom, Joe, Agnes, and Kitty were a handful to stir in the darkness of a wintry morning. In the glorious summer months they would all be out "in the streets, half heard." Sometimes they would be playing before breakfast was ready, and it was always quite the chore to coax them back inside even long after darkness had fallen. It was just a few short weeks past the winter solstice, and the only place they wished to be was in their cozy warm beds.

This was like it used to be back home in Mynish, Mary mused, when in the winter her entire family would be slow to rise but would then stay up late at night at the only warm place in the house which was in front of the homely turf fire where all Irish families assembled and communed. This was yet another trait that seemed to survive their relocation to America, and Mary often pondered upon the word "homely" that was used as a positive attribute in Ireland while in Portland it was most often seen in a negative light, as something that was not attractive. 'What's wrong with your own home?' Mary would ask her children when they used "homely" as a criticism.

The Irish, she believed, are better suited to nature's time than to any artificial human schedules, and that is why she preferred to follow the journey of the sun rather than the instruction from some confounded clock! 'Why do they have clock towers over here, while we always had church towers at home?' This reminded

Mary of the slow air then popular back in Galway, perhaps as much for its evocative title as for its haunting melody,

'Táimse i mo codhladh, 's ná duise mé (I'm sleeping, don't waken me).'

How true, and now "Don't waken me" was indeed the plaintive morning cries of her young ones here on this side of the Atlantic, too!

Coley had taught all his children a favorite little ditty set to a popular Irish tune. He would often gleefully sing this to them on any dark midwinter Sunday morning when they were free from school and he could also celebrate his one day away from the docks:

Oh, it's nice to get up in the morning when the sun begins to shine,
Four or five or six o'clock in the good old summertime.
But when the snow is snowin' and it's murky overhead,
Sure, it's nice to get up in the morning but it's better to stay in bed.

Coley would playfully get the older children laughing by quietly substituting for their less sensitive ears the final phrase, 'Sure, it's nice to get up in the morning, take a pee, and go back to bed!' They thought that was quite risqué, and so they told him. But Coley characteristically responded to their half-hearted protests as he did to so many other things – '*Is cuma* (No bother),' he'd say, but then would cautiously add, 'But please don't tell your Máma!'

Mamie was a great help to her mother. Mary and Mary Magdalene, mother and daughter, had a special bond. She was, of course, the first female in a family divided evenly so far by gender. The expected new child, the cudeen, would break this tie one way or the other. During the past half year, Mamie had taken on the lion's share of the physical care for Míchilín. Once the doctor informed the family that his earlier nausea and continued leg pains were from an actual disease by the name of poliomyelitis, or polio, they knew that the future might be challenging for this lovely child, at least as far as walking was concerned.

Mary wouldn't allow anyone to pity her baby, however, or ever give up hope for his full recovery, unlikely as that might be. Without even so much as being asked, Mamie had taken upon her own shoulders the task of rehabilitating her little brother. She had even temporarily given up her part-time job at the clothing shop for a few months during the previous year, and with it the money that was so desperately needed by the family, in order to devote her full attention to Míchilín.

Coley disapproved. He strenuously voiced the importance of the added income to the family's chances of financial survival. But Mary usually won all battles dealing with her children. Although Coley might bluster and blow hot air for a while, Mary's calm rational thinking usually prevailed. She firmly believed that this was simply her eldest daughter's natural maternal instincts emerging. 'And what," she pointedly put to her befuddled husband, 'would you be knowin' about that?' Case closed – for the moment at least.

For these several months following his dreaded diagnosis in July of the previous year, Mamie had massaged Michael's painful left leg several times a day in addition to giving him a warm bath every morning and evening. Their favorite time together, however, was listening to stories that she had selected to keep his mind occupied during this therapy. Although he was now just over two years of age, Mamie believed that young Michael could understand. He would smile at all the right places in these stories, and he would even chuckle at the same places each time as she read aloud from his favorites.

Like her mother, Mamie was an optimist. Coley ultimately declared this therapy to be a waste of time. Even though he had originally capitulated, after some time he eventually persuaded Mary to coax their daughter back to work by the beginning of November just as the home heating season was approaching. Mamie persisted in her hope for Michael's recovery, however. Every day before leaving for work she would massage the little boy's weak leg that, unfortunately, continued to slowly atrophy. Michael was by now so familiar with her touch that at times he would not stir from his sound sleep during this regular morning ritual, but later in the evenings he often cooed and sighed.

While Mamie's therapy routine for Michael was occurring upstairs, Mary had her own chance to pamper her oldest child in the kitchen. Johnny had attended primary and grammar school until just two years earlier, and then in the autumn of his fourteenth year he had enrolled in one of the nation's oldest public education facilities, Portland High School.

Johnny was a natural scholar and he had relished his years at North School, both Primary and Grammar. His first full year at Portland High School, located within easy walking distance from their home, had truly opened his eyes to the larger world. For Johnny, it had been a tantalizing taste of what his world could become. But his meager earnings were also badly needed, and Coley insisted that he work at least part-time at a local bottling factory whenever they required extra help. Mary questioned Coley as to how that menial employment could positively change her son's life claiming, 'It's only a bottling company, after all, and there's little room for advancement.'

It seemed that the top spots in the Murdock and Freeman Bottling Company had been reserved for family members or their closest friends, mostly all members of the Saint Lawrence Congregational Church on Munjoy Hill. Johnny hadn't been working there very long before he was informed by a supervisor, not that much older than himself, that he would likely never be anything more than a manual laborer.

Johnny had pointedly protested, "But how could you know what talents I may have?"

"What in God's name does talent have to do with anything?" his young boss responded with a smirk that seemed to say everything. "I thought you told me that your family name was Folan, not Murdock or Freeman!"

Mary often counseled her eldest to be patient. 'Perhaps this particular job is not what you are cut out for, but your time will surely come,' she optimistically insisted.

In the meanwhile, the meager wages earned by Johnny and Mamie brought a few extra dollars into the household each week, and that made a huge difference to their growing family. Mary was finally forced to agree with her husband on that crucial point. This was especially true with a new baby due any day now and with the cost of heating by coal increasing with painful regularity.

"Máma, I want to work for myself," Johnny would insist whenever he became frustrated with the limitations placed upon him at work by people with much less ambition and even fewer skills than he possessed. "At least then my efforts would count for something."

Already he had noticed one or two boys nearer to his age who had started work at Murdock and Freeman at about the same time. "Worthless time-servers," he called them, but they had already been promoted ahead of him to easier jobs with slightly better pay. This seemed unfair and, as with his mother, he was keenly aware of injustice.

Mary knew that Coleman would place a great deal of responsibility on the shoulders of both of their eldest children. They both knew that primogeniture had a remarkably long history in Ireland.

"Johnny is the first in our family to be able to read and write in the English language," Coley had often proudly stated.

"Or in any language, for that matter," Mary added with equal pride.

Johnny was the one tasked with deciphering any letters or official notices that the family had received. There were plenty of friends who could help them to write the occasional letter home, in Irish, of course. None of their other children knew Irish, although Johnny at least could understand several common phrases that he had heard since childhood. There was no incentive to teach their children their own native language, as it was spoken in Portland only by those from the Old Country. Few of these children would ever return to the Ireland that their parents had so reluctantly left behind. They had left, after all, with good reason, and these stubborn facts were unlikely to change anytime soon.

John Mulkern owned a small saloon on the corner of India and Fore Streets. He was from Carna, half-way between Mary's Mynish and Coleman's Callowfeenish. He spoke their same dialect, knew most of their relatives at home, and additionally he could read and write both in Irish and English. Coley was quite impressed with Mulkern's skills.

He had once asked his wife, 'Why do we need politicians when we've got our own publicans like John Mulkern who can read and write, give advice, and even loan us money when we're a bit pinched?'

Mary had replied with mild sarcasm, 'If Mulkern ever becomes a politician he wouldn't be the first Irish publican to do so.'

Johnny also admired John Mulkern. Mulkern had made the adjustment from Ireland to Portland almost seamlessly. He was well respected in his own neighborhood, had a large family who all attended Mass every Sunday at the Cathedral, was conversant about politics on both sides of the Atlantic, and was apparently doing quite well in the saloon business. Johnny saw in him a kind of role model – a small businessman working for himself rather than a "skulldraggin" longshoreman working in the interests of the shipping companies or, like him, working in a dead-end job.

Coleman, however, had once sagely warned his eldest son, 'When you work for yourself, Johnny, you often have a tyrant for a boss!'

Although Johnny loved and respected his Daide unconditionally, he also knew only too well that Coley had his own faults and many obvious limitations. Despite these negatives, Johnny was in awe of the man who was expected to keep up the daily grind of a dock worker, day in and day out, especially throughout the frigid winter months when the vast majority of exports were transshipped from Portland's waterfront.

Mary would oft-times speak with Johnny, as one adult to another, even though he was by then only approaching the age of sixteen. Sometimes his mother shared things with Johnny that she didn't think of sharing with her own husband who at forty-two was twenty-six years Johnny's senior. But Johnny loved playing the role of the eldest child, and he especially liked being taken seriously by his Máma. His goal was to live his life in such a way as to bring neither disappointment nor shame to his parents – perhaps this is a trait shared by many first-borns.

It was very upsetting for Mary to acquiesce to Coleman on the question of Johnny deferring his schooling. They both instinctively knew that education was the only guaranteed way to get ahead in America, especially when one was not starting out with a basket full of natural advantages. Back home, in Galway, with his natural gift for learning and conversation, Johnny might have gone to the seminary and, if qualified, prepared for a religious vocation as a priest. It was a great honor for any Irish family, especially in south Connemara, to have a son in the seminary or a daughter in the convent. For poor families in Ireland like the Folans, this might have been a bit like making a virtue of a necessity, as supporting a large family on subsistence farming was never easy. Neither Johnny nor Mamie, however, saw themselves as being cut out for a life of religious commitment, and certainly not celibacy, for that matter.

Portland, although similar to Galway in many ways, was also starkly different in others, such as education. The Sacred Heart School on Cumberland Street adjacent to the Cathedral was an option for the Folan children. But Johnny had always been happy to attend the North School, a public school about the same distance from their home. Bishop Healy, and especially Fathers Dennis O'Brien and Charles Collins at the Cathedral, had often counseled their flock about the desirability, indeed the obligation, of good Catholic families to send their children to parochial schools when one was available. The cost, of course, was one factor, but tuition could often be subsidized by the parish for poorer families. Coleman, a prideful man, never would admit to anyone that the Folans needed financial help in any way.

But there were other intangible factors also involved in their decision concerning schooling. For one thing, many of their neighbors, mostly those from Ireland, had already sent their children to the public schools with no apparent harm other than the occasional bloodied nose – and these hardscrabble children of immigrants always gave as good as they got! Admittedly, they did have to read and recite from the "Protestant" King James Bible in the mornings, but there seemed to be little or no outright proselytizing. Coming from Ireland these families would have recognized that if they saw it! Johnny even thought that the King James Version of the Bible was quite poetic, and he had memorized many elegant verses.

For another thing, if all the Catholic school children from North School should decide to attend Sacred Heart, the smaller school would have been instantly overwhelmed. On this matter, as with many others concerning the rearing of the children, Mary's will had prevailed. Her convincing argument to Coley was, 'How else will our wee ones learn the ways of this new country and learn to get along with their new friends? And besides, we'll see to their religion, lovie, you can rest assured of that. They will all meet their obligations, and that's a given.'

Mary's argument was strengthened by the fact that the North School was beginning to hire single young Irish women, many from their very own neighborhood, to teach the young ones. The school was headed by Elmer E. Parmenter, a hard-nosed principal widely known as a strict disciplinarian. In the kindergarten could be found Miss Octavia O'Connor, and in the primary school Margaret O'Rourke and Mary G. Connolly from just over on Federal Street. And in the grammar school there was Mary Looney from Kellogg Street up on this side of Munjoy Hill. Although Coleman half-heartedly and defensively insisted that they could find sufficient resources for the children to attend the parochial school and that their children would surely find many friends there as well, his arguments seemed to ring hollow, even to himself.

~ ~ ~

Mamie was by now finished with her morning massage of Míchilín's withered leg. She entered the warm kitchen, putting an end to the mutually enjoyable dialog between mother and son. Mary saw a great deal of herself in Mamie, especially her caring manner. But her daughter was clearly already much more of an American girl. This was especially true in her willingness, almost her eagerness at times, to challenge, confront, and confound her Daide. Her fiery nature made her mother smile. Mary sometimes wished that she could also freely speak her mind to Coley, without inhibitions, especially when he became dogmatic or unreasonably intransigent.

This unflattering trait often appeared when Coley seemed to sense that he was on the weaker side of an argument or disagreement with his wife. At times like these, however, Mary would go off in one direction with her husband; but, their daughter, Mamie, would go in quite another. Mary had learned over her nearly two decades of marriage to pick her fights carefully and to judge when she could safely push or at least bend her husband to her way of thinking. This was especially true whenever she could convince Coley that her argument had been his idea all along!

With Mamie, however, when her Da put his foot down, she would stomp squarely on it! At times like these, Mary could see the blood rising in Coley's face, and she would quietly try to intervene. But it would inevitably be too late. Mary feared what Coley might say or do if his anger boiled over. Two entirely irreconcilable points of view were by then out in the public, and predictably neither the adamant father nor the obstinate daughter would ever retreat or compromise.

Any attempt by Mary to intervene at these tense times would usually result in a verbal assault from both fronts. Her habit was to step back and pray that neither would say something that could not be retracted, softened, or forgiven. These increasingly frequent moments of confrontation predictably resulted in an angry daughter leaving the house and slamming the door behind her for the sake of punctuation. Coley, at moments like these, would often turn to his silent wife and exclaim out of exasperation, 'That daughter of yours...' The other children, of course, witnessed these personality battles in awed silence – but they were wit-nessed all the same.

This morning, as was traditional in the Folan home, Mamie combed and braided her mother's long hair which even after all these years of childbirth and care-giving was still vibrant with the colorful auburn hue common among the Joyce family.

"Máma, your hair is lovely today. It's a gorgeous gentle shade of red. I can only hope to still have your color myself when I reach your age."

Mary seldom took notice of such compliments, but quickly interjected, as she had often done before, "Oh, you might think that my hair is a beautiful shade of red, dearie, but you should see my sister Annie in Boston. She has the most beautiful Auburn hair…and Lewiston eyebrows!"

That hilarious comment caught both Mamie and Johnny by complete surprise. They had never heard their mother make this particular pun before, cleverly referencing the twin cities along Maine's Androscoggin River just thirty or so miles north of Portland. They both laughed heartily. Mary pretended to hardly notice their mirth, although she clearly relished this proof of her growing mastery of the English language. To be able to repeat jokes or puns in two languages was indeed proof of her becoming truly bi-lingual. And further, her ability to impress both of her clever oldest children – that was nothing short of a minor miracle!

Mamie's job was as an assistant in a small local clothing shop. She didn't seem to miss attending school as much as Johnny did, in part because a small fraction of her wages didn't go directly to her family but stayed with her. This petty income was a tangible and highly desirable proof of her increasing independence. Mamie was more interested in fashion and style than philosophy or poetry, or any of the other traditional school subjects. Although she might one day be gainfully involved in a business, she didn't envision herself as a business owner. Mamie and Johnny were very close despite their profound personality differences, the most notable being their totally divergent relationships with their father. Mary had a loving nickname for her daughter – she called Mamie her "*Meiriceánach Dána* (Bold American)."

And now Mamie would be off to work in a flash. Unlike her brother, she wasn't much for conversation in the mornings. Just before leaving, she made sure that the four middle children were awake and getting ready to come downstairs where it was much warmer. There they could all dress for school in front of the freshly-stoked coal stove. The kitchen was always the family gathering place. Mary cherished the saying she had once heard locally, 'Wherever I may serve my guests, they always like the kitchen best.'

The unheated upstairs bedrooms were unappealing, especially after being forced to vacate a comfortable warm bed often shared with two or three other siblings. When at home, Mamie had a routine that all the younger children had come to expect. She chanted to them as they marched, almost in military cadence, out of their bedrooms and down the stairway toward the warmth of the kitchen. This martial tramp was always accompanied by a short nearly monosyllabic ditty that Mamie had heard somewhere, heaven only knows where.

Here we come with a nickel drum,
We've just made up an Army.
Hurrah for Cox, hurrah for Cox,
Hurrah for Coxey's Army!

Young Peg, still too young to attend school, witnessed this event each morning from bed, usually along with Michael. She wished that she could join in, it looked like such fun. And indeed, the tactic seemed to work. The children cheerfully processed down to the kitchen, and if anyone should ever approach this moving line of scholars from the other direction, Mamie had yet another saying for that occurrence as well, 'Keep to the right as the law does command, for such is the law of the land!'

After a breakfast, usually consisting of what was called stirabout and warm milk, all four young Folans would walk the short distance over Fore to India Street and then up to the bustling corner of Congress to their own beloved North School. It was an imposing brick structure that housed both the Primary School, including Kindergarten, and the Grammar School.

Presently, two of the Folan children were at each level. Mary and Coley had provided a steady stream of young scholars to North School with a new student nearly every other year. Predictably at the start of such a new year, one of the teachers would remark, 'So, this is Johnny Folan's young brother/sister? We have high hopes for you.'

Tom, supported by the younger Joe, had once protested to their amused but sympathetic mother, 'We don't want to be known as Johnny Folan's younger brothers – it's not fair! We're not all geniuses and teachers' pets in this family like Johnny, you know!'

Once when Agnes had supplied only her given name on the first day of school, her teacher, a Miss Mary Looney from nearby Kellogg Street, had presciently remarked, 'And of course you'd be a Folan – sure don't you have the map of Ireland all over your face!'

Poor Agnes had come straight home from school that afternoon as fast as her short legs would carry her. She went right to the bathroom mirror and searched her face diligently for this tell-tale map! Mary tried to console her daughter by telling her that it was only a manner of speaking and a compliment from someone who recognized a family resemblance. But, alas, poor Agnes never fully compre-hended. For the next several weeks she double-checked her face in the mirror each morning to be sure that the map had not mysteriously re-appeared overnight. Once Mamie told her amused mother that Agnes had checked her face in the mirror, twice that morning, as Mamie comically put it, 'To be sure, to be sure!'

Mary tried to explain to her children that words do not always have an exact meaning. Sometimes, she informed them, they are used creatively, especially in the Irish language. Still, this was no consolation to Agnes. Even the other children did not have the slightest understanding of what their mother meant by "creatively." So Mary further clarified this concept by telling Agnes about a friend who had a piece of antique furniture, a chest of drawers, in her home.

One day a visiting neighbor had humorously suggested, 'I'll wager that old piece of furniture came over on the *Mayflower*.'

Mary's friend's innocent but honest response was, 'No, I bought it just two years ago at Beal's over on Newbury Street!'

Still, there was no reaction from Agnes or the others, with the exception of an amused Mamie who explained, 'Right over their heads, Máma.'

Mary was more than sympathetic with her young ones because she knew only too well herself, as a native Irish speaker, how difficult it can be to understand jokes, puns, or double meanings in any language. But they would have to learn. These linguistic twists and turns were an essential part of any useful conversation, especially the more interesting ones, and without them most communication could be quite boring.

~ ~ ~

Almost before Mary knew it, the morning rush was over. Coley was working on the waterfront; Johnny, or so she thought, was off to Portland High School; Mamie was on her way to work at the clothing shop; and the young students, Tom, Joe, Agnes, and Kitty, after putting on their winter outer garments in the warm kitchen, were by now out of the house and well into their short, frigid walk to the North School.

Mary now whispered to herself, in Irish, "*Suigh síos a Mháire* (Sit down, Mary)." She found a cozy spot in which to rest. She rubbed her lower back and looked down on her immense protruding belly. This new child would not keep her waiting much longer. She could hear Peg crooning softly to Míchilín upstairs –

her two youngest both awake and content for the moment. They called themselves "pals," and they were a great source of entertainment for each other.

Peg sometimes seemed to resent the attention given to young Michael, the *cuidín*, especially since she had reaped the benefits of being the youngest herself for nearly two years. She often pondered how Michael had the effrontery to disrupt the birth order and thus place himself into this vaunted family status over her. And to add injury to insult, Michael had gone out and contracted polio! How would she ever again get any attention from anyone for herself? These musings were only partially formed and largely internalized, however, and to Peg's credit, she showed nothing but love and attention to little Michael.

"Play away, play away, *mo leanbh* (my children)," Mary intoned to herself, "and give me a little more peace, *le cúnamh Dé* (God willing)."

A short time later there was a gentle knock at the front door and the first visitor of the day arrived. It was Nora Ward, one of Mary's favorites. Although much younger than herself and from East Galway, Nora was a kindred spirit. Her Irish was "book Irish," something the native speakers derisively called *Gaeilige bhriste* (broken Irish), but Mary had encouraged her by means of a popular phrase to always try to improve and keep working on her Irish, '*Is fear Gaeilige bhriste nár Bearla chliste i mbéal Gael* (I prefer broken Irish to clever English from the mouth of an Irish person).'

Nora was "far from the land," Mary would remind her closest friends. She was trying her best to survive under difficult circumstances in Portland. With one child already at home and another on the way, Nora had recently lost her young husband Jim to cancer in New York City. After this terrible and unexpected loss and with her daughter in tow, and another on the way, Nora had travelled up to Portland to be with her three sisters, Mary, Chris, and Bridie. They were a great source of comfort and support. But Nora sometimes wanted the attention of some-one else, someone outside of her own family – someone who could understand her without the constraining and sometimes judgmental bonds of family ties. Mary lovingly called her friend, '*An glór neamhspleách* (a true independent).'

Mary Josephine Folan was just such a person. Nora enjoyed holding conversa-tions with older people, even at home in Ireland, and Mary reminded Nora so much of home. With Mary she could vent her frustrations without the familiar restraints that are often applied inadvertently by siblings, even when these are well-meaning.

"What's troubling you today, Nora dear?" Mary was able to size up Nora's frame of mind at a first glance. She had once told Nora that the state of her hair gave away her feelings and thoughts claiming, "Sure can't I judge how you're feeling by one look at the crown of your noggin!" Nora was amused but remained incredulous concerning this preposterous claim.

"It's my sisters again, Mary. They're still trying to find a man to look after me. And now, to make matters worse, even my friends at the Maine General Hospital where I volunteer are starting to do the same."

"But don't you think your children, especially with this new one now on the way, will be needin' a father at home, Nora dear?"

Nora agreed with her older friend's sentiment, but she insisted, "Yes, but I'd rather find one myself. And if I do, it will surely be on my own terms and in my own good time!"

Although things were not easy for Nora, she was not desperate, and she wanted the Portland Irish community to know that she could manage on her own, if need be.

But Mary next offered a further justification for their intervention. "It's only out of their love for you, dear, and their concern for the children."

"I know, Mary. I know. And I appreciate all they are trying to do for me, but it's embarrassing. Last weekend at the ceili at the AOH hall an old man with his face all covered with grey whiskers came up to me and there, right in front of all my friends, he loudly asked, '*An bhfuil aon chance ort, no an bhfuil tú squarailte cheanna?* (Is there any chance with you, or are you already squared off?)' Then everyone laughed, Mary, just as you're doing now!"

"Ah, dear, that was probably only *Philipín bocht* (poor little Philip). Faith, everyone knows he's totally harmless. He thinks he's a Dancing Master, the poor *créatur*. Sure, didn't he ask the same of me once after I being married for seven years and meself at the very time already with three children and another in the kettle? Philipín's harmless, dear, I tell you!"

The thought of Philipín chasing after a mother with three children in tow now caused Nora to giggle, temporarily forgetting her own predicament. That was Mary's effect on Nora and on others. She could put things in their proper perspective. She had a unique and simplifying take on complex issues. She was a great comfort to Nora, almost like a second mother. Although she had a parcel of children of her own, Mary Folan had an endless supply of love, and understanding, and time for others – even those from East Galway!

"Mary, will I ever fit in here in Portland? You know that I'm from near Loughrea. Most of the Irish here are from *Cois Fharraige* or even further out in west Galway, like yourself, from *Iorras Aithneach*, or Joyce's Country, or up in the hills of Cornamóna. They all speak Irish with a *blas* (perfect accent, literally taste). I'll never have anything more than my Rosmuc book Irish."

"But who amongst them has your spirit, Nora, to say nothing of your love of the music and the dancing? I saw you myself at the céili once with your black shoes strapped firmly onto your two small feet, and well they needed to be strapped on the way you were taking turns around the hall! My older friends were all worried that this young Irish *cáilín* (colleen) from Loughrea would break her fool neck if she wasn't careful. Don't trouble yourself, *a stoirín* (my treasure). You're as well loved and looked after here in Portland as you would be if you were still back home."

"But, Mary, only last week Steve Curran told a bunch of my friends that I was living in a *púncán's* (Yankee's) house, just because my sisters have blinds on their windows. He said that I couldn't know much about Ireland because I was from East Galway. He also told them that I murder the Irish language!"

"Ah, dear, don't let Steve trouble you. He has his own strong notions, and faith he's not afraid to share these with anyone within range of his voice. Don't ever ask him for his opinion on the Catholic Church unless you have the better part of a day to spend listening to him rant and rave on about thems that are tryin' to make the Church more modern. But he has a gentle enough soul, and he means you no harm, I'm sure of that. Sure, didn't he even tell me once that you at least have a love for the Irish language, more than his own children do, even though you didn't grow up like him speaking it at home."

"That may be so Mary, and perhaps he doesn't intend to be mean, but I paid him back in good form last week for what he said about my 'book Irish.' When one of my American-born friends asked of him the word in Irish for library, Steve sheepishly answered, 'Sure, I wouldn't know that, dear. You see, we didn't have them things where I was from.' So I quickly jumped in and said, 'Well, we had them all the way over in East Galway, Steve – and the word is *leabharlann*!'"

"Over the bar!" cried a delighted Mary, as if her young companion had scored a point in a hurling match or some other Gaelic game – "The winner and still champeen from the bold eastern edge of our own County Galway!"

They both had a great laugh at Nora's boldness. They were so very much alike, these two, like mother and daughter or actually more like older and younger sisters. It was as if they could each instinctively recognize the many special qualities of the other. At the very least it was apparent that they certainly enjoyed keeping company with each other.

"Well, why on earth am I burdening you with my small cares, Mary, and you with your own many greater concerns? How are you feeling today? Is the midwife close by for you? Your time can't be long off now – am I right in saying that?"

It was Nora's style to turn attention away from herself. She was concerned for the welfare of others, and this, too, was yet another common trait between these two women. Mary recognized this similar characteristic, too. On more than one occasion Mary had remarked on her feeling of closeness with this younger companion by citing a favorite old Irish proverb, "*Aithníonn ciaróg – ciaróg eile* (One beetle attracts another)."

And here they were, these two Portland "ladybugs" – they both seemed to enjoy that image. In the warmth of Mary's kitchen they spoke of many things. Unlike Mary, Nora regularly read the daily newspaper and was up on local affairs.

"What do you think, Mary, of the former mayor, James Phinney Baxter, and his plans to put a public park all the way around the Back Bay? Does that sound like a good idea to you?"

"Well, my Coley told me that some of the longshoremen, at least those who seem to know a lot about these things, feel that Baxter's plans would only benefit the elite, whatever that word is supposed to mean. I think it means that it would only benefit the rich people. But I'm not so sure about that. Wouldn't we all get to use it? Some people only see the good in ideas that would earn them money or create jobs, but what about those ideas that would create beautiful things like parks? It's sort of like my 'hyacinths to feed thy soul.' Sure, the poor people love beautiful things as much as the rich do, I'd say."

Nora didn't immediately understand Mary's reference to hyacinths, as she was unfamiliar with this poem, but she certainly agreed with the gist of Mary's opinion.

Then she added, "He's different from us, this Baxter, I suppose. I don't know any truly rich people. But I've heard that some of them are good and some are bad, just like our own. I heard tell that Mayor Baxter once complained that alcohol in our Bishop's residence seemed 'too strongly of the World, the Flesh, and the Devil,' and that this would not be following the example of 'the lowly Nazarene,' as he put it. Can you imagine our priests doing without their wine or even their tumblers of punch, Mary? I guess we all worship 'the lowly Nazarene,' but in our own peculiar ways."

Mary envied Nora's ability to memorize things she had heard, somewhat similar to her own ability, and that of her Johnny, to recall poetic or colorful phrases. Mary then offered a different spin on this subject of the drink.

"Well, I'm with him as far as alcohol is concerned," she stated emphatically. "I've seen enough of it on both sides of the Atlantic to last a lifetime. I know that Coley thinks they're crazy, but sometimes I think I'd like to join up with the Women's Christian Temperance Union along with Florence Dow and Lillian Stevens – they're on to something, I think."

"I can only imagine what Coley would have to say about that, Mary. I'm not much of a drinker myself, as you know, although I'm not in the total abstinence society or one of Father Mathew's converts, either. But just look at the way alcohol disguises someone who's under its influence. And if they've been drinking for too many years their faces all seem as distorted as those poor ladies with the 'phossy jaw' from working too many years amid phosphorus down at the Portland Star Match Company – it just destroys them."

"Coley thinks that it's the Yankees' way of trying to control us," laughed Mary. "But the ones really doing the controlling, I'd say, are the ones selling the booze and pocketing all the change. I don't like it, and I never will. I just pray that all of my children will learn the lesson from seeing their poor father helpless at times when under its spell, and stay away from the booze themselves."

Now in substantial agreement, Mary and Nora looked to change the topic. "Did you see that automobile in town last year?" Nora asked. "Some say that it's going to be the way we'll all be getting around sooner or later."

"I doubt that," replied Mary. "Sure, aren't the electric streetcars more than enough? Well, I suppose that's depending on if you've got the money to use them, at least. And aren't all them schoolboys hitching rides on them and on the horse-drawn milk carts already, at least on the winter snow? And that's for free. If I catch my oldest doing that I will have Coley warm his behind, even though my Johnny's now nearly a man already himself."

They both laughed at the image of this happening as Johnny was already slightly taller and heavier than his father even at his young age.

Nora then returned to the subject of automobiles by adding, "Well I don't see how they'll work on our cobblestone streets, especially in the ice and snow. Have they thought of that, I wonder? I'm not against all changes, Mary, but them automobiles are big, and loud, and smelly, and dangerous, I'd say. I'd rather use shank's mare, the two good legs that God gives us all."

Then quickly remembering poor Míchilín upstairs, and how hurtful that last comment might have sounded to his poor mother, Nora added contritely, "Or at least those of us lucky enough to have two good legs."

Mary would never fault anyone for such an inadvertent comment, and she instantly relieved Nora of any anxiety by reciting an old axiom, "A slip of the tongue is no fault of the mind."

Mary then challenged Nora. "What says you and I give our own two good legs a wee bit of a stretch now, *girlín* (little girl) – are ye able for that? You're barely pregnant and look at the likes of me. Come on, *a stór*, are ye able or what? I've been cooped up inside this house ever since the latest cold blast arrived several weeks ago and I'm dying for some fresh air and a bit of visiting!"

Mary first checked to see that the two youngest would be well cared for and under the watchful eye of a young neighbor girl, Bridgie Cronin, who had arrived earlier that morning. Bridgie had been helping Mary over these past few weeks with the children and other household chores. Listening carefully upstairs they could hear Mary's youngest cooing, "Tapioca tea, a bedbug, and a flea…"

It was one of Míchilín's favorites at the moment and represented only the smallest part of a ditty that one of the older Folans had heard at school recess from one of the Hanley boys and brought back home, at least partially. It now caused Mary to smile at the prospect of yet another budding young poet in her family. She was well pleased.

Now that the children were content and well attended, and all seemed in order in her home, Mary Folan and Nora Ward were free agents – it was a totally thrilling prospect for them both!

Chapter 5

The World's a Bubble

"A mind can tour the world at little cost,
and visions once perceived are never lost."

– Sonnet by Carolyn Stuart, "To a Weathered Wanderer"

Several old abandoned pilings near the Grand Trunk sheds had taken on the appearance of tall sticks of dark chocolate sticking straight out of the ocean bed. They were now coated with a heavy, sticky snow that stuck to the top of the pilings down to the high tide mark giving them the appearance of having been dipped into a creamy, white topping. They were surprisingly beautiful – almost edible.

Coleman Folan's longshore work gang was too busy unloading the *Avona* to notice any such thing, nor was it likely that these dockworkers had ever perceived the Portland waterfront as anything other than a place of toil and sacrifice. The view of a casual observer versus that of a common laborer would be a study in contrast.

~ ~ ~

In another part of town, young Johnny Folan had now been joined by two of his best buddies for a jaunt around the east end of town. The main bottling machine had broken down again at the Murdock and Freeman Bottling Company, Johnny's place of part-time work located at 7 Franklin Street, only three doors down from his home. In any case, it was a quiet season for this type of manufacturing as demand for the product was predictably low. Therefore, Johnny's labor, along with that of other part-time workers, was not needed on this day.

Johnny had promised his mother that on a day such as this, when there was no work, he would attend Portland High School. This might allow him to catch up on missed school work and possibly even graduate on schedule in another year and a half. Many of the younger full-time workers at Murdock and Freeman were also given the day off, without pay of course, while the older employees busied themselves with inventory and fixing the mechanical problem in their own piecemeal fashion.

The full-time workers relied on their limited technological expertise since there was not even one mechanical specialist employed by the company. The company owners had argued that they shouldn't be forced to pay for such an expert to simply sit around and wait for a problem to develop. As a result, no one would be paid until the machinery was properly functioning – 'No work, no pay!' the manager had declared. Since that was the owners' position, what could the workers do other than accept and comply, and lose significant pay?

Murdock and Freeman was Maine's largest bottling company of soda and mineral water, and it specialized in the production of the very popular ginger ale. David Murdock kept his main office on site, even though the company had other business branches in Bangor and Rumford Falls. It amazed Johnny that any business could be profitable when its major machinery seemed to fail so frequently, which predictably created a redundant work force sometimes for days on end. Johnny and many of his younger fellow workers didn't seem to mind these work stoppages. In fact, they often seemed to relish their time away from the tedious and fast-paced conveyor line.

It struck Johnny that the pace of work on the conveyors was set to be as fast as any human could possibly respond, and then just a bit faster than that. In order to determine what that pace should be, the speed was often increased until the workers on the line ultimately failed to keep up with the workload. At times like this, bottles either backed up or were lost over the edge of the conveyor belt, creating loud popping noises as they smashed on the wet cement floor sounding much like a series of minor explosions.

Johnny caught on to this curious way of doing things, and he occasionally allowed the bottles to back up and even spill over. His actions would create quite a commotion, and in the worst incident, had temporarily caused the whole production line to shut down. That had warranted a visit from a very animated chief supervisor. When Johnny informed his boss, 'I'm working as fast as I possibly can,' his protest was greeted by an angry and skeptical stare.

Thereafter, Johnny was observed with suspicion. Ultimately, later that same day, he was taken off this line job for slower paced work. That suited him just fine. Johnny had earned the unwanted attention of his supervisor, but simultaneously he earned the admiration of his fellow workers. Many of these factory laborers had long wanted to take such a stand themselves. Johnny was warned by those in the know that another such incident would probably result in his being permanently let go. He could easily be replaced by a more compliant worker.

'We'll never have any rights as long as there are so many others desperate for work under any conditions,' Johnny was told by one of his fellow workers who seemed to have his finger on the pulse of factory work.

The older workers at Murdock and Freeman seemed to be better adjusted to the mind-numbing pace of work than the novices. Johnny felt sorry for those with families and mouths to feed. Some of them needed the work and income even more than he and his family did. Yet again this week their families would have to get by with even less money and therefore less food and coal. One man, a Yankee from somewhere in upstate Maine, had recently told Johnny that he planned to leave Murdock and Freeman soon in order to take a job next door at the Burnham and Morrill Company. That food processing factory was located at 13-19 Franklin Street which abutted Johnny's own back yard.

'B&M,' this man optimistically stated, 'will promise to give me steadier work. If the production line ever breaks down they always keep the laborers busy doing other tasks, and they never slow down even in the winter. They ship canned goods of many types all over the world. I think I'll have a better future working there – but please don't say anything to anyone until after I've gone.'

B&M called their products "hermetically sealed goods." Johnny had once provocatively asked his Daide if he'd ever shipped out any B&M "hermetically sealed goods" from the waterfront. Coleman, as he predicted, had innocently replied, 'No, son, we only ship out B&M products in cans.'

Johnny had several choices when it came to employment. There was even another bottling company, Ingalls Brothers, closer to downtown Portland on Plum Street. They specialized in mineral waters and syrups, including something peculiarly called "Moxie Nerve Food." Most of the Irish in Portland greatly disliked the taste of this Moxie, as well as something that was called "Root Beer." They mostly agreed that these both reminded them of some kind of bitter medicine. Malachy Mulkerrin was particularly disgusted with these new-fangled beverages. He had once dismissed this root beer most emphatically, as if speaking for them all, declaring, 'If youse wants to give me beer, then give me beer – not cough syrup!'

Like Murdock and Freeman, Ingalls bottled a great deal of ginger ale, but they also produced cream ginger beer and hop bitter ale, together with other kinds of beers. Because of the alcohol involved, workers at Ingalls had to be slightly older, so this was only a possibility for Johnny in the future. B&M was another appealing prospect, not only because he could almost roll out of bed and into work, but also because of the specialty items that were canned there, including Machias Bay lobsters, Scarboro Beach clams, and Portland golden corn. Johnny loved the sound and especially the taste of all of these local delicacies, as did his mother.

'The Maine lobsters,' Mary reminisced, 'always remind me of the smaller ones that we called *gliomaigh* that my older brother Patrick and I would catch off Mynish Island when we were young. I must admit, however, that these Maine lobsters are certainly larger and possibly even a bit tastier.'

This was one of the few times that Johnny had ever heard his mother compare Maine favorably to her beloved Galway. When he cutely informed her of that positive comparison, Mary grinned but then quickly retorted, 'Don't get used to it, sonny boy!'

Johnny had been told that the B&M factory was obligated to test at least one can from every batch of food that it produced in order to make sure that the seals had not leaked. The opened cans from every new batch, thus tested every few minutes for both smell and taste, would be casually stacked outside the warehouse and often spirited home by workers while their supervisors turned a blind eye. Johnny and his friends, however, sometimes got there first. They knew that during the overnight third shift they were faster than the night watchman, an older man working out the last few years of his career at B&M.

One night they had slyly sent in a young neighborhood boy who suffered from the crippling disability of polio. They had told him that it was quite alright for him to take whatever he wanted. Predictably though, he could not outrun the night watchman. According to their sinister plan, by the time the youngster had been caught by the watchman and hurried off to his irate parents, Johnny and his friend, Dara Loftus, had nearly cleaned out all the rest of this unguarded treasure long before danger returned. They were quite proud of their brilliant plan. To assuage their guilt at having used such an innocent young lad in their clever scheme, they offered to share some of the booty with this young boy over the next few days. This act of kindness had helped him to more quickly earn back his parents' love and respect, and it relieved Johnny of his minor guilt.

Mary was always thrilled to get this "free" bounty, which was accepted nearly without question. Whenever there was lobster involved, Johnny's story of the "kindness" of the B&M Company was conveniently believed. There would be lobster stew for all of the Folan family in the double boiler on the kitchen stove that Mary always kept full of something warm and delicious. It was most often oyster stew which Johnny ate by the gallon. He especially relished the tasty oyster broth that he would ladle over the dry salted crackers; but, lobster would be a welcome change for the others.

Coleman was a little more than suspicious when he heard Mary's explanation of this lobster bonanza, but he also craved these crustaceans. Therefore, he never followed up on his suspicions regarding their method of procurement. Once, before slurping down a big spoonful of the delicious chowder laced with big chunks of lobster, he looked in Johnny's general direction and sheepishly intoned, 'God, I suppose, takes care of thems that takes care of themselves!'

Johnny's best friend, Dara Loftus, lived just across from the Folans at 235 Fore Street on the corner of Hampshire. The two of them had no trouble convincing their older buddy, Frank Feeney from Danforth Street near Gorham's Corner, to join them while skipping school, "mitching" as they called it. These three had done this many times over the years. The three young and curious Irish boys were thus off on another adventure.

Dara's dad, Joe Loftus, was also Coleman's best friend. Mary said that friendship seemed to pass along from father to son between these two families. In Ireland, the Loftus family originated from Dinish, an island just across the bay from Callowfeenish at the far end of a larger island known as Lettermore. Like many coastal Maine towns and villages, Dinish was much easier to reach by sea than by land because the roads in the outlying parts of both of these regions were nearly nonexistent, and where they did exist they were thoroughly narrow and rutted. Dara's mother's side of the family, the Breathnachs, or Welchs as they were called here in Portland, came from the south side of Carna near Half Mace. This was even closer to the places of birth of both Coleman and Mary. Coleman had often spoken to Mary of his astonishment that family ties and affections could survive over several generations and journeys of thousands of miles.

'These ties were meant to be,' he once opined, 'so long may they continue.'

To which Mary replied, 'You're right, Coley. And as I've heard the local Protestants here in Portland sing, blest be the tie that binds.'

To Johnny, these familial bonds of friendship were natural. He and Dara were kindred spirits – brothers, really. They shared similar family ties to Galway, of course, and all four of their parents were native Irish speakers, but beyond that they had compatible opinions on politics, religion, work, relationships, and most other important subjects.

Whenever Mary would see these two "scoundrels" or "scalawags," as she called them, together, she would whisper to herself, '*fir chomh maith le na athair* (men as good as their fathers).'

Frank Feeney, on the other hand, was bolder and a bit of risk taker. This made him an interesting companion for the two younger and more cerebral adventurers. What unexpected experiences would this day present? It was rumored that the Feeneys were considering a move to Munjoy Hill in the city's east end from their current west end rental at 48 Danforth Street. Their present home was in an equally Irish working-class neighborhood surrounding Portland's oldest Catholic Church, Saint Dominic's, and including the always vibrant Gorham's Corner. Frank was, therefore, in the process of seeking a new set of east end mates.

Frank's father, John Augustine Feeney, owned a "grocery" in the west end that was well known for selling illegal alcohol from the rear of the building, a very common practice in these days. Both John Feeney and his wife, Barbara "Abby," nee Curran, were from just west of Spiddal in *Cois Fharraige*. Like Johnny and Larry's parents, they were both native Irish speakers. This was quite normal for both the east- and the west-end Irish of Portland, given their common place of origin in the Galway *Gaeltacht* (Irish-speaking district). None of the children of these three families had yet learned to speak Irish fluently, even though they all recognized the meaning of certain choice commands in Gaelic, having heard these since childhood. These included such gentle phrases as *suigh síos* (sit down) or *dún do chlób* (shut your mouth).

Frank, aged nineteen, was not attending school. He described himself as being "between jobs." He hadn't exactly distinguished himself at Portland High School and since leaving school had bounced from job to job. His father was adamant about not allowing Frank to become involved, in any way, shape, or form, in the alcohol business. Frank had already demonstrated on a few occasions his love of the "water of life" and "demon rum."

Being three years older than the other boys, Frank was more experienced in many realms, including the mysterious arena of romance. He was thought to be quite handsome, and never had trouble attracting female companionship. His tales of courtship often excited the more innocent younger boys, sometimes leaving them wide-eyed and wondering if his stories were true or just some fantastic creation of their worldlier pal's over-active imagination.

Frank's latest conquest was an attractive Yankee girl from South Portland who was smitten by his dashing manner and titillating tales of adventure.

'Why are these girls attracted to such flirtatious boys?' Johnny once queried Dara. 'What could someone like Frank offer them? He's hardly even left his own parish for most of his life. He doesn't even have a part-time job, for Christ sake! But with all of his fantastic tales, wouldn't the two of us seem dull by comparison to the likes of him? We're just not in the running, I'm sorry to say!'

At Portland High School, Frank's teachers had advised him to see the world beyond, sensing that Portland was too small for his adventurous personality. Frank appeared to be imprisoned in their small classrooms, and they wanted him to see what a taste of freedom might bring.

Finally, this unholy trio was off. Frank had something in mind, something tantalizing he insisted – a chance to get some "free" alcohol. Intrigued, Johnny and Dara followed along heading east toward Munjoy Hill by way of Federal Street. After crossing India Street, they spotted the well-known Sheriff Emerson Doughty with a neighborhood street urchin firmly in hand.

"I'll teach this one a lesson," he told the three of them as they passed by. It seemed as if he was issuing a warning to the older boys, too. "And shouldn't the three of you be in school today yourselves?" he inquired. The sheriff was too busy with his young unhappy captive to follow up on his own question, however, so mercifully it simply hung in the air.

The pack of three continued eastward, unobstructed. They learned shortly afterward that the young boy had been part of a larger group of mostly older boys who had been taunting Sheriff Doughty from the top of the tall stone wall along Federal Street that held back the old Eastern Cemetery. One of them had even dropped his trousers and proceeded to urinate on the unsuspecting and humiliated sheriff beneath them before running off through the cemetery and from there up to the relative safety of Congress Street. Unfortunately, the youngest boy was not as nimble or as skilled in retreat as the older boys, and he was easily apprehended by the indignant Sheriff Doughty.

His arrest would represent one small bite out of crime – a very small morsel indeed. The youngster had essentially been a sacrificial lamb. Unwittingly, he had allowed the others to escape while facing the sole punishment for their bawdy antics.

"Live and learn," Johnny remarked rather flippantly, "like the boy we sent into B&M for the cans of lobster stew. Someone always has to pay the price, I suppose, just as long as it's not us!"

The bold threesome then turned onto Mountfort Street, just above the area known as "The Bight." It was the kind of rough neighborhood where illegal activity was known to occur and whose impoverished residents survived by whatever means were at their hand. They passed by the AME Zion Mission, a tiny storefront used by some of Portland's tiny Negro population.

Dara then asked, "Why do they have this church here with the Abyssinian Church just around the corner on Newbury Street? I wouldn't think there would be hardly enough of a call for two Negro churches in the same neighborhood."

Johnny attempted to answer Dara's question by suggesting, "I think this church is run by the Methodists, or at least 'supplied,' whatever that means. The Abyssinian, I've heard, is independent and is therefore on its own. Did you see the black bunting on the Abyssinian? That's been there ever since the *Portland* went down just over a year ago. They lost several of their members, I heard, and the Church has fallen on hard times ever since. But, I think this building here is for a slightly different group. Don't ask me any further, 'cause it's confusing to me. The Protestants are not like us, you know. They have lots of different choices, denominations they call them. They have almost a new one every year, or so Father Draine once told me. I even heard that some of the Italians who have arrived in this same neighborhood only recently are now attending the Seamen's Bethel over at 283 Fore Street between Deer and Chatham instead of the Cathedral – now how's that for a twist?"

They travelled up Mountfort with the Eastern Cemetery on their left. It contained the earthly remains of many of the older original settlers of Portland, along with the two opposing captains of the HMS *Boxer* and the USS *Enterprise*, both having been killed in an epic sea battle back in 1814 somewhere off Monhegan Island. At this spot, they were buried side by side with full military honors.

Upon hearing of this, Frank's father had once remarked to his family,'"Don't ever let them bury me next to an Englishman!'

To which his wife, Abby, had replied, 'Little chance of that happening – you're too stubborn to die, and you'll probably outlive the lot of us!'

According to local family lore, the Feeneys had an uncle by the name of Mike Connolly who had lived the romantic life of a world traveler before settling down in Portland. Perhaps Frank's uncle had indeed experienced all of these adventures in reality, but more likely he may have done or seen many of these things only in his mind's eye. Regardless, his visions were most intriguing and seemed all too real to those who heard of them. Here he married a wealthy widow who owned and operated a boarding house. Connolly supplemented his income through bootlegging. Uncle Mike was supposedly the person credited with convincing Frank's father to leave Spiddal and come over to Portland by painting a rather enticing picture of life in America. Frank once told Johnny and Dara a comical story about Uncle Mike and this particular spot.

"Uncle Mike was once shown this gravesite in the Eastern Cemetery. He quickly spotted a hand-drawn wooden marker placed next to the burial site designated by some admiring local Englishman as holding the remains of the British Captain Samuel Blyth. The marker read, 'Here lies an English officer and a gentleman.' Upon reading these words, Mike Connolly turned to my father and exclaimed in near total disbelief, 'You wouldn't think they'd be room for two people in that one small plot!'"

At Congress Street, the boys spotted the older delinquents who were still keenly watching out for Sheriff Emerson Doughty.

"You're in the clear boys," Dara informed them, "but I can't say the same for the young one."

They all chuckled upon hearing that and one of them gruffly and uncaringly shouted back, "We've all been nabbed by Doughty at least once – it was just his time, I guess. I'm sure he'll survive."

The boys proceeded up Munjoy Hill. The Hill was highlighted by the stately and beautiful maritime signal tower called the Observatory on its summit. The Observatory was a symbol not only of the Hill but of Portland's entire maritime history and the importance of the sea to this city. Henry Wadsworth Longfellow had once poetically described Portland, his birthplace, as, "the beautiful town that is seated by the sea." The Observatory had been constructed in 1807 during the Embargo period when few ships could either enter or leave port legally. Therefore, it was often cited as an example of Portland's optimism and boundless energy as well as its ability to overcome serious obstacles.

Just beside the Observatory was the simple but elegantly beautiful red brick fire barn with its enormous doors, wide enough to accommodate the house-drawn fire apparatus, and with sleeping quarters for the firemen on the second floor. This building also served as a voting place during municipal elections. It was located here, people said, in order to assure Munjoy Hill of protection even in the winter months when travel up the somewhat steep Congress Street could be tricky when coated with snow or ice.

Next to the fire barn, all the way over to the corner of St. Lawrence Street, stood the Congress Street Methodist Church with its stately tall white steeple. Most New England towns seemed to have such a Protestant church that was almost always located, or so it appeared, on the highest point of ground.

Johnny's father, Coley, had once half seriously joked, 'Sure they're just trying to keep an eye on us!'

Across St. Lawrence, on the other corner of Congress Street, stood one of the signature buildings of the entire city, the "Carleton Castle," as it was called. A wooden structure that looked like a medieval fortress or nobleman's keep, it was the residence of Samuel L. Carlton. Frankie, as his friends called him, loved to stare at this building, dreaming what it would be like to have enough money to live in a home like this.

These four imposing adjacent structures viewed in tandem on the summit of Munjoy Hill gave the entire neighborhood an elegant and unique definition. In the entire city of Portland, there was nothing else quite like these buildings all in one location, not even along the Western Promenade, in their opinion. The residents of Munjoy Hill were proud of these structures and of their own neighborhood, and Frank was quickly coming to love the Hill that might soon become his new home. The Irish were moving on up!

But the appreciation of architecture was not the reason that Frank had enticed his pals up the Hill on this particular day. He had heard about a small dingy home on Munjoy Street that was occupied by a neighborhood drunk. There just might be some booze located there free for the taking. All that one needed was the gumption to go in and grab it, and Frankie was the boy for that mission.

When they arrived at the location, Dara suddenly recoiled in shock shouting, "Christ, what are you doing? That's my uncle's house!"

And so it was. The brother of Joe Loftus was widely known as a heavy drinker. Joe had once colorfully said of his brother, 'He gets a lot out of his booze. He can make one drink last all afternoon. He'll get one drink at noon and he'll be *maith go leor* (drunk) all afternoon. Yes, he gives the booze quite a wrestle.'

Dara stated firmly, "You boys can count me out of this."

Although the other two understood completely, this partial withdrawal wasn't about to deter Frank from his "mission." It would be easy pickings, and Frank acted like an Army drill sergeant setting out their respective assignments.

"Come on then, Johnny, it's you and me then. Dara can keep watch out here."

Even that seemed too much like family disloyalty for Dara, so he deferred and wandered up to the corner of Wilson Street. With his hands deep in his pockets and his eyes sheepishly to the ground, he waited for the return of his pals who were intent on petty larceny. He didn't even intend to drink any of the pilfered alcohol – that just wouldn't be right, he thought to himself.

Dara was often embarrassed by his uncle's antics, as was Dara's father. Everyone in Portland seemed to know of this man's weakness for booze. But Dara had seen his uncle at other family occasions while not *ar meisce* (drunk), as they'd say in Irish, and he could be a jovial and fun-loving person when sober. He had never married but possessed a sensitive nature and seemed to care deeply about things.

Dara's mother had once attempted to explain this to her son, sympathetically suggesting, 'That's probably why he drinks so much. The world's a comedy for those who think, but it's a tragedy for those who feel.'

This was a bit of philosophy that Dara always remembered. It was quite an unusual statement from his mother who was normally quite Spartan with her words in public and reticent to state her own thoughts or feelings about most things. That was probably why this particular axiom had made such an impression on Dara. From what he had personally observed, his uncle was a caring person when not under the influence. Problem was, those times seemed to be few and far between.

Distracted by these matters, Dara failed to detect movement coming up the street – the return of his uncle, who was by then more than halfway up Munjoy Street from the Eastern Promenade. By the time Dara spotted him, it was too late to warn his unsuspecting pals by then already rummaging inside his home.

"What the Hell is going on in here?" Loftus roared, spotting the two boys each holding a bottle of his precious whiskey. "Who in the hell let youse into my house, you little bastards?"

He lurched toward Frank, but was too slow. Dropping the whiskey bottle which loudly smashed on the floor, the older thief made his own clean escape. Unfortunately, things didn't go as smoothly for Johnny. Just as he reached the door and thought he had also gained his freedom, he felt a strong hand firmly gripping at his shoulder. Johnny was roughly jerked back into the house and then propelled all the way across the room and up against the far wall. There the second bottle of whiskey that he firmly held in his hand also smashed. The surprising speed of this frightening development plus the solid contact with the wall had nearly paralyzed Johnny. His breath was knocked out of him.

The loss of not one but now two of his precious bottles had turned the eyes of Loftus into a bright shade of red. His glare was entirely menacing. As Johnny was about to be grabbed by the irate man a second time, he skillfully maneuvered under Loftus's arm. Unencumbered by any of the alcoholic booty, Johnny was finally able to narrowly beat the inebriated home owner in a race to the door through which he now desperately darted for his very life.

Frankie thought that the episode was entirely hilarious. "Did you see his red eyes when he saw the two of us each with a bottle in our hands? We came so close to pulling off the crime of the century – why the hell didn't you give us a warning, Dara?"

Neither Dara nor Johnny took such a sanguine view of what had just occurred. Johnny was still out of breath and more than a little woozy from the shock he had just received.

"I'm lucky I didn't get killed, or worse!" Johnny cried. "Christ, you were out of there in a heartbeat, so where were you to give me a hand? Some pal you are!"

Mimicking the young trouble-making boys on the corner of Mountfort and Congress Streets who had earlier that morning escaped Sheriff Doughty, Frankie rationalized to his frustrated partner in crime, "It was just your time, I guess!"

"And what about me?" Dara blurted out. "What if my uncle had recognized me or seen me run off with the likes of the two of you? How long before my Da would have taken out his belt to teach me a lesson about stealing, especially from my own family?"

"Well, we all take our chances," was Frank's cold and unsatisfying reply.

It had been quite a start to their day. The two younger lads had learned a lesson about their pal Frank, about chumming around with older boys, and also about themselves. They were beginning to understand a little better their mothers' concerns about who they chose to hang out with and what that might mean for their own reputations. Frank was, to be sure, not the worst kid in Portland, they both knew that, but he clearly was a risk-taker. To both Johnny and Dara, he still had an endearing side all the same, and they would both probably continue their friendship with Frank, though perhaps more guardedly now.

Before heading off on their own separate ways, Frank asked the others if they would accompany him to the Cathedral. He had promised his mother that he would go to Confession daily, at least until he was working again. Given the morning's thrilling start, who could blame him? Johnny and Dara both thought that daily Confession was a bit excessive, but for Frank a promise to Abby was like a promise to God. As bold as he might otherwise be, Frank and all the Feeneys worshipped their mother almost as a saint. They would never tell her an outright lie or knowingly do anything likely to disappoint her. It was lucky for Frankie that he was quicker on his feet than Dara's uncle – Frank seemed to reason that it wouldn't disappoint his mother unless he was actually caught doing something wrong!

Frank's mother, Barbara Feeney – known by most as Abby – and her family had only recently returned to Portland from an absolutely idyllic rural setting along the coast of Cape Elizabeth, just south of Portland. A few of the younger Feeney children had even been born there. The youngest surviving child was John Martin whose sixth birthday was tomorrow. John had recently come down with diphtheria which caused him to miss several months of school. An older sister, Mary Agnes Ridge, who like Johnny's sister was also called Mamie, had herself only recently become a widow. Thus, she was free to assist Abby with her sickly child.

By this time, Abby Feeney was nearly forty-five years of age. She had labored through eleven childbirths, five of whom had not survived beyond infancy. Young John Martin was number ten. Not long after John's birth, in 1894, Abby had suffered yet another infant death with the loss of the infant Martin. She felt that she was too old and weak for this to continue. Abby fervently prayed that Martin would be her last pregnancy and that John Martin would always remain the baby of the large Feeney family, and thus, at least, the name of Martin would survive in the family.

Mamie Ridge, nee Feeney, would continue her loving care of John Martin, thereby allowing Abby to attend to other important yet less taxing family matters. The similarity between her care of John Martin and Mamie Folan's care of young Míchilín was not lost on their two appreciative mothers. Family members simply did what was needed – they were in it together and they instinctively knew this to be true. Mamie Ridge also read to young John Martin from tales of adventure and travel. These were things that she had not had the time for herself when she was his age. She enjoyed these adventure stories as much as did her baby brother. It was like a second chance at youth!

This was a more personal education, Mamie Ridge thought, than John Martin might have received at the east end public schools, such as Monument Street School and Emerson Grammar School, if they were to move to Munjoy Hill. Even so, the principal of Emerson, Miss Marada Adams, had a wonderful reputation of sharing with her students the many adventures she experienced on her frequent trips to Europe and other exotic places. Mamie wondered how much young John Martin could understand of what she was reading to him, or even if they understood these stories in the same way. John absolutely soaked up these stories, and he remembered the details vividly, created pictures of far-away places in his mind. He would often ask his sister to repeat his favorite passages over and over again whenever she finished another new book. This type of travel cost the Feeney's nothing more than time, but it had provided a vision of the world that John Martin likely would never lose.

Young John Martin Feeney obviously relished his role as the *cuidín*, or baby of the family, as did young Míchilín Folan. As much as he would have liked another younger sibling to play with, John Martin seemed more than content to have the undivided attention of his sister and his mother, not to mention all the older Feeney children, squarely focused upon him and him alone.

True to his word to Abby, Frank then led Johnny and Dara off the Hill and down to the Cathedral, just a fifteen minute walk from the summit along Congress Street, Portland's major thoroughfare. Since the Cathedral's main entrance faced away from Congress Street, the boys always entered from a smaller side door. They watched while Frank blessed himself at the font of holy water and patiently waited for Father Draine's confessional line to recede. Frank could have gone into Father Collins's much shorter line, but like all the others, he knew that Collins's nature was far stricter and his penances, therefore, much more severe. More importantly, Father Collins's voice was much louder than Father Draine's. When agitated, he could be heard bellowing throughout the Cathedral, something that no one cherished. Dara had once complained to Johnny, 'Father Collins appears to take our confessed sins quite personally!'

While waiting for Frank, the other two boys sat quietly in the rear of the Cathedral. That's where many of the unmarried men would congregate. The boys then heard the Rector, Father Dennis O'Brien, reluctantly greet Malachy Mulkerrin, a harmless but perpetual drunk who was well known to all in the Cathedral parish. Malachy came to Confession daily, and it was commonly said that he was never lacking in cause to be there.

Father O'Brien now cautiously addressed him by tentatively asking, "Drunk again, Malachy?"

"Yes, Father, me too!" Malachy immediately responded with absolute innocence.

It took all of the self-control that the two boys and the rest of the congregants could muster to keep from laughing out loud. If they had disturbed the solemn atmosphere of the Mass with their laughter, then they would all have something additional to confess themselves.

Father Draine's line was still quite long. Before it was Frank's turn, Father O'Brien had already started the morning Mass. This ritual was more than familiar to both Johnny and Dara. They had been raised entirely within this Church and in this parish. Each of them had recently stopped attending, however, much to the disappointment of their parents, especially their mothers. Religion remained one of their favorite subjects of conversation, but they had simultaneously come to the conclusion that neither of them could ever be what was referred to as "good Catholics."

Johnny and Dara had both experienced disappointment and then anger when, a few months earlier, the deceased father of one of their best friends was not allowed to be buried at Calvary Cemetery, the primary Catholic burial ground located over Cassidy's Hill in South Portland. This allegedly was because he had not regularly attended to his religious duties. The fact that this man's own mother and father, along with several of his siblings, were buried in their family plot at

Calvary that was paid for and maintained by his family seemed to make little difference. Both Johnny and Dara had considered this to be a travesty.

Their friend had tried very hard to overlook the affront to the family and the embarrassment that had been caused at having to bury their father in a new plot at Evergreen Cemetery. This old public cemetery held the remains of many of Portland's most prominent families. Evergreen was located all the way across town on Stevens Avenue, almost opposite from the spot where the Dublin-based Sisters of Mercy had opened Saint Joseph's Academy for girls back in 1882 under Sister Mary Petronilla O'Grady. Johnny and Dara had taken great offense, as if this affront to their friend's family had happened to their own families – this action felt most unchristian and they took it personally.

Another conflict with the Catholic hierarchy had also troubled the boys. Bishop James Augustine Healy was well loved by his congregation. By now he was aging and in his twenty-fifth year of service as the second bishop of the Diocese of Portland, which had been separated from Boston only since 1855. Healy had earlier issued a strongly-worded letter condemning Catholic parents who did not send their children to parish schools, when available, but rather to the Portland public schools. Neither Johnny nor Dara, nor Frank for that matter, had attended the parochial schools. All of these boys were highly intelligent and they very much enjoyed schooling, but like so many of their neighborhood friends they were unlikely to graduate from high school. Johnny wanted to attend a manual training school, but none was yet operational in Portland. There he might have obtained several skills that would have been useful in the construction industry. But for now, he was only attending school, even if only sporadically.

Dara Loftus, although still enrolled at Portland High School, had recently left to briefly ship out to sea on one of the many English steamers then sailing out of Portland. That intriguing episode had lasted only a precious few months until his actual age of fifteen had been discovered by a discerning steamship official.

The parish would often subsidize the families of young scholars like Johnny and Dara, but both sets of parents, at least the mothers, believed that the public schools were more than adequate. Unlike the Bishop, they did not fear the loss of their mortal souls should their children decide to attend them. In the case of the two boys, the reasons for not attending the Sacred Heart School on Cumberland Street were largely personal.

And then, quite suddenly, from the rear of the sanctuary, Malachy Mulkerrin awoke from his somnambulant state. He was still disoriented and wished to continue his unfinished dialogue with Father O'Brien who, unfortunately, was by now serving Mass from the altar! The good priest had just finished praying for the protection of Bishop Healy, along with the souls of all the other priests in the Diocese, and for the survival and growth of the Catholic Church throughout the entire world.

It was precisely at that point that an obviously frustrated Malachy barked out, "Sure what do you know of the entire wor'uld, Father dear? Have you been there? What about the entire wor'uld does any of ye really know?"

Snickers of laughter could be heard throughout the sanctuary. One of the sextants serving at Mass that morning had worked with Malachy during his time as an active longshoreman, but this was before booze had rendered him a threat to his own safety and that of his fellow dock workers. Malachy was actually still a dues-paying member of the union, but for obvious reasons he was rarely chosen at the shape-ups for any of the regular gangs.

The sextant tried heroically to quiet and calm him down by imploring, "Malachy, you shouldn't interrupt Father O'Brien again. Please, Malachy."

"Ah, sure, but he's up there preachin' about the whole wor'uld, and what would he be knowin' about that? What does any of us know about what the entire wor'uld is? Sure the wor'uld's a bubble! And what's a bubble? Only air..."

That was too much for the two boys. They couldn't control their laughter any longer, nor could many of the others present and within earshot. So now they immediately exited by the same side door they had earlier entered only a short time before. From this outside location, they could hear the sextant still trying to reason with Malachy, who by now had become even more agitated and therefore had to be gingerly escorted from the sanctuary.

In an attempt to calm Malachy down, the sextant reasoned, "I don't see why you need to disturb Father O'Brien, Malachy. Sure you even recently told him that you are living a good Christian life!"

Without missing a beat, Malachy turned his eyes plaintively toward the sextant and implored, "Then would you ever give this poor Christian a drink!"

Soon thereafter, the boys were joined by Frank. He had worked his way up the queue and had been next in line to give his confession to Father Draine. Frank reported to them, however, that Malachy's comical outburst had caused even the priest himself to lose his composure. From inside the confessional booth Frank had heard Father Draine's loud guffaw, along with that of the otherwise innocent and unsuspecting confessant.

Frankie had therefore exited the church without confessing, causing Dara to ask in all sincerity, "But what of the promise to your mother, Frank?"

Frank cleverly replied, "If this would be a sin, surely it's only a sin of omission and not one of commission. Isn't it my intention that really matters?"

"Ah, sure, and doesn't Frank have a way with the English?" cried Dara to Johnny. They both admired Frank for his boldness and his quick wit. And who could now argue with his line of reasoning?

From the front door of the Cathedral on Cumberland Street near the corner of Franklin, the boys proceeded north down Franklin and away from their homes and also Portland High School located just a few blocks further to the west. They were headed in the direction of the partially-frozen Back Bay, and the wind still coming off the Atlantic seemed to funnel itself along Franklin Street with increasing velocity. It takes an intense winter to freeze salt water, but that is what they now witnessed.

The Bay, neatly forming the northern border of Portland's peninsula, glistened in the cold dim sunshine of this late January morning. The sun had broken through the thick clouds, but just barely. Most of Johnny's young life had been lived on the south side of the peninsula, facing eastward toward the Atlantic – "facing home" as his mother always insisted.

Mary loved to remind her son, 'The next parish east is Galway, and don't forget to raise your oars and lower your sails when you pass by Macdara's Island!' This was one of Mary's favorite sayings issued whenever one of her children was leaving the house.

It would become one of Johnny's, too. Whatever this Macdara's Island was, it had already become a part of Johnny's inherited persona and familiar geography, even though he would likely never actually see or set as much as one foot upon it. It reminded him of a verse he had once learned in literature class at the high school, "A mind can tour the world at little cost, and visions once perceived are never lost."

Johnny had envisioned Macdara's Island and indeed all of Connemara itself many times. He often wondered if he would live to see any of these hallowed places so sacred to his imagination. He would always revere them.

And so this trip to the nearby Back Bay, as short a journey as it represented, became a minor adventure for them all. This was *terra incognita* (the unknown land)! Heading further down Franklin, this was clearly not an Irish neighborhood on this north side of Congress Street. At least it was neither like Munjoy Hill nor Gorham's Corner, this much was clear to them all. The names on the mailboxes, although occasionally an Irish surname would appear, sounded mostly Yankee to the boys. These included such surnames as Mayberry, Foss, Trefethen, Libby, Curtis, and Mountfort.

Before arriving at the corner of Oxford Street, they spotted the Open Door Mission. That was intriguing to them all, but it was bold Frank who was first to stick his head inside the front door. There he spied what appeared to be a sparse congregation, really only a small handful of congregants, all of them deep in prayer, even though it was a Wednesday morning.

"Maybe the confessional line will be shorter here," Frank joked as he stuck his head back out and winked to the others. "And now, at long last, my promise to my mother might yet be fulfilled!"

Yes, Frank was indeed the bold boy, but they thought he was only joking until he then took the next daring step inside. Again, turning to his amused pals, he now whispered with a sly grin, "Once the camel's nose is under the tent, it isn't long before the camel itself is inside! So follow me, me buckos!"

Before Johnny knew what he was doing he had indeed followed Frank and Dara into the Mission whereupon he quickly realized, only after it was too late, that he had inadvertently entered into a Protestant Church for the very first time in his life. He cautiously whispered to Dara, "Well, if the two of us get in trouble for mitching from school today, at least, our souls will be provided for."

Dara responded in all seriousness, "That is unless our dear Father Draine hears about this transgression."

The three buccaneers sat quietly in a pew near the rear of the small Mission. The pastor with his eyes firmly closed was fervently in the midst of prayer with his hands on the head of another man then kneeling before him at the small altar.

"Oh loving God, grant this man the strength to do what is pleasing in Thy sight. Help him to turn away from the horrors and the perverse sin of alcohol. Help him to be the support that his wife and family so need. Help him to gain the sobriety that he has so earnestly prayed for before us today in this place. We ask all of this in His name, and we ask all of you to pray for this and to now say together, AMEN!"

Shortly thereafter, when the penitent man turned to retake his seat in the front pew, tears were streaming from his down-turned eyes and down his rugged cheeks. Frank's jaw suddenly dropped. He instantly recognized this man's face. He was the father of one of his most recent girlfriends!

Frankie whispered ardently to his friends, "Oh, God, please don't let him recognize me. No wonder she wouldn't touch my booze. I feel so stupid now for even offering it to her. She only told me that her Da had been sick lately. How was I to know?"

There wasn't much of a risk of Frank being noticed, however, as the penitent and weeping man was deep in his public shame and purposefully made no eye contact with anyone. His sincere repentance was as apparent as his anguish.

Dara then spoke as if he had just discovered a new law of physics, "Jesus, they must have the same trouble with booze that we Irish do!"

The three quietly and respectfully slid out of the Mission before their presence could be detected. Frank told the others that this man's daughter had been highly distracted recently over what she called trouble at home. She was "at sixes and sevens" because her dad, he found out later, had been fired from his job for stealing from the cash register in order to feed his craving for alcohol. The family was too proud to ask for any public assistance even just to tide them over. They were now living day-to-day, just barely getting by on the generosity of neighbors.

Frank was still in total disbelief. "This was the last thing I expected to see today!"

All three of their families had been strongly and negatively affected by alcohol in one way or another. Johnny, sounding more religious than was usual for him, now ventured to his pals, "Maybe God is sending us all a message!"

Dara quickly reminded him, only half in jest, "I thought we had agreed that God had disengaged after the Creation. Have you already forgotten about that book that you said you loved, *The Age of Reason*?"

"Jesus, I only meant it as a figure of speech," replied a slightly perturbed Johnny. He had clearly been caught out by Dara at his own game of semantics – and didn't that irk him?

As they passed over Lancaster Street, somewhat further along Franklin, they could smell an enticing aroma of cured fish coming from the Mortenson Smoke-House and also competing smells from the Wyer Smoke-House just across from that. Watson Gribbin lived next to the small store that the family ran there, and all the boys knew many of the Gribbins from Portland High School.

Johnny's mouth watered, and he optimistically exclaimed, "Wouldn't that be a nice treat? I wonder if they have any dented cans of that stuff over there. No such luck, I suppose, at least not today, boys. We'll have to settle for the smells alone and then just let our imaginations do the rest."

Beyond Fox Street, they now crossed over the tracks of the Boston and Maine Railroad whose Portland terminus was the stately Union Station in the west end. The two younger boys had never been to that depot, or anything else that far west in this town, but Frank had been once a few years ago to greet his dad returning from a visit to see family in Spiddal and Galway. He would take Frank back to Ireland one day, the elder Feeney had sincerely promised – but Frank was still waiting. Frankie was beginning to believe that the honor might more likely fall to one of his younger siblings.

Finally, they reached the end of the line, the Bates Ice Company, which was on the water side of what was called the Marginal Way. This was all filled land, or so they had been told in school. Often at the highest astronomical tides, according to their science teacher, the ocean would temporarily reclaim at least part of its own.

'If the sea level were to rise even a few feet,' Dara had once instructed Johnny after attending a particularly interesting Earth Science class at Portland High School, 'Portland would revert to its original boundaries, and would then lose much of this marginal area near the Back Bay and nearly all of Commercial Street.'

Dara then added his own secular postscript to this lesson, 'Nature giveth and Nature taketh away – blessed be the name of Mother Nature!'

The ice company was a favorite spot for neighborhood children during the withering summer months, especially the dog days of late July and August. But now they were in the midst of a deep mid-winter freeze, and Dara noted the irony of this by proclaiming, "Selling ice in January in Portland, Maine – it's a little like selling coal to Newcastle!"

Dara and all of the boys loved to use expressions as they served to make them feel more mature, and worldlier. Dara also knew many other wise proverbs and more than a few vulgar sayings he had picked up from the older able-bodied seamen he had met during his brief stint on the English steamships.

Frank, never one to be outdone by his juniors, interjected a bit of mild blasphemy of his own, "Wouldn't all those souls now writhing in Hell's fires give their eye-teeth for just one hour of relief back here at the good old Bates Ice House?"

They all grinned and nodded their heads in general agreement. This signaled that a morning spent walking about and taking in the sights of Portland would surely beat anything that the high school or the bottling company, or most other options for that matter, could match. They were three kindred spirits freely imbibing in whatever their erstwhile tranquil Portland home could offer. These three didn't have to look very far to find adventure, even along the narrow streets of their dear little town. Adventure often came looking for them – and the best news was that this day was still young!

Chapter 6

Why Women Sin

"Míle grá le m'anam í is gear go mbeidh sí mór!"

(A thousand loves of my soul, it's not long before she'll be grown!)

– from the Irish song *Peigín Leitir Móir*

The day, finally, was becoming somewhat brighter. The coldest days and nights in winter were often the very ones accompanied by the clearest skies. It seemed a fair trade-off to Mary who reasoned, "In this life you can have the one or the other, but usually not the both!"

The sun, now dimly shining through the windows, was warm to the face. Mary, like most of Portland's Irish, had difficulty dealing with the local extremes of weather. Galway's weather was moderated by the Gulf Stream, but here in America it seemed that things were often taken to the extreme, including the weather.

"I guess the Gulf Stream, or whatever it's called, missed us here in Portland yet again on its long journey over to Ireland," Mary sighed to Nora. "How could such a day, even if only with its few bright spells, be so god-awful cold, I've often wondered?"

Mary had been speaking with her friend Nora in the warm kitchen for well over an hour by this time. It was nearing mid-morning and she figured that if she was going to get any fresh air this day it had better happen soon. Nora was free to join her because one day each week her older sister, Mary, agreed to watch over her daughter. This gave Nora at least one full morning for herself. And so on this Wednesday she was away from the cares of home and the constant demands of running a small household nearly entirely on her own. She felt like a bird that had been freed from its cage, if only briefly.

Before these two could set off, however, Mary would need to be sure that all was in order with her two youngest children and that preparations had been made for the mid-day dinner. The noontime meal at the Folans was called dinner, and it would feed not only the two youngest children still at home, along with the four young scholars who would be returning home from North School for their dinner, but also several longshoremen who came regularly to eat here during their hour-long break from work. These men, mostly young bachelors with no family ties in Portland, appreciated a home-cooked meal in a warm room fairly close to the docks. Some of them were newly arrived, "just off the boat." Thus the atmosphere of this home, and in particular the widespread use of the Irish language, was especially welcome.

'This is a homely place,' several of them had told Mary on different occasions. This caused Mary to explain to her domestic helper, Brígid Cronin, that this word had a completely different meaning in Ireland from its more negative connotation over here.

'Homely to these Irish, dear, simply means like home – something that's welcoming, familiar, and comfortable to them. That's exactly what they are all searching for here in Portland – in addition to the generous portions of good healthy food that we give them every day, especially the required meat and potatoes. Potatoes cooked every way imaginable, Bridgie – baked, boiled, roasted, fried, mashed with scallions or with bits of cabbage, broiled…whenever there are plenty of spuds, *prátaí* in Irish or *fátaí* as they usually call them in Connemara, the meal will always be a roaring success. But run out of spuds, and the meal's sure to be a complete failure, regardless of what else is served! Now keep that in mind.'

The small amount of money that Mary charged for serving these meals would pay for the food and the help needed to cook and serve them, and whatever little bit was left over would go into Mary's "emergency fund," her kitty.

'Every little bit helps,' Mary often whispered, as if trying to convince herself. This was one of Mary's many mottos from an endless store of gems of wisdom which all appeared to have the ring of truth to them. She had a saying for nearly every occasion, both in English and in Irish, and so her children had come to accept them all as the gospel truth, even though they could only understand the half of them.

'In for the penny, in for the pound,' she had once reasoned to Nora regarding these extra mouths to feed. 'Once the stove is hot from the wood that starts the fire and the coal that keeps it going, and the potatoes are all boiling away, you might as well feed a small army as a small handful.'

Up to her sixth month or so, Mary had handled most of the cooking and nearly all the cleaning, together with the many other household chores that she completed almost entirely on her own. But now that she was nearly full term, she sorely needed the assistance of young Brígid Cronin, Catherine Cronin's fifteen-year-old daughter from just a ways down Fore Street over by the corner of India. Bridgie, as she was known, would arrive each morning around 10:30 a.m., or "half-ten" as Mary still called it. She would immediately see what needed to be done in the kitchen or for the two young ones upstairs. She was a natural. Mary often told her that she'd make a lovely wife for someone and a wonderful mother herself one day.

'God bless all here,' Bridgie would greet Mary each morning in the style of speaking that she had picked up from both her mother and her grandmother who also lived in Portland. Even the native borns who could not speak Irish themselves still had a pattern of speech that reflected the Gaelic roots of their families.

These traditions and speaking patterns went far back into the primordial past – further back than could ever be recorded or even imagined. But still this unknown past would influence those now living, often in ways unknown and mysterious these many years later. Bridgie informed Mary that she had a "special treat" in store for them all at dinner, something that her grandmother had taught her to cook.

"It's lucky for you," Mary lightheartedly stated, "that my Coley won't be home for dinner, as my husband is none too big on surprises when it comes to his food."

As soon as Bridgie was settled in and playing with Peg and young Michael, Mary and Nora had quietly escaped out the door. They were both well bundled against the extreme cold. It was Mary's first day out for several weeks, and this break from her daily routine was much anticipated. She nearly bounded onto the sidewalk and paused to take a deep breath of the frigid cold air which seemed to tickle the inside of her throat.

"Layers, they say, is the trick over here. But I'd give up three or four layers of these thin cotton threads for just one nice Connemara *báinín*," Mary exclaimed as the cold wind smacked her face like a slap.

Báinín is the thick, lanolin-saturated, woolen flannel material from which the sweaters or "jumpers" of most Galwegians are painstakingly woven. These outer garments were worn in Ireland throughout the year, including all but the few warmest days in the middle of summer. Even then they were never put very far away. The Irish cold or the dampness was never that far off, and there was nothing to be gained by tempting their premature return.

Of all the difficult questions that any mother must answer on a daily or even hourly basis, Mary was now confronted by a relatively easy decision. Would they go left or right, west or east? How could they ever decide?

These two women briefly looked at each other in mocked amusement at this simplest of dilemmas that they now faced before Nora took the lead and announced, "Fair enough then, Mary, we'll go straight – that's usually the safest path. You lead, and I'll follow."

Nora knew her friend well enough to know that it would be Mary's desire to pass closely by Carlo Toney's small family restaurant on the opposite corner just across Fore Street from her own apartment. The smells that emanated from Tony's place were strange but always delightful.

'What's your secret?' Mary had often asked of him.

Carlo would smile and give her the same simple answer each and every time, 'Garlic, Mrs. Folan, a lots a garlic. It's a the besta spiceah, you know. No garlic, no tastah! Everybody's a likes a garlic!'

Tony's broad smile encompassed his entire face, and it usually spread to the faces of all in his presence. Neither Mary nor any of her Irish friends had ever tried this garlic, nor had they even heard of it before arriving in Portland. The aroma of simmering garlic had never wafted along the streets or boreens, the small streets, of Galway. Mary was quite sure of that.

There was that one exception when Mary had fried up several garlic cloves which Carlo had given to her for Coley's Sunday roast together with some onions. She could see her husband curiously sniffing at the unfamiliar aromas emerging from the kitchen, but Coley hadn't given in to his suspicions except to ask her the next day if yesterday's roast had been entirely fresh. She noticed, however, that he had eaten his entire meal, except for that one small bite that he habitually left on his plate, day in and day out.

Coleman never explained this unusual habit to anyone. But Mary had reasoned that it was probably meant to show her or anyone else who might notice that the Folans always had more than enough food to eat. It appeared to be a kind of protest or challenge to the multiple famines that had plagued both of their families back home for centuries. Coleman did this, Mary believed, and had once confided to her daughter Mamie, as if to say, 'We're over here now, and you can't harm us any more!'

Carlo Toney always had a full house at dinner time, but Mary had never seen a single Irish longshoreman coming out of his small restaurant, only Italian freight handlers. Apparently, these manual laborers were segregated both at work and at the dinner table! This seemed a peculiar behavior, she thought, but easily understandable. For their part, the Irish were particularly clannish. Many of them even wanted to know exactly what section of County Galway you came from before openly befriending you. One of the second-generation native borns had once assuredly declared to Mary, 'You simply can't trust them Connemaras!'

But this had been stated without the knowledge that his very own family was firmly rooted in that exact same region of Galway going back several generations on both sides! Shortly after being enlightened about his family roots, this "corner boy" had moderated his opinion of this region and all those who hailed from Connemara!

In more recent times, the Italians were starting to arrive in Portland in ever-increasing numbers. There were not yet enough of them to support an entirely separate church of their own, but they wanted one. And they would probably get one as soon as their numbers on and around the base of Munjoy Hill would justify the building and maintenance of such a structure. This would occur, of course, only assuming that the Bishop would agree to it.

Both of the Bishops of the Diocese of Portland so far had been Irish. Assimilation into the dominant culture seemed to be a common theme here and in the Catholic Church throughout America. All three of Portland's Catholic Churches, at least up until now, were overwhelmingly Irish. These churches included Saint Dom's, the oldest; the Cathedral, the Folans' parish; and Sacred Heart, the newest church in the fast-growing west end and located only two blocks up from Deering Oaks.

The two women passed Carlo Toney's and hurried up Franklin Street with the wind at their backs coming off the water as it often did in the winter. They were soon near the block that had in earlier times been known locally as "Sebastopol." It was bordered by Franklin, Middle, Hampshire, and Fore.

As they reached the corner of Newbury, where the Clancys and the Joyces lived, Mary predictably asked the same old question, "Where on earth did Baraba

Joyce get his peculiar name, a'tall? I never heard of a Baraba on Mynish or anywhere else back home in Joyce's Country right up to the Twelve Pins. What manner of name is that, a'tall?"

Nora had always thought that this was simply a corruption or misspelling of the female name of his mother Barbara. Immigration officials had notoriously butchered many surnames, so perhaps they were now going after one's Christian or given name as well!

Nora, even with her logical suspicions, would simply shrug her shoulders as always and say in Irish, "*Níl fhíos agam, a Mháire* (literally, knowledge is not on me, or I don't know, Mary)."

Nora's well-intentioned use of the Irish would only make Mary smile and respond critically yet lovingly, "Sure you murder the Irish language!" Mary's thick brogue and over-emphasis stretched out the word "mooradurrah" and made it sound as if it had many more that just two syllables.

At the corner of Newbury and India they could have headed south and back toward home, but Mary pressed on. She sensed that this might be her last long walk outside for a few weeks, especially if the little kicker inside of her decided to emerge to take in the sights and sounds of Portland for the first time. This caused Mary to wonder again whether the new child was to be a "herself" or a "himself."

Looking south down India Street they could see patrons bringing their soiled clothing into Hip Lunn's Laundry. This was one of several Chinese laundries in the city. The Chinese, it seemed, were concentrated in that line of work just as the Italians were in freight handling and on the railroads, and the Irish were in the longshore for their men and domestic work for their women.

"Do one job and do it well, Nora!" Mary pontificated in an attempt to try to explain these separate work patterns.

Mary seemed to enjoy playing the role of the wise older sage to the young *girlín*. Mary had lovingly mentored this innocent young widow from East Galway since they first met. She believed that she had learned as much herself from this clever and vivacious young mother as she had taught.

Mary had a certain feeling in her heart about this one, and had once told Nora, 'You will have no trouble in adapting to life here in America, or doing anything else that you set your mind on doing.' She saw much of herself in her companion, although Nora was now several years younger and so far much less encumbered by a growing tribe of children.

Passing by the corner of Hancock, they arrived at the rear of the Thomas Laughlin Company. Here they could see and hear the busy marine hardware factory and the forge with its rhythmic beat that dominated the entire eastern half of the city. This sprawling factory ran down to Fore Street, between India and Mountfort. It specialized in a process known as "galvanizing," which was done on a daily basis. Thomas Laughlin advertised itself as the only factory of its kind in the entire state of Maine.

Across Fore Street was the Portland Company that produced locomotives and other heavy machinery. These two companies were good sources of industrial employment for Portland's working men, if one was lucky enough to land a job there. But this presented a certain dilemma – how does one acquire the skills necessary to gain employment at such a business? Most of the young Portland Irish had not yet solved that particular riddle.

As the two ladies approached Mountfort Street they could see the Abyssinian Church ahead on the left-hand side located at 73 Newbury Street. The Abyssinian had been built in 1828 and was one of the oldest African-American meeting houses in America. It had always served as the central meeting place for Portland's small but important Negro community.

Prior to the arrival of the Irish, this small group had done much of the menial dock work on the Portland waterfront given its strong maritime connection to the West Indies and its lucrative molasses trade. Two of Portland's most important early businesses were entirely dependent on that pungent black syrup – locally transformed into either refined sugar or rum, or "Demon Rum" as the local temperance societies called it. The support for the prohibition of alcohol had long and deep roots in Maine, but so did the tradition of making profits from the transportation of goods of all types and description. Now that the Negro dock hands in Portland had been displaced by the more numerous Irish, they were forced into several other service-related jobs around the city or on the railroad cars and passenger steamers then serving this region.

Mary and Nora could hardly help but notice that the Abyssinian was still draped in black bunting ever since that disastrous day of November 17, 1898, just a little over one year earlier. It was on that horrific day that the steamship *Portland* was lost at sea off Cape Cod in what would be forever known as the "Portland Gale."

Ironically, earlier that very same year, another ship also with a Maine connection had sunk, albeit under far different circumstances. On February 15, 1898, the battleship USS *Maine* exploded in Havana, Cuba, with the loss of 258 out of a crew of 350. The only Maine native on the crew, one J. M. Douloff of Portland, had mercifully survived. This explosion, even though its origin or cause largely remained unknown, had been used as the pretext propelling the United States into its first major overseas war of conquest, the Spanish-American War. Because of this war, the *Montauk* was now patrolling Portland harbor purportedly to protect the city from any foreign intrusion.

As Portland was a maritime city, shipping disasters were to be expected. On February 22, 1864, the RMS *Bohemian*, carrying mostly Irish steerage passengers, had gone down with the loss of forty-two lives. Nearly twenty-three years later, on December 24, 1886, the *Annie C. Maguire* had wrecked off Portland Head. But it was the "Portland Gale" of November 26, 1898, known both regionally and nationally, that had a far greater impact locally. The ship's captain, Hollis Blanchard, had apparently ignored warnings of gale-force winds. Among the nearly 200 lives lost were sixty-five crew members, many of whom hailed from Portland's small Negro community at the base of Munjoy Hill. Between the Abyssinian and the nearby AME Zion Mission, nearly twenty members had been lost, including two of their trustees. The Abyssinian had taken a severe financial shock from which many worried they could not recover.

It was believed that the house nearly adjacent to the Abyssinian, that formerly of the Eastman and Stephenson families, had served as a conduit for the Underground Railroad before the Civil War. Portland's Negro community, though small in number, was strategically placed on a major deep-water Atlantic port close to Canada. Additionally, it was served by several major railroad links. This transportation hub allowed sympathetic Portlanders to assist runaway or fugitive slaves from the South and the Border States to "follow the drinking gourd," and thus gain their freedom further to the North. As these two sojourners approached the corner of Newbury and Mountfort Streets near the now decaying neighborhood known locally as "The Bight," Mary paused and looked sadly back toward the Abyssinian.

"You know, Nora, the Negroes of Portland have not had an easy time of it. They are so few in number and are forced to work at whatever poor jobs others won't take, especially our own people. Coley tells me that they were once an important group of dockworkers in Portland before the railroad connected us to Montreal in the early 1850s. By the time he and I arrived in Portland, the Irish owned the longshore work. Coley says that the PLSBS Bylaws written in the same year that he arrived exclude Negroes from working longshore. He told me that these Bylaws state clearly that 'No colored man shall be a member of this Society.' Now what do you think of that, dear?"

"I don't know anything about longshore work, Mary, but it just doesn't seem fair. After all, there are so few Negroes, and don't they need to feed their families, too? What does Coley say about it?"

Mary replied sadly, "He says that they should find work with their own kind and that we should work with our own kind, and that is that! The few times I've tried to discuss this with him a row and a ruction usually breaks out. He will listen only up to a certain point, but then he always brings out the same tired old argument, 'It's in our Bylaws, Mary! What would you have me to do?'"

"What would be the harm, Mary," Nora asked, "of letting a few colored workers on the waterfront with all of our boys? Sure those families that I know work as hard as any of ours, and the women are real easy to talk with – no airs to them at all. I hear that some, like Moses Green, a porter at the Union Station, give nearly their entire earnings every month just to keep their Church going. Then there's the Ruby family, too, that I know. They're all fine people, much like our own. They once told me that one of their relatives, a John Suggs from Munjoy Hill who was sometimes called Siggs, used to work regularly on the waterfront before our boys took over. He was once ridiculed and called 'wooly headed' just because he supported the temperance campaign of Mayor Dow. It seems to me that many of our own people here in Portland don't want to give these poor Negroes a fighting chance!"

"I'm glad you see it that way, Nora. I thought you would. It's in your nature to judge people by what they do and say and not for less important reasons. But I'm sure you know that not all of our kind would see things that way. For the life of me, I can't understand why the Irish, of all people, would make life more difficult for any other group. Sure, wasn't life made plenty difficult for us back home?"

Nora agreed with her older mentor and then added, "I've heard from some who say that the Abyssinian and this very house that we're standing beside now, the Eastman House, were both used by Negroes trying to flee their slave-owning masters around the time of the Civil War, and that they were both part of what was called the Underground Railroad. But here it is, Mary, very much above ground for all now to see. Don't you think that the Negroes here and everywhere want freedom just as much as we Irish want it for ourselves in Ireland and in America?"

Nora's question hung in the cold air, unanswered. The two women continued to stare at the bleak Abyssinian with its torn and faded black bunting flapping loudly in the frigid breeze that was still coming off the cold Atlantic only a couple hundred yards away.

Nora seemed paralyzed by the sound of the bunting, but then sighed, "The Portland Gale took possession of so many of their beloved, and now it appears to want to even claim their bunting as well – the last sad memory of their loss!"

It almost seemed as though the bunting was still trying to sharply call out the names of all those who had been lost just over a year ago, lest they be forgotten. The staccato snapping sound was not only terribly sad but also painfully haunting. It caused Mary to reveal her ultimate concern.

"It would be a tragedy upon a tragedy if they lost their most important Church as a result of this calamity and its heavy loss of life. Haven't they suffered enough already? As my Johnny says, with all of his fine English, 'That would be adding insult to injury!'"

As the ladies were about to continue their walk-about, the front door of the Church creaked open and an older man, decked out in a dark woolen coat stepped outside and slowly closed the door behind him. He respectfully tipped his hat in the general direction of Mary and Nora and started to make his way west along Newbury Street. Just then Nora did something unexpectedly that caught Mary by complete surprise.

"Mr. Ruby?" Nora inquired.

He stopped, turned toward them and politely asked, "Do I know you?"

"No," Nora confidently stated, "but I have one or two women friends from this congregation and I thought I recognized you from the memorial service for those lost in the Portland Gale."

"Thank you for attending that service, young lady. It was a very sad day for the Abyssinian and for the entire city. We were delighted that so many came out to mourn with us on that day."

"Mr. Ruby, this is my dear friend, Mary Folan. I believe that her husband,

Coleman Folan, and some of his other longshore workers have been to your restaurant on Free Street."

"That's true," Mary happily responded and then added, "My husband told me how much he enjoyed your home-style of cooking, and that one of his mates later claimed, 'A 25 cent dinner there is equal to a 50 cent one in almost any other eating house in New England!'"

"Well, well," Mr. Ruby thanked Mary and added, "I'm thrilled to hear that, my dear, and coming from a group of longshoremen with their reputation for having hearty appetites, I'd say that is high praise indeed."

This impromptu meeting was off to a most congenial start, but Nora felt the need to again express her sincere condolences to him, and in this she was quickly joined by Mary.

"Yes, thank you both for saying that. The year 1898 was a most challenging one for me and my family. In June, I came very close to losing my son, William Wilberforce Ruby, Jr., to a lynch party in Kentucky where he was then serving as a private in Company A of the First Maine Regiment. He and two friends were out for a walk when they approached and attempted to cross the lines of a Kentucky Regiment. After being abruptly halted, a war of words ensued. Before long a mob from the Second Kentucky Regiment had gathered with even some yelling, 'Hang him. Hang him.'

"My son was only saved by the timely arrival of a few of his own officers who had a difficult time subduing him as they claimed that he was 'full of fight.' William was lucky to escape with just a court martial.

"And then, just five months after this, we had the terrible maritime disaster. I can hardly think of a worse way to perish than aboard a sinking ship in such a devastating storm at sea. My heart bleeds every day for all of the families of the lost, and especially those dear friends from the Abyssinian, as well as those from the AME Zion Mission just around the corner on Mountfort Street. Perhaps they lost even more members in the great storm than we did as they have a younger congregation."

This caused Nora, never one to be shy about asking questions, to inquire as to why two Negro churches existed so close to each other, using an unusual phrase 'cheek by jowl.'

William Ruby replied that he could only guess at the answer to that. "Well, first, this is our neighborhood. I suppose it might be because the Abyssinian is older with roots going back to my father before 1830 when we split from Congregational churches that did not treat us fairly. Over the years since then, we have become a bit too conservative ourselves, perhaps, and even forced out some of our younger and more energetic members for seemingly minor infractions. Our loss became the AME Mission's gain, I'd say. But it's no less true for the white Protestant churches here in Portland, ladies. Just look at the number of different denominations we have even in a small city like ours."

The three of them paused to let all these thoughts sink in. This story of his son's near miss was a complete surprise to both women, but they seemed to have an instinctual sense of the precarious nature of being identified as a minority, even within one's own country – Ireland had taught them that tough lesson.

After an interval of time, Nora inquired of Mr. Ruby about the origin of his unusual full name. She guessed, "I suppose it comes from other generations of your family?"

"Well, not really, dear. In fact, both my son and I carry the name of one of England's most famous abolitionist leaders, William Wilberforce."

Neither lady knew anything of him, however. So, Mary added sympathetically, "It's that way for us, too, Mr. Ruby, as many Irish children over the years have been named in honor of our many heroes from O'Connell and Parnell, including some well-known religious leaders, and even a few saints to boot."

The image of "booting" a saint seemed to strike Mr. Ruby's sense of humor and so he informed them that was why he chuckled at this mention. It had been a short but most enjoyable meeting of chance.

As Mr. Ruby took his leave and proceeded toward town, Mary could not help but notice that, by his slow gait and carefully placed steps, he was starting to show his age. She estimated he might be in his mid-60s. He still had a handsome face, now fringed in gray, and she could easily imagine his imposing presence when he was in his prime.

After he was a ways off, Nora informed Mary that it was he who reportedly had given the first notice of the Great Portland Fire of July 4, 1866, and was also often credited with saving his beloved Abyssinian Church by applying wetted blankets to the roof, thus protecting it from the countless blazing embers that scattered all over the city from west to east by a steady hot July wind. The fire destroyed an estimated 1,500 buildings, including nearly everything in the area in which they were now standing. Ironically, the swath of destruction closely paralleled that lost in the earlier burning of Falmouth (Portland) by the British back in 1775.

As they turned again to watch William Wilberforce Ruby depart, they smiled at each other in obvious admiration for a man who had lived his time on this earth to the fullest. It would be Mary who put words to their shared feeling. "His likes will not be seen again!"

"It's true for you," Nora whispered in agreement. "It's true for you."

Slowly, as they turned their gazes eastward and into the wind, the women could see Portland Harbor and the Casco Bay islands in the near distance – one for every day in the calendar it was popularly claimed. How much this vantage point reminded Mary of her own beautiful Mynish Island at home, and the similarly gorgeous view out to Finish and Macdara's Island, or even further over to Gorumna, Lettermullen and Lettermore, Furnace, and even tiny Dinish, the birthplace of the Loftus family.

Mary purposely decided to change the somber mood as she now thought of the popular song *Peigín Leitir Móir* (Peggy of Lettermore) and wondered aloud to her bemused companion, "How do you think young Peggy of Lettermore is getting on these days?" As if she had plucked it out of thin air, Mary began to softly sing,

> *"Tá iascairí na Gaillimhe ag teach anoir le coir.*
> *Le solas gealaí gile nó go bheicidís an tseoid..."*
> (The fishermen of Galway are coming west at the ready
> With bright lights so that they could see the beauty...)

And with this musical introduction bringing a full smile to Nora's face, she joined in heartily on the refrain,

> *"'s ó, gairim, gairim í, 'gus gairim í mó stór,*
> *Míle grá le m'anam í 's í Peigín Leitir Móir!"*
> (Calling out to her, Peggy is my treasure,
> A thousand loves is she to me in my soul, Peggy of Lettermore)

And then, once again for good measure and with even more enthusiasm and volume this time, both of these Galway women slightly changed the final phrase as by tradition,

"'s ó, gairim, gairim í, 'gus gairim í mó stór,
Míle grá le m'anam í is gear go mbeidh sí mór!"
(Calling out to her, Peggy is my treasure,
A thousand loves of my soul, it's not long before she'll be grown!)

They laughed heartily and long at their rakishness, both, of course, having already carefully determined that there was no other person anywhere around to hear or see them acting up in such a manner.

With tears welling in their eyes both from the nostalgia and the joviality of the moment, it was Nora who finally brought them back to this side of the Atlantic with a light-hearted warning, "Mary, they'll send us both to Ballinasloe (Galway's asylum for the 'feeble minded') if they catch us howling on the streets like this, and with you about to deliver your tenth child! Sometimes I forget which one of us is the young one. Get a move on before *na iascairí Portland* (the Portland fishermen) find us and judge us both, with good reason, to be *craicailte* (cracked, or crazy) – a couple of *oinseachaí* (foolish women)!"

Neither had noticed the cold while they were walking or singing. But now it was becoming quite clear to them that they should be returning home again soon to where the coal stove would be working overtime. There they could also eat whatever the voracious young longshoremen and young Bridgie would have left for them. And what was Bridgie's "surprise," Mary now wondered?

They were now heading west along Fore Street, and Mary couldn't help but ask if Nora had heard the story about Longfellow's birthplace. Nora gracefully said no, even though she had already heard this story from Mary at least a dozen times. Why stop her? Mary obviously loved telling this story, and it was presented a little differently each time in any case. They arrived at the somewhat dilapidated building at the corner of Fore and Hancock, the actual place where the poet Henry Wadsworth Longfellow had been born nearly one hundred years earlier.

As expected, Mary shook her head, set her jaw in a kind of scolding manner, and sternly declared, "Well, Catherine Foley and Patrick Greely are in there now, along with several others I hardly even know, where the Connors also once lived. But my Johnny told me a few years back this story from one of his favorite teachers at the North School, Miss Mary Connolly who lived over on Federal Street. It seems that a teacher there had once asked her young students if anyone could tell her exactly where the poet had been born. She would have been content; I'm sure, with a simple answer, such as 'in Portland, Maine.' But the scholars searched their young and still developing brains more diligently until one finally burst out with what he confidently knew to be the precise answer his teacher was searching for. And then, with the kind of enthusiasm that only accompanies the assuredness that you are one hundred percent correct, the young scholar shouted out, 'Longfellow was born in Patsy Connor's bedroom!'"

Nora laughed as if she was hearing this story for the very first time.

Mary added, "How the times have changed, Nora. Just think of it. Two of our own now living in the very place where America's most famous poet was born! I must get onto Catherine Foley and Patrick Greely about doing something with this place before it falls into total disrepair entirely."

Nora loved the way that Mary took ownership of all things great and small. It was as if she had a personal stake in resolving all of the world's crises, or at least these local problems, to the betterment of her newly-adopted city and all of its inhabitants. Just before coming to the corner of India Street, they both stopped. Despite the chilling winds they paused to briefly admire the stunning beauty of the Grand Trunk Railroad depot. One would hardly find a finer building on either side of the ocean.

And then in yet another sign of Mary's own parochial nature, she now declared, as she had regularly done in the past, with both sincerity and full passion, "Stone for stone our train station is a far grander building than the mighty Union Station in the west end. I'll even give them credit for their taller clock tower!"

The Grand Trunk was indeed the transportation hub of Portland's east end with people coming and going around the clock. When travelers from northern or western locales arrived in the city, they could stay at the comfortable and elegant Atlantic House directly across from this same corner. But now, Nora grimaced as she looked up at a commercial billboard announcing a public address to be given on the burning issue, "Why Women Sin!"

Nora then irreverently asserted, "It must be a man giving that talk. He probably thinks that he came into this world by Immaculate Conception – only for the second time on record over the past two thousand years!"

Mary laughed at Nora's witty comment even though she thought to herself that she shouldn't be encouraging the younger woman's blasphemy, mild as it was. These things never sounded wrong, however, when Nora said them. She didn't have a mean bone in her body. But don't get her going on the perks and privileges of the priests, especially those pompous ones who seemed to think that the world owes them a living.

Most of the priests that Mary knew were, like themselves, from humble Irish homes, but occasionally one would come along who must have traced his pedigree directly back to the City of David, or at the very least to Ireland's Hill of Tara. These haughty souls raised Nora's hackles. Although Mary never openly encouraged Nora in her inherently strong passion against both pretense and privilege, she felt exactly the same way – if only less publicly.

Crossing India Street, they were nearly home now, and they could once again sense the exotic smells still wafting from Carlo Toney's. The Irish longshoremen that the Folans fed on a daily basis would have to get by on more basic fare, such as stews of all kind, roasts, and potatoes served in a myriad of different ways. Indeed, meat and potatoes would always be the standard Irish bill of fare. That is what they wanted simply because it was what they were used to.

"You can take a boy out of Ireland but the smell of turf stays with him all the same," declared Mary who was looking over at Nora but thinking of her hungry longshoremen.

Mary was more convinced than ever that Irishness is much more than simply a matter of blood or where one is from – she long ago had concluded that Irishness is a style of life, a series of choices that are made often without thinking and usually almost minute-by-minute. Her own Coley, she was convinced, had changed his place of abode but not the essence of who he was. And to Mary, he was essentially the same man who had arrived from the rocky shores of Connemara to the rocky shores of Maine some twenty years ago.

To Mary Folan, Portland was and had always been a little bit of Galway that had somehow dislodged and floated across the Atlantic, forced ever westward possibly by some great Atlantic gale. She was content here. She felt at home here. But at the same time she was also intrigued by those stimulating and foreign smells of garlic coming from Carlo Toney's! This strange and endearing place, with all of its differences and extraordinary customs, was now her home away from home – for better or for worse.

Why Women Sin

Part II ~ Afternoon

"Let the Echoes Ring"

Lo, little bark on twin-horned Rhine, From forest hewn to skim the brine,
    Heave, lads, and let the echoes ring!
The tempests howl, the storms dismay, But manly strength can win the day,
    Heave, lads, and let the echoes ring!
For clouds and squalls will soon pass on, And victory lies with work well done,
    Heave, lads, and let the echoes ring!

From "The Boat Song" of Saint Columbanus
Irish missionary monk of the 6th – 7th c. from Bangor in Ulster
Translation taken from Tomás Ó Fiaich, *Columbanus in his own words*

Chapter 7

Strange Bedfellows

"Destiny is no matter of chance. It is a matter of choice:
It is not a thing to be waited for, it is a thing to be achieved."

– William Jennings Bryan

It seemed to Johnny and Dara like the Second Coming of Christ. "The Great Commoner" himself in little Portland, Maine, and there he was in the flesh – the silver-tongued Prophet from the Great Plains.

Johnny Folan and Dara Loftus had left their friend, Frank Feeney, down by the Back Bay. Frank, as usual, seemed more interested in locating his current girlfriend than in the political adventure of a lifetime that the younger two were now planning. Just after noon, on this last day of January in the year 1900, Johnny and Dara were in the very midst of a real live, albeit small, political rally right in their own home town. It was a thrilling sight to behold.

William Jennings Bryan had led the Democratic Party and the Populists just over three years earlier in an anti-corporate crusade for the highest elective office in the land. Now at the still tender age of forty, he was again on the campaign trail. Perhaps he would be the Democratic nominee one more time later this same year. Hadn't his "Free Silver" platform of 1896 caught the attention and won the hearts of America's farmers and working poor? Hadn't he electrified the Democratic National Convention that same year on July 9th, when he delivered his now-famous "Cross of Gold" speech?

"You shall not press down upon the brow of labor this crown of thorns. You shall not crucify mankind upon a cross of gold!"

Hadn't Bryan repeated the now iconic speech to enthusiastic crowds at Chautauqua and countless other venues across the country, and couldn't every school child in America recite those stirring words by heart? He was possibly the greatest American public orator of his day, and, as hard as it was for the two boys to believe, here he was right in the very heart of Portland!

"I guess we aren't the end of the line after all!" said Johnny to his friend, alluding to the viewpoint then common in their home town that Portland was, and probably would always remain, a mere backwater. This widely-held opinion defined Portland as a poor cousin to the larger and more prosperous cities to its south and west, particularly Boston, New York, and Chicago.

Bryan was in Maine on this frigid January day for several reasons. Firstly, his Vice Presidential candidate in 1896 had been Arthur Sewall of Bath, Maine, just a few miles down-east of Portland. Of course, Sewell would be expected to be here to greet his standard-bearer on his own home turf. Secondly, and quite perplexing to both Johnny and Dara, Bryan was about to enter the home of Maine's most identifiable Republican – Thomas Brackett Reed.

As the all-powerful Speaker of the House of Representatives, until his recent resignation, "Czar Reed" had wielded near absolute control over that chamber for most of the last decade having promulgated "Reed's Rules." These rules had changed the *modus operandi* of the House and drastically reformed the previously slow and cumbersome manner of doing the business of "the People's House." Simultaneously, however, they also guaranteed near absolute control by the dominant Republican Party that was led in that chamber by Reed himself. But now, following his resignation, Reed was again a private citizen.

"What on earth would Bryan want with a man like Reed?" Dara asked. "What could they possibly have in common? It's hard to believe that a rock-ribbed Republican like Reed could be of any help to someone like Bryan, or that they'd even have much of anything to talk about with each other."

Johnny agreed adding, "That seems right to me – Maine supported Bryan's Republican opponent, President William McKinley, in the last election and will probably do so again should he choose to run for re-election this year, or any other Republican for that matter should McKinley choose not to run. Maine votes Republican and that's that – as it was in the beginning, is now and ever shall be… Republican without end, Amen!"

Both of these boys came from homes where politics, Democratic politics that is, was the daily bill of fare and was spoken on a regular basis, almost like a secular religion. They seemed to know instinctively what side their bread was buttered on, or at least what party was more likely to provide them with the bread and butter that poor families like theirs so badly needed.

As perplexing as it seemed, here was William Jennings Bryan on the corner of State and Deering Streets, at the home of "Czar Reed." And here were Johnny and

Dara about to get a bird's-eye view of these two towering national figures – and quite a figure it was in the case of Reed who stood six foot three inches tall and weighed very nearly 300 pounds!

"What a statue that man would make!" Johnny quipped. "And you'd have to be sure that its pedestal consisted of solid granite!"

If the boys' bold scheme worked, not merely would they have a birds-eye view from the street but also from the very bird's nest itself. Dara Loftus's mother was a Welch (a Breathnach) who had come to Portland several years back from Half-Mace, a rugged townland that bravely clung to the rocky coast of south Connemara quite near Carna and Callowfeenish in far western County Galway. Delia Welch, ironically no relation but a friend of his mother, hailed from nearby Feenish Island. Delia was now working as a domestic in service to the former Susan Prentice Merrill – none other than the present Mrs. Thomas Brackett Reed!

Delia Welch had often invited Dara, and sometimes even Johnny, into the Reed kitchen when extra help was needed, particularly for large dinner parties. There had been many such events over the years while Reed was in power – power, it seems, is attractive. But these had been almost entirely Republican "blue blood" affairs, and therefore of no particular interest to these true-blue Democratic boys. Once, curiously, the Catholic Bishop, James Augustine Healy, had been an invited guest. When he came into the kitchen to thank the help, these two boys were greeted by their Bishop as if they were members of the great man's household. Their mothers were, of course, both proud and thrilled at this news.

But today would be different. The "Great Commoner" was about to enter through the front door – something that neither Delia nor indeed any of the domestic staff would have dreamed of themselves. Dara and Johnny now hurried around to the back of the house. This entrance was being patrolled by the head servant, a trusted older Yankee, but one who recognized both of these boys and therefore allowed them to pass along unhindered, assuming that they were there again to assist the kitchen staff. Thus they passed freely, albeit surreptitiously, into the home of the former Speaker. Johnny had long since learned the important life lesson that confidence, or at least a feigned show of public confidence, could open many doors. These same doors would otherwise be closed and locked to him and most members of his social class.

'In for the penny, in for the pound,' he had often heard his mother declare, and he now swore by this axiom, finding that it had usually worked in his favor. Dara, always a bit more skeptical or at least more reticent, was by now learning to follow suit.

Delia appeared to be a bit miffed upon seeing them as there had obviously been no invitation extended for this particular occasion. There were only a small handful of guests to be admitted and served on this day. It was to be a nearly private meeting between the man from Nebraska and the man from Maine. Delia had neither the time nor the inclination, however, to cause any kind of scene about this small but unwarranted intrusion. She gave both boys a stern look that they correctly took to mean, 'OK boys, this time, but watch your step and keep out of everyone's way!'

The liaison who had promoted and organized this unusual meeting was himself an unlikely facilitator, Arthur Sewall of Bath. Sewall at this time was Maine's leading Democrat. He was a major banker from the mid-coast who had amassed quite a small fortune for his family. He had financed the building of the country's first steel sailing ship in 1894, and he was currently helping to maintain the historic prominence of Bath and, by extension, all of coastal Maine on the national maritime stage.

Bryan's choice of Sewall in 1896 as his Vice Presidential candidate on the Democratic ticket had at first seemed to be a curious one. Perhaps Bryan was attempting to balance his ticket. He was a populist mid-westerner and only thirty-six years of age in that year, barely meeting the Constitutional age test and the youngest candidate of a major party in American history. Sewall, by contrast, was a more mature and well-heeled New Englander with considerable business experience. Bryan, from Nebraska, could hardly have gone further east to geographically balance the ticket.

The choice of Sewall, however, had alienated many Populists who would ultimately be crucial to the success of any Bryan coalition. Some Populists, especially those from the South, had responded to the choice of the Yankee Sewall by nominating their own candidate for Vice President, Thomas E. Watson of Georgia. Nationally, voters could support Bryan and simultaneously split their vote at the bottom of the ticket, supporting whichever of these two highly different vice-presidential candidates they preferred. That's American practicality for you.

Listening from the kitchen pass-through into the dining room, Johnny and Dara soon learned that Sewall's presence in the room was more than a mere formality. Almost instantly upon entering the room, Bryan button-holed Sewall to ascertain whether he could count on the Mainer's unqualified support should he decide to run again for the presidency later that year. Perhaps Bryan's suspicions had been heightened by the well-publicized and embarrassing revelation that in 1896 Sewall's son, Harold M. Sewall, had become a delegate to the Republican National Convention, and further that he had strongly thrown his support to its nominee, William McKinley! Bryan wanted to avoid compounding this earlier internecine embarrassment by at least confirming that he could still be assured of the endorsement of his former running mate.

"Can I count on your support, Arthur, in July at our National Convention?"

"Of course you may. I'm a loyal Democrat and I don't consult with my son for political advice, I can assure you."

"Can I count on your *strong* support?" Bryan further inquired with emphasis and now with his eyes directly probing Sewall's for an indication of his true feelings.

"When the time is right, I shall reaffirm my undiminished enthusiasm for the Democratic Party and declare that you, Mr. Bryan, have no stronger friend or more loyal supporter in the country than you have in me."

Bryan was by now two and one-half months shy of his fortieth birthday. His political skills were finely developed, as he had already gone through the earlier political trial by fire in 1896 by pushing for inflated currency and the free coinage of silver at a 16:1 ratio to gold. These positions would be beneficial to heavily indebted farmers, among others, thus earning Bryan the title, "The Great Commoner." Bryan's failed campaign had not diminished in the slightest his zeal to serve in the nation's highest office.

"Thank you, Arthur. That means a great deal to me and to Mary as well, it should go without saying. I give you thanks, my good friend. I cherish your support and your loyalty, and I look forward to your continued good counsel in the months and years ahead. I know well that our campaign together was both personally and professionally difficult for you – would that the results could have been different..."

Bryan had impressively dispatched this important piece of business in short order. By this time Reed himself entered the dining room, having been briefly detained at his front stairway by political favor-seekers who wished at least to cast a cold eye upon his household guest. Some, perhaps the most fervent Republicans in the state, would have liked to crucify Bryan themselves upon that very same conjured "cross of gold" that had made him so famous. It was an oration that many had heard Bryan repeat with his booming voice time and again, quite willingly it seemed, at tent meetings, Democratic political rallies, and at public gatherings all over the nation.

These Maine Republican stalwarts were curious as to why these political polar opposites were meeting at all. It was the same question that Johnny and Dara had earlier posed to each other.

Dara whispered to Johnny a phrase that he had heard while shipping out a year earlier, and he thought it appropriate for this occasion, "Politics makes strange bedfellows."

The answer to all of their questions was not long in coming. Mr. Bryan could be quite direct when matters called for it, as in the case of the just concluded conversation with Arthur Sewall.

"Tom, if I may call you that?"

"Of course, Mr. Bryan, no courtship, no ceremony – no formality is necessary while you're a guest here in my home."

"Tom, I've come to Maine, in the midst of this bone-chilling weather that you've so kindly provided, for several important reasons. As has been widely speculated upon, I am indeed seriously considering another run for the presidency. I'm sure this will come as no surprise to you – you were touched at least once by the presidential bug yourself, I believe?"

"That's in the past now. But as you say, your plans are hardly a surprise – I had always assumed this to be well within the realm of the possible."

"I wish to travel to all forty-five states in the Union, Tom, before our Democratic National Convention this coming July. It's important that I familiarize myself with party leaders, strong supporters, and important opinion-makers in all parts of the nation."

"Well," Reed acknowledged, "that would explain Arthur's presence here and your engagement to speak this evening at our City Hall Auditorium, but…" Reed then hesitated, throwing the ball back into Bryan's court.

"Yes, Tom, that does get us to the obvious unanswered question – why I specifically asked to meet with you during this trip to Portland."

"Perhaps you hadn't heard that I have only recently relinquished the Speaker's gavel and am no longer a great man?" Reed asked with a straight face, causing Sewall to almost choke on his drink. "I have also retired the title of 'Czar' and all the glitter associated with that elevated position of power. My realm has greatly diminished and my court is now the court of law alone – I am but a simple lawyer these days." Sewall searched Bryan's face to see how he would react to Reed's notoriously Yankee tendency to trivialize the complex and accentuate the mundane.

"Yes, Tom, that news had indeed reached even as far as my humble home on the Great Plains. And although you may no longer wield the gavel, you are still a formidable political and moral force greatly to be reckoned with. You will, I'm sure, continue to be one of the most highly respected voices in American politics. It was never the mere possession of the Speaker's gavel that ultimately gave you respect and power, rather it was, I sincerely believe, your intellect and your strict adherence to principle. It has been widely reported that your reason for voluntarily surrendering the Speakership of the House, an office that you once referred to as being 'second only to one and without equal by any other,' was solely on the grounds of conscience. It is generally believed that you could no longer go along with the direction in which your party and our country were then heading in terms of expansionism."

"It was not an easy decision for me, I'll grant you that. I had served my party for sixteen years as either majority or minority leader in the House, several of these years, as you've noted, as its Speaker."

"Tom, that brings me to my major reason for asking for this meeting today. Again, I give thanks to you, Arthur, for arranging this to happen."

Reed's interest was now clearly piqued, and Bryan had everyone's full attention. Just on the other side of the wall from where this fascinating conversation was occurring, Johnny and Dara were also all ears. Something of interest was soon to follow…

"Along with the crowd outside this house, I had wondered, Mr. Bryan, as to your purpose in proposing this unorthodox meeting. Some fellow Republicans out on the street have even this day asked me why I would 'sup with the Devil.' More than one of my friends has mentioned that several representatives of the nation's most influential newspapers are here today in our fair city to satisfy their curiosity on this same question."

"Well, Tom, you've brought us to the crux of the matter, and with the elegance and directness I have come to expect from you. Along with the entire country, I was greatly moved by your courageous withdrawal from the Speakership earlier last year, a position that was yours to keep simply for the asking, and simultaneously giving up this safest of seats representing Maine's First Congressional District. I've been told that you were regularly returned with ever-increasing majorities since first being elected in 1876 replacing, as I recall, the 'Plumbed Knight' himself, Maine's own James Gillespie Blaine, when he was elevated to the Senate."

Reed wittily interrupted his guest, "Are you sure you meant to say 'elevated'?"

All present laughed, knowing well of "Czar Reed's" famous contempt for the "upper chamber" of the Congress, pejoratively labeled by Reed as the "uppity chamber." Members of the Senate were elected by the various state legislatures rather than by the direct vote of the people, as in the case of the House, the "lower chamber." Reed had once joked, "If the Senate was ever permitted to nominate and vote for candidates for the presidency, there would certainly be ninety votes returned for ninety entirely different nominees – with each Senator humbly yet predictably supporting his own most worthy candidacy!"

Bryan then continued, "As Shakespeare once wrote, 'Nothing in his life became him so much as the leaving of it….' In that regard, Tom, I'd say that your surrendering of this office nine months ago was an act of supreme courage and honor. It was universally praised and judged to be a principled decision, just as when you stood firmly against the annexation of Hawaii in June of 1898 – and in that you were almost alone within your own party. As I recall, you were absent on the day of the vote due to illness, and yet you determined to have the acting chair inform the House that if you had been there you would have voted 'NO'! You didn't have to do that, and yet you did. These acts of conscience are, I fear, all too rare in American political life today. Even *The Nation* opined on what it called your 'uncommon virtue' in opposing both the 'popular mania' and the overwhelming consensus of your own party."

"It was not a happy time for me, Mr. Bryan, as I'm sure you will understand."

Bryan certainly did understand. He agreed wholeheartedly and then added, "The war with Spain, the annexation of Hawaii, and the final straw of the Treaty of Paris less than one year ago, which thereby transferred the sovereignty of the

Philippines from Spain to the United States, and sweetened, as it was, by a $20 million cash 'settlement' – these things should have been repugnant to all Americans, Republicans and Democrats alike."

The silence that betokens consent briefly ensued. After a proper pause, Arthur Sewall, who had been nearly silent although deeply contemplative up to this point, now added his own note of respect for the former Speaker in an intentionally reverential but ultimately comical tribute.

"Tom, I would like to add my own personal admiration for your comportment during those recent trying times. Mr. Bryan is meant to be the silver-tongued orator among us, but on several occasions during these debates you hit the nail on the head with such passion and succinctness that should have impressed and convinced any open-minded listener. During the Treaty debate you wrote, 'The quarrels which other nations have we did not have. The sun did set on our dominions and our drum-beat did not encircle the world with our martial airs. Our guns were not likely to be called upon to throw projectiles which cost, each of them, the price of a happy home...' That analysis of expansionism should have been committed to memory by school children throughout the country. And finally, Tom, your comment during this same debate that was often quoted will prove, I'm sorry to say, prophetic when you stated, 'We have bought ten million Malays at $2.00 a head unpicked...and nobody knows what it will cost to pick them.'"

In the kitchen, Dara couldn't control his laughter at this hilarious quote that he had not heard before. Johnny, fearing discovery, quietly shut the wooden door of the pass-through so that he could join undetected in Dara's mirth.

"I had no idea that Reed was such a wit, or that he was so strong against imperialism," Johnny finally whispered to Dara. "Christ, he almost sounds like a good Democrat – even better than many of them! I had no idea. Could it be that both of our dads got this fellow all wrong?"

"Maybe we all had him judged wrongly," added Dara. "But my dad and yours would box our ears if they heard us saying something nice about any Republican, especially a powerful one like Reed. I'll tell you something, though – to me, this fellow seems alright!"

By the time that Johnny dared to slowly slide the pass-through window slightly open again, the topic of these three gentlemen had changed from the past to the present. Bryan, it seemed, had come to Portland to discern what Reed's position would be on the important issues during the upcoming election of 1900, now less than ten months away.

Bryan was now publicly justifying his own mystifying and ultimately influential support for the Treaty of Paris. Many within his own party claimed that Bryan had helped to put it over the daunting two-thirds vote needed for passage in the Senate. Bryan nationally had defended his claim that such a move, although controversial at the time as well as very divisive especially within his own party, was necessary in order to unite the country and to end the war.

Arthur Sewall now stated his opinion that Bryan would soon have to articulate a new issue to campaign on in 1900, with "free silver" having apparently run its course. It had become a loose plank in a failed platform that the two had unsuccessfully promoted and defended three years earlier.

"As one Democrat to another," Sewall then openly criticized Bryan, "I couldn't believe you would join forces with Senator Lodge and the other Jingoists. Your support for the Treaty was credited with moving one or two un-committed Democrats to the 'YEA' side which passed, as we all now know, by a vote of 57-27 – a margin of victory of the number constitutionally required of only one vote!"

"I understand your incredulity, Arthur, and yours too, I suspect, Tom. That position may yet again cost me later this year even if I should be fortunate enough to garner enough support from our divided Democrats to be re-nominated. I seem to have split my own party. There again, Tom, we have something more in com-mon. Thankfully, I'm young and still have my strength and the will to fight a few more political battles. I took a chance last time in nominating you, Arthur, as my Vice President. We lost the support of some of the Southern Populists, even though many eventually voted for a Bryan-Watson ticket. Politics is not a game for the weak-hearted or for those simply trying to please everybody, that's a certainty. I recall the *Los Angeles Times* writing, 'Millionaire Arthur Sewall of Maine Placed at the Rear of the Ticket' and then gratuitously adding, 'The tail was stronger than the head.' That one stung, I'll admit to you now. Sometimes in politics one can't win for losing."

Tom Reed had listened attentively to this intra-Democratic dialogue, but now he interjected his own opinion on the matter. "Well, Mr. Bryan, I'd have to concur with your last sentiment. Last year, and for one of the first times in my life, I felt distinctly at odds with my own party. I told my secretary, Asher Hinds, 'I have tried, perhaps not always successfully, to make the acts of my public life accord with my conscience, and I cannot now do this thing.' I suppose I felt a greater despair at that moment than at any other time in my entire political career. But strangely, it was also a moment of clarity and calmness. Since retiring, I've been able to do some lawyering, start to replenish my family's treasury a bit, relax some, and even enjoy some good company in New York with Mark Twain, among others. Twain's natural instincts, especially his decidedly anti-imperialist and anti-expansionist views, seem quite in accord with my own. While I am said to be sardonic and sarcastic, Twain is witty and even self-effacing. His barbs usually hit the mark with more subtlety and accuracy than my own. I've told him that I could have used him in the great debates in the House over these past two years!"

Reed sighed and looked somewhat weary. Sensing that he had intruded upon the hospitality of this gracious man quite long enough, Bryan complimented Reed and then added, "Well, Tom, I've very much enjoyed this time with you today. I know we've both watched with interest and sadness as American and Filipino casualties have mounted over recent months, along with unfortunate atrocities on both sides of this sad struggle. Aguinaldo should be our ally, not the target of our young troopers who are only following orders. He wanted freedom for his own country from an imperial power. And today, I'm pained to admit, he is still looking for that freedom. It's the same fight, only now with a new and more powerful contestant! How did we ever allow ourselves to replace Spain as the party with a whip in its hand? Weren't we meant to be the liberators? Isn't that the message and the proper image that America needs to be sending to the world?"

"I've always maintained," agreed Reed, "that self-government is preferable to any imposed government, even that of well-meaning, highly intelligent people. I'm sure that many of our agents in the Philippines are well intentioned. Even William Howard Taft seems to have honorable ideals. But the whole bloody affair is a dishonor to our traditional republican values that go back all the way to Washington and Jefferson. These ideals are represented by both of our great political parties. I'd always thought, at least until just recently, that these values should be bi-partisan and nearly universal. How did things become so partisan, and how did they get out of control so quickly?"

"Money is a powerful agent," Bryan mused, "whether in the form of gold or silver – and sugar is always sweet! The monopolists could sense a windfall in

Hawaii. And then Admiral Mahan presented a cogent argument for naval superiority if we ever wanted to challenge the naval dominance of Great Britain or the other great European powers, and especially if we wanted to have a future significant maritime and naval presence in the Pacific. Of course, within your own Republican Party, Tom, there were eloquent voices in favor of expansion, such as Lodge, young Roosevelt, and let us not forget Indiana's Albert Beveridge. That man is never at a loss for hyperbole! That poem by Rudyard Kipling, 'The White Man's Burden,' that appeared in *McClure's Magazine* last February seemed to be timed for maximum impact, it seemed to me. It came out less than one week before the narrow Senate ratification vote on the Paris Treaty..."

"Which you endorsed yourself, Mr. Bryan," Arthur Sewall again pointedly interjected.

"It was neither my easiest nor my happiest political decision. I hope you can both believe me when I say that. To be quite candid with you both, I felt then and I still feel now quite trapped by this wholesale drive for expansion. It seems to feed on itself and it grows by leaps and bounds. My instincts were, and continue to be, against imperialism. But from a practical point of view the war needed to be ended – God only knows that it hasn't yet worked out the way that I had wished. And I needed to be where the country seemed to be going if I were to have any influence at all for the rest of this year and beyond. I know it sounds like expediency, even to me it sounds that way, and if so I'll plead guilty to the two of you on that count!"

"Well, I appreciate your candor with us, Mr. Bryan," Reed volunteered approvingly. "I've been trapped in political boxes more than once myself, and oftentimes the best way out seems to be the most unpalatable. But there is a somewhat obscure Celtic verse that I have always subscribed to that maintains that 'Truth is a fixed star.' And I will always try to attach my hopes to that star!"

"Thank you, Tom. You know that my party is still in disarray. There are many who will never forgive me for supporting the war or the Treaty, I know that! Even Carl Schurz called me 'the evil genius of the anti-imperialist cause.' With friends like that... You both know, I'm sure, that earlier this month a meeting was held in New York by the Anti-Imperialist League, among others, to look into forming a third party. One of their stated goals is to try to avoid the choice, as they put it, 'between two evils.' Your name, Tom, has been prominently mentioned as a potential leading candidate among some of the supporters of that effort – even

Andrew Carnegie supposedly has contributed $25,000 to this cause. Could I be so bold as to ask you directly of your intentions concerning this, Tom?"

"Mr. Bryan, let me totally reassure you on this matter. I was born into a Republican home in a Republican city and state, and despite all of my recent disappointments I'll be buried a Republican, albeit a chastened one – but not before my time, I hope! We Republicans all remember, or at least we should, what happened to our party in 1884. When our party split, we got the first of two terms of Grover Cleveland. At least he was a man of principle. Possibly because of his girth we were sometimes confused for each other by visitors to Washington – and that was no compliment to the President. Party splitting and intrigue have never been a part of my political philosophy, I can assure you. And unlike your own Democratic Party, Mr. Bryan, Republicans tend to stick together, for better or for worse. Lately, I'm afraid, it's been for worse. Should you decide to run again this year, and be fortunate enough to gain the nomination of your party, I can assure you of one thing – you won't have to concern yourself with Tom Reed as a candidate, fringe or otherwise. I'll content myself with besting Mr. Twain in our regular games of poker. I've made my political bed, and now I'll have to lie in it – even if it's positioned in the political wilderness for the time being. Yes, the atmosphere of New York suits me just now, as does the legal profession. It's where I got my start. As well, I now have some time to reacquaint myself with a few of my favorite Bowdoin College alumni. I've had precious few opportunities to demonstrate my legal bona fides, at least until recently, or to earn for my family anything more than merely an adequate salary."

"And what of your support for McKinley, Tom?"

"I shall continue to support my party, even if it must by circumstances be with neither my former enthusiasm nor energy. Young Roosevelt may stiffen McKinley's spine, perhaps, and I pray that after this latest ill-conceived and ill-advised episode in the Philippines has ended, as end it must, we may all return to some semblance of our basic republican ideals that you and I, and you, Arthur, regardless of any partisan politics, have always shared."

"I pray, Tom that you are right in this. I fear, however, that once down this road to expansion it may be difficult to change direction. The forces arrayed against us are formidable. Sadly they seem to be in the ascendant. Would you mind, Tom, if I asked you a personal question that's been bothering me, given that in just two weeks we'll all be commemorating the second anniversary of the sinking of the USS *Maine*? I have always wondered as to your opinion on the question, 'Who sank the *Maine*?' For the life of me I can not see that it would have been in any way advantageous to Spain, or for any of its interests in Cuba or beyond."

"I would have to concur with you on that assessment, Mr. Bryan. I have harbored the strongest suspicion in that regard. It seems to me far more likely to have been the result of an internal explosion, perhaps an accident, rather than any type of external explosion caused by the empire of Spain. Surely, that event was the catalyst that set us off on this imperial venture. Clearly, we were already well primed by 'yellow journalism' and jingoism in general. We only needed one spark – and that spark, unfortunately, was the *Maine*. Once commenced and released from any domestic shackles, the forces of war and expansion seem almost impossible to corral. I have no special knowledge concerning the *Maine* or the 261 naval fatalities aboard that ship, and I fear we may never know with any certainty the true details of its sinking. But this I can tell you with absolute certainty – it is always very bad policy to commence any major foreign policy initiative, let alone a war, on such shaky and unsure grounds. The correct political axiom is that 'something poorly started is often poorly finished.' I fear for our Republic and think that it is incompatible with expansionism and overseas ad-ventures. We should grant to others what we demand for ourselves – democracy, even when we disagree with others' decisions. I once wrote that, 'The best gov-ernment of which a people are capable is a government which they establish for themselves. With all its imperfections, with all its short-comings, it is always better adapted to them than any other government.' This I still believe with all my core values and instincts."

"One of my greatest regrets, Tom, is that in this upcoming election, which will certainly be fought out largely on the issue of imperialism and expansion as opposed to traditional American republicanism, you and I could not somehow be allied."

"Wouldn't our friends at *Punch* and in the domestic political cartoon industry sell a few million extra copies of any edition with that headline and image, Mr. Bryan? I'm convinced that we would certainly make strange bedfellows. I can see their flashing headlines now, 'The Prophet and the Czar!' It's not a pretty image, I'm afraid. Two mavericks speaking the truth as they see it – what a novelty that would be! Would this country of ours, I wonder, ever be prepared to face that kind of political campaign?"

Chapter 8

Coxey's Army

"To the wren, her nest is enough."

– Old Gaelic proverb

"Here we come with a nickel drum, we've just made up an army.
Hurrah for Cox, hurrah for Cox, hurrah for Coxey's Army!"

All the way home from North School a few minutes after noon, Agnes Folan chanted this little ditty that she had just learned that morning in Miss Mary G. Connolly's civics class, as all the older Folans had done previously. It was learned at school and then reinforced at home through their morning rising ritual led by their eldest sister, Mamie. As always, the Folan children first waited for Tom to finish his duties as a crossing guide before now all marching home in martial time for their noontime dinner – Tom, Joe, and Kitty, but all of them led by the youngest and most enthusiastic, Agnes, making the short pleasant tramp down India and over Fore.

The distance somehow felt much shorter when accompanied by this marching tune that they all knew by heart. Given the freezing temperatures on this day, "Coxey's Army" buoyed their spirits and warmed their insides, or so it seemed. A good marching tune could make any journey less daunting and more uplifting. Agnes smiled as she counted out the cadence as her older siblings had done in years past. "Coxey's Army" would predictably be an essential part of the Folan family for generations to come. Even young Peg, though still at home, was already showing a keen interest in learning and reciting it. She regularly practiced on the baby Míchilín.

Mamie and Johnny were by now largely free from attendance at Portland High School, one of the oldest public high schools in the country. They both had intermittent or part-time jobs, at least when they were needed by their employers. Mamie, by her own choice, was finished with schooling, and Johnny's high school attendance had recently become much more off than on, although his parents were as yet unaware of his increasing truancy. In spite of this reality, public education, according to their mother, was a pure godsend. Having had little formal education in Ireland themselves, both Mary and Coleman cherished the dream of all of their children becoming educated, or at the very least being able to read and write.

Mary was particularly firm on this question. But Coley sometimes vacillated on exactly how much education was needed. He was unsure about what to do when his children's schooling interfered with the possibility of a good-paying job. Most notably, he was conflicted about just how much "book learning," as he called it, was needed for the girls in the family. Mary had often quipped, 'A little education is a dangerous thing....' By this she meant to say more education was better, especially for girls.

As in most family-related or domestic questions like this, Coleman would always have his say, but Mary would usually have her way!

The North School was located near the corner of Congress and India Streets and served nearly one thousand mostly immigrant children. The principal was Elmer E. Parmenter, although no one had ever dared to utter his first name in public. He was a strict disciplinarian, to be sure, and was not known to spare the rod – there would not be many spoiled children under his tutelage, you could count on that. But to the Folan children, especially the boys, Mr. Parmenter had always been more than fair. Previously, Johnny and now Tom served as street crossing guides under his careful supervision. This was quite an important distinction and a crucial responsibility, given the very busy nature of both Congress and India Streets in the bustling east end of Portland. It was a location that witnessed many hundreds of young children crossing these crowded streets on a daily basis.

"Did you see Mr. Parmenter rap the Duddy boy behind the ears this morning, Tom?" young Joe asked his slightly older brother.

"I did. And didn't he deserve exactly what he got?" Tom answered with the authority that comes from a superior age. As always, Tom conscientiously tried to demonstrate to Joe that their slight difference in age was indeed significant.

"He's always crossing from the corner of Montgomery Street without waiting for my signal or even looking both ways. Today, just like once last week, he was nearly clipped by a delivery carriage. That would have made mince-meat of him, and he hardly seemed to notice or care. But Mr. Parmenter noticed, and Duddy then surely noticed Mr. Parmenter's knuckles on the back of his ears, he did indeed. He let out a yelp that made it seem like his ear had been removed from his skull and replaced back in a slightly different location. Good for Mr. Parmenter, I say. Can you imagine the trouble that I'd have been in if young Duddy had been struck or injured, or even killed perhaps all on my watch?"

"I hadn't thought of it like that, Tom," Joe replied, already feeling much more than a year younger – yet again. "It's just that the other kids seem to think that the principal is mean, that's all I'm saying."

"How'd you like to be responsible for one thousand little Duddys all crossing over Congress wherever or whenever they liked? And don't forget, you may be next in line for crossing guide after me – Johnny did it before, remember?"

"O.k., O.k. You're right…again," Joe relented, murmuring almost inaudibly that last word under his breath. "But I'll never change my friends' minds about how tough Mr. Parmenter is."

In a further effort to demonstrate to Joe what he meant about the principal, Tom then related to him a specific example. "One of my friends complained to his dad once about being sternly disciplined in the principal's office, and his dad then threatened to transfer his son to the Sacred Heart School. Mr. Parmenter told the father to do so if that was what he and his boy really wanted. The principal then added, 'Go ahead and do so with my blessings, but be prepared to have your son's knuckles rapped on a daily basis there by the nuns, and for much lesser crimes than simply crossing the street against orders. He'll learn discipline there, by gory, and maybe that is just what your boy needs.' The father never removed him and, not surprisingly, his son never again crossed against our instructions either. And he was right, too," Tom declared with obvious pride. "Yes, he's tough, sure enough, but them nuns are tougher still, from all that I've heard."

The girls continued to chant "Coxey's Army" nearly right up to the stepstone of their flat. As always, the trip had gone quickly, but now hunger was foremost on their minds and their small bellies. As they bounded into their kitchen by the back door, they spied Bridgie dressed in an apron and with a welcoming smile on her face.

"What's for dinner?" the younger Folans all chirped. Their mother was usually the one to greet her children as they arrived home for this noontime meal. But on this day, Mary and her young friend Nora Ward had not yet returned from their small odyssey through town. The children were about to discover that things in the kitchen would not be the same in their mother's absence.

"Smoked Creamed Finnan Haddie," was Bridgie's optimistic reply, but that only brought out quizzical expressions on the faces of each of these famished children. Young Bridgie Cronin, although only fifteen years of age, had been preparing meals for the children and also for the non-married longshoremen, "half-boarders" as they were called, over the past several weeks as Mary was nearing full term and not always able to stand comfortably for long stretches of time. It had become increasingly difficult for Mary alone to find the hours needed to cook, clean, and care for her large family, to say nothing of the increased demands from the half-boarders.

"What's that?" they queried almost in unison. They then turned up their noses at the strange and unfamiliar smell emanating from the kitchen stove. All the Folans loved fish in general, to be sure, and haddock specifically, especially on Fridays – but this was only Wednesday. So now they each wondered what in the world Bridgie could have done to the poor fishes to make them smell as foul as this.

"How long was the poor creature dead before you cooked it?" asked Joe, knowing full well that he was being cute.

The others laughed – all but Bridgie, that is. The children had no way of knowing that the longshoremen had likewise turned up their noses at her culinary offering only a few minutes earlier. Bridgie was simply trying to provide an alternative to the usual boiled or fried haddock, or the meat and potatoes that they were all used to getting at noontime. But this attempt at creating a culinary novelty had apparently fallen completely on its face, much to her chagrin.

As if by instinct and without any prompting, the three youngest, Kitty, Agnes, and Joe, turned on their heels in unison and proceeded to head over to Mrs. Loftus just across the street where they were always welcome for a meal with no questions asked – and no experiments with good wholesome food, either! Mrs. Loftus's only requirement was that they should all wash their hands first before eating.

Therefore, when Joe headed for the kitchen sink to complete this chore, Mrs. Loftus chided him by asking, "Where's your manners, young man? Take yourself over to the *Teach an Asal* (literally the house of the ass or donkey, better known as the bathroom).

For poor Tom, unfortunately, his timing was off. He had been slightly delayed in his arrival home, and therefore was not privy to these earlier episodes in his family kitchen. It was Tom's daily ritual to stop at a local Italian butcher's shop on the way home for dinner to ask if there might be an end of bologna or some other scrap of unsold meat that he could chew on as an appetizer for his regular meal. It never hurt his appetite as he was always hungry and never turned down a chance to eat. That particular day, however, there was nothing to be had, and so his hunger had peaked. When he entered the kitchen, by now empty except for the poor forlorn young cook, he found Bridgie with a look of exasperation on her otherwise attractive face.

It was then that Tom made the fateful mistake of asking her, "What on earth is that god-awful smell?"

With that, in the flash of an eye, a pre-loaded plateful of mashed potatoes smothered in a rich and pungent Finnan Haddie sauce was launched by the consternated young cook in his general direction. Fortunately, it missed Tom, though not by much. The Finnan Haddie hit the wall just above Tom's ducked head, splattering all over the wall and even in between the individual metal slats of the highly-prized Venetian blinds that covered the two kitchen windows.

There they both stood glaring at each other for a few seconds. Then Tom, seeing that Bridgie was apparently re-loading for another salvo, swiftly turned on his heels and like his younger siblings removed himself from the battlefield. He, too, now headed out the back door and toward the relative sanctuary of Mrs. Loftus's kitchen. He would never inform on young Bridgie, nor would any of the others, partly because it was completely out of character and it might well have cost her a position that she and her family sorely needed. And not to mention that such a disruption now would have placed an additional strain on their mother at this very delicate time for her.

Secretly, Tom admired Bridgie's spirit. For her part, Brígid Cronin would have to spend much of that afternoon cleaning the kitchen and, painstakingly, the partially encrusted individual slats of the window blinds. Tom would firmly believe for years to come that he could still sense the odor of smoked fish slightly permeating his mother's kitchen – but nothing more would ever be said of this incident, to Bridgie's enormous relief.

Mrs. Loftus thought nothing of this Folan invasion, as the children of both households would often try out the offerings at the other locale when the menu at home was not to their liking – it was a normal neighborhood expectation. As the Folan children prepared for their short journey back to North School, Tom turned to Mrs. Loftus. With typical Irish bravado, mimicking the teasing style of his father, Tom then paid his benefactor what his mother always referred to as a "back-handed compliment."

He winked to his siblings and from the safety of the doorway turned and proclaimed, "Thank God for that small portion of food. Many's the hungry man would call that a meal!"

The children all chuckled at their brother's boldness, even as Mrs. Loftus pretended to swing an empty frying pan in Tom's general direction.

"Be off with ye now. You're nothing but a bunch of bold scalawags!"

As they left they were all cheerfully in agreement with Joe who now parodied his older brother by stating, "Thank God for Mrs. Loftus. Many's the hungry Folan can now call that a meal!"

"Here we come with a nickel drum..." the children again led by Agnes's chanting began to make their way back to North School. The two boys, however, quickly decided that they had heard enough of this particular ditty and so they substituted one of Coley's favorites until all the others had joined in, even the slightly perturbed Agnes. Soon they were again counting out their steps to the measured tempo of yet another pithy tune, a comical call and response, "Where was Moses when the lights went out?" This familiar question was followed in unison by the children, "Down in the cellar with his shirt tails out!"

All four Folans had been fortified by Mrs. Loftus for the afternoon of school work. Except for Tom, they all were oblivious to the mortal combat that had just transpired in their very own kitchen. Mrs. Loftus hadn't sought an explanation for their presence, as neighbors were just like that – where there was a need, there was always a local solution. There was never talk about pay back as it would all come out in the wash anyway. Mary and Coleman had often assisted the Loftus family in a myriad of other different ways, and their son, Dara, was as much a part of the Folan family as his own – in fact many at Portland High School thought of Dara as a Folan. As it was for her own family in Galway, Mary had often stated the truth about Portland, 'Sure, aren't we all just one big happy family anyway?'

Mary believed this to be entirely true. For her it wasn't just something that was only said at a weekly Mass or in catechism class for the children, rather it was a true and genuine guideline for living. Back in Connemara and now here in

Portland, the Folans and the Joyces, the Connollys, the Mulkerrins and the Loftus families all needed each other's help and they would give it freely whenever they could. None of these families were wealthy enough to meet all of their obligations on their own. Rather, they were dependent upon their larger family – the neighborhood, the schools, the church – to look out after one another. How else could it have been when most local families, like the Folans, had seven or eight children, or even more?

~ ~ ~

Johnny was well aware of this "shared parenting" concept among the mothers of Munjoy Hill. He had once confided to Tom a story that clearly illustrated this concept. The story started during recess at school when Johnny had accidentally crashed into one of the toughest Italian boys in the playground during a game of punch ball. They were each trying to catch the same fly ball with their eyes in the air and not on the ground or on each other. The result was a memorable collision, and years later the school kids could still recall this event. A stunned Nicky Donatelli ended up with half of one of Johnny's bottom front teeth firmly implanted in the middle of his forehead.

Nicky was much smaller than Johnny, but he was much tougher. Nicky's instinct was to strike out at the perpetrator of his pain, but this thought was immediately mitigated by the sight of Johnny's bloody mouth and a triangular half of his front tooth clearly missing. Perhaps Nicky still would have struck out at Johnny had he only known where that half tooth had, in fact, ended up. One of Johnny's friends quickly and stealthily yanked the tooth fragment from Nicky's forehead before the dazed schoolboy even knew what was happening to him. Thankfully, Nicky's small scar healed quickly and Johnny's front teeth, overcrowded as they already were, hardly seemed to miss their fallen comrade. The extraction of the remaining half tooth by a dentist the following week was certainly more traumatic than the original accident. When Johnny heard the grunts and groans of the struggling dentist, along with the troubling sight of his profusely sweating face, he wondered who was suffering the most, the patient or the doctor.

Later that very same afternoon, as his story to Tom further unfolded, Johnny and a friend found themselves in the backyard of an abandoned storefront then located between their school and their homes. His friend reasoned that since the store had been long abandoned it would surely be no crime to put out a few more of its last remaining window panes. Johnny had agreed with this rationale. They then proceeded to sling several rocks in the general direction of the store until a voice from an unseen but concerned witness loudly called out, 'What the hell are ye boys up to?'

Neither of them stayed long enough to answer this posed question and indictment. Hightailing it away, they headed off in different directions with Johnny running down a series of small lanes. He found himself outside the home of a school chum who lived only a block or so from his own home. He'd been specifically warned by his mother to stay away from this boy, Jamsie Devine, who was always in trouble for one thing or another. But Johnny was obviously on a roll this day, and so he then figured, sure what's the harm? Young Jamsie didn't seem to Johnny to be a particularly bad boy, but in truth Jamsie had found himself in the midst of trouble more times than not.

Much later that same afternoon, after a day filled with both adventure and plenty of misadventure, Johnny finally returned home and entered his own front doorway where he was immediately greeted with a massive swat across his face from his none-too-pleased mother. It stung and surprised him and he burst into tears, less from the pain than from the shock. Their mother had rarely punished any of her children so severely.

Between the broken tooth, the broken windows, and the visit to his forbidden friend, however, Johnny figured that he probably had richly deserved this treatment. He quickly began to wonder which of these misadventures had most angered his mother. As it turned out, Mary was completely unaware of the former and the latter, learning from another neighborhood mother of the middle transgression, the broken windows at the vacant store. Johnny then explained to his brother Tom that this neighbor was clearly part of what he called "a network of informers."

He then complained, 'Sure one doesn't stand a chance against the combined vigilance of Portland's east end mothers with them all acting together to our great disadvantage!'

Johnny now further warned Tom that if he or any of his friends ever did something wrong the word would very likely pass along, almost as quickly and surely as Indian smoke signals, from one mother to another. The consequences, he informed his younger sibling, would be waiting for you as soon as you returned home, to your great dismay.

Johnny finally concluded his tale of woe and warning to Tom by sighing, 'If this is what a neighborhood is all about, I could live without it!'

But, even Johnny had eventually come to realize that this indeed was what a neighborhood was all about – despite the pain it had often caused to transgressors. It was an incredibly effective policing measure. The powers of the mothers, already legion in number and scope, were thus multiplied exponentially. They not only had "eyes in the back of their heads," as every schoolchild already instinctively knew; now they were also Hydra-headed! What chance had any one risk-taking boy or girl against such a potent female army, so well equipped and highly motivated? It was clearly an unequal contest. The mothers of Munjoy Hill were almost biblically omniscient, omnipresent, and omnipotent – all-knowing, all-present, and all-powerful!

In Johnny's particular case, however, things had turned in his favor. Unaware as Mary was of the earlier incident in the school yard, she was moved to tears when she saw Johnny's half-missing tooth, thinking that the firm swat that she had just planted across his face had dislodged the tooth. As she saw a trickle of blood now re-emerge from Johnny's mouth, Mary was instantly remorseful and overly apologetic, surprised at her severe physical punishment.

Johnny, ever playing the innocent fool, never told his mother the truth of the matter. Let that be a lesson to you, he reasoned to himself, and to all the mothers on the Hill. He continued to play the victim and milked it for all it was worth, just praying that the whole truth would never fully emerge. This once, at least, youth had been served, and in the Folan household Johnny, for quite some time, enjoyed the fruits of this "victory" over all of the "spies" and "informers." He had lost a tooth, after all, so why add insult to injury? Johnny was unsure as to whether his mother would ever discover the truth, but what matter whatever the future may bring – this day, at least, had been his to enjoy!

Mary would often ask questions of her eldest son, almost in the manner of a lawyer in court, just to see how he would process these conundrums. She also encouraged Johnny to put similar questions to her, even though due to his youth these questions might sometimes seem quite simplistic or at least not very well constructed. Johnny, for example, had often wondered why some of his high school classmates, the ones from the Western or Eastern Promenades or from the other wealthier families in the downtown area, all seemed to have perfectly straight teeth. He once asked Mary, 'Why should poorer families like ours and

Larry's all have to suffer in so many ways, such as wearing ragged 'hand-me-down' clothes, and on top of that have crooked, crowded teeth to deal with? It just doesn't seem fair.'

'God never gives you more than you can handle,' Mary had often counseled her eldest son. But Johnny sometimes wondered if his mother truly believed this in her own heart of hearts. In this specific case, at least, hadn't God given him more teeth than his mouth could handle? Well, using Mary's logic, perhaps young Nicky in the schoolyard mishap had done Johnny a favor by cutting down the surplus by one-half of a tooth, at the very least.

To be fair, Mary rarely complained about anything. Even the snow in the winter that Coleman said only looked good when melting and running down the gutter, was more optimistically referred to by Mary as the "poor man's fertilizer." Mary had taught Johnny and all of her children to be thankful for what they had, and not to covet the wealth or mere possessions of others. She said that this was not only from the Bible but also from ancient Gaelic wisdom. She sometimes cited for them one of her many favorite Irish axioms, '*Is leor don dreoilín a nead* (To the wren, her nest is enough).'

If Johnny had even one ounce of optimism about humanity in his bones, a good portion of that had clearly come from his mother's side of the family. Mary seemed like a saint to all the young Folan clan.

~ ~ ~

And now, back to the present and finished with their noontime meal, the Folan scholars continued to traipse back up India Street toward their school yard. They were now additionally attracted by the anticipated warmth of their classrooms. Tom uniformly arrived back at his Congress Street crossing post fifteen minutes before any of the other students as was required of him. There, predictably, was Mr. E.E. Parmenter at his post, as always. The principal looked approvingly at his young protégé. Why had he favored the Folan boys, Tom wondered. Why did others see this responsible man as mean or even vindictive? To Tom and his brother Johnny, and perhaps eventually to other younger Folans as well, Mr. Parmenter represented a just and caring presence in a sea of change. This public servant cared for one thousand challenged and challenging young students, and he thereby allowed their parents to pursue the difficult labors that were needed to keep life and limb together here on the northeastern fringe of the country. To the

Folans, Mr. Elmer Parmenter was a friend.

Entering his classroom shortly after all the other students had been accounted for, and with a reassuring nod from his teacher, Tom joined his classmates in constructing an essay based on an Abraham Lincoln quote, "I like to see a man proud of the place in which he lives. I like to see a man live so that his place will be proud of him."

~ ~ ~

In the meantime, Nora and Mary had returned home only to find the dining room empty except for Johnny who was just finishing his meal. He quickly explained to his mother that he had not attended school that morning because of taking the opportunity to see his Democratic political hero, William Jennings Bryan, in the flesh. He spoke briefly but with great enthusiasm to his mother about this encounter. Mary seemed to be more concerned with his truancy and also his sneaky entry into the home of Thomas Brackett Reed.

Following her somewhat skeptical exchange with her eldest, Mary joined Nora in the kitchen. She could hear Peg and Míchilín upstairs arguing as usual about some small thing or other. Bridgie was also busy in the kitchen, apparently cleaning the walls and window blinds. That seemed unusual to Mary who whispered to Nora, "She's a marvel, that girl. Look at her taking on another task without even being asked – isn't she a treasure?"

Mary intentionally spoke only loud enough for Nora to hear, as the young Bridgie was always easily embarrassed by attention. Nora couldn't have agreed more with Mary, especially after sensing the enticing aroma of one of her favorite dishes, Finnan Haddie, still emanating from the kitchen. The two ladies then eagerly ate all that Bridgie placed before them. For some reason there seemed to be plenty left over even after they had eaten their fill.

"You needn't do all that extra cleaning work, dear," Mary reasoned with Bridgie. "Sure haven't you enough with the cooking, cleaning, and minding of the two young ones?"

"It's no bother to me, Mary. Sure it's part of my job, I'd say," Bridgie murmured somewhat sheepishly.

"Well, this dinner is truly excellent," exclaimed Nora. "The longshoremen and children must have devoured it."

Bridgie seemed to blush and could only mutter, "Well, it seemed to get a mixed reception in this house today. Everybody, I suppose, to their own taste…"

After finishing her large plate of smoked fish, Mary was fully engaged and energized again. She then boldly enticed Nora by challenging her to spend part of the afternoon continuing their odyssey around town.

Mary plaintively urged her friend, "Sure wouldn't you love to join me in visiting Catta Bheathnach (Catherine Welch) on our way up to the Convent, Nora dear?"

"You lead, Mary, and I'll follow!"

Chapter 9

Between a Rock and a Hard Place

"Aithníonn ciaróg – ciaróg eile"

(One beetle knows another, or to each his own)

The morning's work alongshore had gone well. After twenty years of demanding, often painful, back-breaking lifting and shoveling, Coleman had settled into a regimen whereby the mornings progressed fairly quickly, even though the afternoons often seemed to wear on and on. His work was becoming more and more of a physical strain. Even though he was not yet forty-two years of age, his body certainly felt much older. A good night's sleep the night before, a very welcome hot breakfast with Mary, and the promise of a dinner break among his best friends on the docks often helped to speed the mornings along. No single hour of the day, or so it seemed to Coleman, ever went by more quickly than this one-hour dinner break at noon. Good times and camaraderie always seem fleeting, but the drudgery of heavy manual labor always wears on and taxes the body.

One of the highlights of the noontime break was the cherished opportunity to speak his own beloved Irish language with those for whom, like himself, it was their first language. '*Aithníonn ciaróg – ciaróg eile* (One beetle knows another, or to each his own),' Coley had often proclaimed to his good friend Joe Loftus regarding these precious times shared with their own kind.

As valued as those lunch hours were to Coley, there were forces at work trying to take away even this simple pleasure. There was always a large backlog of materials to be handled, especially in this busy mid-winter season. Huge quantities of coal were coming in and grain was going out of Portland. Some stevedores, particularly those representing the firm of Mills and McMasters, were keen on keeping the longshoremen working steadily through their traditional noontime break.

To compound the grievance, they didn't even offer to pay the going rate of double time for work demanded during this meal hour. Coley and his gang, and most all of the older longshoremen, were dead set against any concession on this

142

important work rule. It was a concession that they had fought long and hard to achieve over many years. If it were up to Coley, he would sacrifice that much needed break neither for love nor money. But, if forced by the shipping companies and his union to work it, he wanted to be fairly compensated at the very least.

Surprisingly, not all longshoremen felt this same way. Most of the younger men wanted as many hours as they could get, especially as this busy winter work season represented only a half year between November and April.

'Make your money while the ice clogs the Saint Lawrence,' one of them had recently argued to Coley in what seemed like a seasonally-adjusted version of the old local saying. 'Make hay while the sun shines.'

But now it was time to eat and talk and rest – the precious noon hour had finally arrived. Coley exclaimed to his work mates, "Come on boys, out of the wind and into the sun!"

To which this caused Joe Loftus to proclaim, "You're a natural poet, Coley – and wouldn't that make a lovely title for a verse or a song?"

The gang all knew Coley's meaning as they instinctively headed for one of their two favorite perches on the decaying docks, specifically dependent upon the direction of the wind. They uniformly opened their lunch pails after placing their backs against the decrepit wooden sheds that now fortuitously would be blocking the worst of the cold ocean breezes coming directly off the Atlantic. This was an ideal spot for taking their lunch break. It was on the west-facing side of an old pier that had seen its better days, but the location clearly met Coley's criteria – they were now out of the bitter wind and facing into a dim winter sun.

The gang could thus be slightly warmed by a pale late January sun. They all agreed that it seemed a good twenty degrees warmer than at the end of the pier that they were presently working. They called this time of day the "Longshoremen's Noon." It was always the most pleasant time for them and stories flowed galore.

From this protected perch, they could watch the *Governor Dingley* or any of the other eight steam vessels that called Portland their home port. These vessels served sixteen steamship companies, fully six of which were transatlantic.

"Yes," Coley sighed as he settled into place along with his workmates, "Out of the wind and into the sun!"

Mike O'Tuarisc opened his lunch bucket, pondered its contents, and predictably uttered his daily salutation to the anticipated delight of all present, "I wonder what would interest me the most."

Usually most disagreements between the longshoremen could be worked out by vigorous and sometimes heated debates during their weekly Wednesday night union meetings at the PLSBS hall located at 374 Fore Street. This particular issue of the lunch hour, however, was proving to be more divisive than most as it seemed to pit one group against another. It was driving their beloved union into disorder with factions forming. It was becoming older versus younger, first generation versus second generation, Irish versus English speakers, fathers versus sons, and uncles versus nephews.

Money was at the root of this dispute, as it often is. But, ironically, the younger dockworkers had shown a willingness, which some perceived almost as an eagerness, to work at a lesser wage, which meant they were willing to consider working for one and a-half times the standard hourly wage versus what had long been the traditional double time wage for work required during their sacred lunch hour.

The real issue for Coley was union solidarity – this he defined as standing up to the shipping companies and their local stevedores as one group, and that group to be united! This was the only way the PLSBS, since its inception in 1881, had achieved the favorable wages and work rules already in place. And now with certain stevedores trying to weaken these collectively bargained rules, which were really the life blood of any union, it was the younger members who seemed to be deserting the central principles cherished by the older more experienced laborers. They were using terms like "concession" and "compromise." But Coley and most other charter members wondered aloud where their militancy was or their willingness to take on the power of their employers and, if necessary, to fight them or even go out on strike. Did the younger workers understand these things?

The defense of the meal hour was central, but it was also divisive as it exposed so many fault lines within the Society. No longshoreman, old or young, would ever admit to being tired or in need of a break – it just was not in the nature of the beast. But, nevertheless, tired they often were, and Coley personally felt it deep in his bones. He needed this lunch break to prepare for the rigors of the long and difficult afternoon ahead.

Coley's regular gang consisted entirely of first-generation Irish and was therefore all Irish speaking. The gang boss was a Gorham from Rusheenamanagh, the next townland over from Coley's birthplace in Callowfeenish. Coley's closest friend was Joe Loftus who was about the same age as Coley and, like him, was a charter member of the union having also joined in 1880 shortly after his arrival in Portland.

"What's the matter with these young pups, Coley?" Joe now asked in a low almost inaudible tone, as if not wanting to disturb the peace any further.

"I'm not sure I can say for myself," Coley admitted. "It seems they don't know how tough it was in the first place to force these work rules and other concessions from the steamship companies and the local stevedores. If they had any idea of what we had to go through to get this double-time rule, they would likely join with us in not allowing any changes now. Recent times have been tricky, don't you remember? Sure, the tough times during the early '90s dropped our membership below 400. Even though we've doubled in the last six years since then, who knows how long the good times will last? The young ones don't see that. Their vision is shorter. I guess they think it'll be boom times from here on out."

Joe nodded his head in complete agreement with Coley and then, after some time, he added a worry of his own. "Maybe we made a mistake taking on so many new members so quickly, over 400 in just one year a couple of years back, remember? Maybe these new members have changed our union, do you think? How can we teach them something that they've not yet experienced for themselves? We only took in half as many last year, but we've still got too many youngsters on the rolls, I'm sorry to say. It's nice to get their initiation fees and dues, and their strong backs – but what's the price we'll all have to pay?"

Coley and Joe were typical of the older members of the PLSBS in many ways. Neither one had any formal education. As it was with Coley, Joe couldn't even write his own name when he joined the PLSBS twenty years earlier. But this group had plenty of practical judgment gained through many years of labor, and common sense. They had brought with them from Ireland a keen awareness of oppression on many levels. Here in America the conditions were so much better, but this had not come without struggle! This they knew in their very bones – but did the younger longshoremen? How could they?

These workers had learned that before they formed the union in 1880 conditions on the docks of Portland were acceptable during boom times when labor was at a premium, but that the steamship agents and their stevedore representatives could often turn on a dime. When things started to slow down, as periodically they always had, these employers showed no hesitancy in letting hundreds of workers go with not so much as a "by your leave." During the Civil War boom years, munitions and

Maine-grown produce were being shipped out of Portland in impressive volumes. Thus, a Portland Longshoremen's Association had been formed and had successfully struck for higher wages.

This Association was good, as far as it went. In the 1870s, however, another of the all too predictable economic "panics" had disrupted the post-Civil War boom. By 1880, shortly after setting foot in the city, Coleman was invited to join the newly-forming Portland Longshoremen's Benevolent Society (PLSBS). Within just a couple of years its membership had soared to over 600. After suffering through more than a decade of decline, especially around the Panic of 1893, union membership had again picked up in the late 1890s due to increasing shipping demand caused by both the Spanish-American War and the British Boer War in South Africa. Now at the turn of the twentieth century, the union represented fully 850 members. The tide seemed to be high and still rising!

"Here's hoping the good times are here to stay, Joe, me *buachaillín bán* (fair-haired boy – a term of endearment)," Coley now joked.

"Yeah and here's hoping that the new members will listen to reason about the meal hour pay at our meeting tonight," Joe added cautiously.

On that note of agreement, they both got ready to concentrate on the meals their wives had prepared for them. Coley's dinner usually consisted of a sandwich or two, made from whatever leftover meat was saved from the supper meal from the night before. He marveled at how this often tasted better the second time around.

Just as the lunch break was underway that day, Coley's gang heard what sounded like a series of loud "Hurrahs!" coming from a neighboring wharf. They sent one of their members over to check out what was happening, and when he promptly returned with a broad smile on his face, they all knew there might be a good story to follow.

It seemed that the gang on the next wharf over was celebrating the return to service of young "Boozy" Griffin. "Boozy" was a nickname only recently earned by this young longshoreman because of an incident that was already becoming legendary among his fellow workers. The nickname was somewhat ironic given that "Boozy" himself was a fully abstaining teetotaler, as were his father and grandfather before him. But he would now and forever always be associated with bonded Scotch whisky.

Just one week earlier, crates of this bonded alcohol were being unloaded from an

English schooner. Young "Boozy," whose real name was Declan, had supposedly slipped and broken his leg when a crate of the *uisce beatha* (the "water of life") landed on him. He was immediately placed on a stretcher by his fellow workers and quickly transported up to State Street and the local doctor who handled all longshore cases. "Boozy" had appeared to be in great distress. Although the doctor could find no outward signs of a break, he placed young Declan's leg in a full length cast just to be safe. Now, after only one week of "recuperation," Griffin was already back at work, seemingly showing no ill effects, along with his new nickname and a new-found respect from his co-workers.

The whole incident had been a complete ruse. It was concocted by some of the older longshoremen. They thought it was unfair that all of this fine booze would be going to the elites of Portland, throughout Maine and the rest of New England, while those like themselves who handled it, and treated it with the proper reverence that they believed it deserved, were left to drink only the cheaper brands and the harsh locally-distilled rum. According to this clever and successful scheme, as soon as young Declan hit the ground writhing in pain, he was placed on a stretcher and his "injured" leg was immediately covered with a woolen blanket. This blanket also conveniently covered the two cases of valuable bonded Scotch whisky that were placed on either side of young Boozy's "crippled" leg. That way this highly desired liquor would be out of sight of any of the suspicious stevedores or their watchmen. These waterfront officials had never figured out how they were two cases short at the end of that work day.

The legend of "Boozy" Griffin was thus born. That same afternoon, according to one longshoreman who was there and who had participated in this marvelous scheme, some of the workers went over the top in their celebration and consumption. In his descriptive words, "there were handsprings and uppercuts" all along the docks. One desperate stevedore even threatened to summon the police to regain order and to protect the remaining supply of this potable cargo.

This episode had all the hallmarks of another potential "Rum Riot" such as the notorious City Hall incident of 1855. At that time the local militia was protecting a supply of bonded or "medicinal" alcohol in the basement of the City Hall, ironically at the behest of Mayor Neal Dow, a Quaker and a Prohibitionist. The militia had fired into the angry and unruly crowd with deadly effect.

Cooler heads prevailed along the waterfront on this day, however. The union walking boss told the stevedore in no uncertain terms that, if any policeman or sheriff appeared on the dock, his gang would knock off the ship altogether and there would be no more work concluded for the rest of that entire day. Discretion being the better part of valor, the stevedore backed down from his threat and the giddy longshoremen, albeit in a somewhat altered state of consciousness, somehow completed their tasks – and along with that the remaining bottles of some of the finest bonded alcohol ever consumed on the docks of Portland. Some would say, even many years later, that it was the most enjoyable afternoon of work these men had ever performed. This entire story had by now already entered into the realm of legend, and no one ever dared to let mere facts or details get in the way of such an entertaining tale.

But business could wait. Joe Loftus hailed Steve Curran from another nearby gang because he was a story-teller of local renown. "Hey, Steve, tell us about 'no stir a'tall!'"

With that, Steve Curran brought his lunch pail over to Coley's gang and proceeded to tell the already well-known story of when he was working with an Italian laborer on a construction site long before he ever had become a longshoreman. The poor Italian had only the most basic English, but he was trying to arrange to meet Steve on a Sunday in downtown Portland on their only day off. He wanted to meet Steve at Longfellow Square, so named after Portland's pre-eminent poet whose statue sat there at the corner of Congress and State Streets.

After several noble attempts to recall the name "Longfellow," but alas with no success, the Italian laborer out of sheer exasperation finally blurted out, "Steve, I see you tomorrow on a the Sunday morning, you know, where the bigga the man, sit in the chair – no stir a'tall!"

Howls of laughter ensued, even though many of these Irishmen hardly had any firmer grasp of the English language themselves. Maybe that was what made this particular story so amusing to them – they had all been in that situation before and the same story could have been told about them.

Now on somewhat of a roll, Joe prompted Steve to continue, "Tell us about the cat and the dog, Steve."

"I just told you that one last week," Steve protested.

"Well, tell it again then."

So reluctantly, Steve began to tell the well-worn story about the young Irish couple that was having marital difficulties after being married for only a few months. The priest was called in to referee and counsel them. But the newlyweds had legitimate complaints against each other, and so he was at a complete loss as to how to proceed. Fortuitously, just then the priest spied the couple's dog which had curled up next to the fireplace along with their cat likewise sleeping peacefully and partially on top of the dog.

Armed with this new inspiration, the priest then continued, 'Now just look at those two creatures. Nature has determined that they are enemies, or at least rivals of each other, but look at them both sleeping next to each other in perfect harmony. That is precisely what matrimony is supposed to be.'

The young husband was obviously unconvinced, and he sheepishly addressed the priest expressing these doubts. 'Yes, Father, that's all well and good. But you just try tying the two of them together and see how long the peace and quiet will last!'

Jokes and stories about spouses and marriage were the standard fare at these lunch breaks. Before returning to work for the afternoon, however, Coley had to conclude two more serious bits of business. He took Joe Loftus aside and asked him about the trouble Coley had recently heard concerning his best friend and Roger McCarthy, an assistant stevedore at the Maine Steam Ship Company on Franklin Wharf. This company provided the direct passenger and freight service between Portland and New York. McCarthy happened to live at the same building as the Loftus family at 235 Fore Street. Although the two rarely spoke about business, McCarthy had recently attempted to convince Joe of the need for the longshoremen to make concessions on the question of working the lunch hour. This was the unified demand of all the steamship companies in Portland expressed through their local stevedores.

Joe informed Coley that he had curtly replied to McCarthy, "You keep to your business and I'll keep to mine. And if you know what's good for you, you'll keep your opinions at the Franklin Wharf and not be draggin' them all the way over to Fore Street."

Coley nodded in approval to his old friend and told Joe that he would have said much the same. He then warned Joe to be careful not to put his rental status in danger.

Coley's gang was working the coal schooner *Avona* which had only recently made a rough crossing in frigid near white-out conditions. The *Avona* was but one of several ships then in port. Most of these vessels were discharging coal, Maine's winter lifeblood. The *Avona* was off-loading its coal for the H. H. Nevens Company located at 233 Commercial Street. This was a fairly small company that took on coal when needed but which usually specialized in the sale of imported fine teas, coffees, and spices.

On his way back to the *Avona*, out of the corner of his eye, Coley spotted young John Walsh, better known by all on the waterfront as Moses.

"Moses, I believe it's time for another mission of mercy, and be sure to bring Major along just in case we might have need of him."

Walsh readily acknowledged Coley's request. He knew, of course, that it was code for another planned pilfering of coal at the end of their work day. They had both done this together before and had a technique already worked out. "Major" was Walsh's scruffy mean dog that followed him everywhere and didn't seem to tolerate any human soul other than his master. Major would be their insurance policy in case they were spotted by anyone and challenged.

All too soon, it was back to reality. Coley's afternoon of work alongshore this day went quickly and smoothly as he remained pre-occupied by the issue of the union meeting that evening. A frozen hatch aboard the collier had given his gang an unexpected but welcome respite in the middle of the afternoon shift, the latter part of which was now being worked in the ever present mid-winter darkness. They were by now only a month or so past the winter solstice.

This break allowed for some conversation about the recent political talk of the town. That very night William Jennings Bryan, the Democratic Party presidential nominee in the previous election of 1896 and a possible candidate again in 1900, was in Portland. He was scheduled to give a major address that very evening at City Hall. Several of the younger longshoremen had voiced a strong interest in attending this gathering, and some had even suggested a postponement of the regular weekly PLSBS meeting. Some of them had stated that they would attend the City Hall political rally even if the Society went ahead with its own meeting as scheduled, which they took to be a foregone conclusion.

Coleman and most of the older longshoremen were much more likely to attend the Society's meeting in the union hall. They could see the immediacy of the issues involved in that meeting, but they couldn't quite understand the greater interest of the younger members in a silver-throated orator from Nebraska. For most of this older group, politics was local and played out daily on the docks. The waterfront piers of Portland were their political arena. Although most of them, young and old, had voted for the Democrat in the most recent election of 1896 over Republican William McKinley, Bryan's positions, although apparently sympathetic to the working classes, seemed somehow more distant to Coley and the senior longshoremen than their union's work rules.

During this brief unexpected break, one of the younger native-born longshoremen read aloud from a recent edition of the *Eastern Argus*, the local Democratic newspaper in Portland. The *Argus* was not a pro-labor paper, but it was the best that Portland had to offer. The gang all got a good laugh at this second-generation Irishman and his comically affected reading of an article featuring Mr. Dooley of Chicago. Although a country-born, his imitation of the Irish accent was dead on, and that caused more laughter than a straightforward reading alone might have produced.

In this case, Finley Peter Dunne, the writer and creator of the "Mr. Dooley" character, was reporting on a speech by Senator Albert J. Beveridge, Republican of Indiana, about administering the Philippines after the conclusion of the Spanish-American War. The paper stated that it was "Ably condensed by Mr. Dooley of Chicago" who humorously gave his opinion:

> "This is no mere man's wurruk. A Higher Power even than Mack [President McKinley], much as I rayspict him, is in this here job. We cannot pause, we cannot hesitate, we cannot delay, we cannot even stop! We must, in other wurruds, go on with a holy purpose in our hearts, th' flag over our heads, an' th' inspired wurruds iv A. Jeremiah Beveridge in our ears."

Although this article concerned political events about which Coleman and many of his generation had little or no direct knowledge, and even less interest, the longshoremen especially enjoyed Mr. Dooley when he spoke about immigrants like themselves often using their own jargon and speech patterns.

Once when told that foreigners did not assimilate well into American culture, Mr. Dooley had replied, 'If we'd lave off thryin' to digest Rockyfellar an' thry a simple diet like Schwartzmeister, we wudden't feel th' effects iv our vittels.'

Along this same line, Mr. Dooley had once given advice regarding the increasing number of immigrants in America, quite similar to a suggestion about overpopulation in Ireland offered a few hundred years earlier in *A Modest Proposal* by the famous writer and satirist, Jonathan Swift. In this case, Mr.

Dooley had also modestly suggested, 'Maybe if we'd season th' immygrants a little or cook thim thurly, they'd go down betther,' I says... 'But what wud ye do with th' offscourin' iv Europe?' says he. 'I'd scour thim some more,' says I.'

They all roared again with laughter, Coleman foremost among them. Most of the Irish in Portland seemed to enjoy hearing the opinions of Mr. Dooley, but especially Coley and those like him who could not read the newspaper for themselves. At home after supper, Coley would often ask Johnny to read that section of the newspaper, and he usually agreed with the sentiments expressed by Mr. Dunne.

Coley told his eldest on many occasions that, if it were not for the local ward captains of the Democratic Party, more and more of whom were themselves Irish, Coley and other illiterate union members may well have been denied American citizenship or at least delayed in achieving it. These party bosses often took members like Coley to sympathetic aldermen or justices of the peace who would verify their ability to read on the basis of an agreed upon and previously memorized piece of verse, thus insuring the city of yet another Democratic voter at both municipal and national elections.

Just as the frozen hatch was finally pried open, and his shift was about to recommence, Coleman asked one of his younger friends who also came from a very large family to meet him and John Walsh at the head of the pier directly after work this day. At six o'clock the three men quietly gathered and Coleman informed them of the plan to "rescue" some of the coal that had somehow inadvertently slipped onto the skirt of the wharf while being shoveled that very afternoon from the hold of the ship. In a small rowboat procured earlier by Walsh, the three quickly gathered up as many pieces as possible of this precious fuel in a very short period of time. They then divided it equitably amongst themselves for the purpose of heating their own cold and drafty homes.

This "bonus" coal would be a most welcome addition to their hourly wages. To feed, house, and clothe such large and growing families on thirty cents an hour, veteran coal shovellers like Coleman often found it necessary to supplement their incomes in other creative ways. Like "Boozy" Griffin's creatively pilfered Scotch whisky, this coal was considered a fringe benefit for their challenging manual labor. But Coleman was always overly cautious. Even on this frigid day, he was highly conscious not to push this too far, and thus kill the goose that was laying these shiny black and highly coveted eggs.

Chapter 10

Broken Irish

"Is your mother at home; is your father working?"

– Typical Irish greeting in Portland

With this standard greeting predictably uttered, almost without exception, Mary Folan and Nora Ward entered the homes of friends and neighbors in Portland. This was all that Mary or indeed anyone else really needed to know. If the mother was at home, there was sure to be a good cup of strong Irish tea brewed or waiting to be brewed for visitors – surely two cups at a minimum per visit.

Tradition held that the guest would first politely refuse the offer of hospitality at least twice before finally, and seemingly reluctantly, accepting the host's gracious offer. This tradition of politeness could sometimes backfire, however. Once while visiting the home of a Yankee neighbor, Mary had followed this pattern by turning down the offer of a cup of coffee. Only in this case it was never offered again, thirsty as she was. 'That was a sobering lesson,' she later admitted to her daughter Mamie.

If the father was working, that was even better news. It would mean more time for the ladies to visit and importantly a more relaxed atmosphere, since there would be some financial stability for the family. This was even more crucial during the coldest months of the year for it was in winter that the constantly rising price of wood and coal further burdened their already over-stretched family budgets. What parent could ever intentionally deny their children the security of a warm place to sleep?

"My mommy's in the kitchen and Daide's on the grain," replied the wee ragamuffin who answered the door at the Walsh's home.

"That's ideal," exclaimed Mary to Nora. "The grain boats take the longest time to load and trim, and Catta's husband is a gang boss – all the more income for them during this week, at least."

Kate Walsh, better known locally by her Irish friends as Ceata (or Catta) Bhreathnach, warmly greeted her two visitors in the traditional Irish form, *"Dia dhaoibh, a chairde* (God be with ye)."

"*Dia's Mhuire dhuit, a Chaite* (God and Mary be with you, Ceata)," replied Mary.

Nora then appropriately added, "*Dia's Mhuire dhuit is Phádraig* (God and Mary and Patrick be with you)" to the salutation.

Nora thus invoked both the name of the Blessed Virgin Mary and the name of Ireland's patron saint, Patrick. In more formal settings these greetings could go on and on almost interminably simply by continually adding yet another saint's name to the already long list. One must always keep them in the proper order, of course. This tradition had been brought over directly from Ireland, and it seemed to be almost as much a test of one's memory as it was a demonstration of one's knowledge of the lesser-known saints.

The usual order of the names of saints following Mary and Patrick could then include: Brígid (Bríd); Colmcille (Columba); Kevin; Columbanus; Brendan; Finian; Kieran (Ciarán); Kilian; Molaise; and even Colmán. Although uncommon in Ireland and not technically a saint, it was popular at least here in Portland to often add the name of Catherine McAuley – the Irish foundress of the Sisters of Mercy. This could sometimes serve almost as a parlor game and thus became a wonderful way of teaching the young ones a bit of Catholic tradition and, simultaneously, Irish history. Both Mary and Nora were locally famous for their ability to go quite far into this list, and so with characteristic humility Catta quit while she was still ahead quite early in the naming contest.

Nora's recitation reminded Mary of a comical story dealing with her young son, Thomas, always the doubtful skeptic of the family. "Once after hearing this long list of saints recited, my Thomas asked if his father was now truly named after a saint. I told him that there were several by the name of Colmán, and that one of them was even known as Colmán *bocht* (poor Coleman). This seemed to satisfy my young son who then proclaimed, 'Yes, that would be the one that my Daide is named after!'"

"I see you've come again, Mary, with one arm as long as the other," Catta then teased her guests in the Galway style of playfully chiding any visitor for failing to bring along any food or drink when calling on the home of friends or family.

"*Muise*, I didn't even have to knock on your door with my elbow," Mary replied in kind, "as I heard that your Stephen is working the grain boat this season and you'll surely now be living in the lap of luxury."

Catta took the joke in stride and then inquired of her visitors, "When will you be leaving?"

Although to the untrained ear this question might have sounded almost rude, it was in fact the Irish way of determining exactly how long one might have the pleasure of your company.

"It will have to be a hasty visit I'm sorry to say, Catta. I've already been away gallivanting nearly the entire morning with my young friend Nora, and now here we are on the move again on our way up to the Convent of the Sisters of Mercy. She's a bad influence on me this one, surely. And me in my condition – ah but what's the harm in it? Sure we all only have the one life to live!"

"No harm in it a'tall, and you'll at least be havin' a strong cup of tea, of course?"

"Why wouldn't we? Aren't we freezin' with the cold and dying of the thirst?" Mary exclaimed with playful exaggeration and accompanied by the omnipresent twinkle in her eye.

And it really was a twinkle, as Nora had observed on more than one occasion. She had once asked Mary, 'How do you make your eyes twinkle like that?'

Mary's reply to the innocent and unsuspecting Nora was, 'Well dear, you see we women from the west of Galway are gifted in that way!'

Mary's jesting with Nora about her East Galway origins were always playful, unlike many in Portland who were so parochial that they hardly would speak in a civil manner to anyone who might not be from their same parish, or worse still not from the same end of their own small townland! Once when Nora inquired of Mary why some of the Portland Irish seemed to despise her because of this accident of birth, she was comforted by Mary's loving and understanding reassurance, 'Sure, isn't it their loss, dear?' And then to further buoy the spirit of her young companion, Mary teasingly added, 'I'm sure that if we searched hard enough we could find some important person who has come from East Galway!'

Mary was well known for these so-called "back-handed compliments." This trait once prompted an old Portland wag to humorously proclaim, 'Mary Folan giveth, and Mary Folan taketh away – blessed be the name of Mary Folan!'

"So, your Stephen's on the grain again?" Mary now inquired of Catta.

"Thanks be to Jesus," was Catta's response. "Anything to get us through the worst of this winter, and isn't it a fierce one this year? But they'll be a while longer trimming this particular boat, I'd say, as the stevedore complained bitterly to my Stephen that one of the last grain boats out of Portland was already listing to one side before it even hit the open ocean beyond Portland Head. This must have been true because Steve told me that he had prayed for that crew every night for a fortnight until he heard just recently that they had safely arrived in England. Can you imagine a load of grain shifting on you in the middle of a ferocious North Atlantic gale? That would surely send you to your Maker, but only after a cold and frightening death!"

"Coleman has often told me the same," replied Mary. "But that doesn't seem to keep the shipping companies or their local agents and stevedores from always trying to get our men to shorten the time that these ships are in Portland. Coley once asked me, 'What would an extra half-day of wages be compared to the lives of an entire crew?' And that's to say nothing of the ship itself."

"Well, Nora," Catta asked, "are ye watching out for our Mary? Sure she'll be having this next child most any hour now I'd expect by the size of her, but hopefully not while the two of ye are here visiting. You can see, dear, that we're already a bit overcrowded as it is, and we're not really well suited for any long-term entertaining!"

Nora was always keen to play her proper role in these playful conversations. So now she proceeded to tell a story about another recent pregnancy in town, this time of a young Yankee woman from her own neighborhood.

"Did you hear about Mrs. Gowan whose husband has a corner grocery over by my apartment? Well, she and her husband have been trying to have children for over five years, but they'd had no success. I remember consoling her once by telling her the old saying, 'If you don't share the joy of having children, at least you won't feel the pains.' So, they finally decided it was time to adopt from the altar down at Saint Dominic's. But wasn't this new child home with them only a few weeks before she became pregnant herself – and with twins, no less! They were born just a couple of weeks ago. So now all of a sudden it's gone from a family of just two to one of five!"

"Now that's a yarn you're telling us, I'd wager," protested Catta.

"Sure it's the holy truth, I'm positive of that," declared Mary in Nora's defense. "I don't know Mrs. Gowan at all, but I know that this same thing happened to two different families back in Galway. One had adopted and the other took a child through fosterage from a nearby relative, and both of them conceived within only a few weeks of getting the first child home. How often did you hear of the priest over at Saint Dominic's who would place an orphaned child up for adoption from the altar with his well-known plea – 'Who will take this child?' I suppose this could happen because of the relief for the mother. Having her first child home with her would cut down on her worries, I'd say, or maybe it just awakens her own maternal instincts. Whatever it is, and as strange as it may seem, I'd say it's not that unusual."

Catta meanwhile had prepared the first cup of tea, properly scalding the pot first, and was preparing to pour it when Mary pre-empted her efforts by tipping back the pot and replacing the cozy over it.

And then with that provocative gesture she issued a playful but gentle admonition to her good friend, "When I wants water, I wants water; but when I wants tea, I wants tea! Sure we're not in that much of a rush – all things in God's good time!"

And so the tea was left to brew to a proper hue as the ladies continued their banter. One can only get away with such criticism among the best of friends, so they all laughed as Mary again chided Catta as if speaking to a novice, "You must always wait, dear, for the tea to properly brew."

While they all now waited, Mary told Catta about the first time that Nora had scalded the pot in her kitchen. This was customary, of course, but Nora in her effort to impress her hostess had forgotten to throw out the old water before spooning the loose tea into the pot. Catta reacted to this story as if in total shock.

She then roundly condemned young Nora by scolding her, "Sure don't you know, dear, we've oceans full of water here in Portland, so there's no need for you to be saving the water from the first go-round."

Nora took all of this playful ribbing in stride, as always, but when she next put two heaping teaspoons of sugar and a huge lashing of milk into her mug before the tea had even been poured, both of the older women looked on with apparent disapproval.

It was left to Catta to commiserate, "I've heard it said, and it must be true, that youth is wasted on the young. And now I see the proof of this."

But when the sweet buttery biscuits appeared they all hungrily devoured them with equal vigor, old and young alike, and with equal disdain for tradition and propriety.

"The first of the day, and sorely needed," declared Mary as she slowly swallowed the first sip of tea that she had allowed to cool in her saucer.

"I enjoyed that immenstedly," declared Nora, in the manner of speaking of one of their dear older friends that was instantly recognizable to the others.

The laughter again rolled out. Laughter was the coin of the realm of these gatherings. Nora loved being in the presence of older women – their sense of humor seemed more in tune with her own. Her own age group here in Portland was keener on quickly becoming American in style, language, and habit. Nora loved her new home as much as any of them, but she also loved Ireland and Irish ways. She fought to preserve the memory and meaning of these traditions in whatever simple ways she could. Nora's mother had often counseled her back in *Cill Chríost*, '*Briseann an dúchas tré suile an cáit* (culture breaks out through the eye of a cat, or, what is bred in the bone will emerge).'

These sojourns around town with Mary were always among Nora's happiest times. Even though her own stomping ground in East Galway was outside of the Irish-speaking Gaeltacht area, Nora had learned to speak Irish fairly well, along with other younger students, by visiting Rosmuc on the very edge of Connemara. *Gaeilgoirí*, they were called, these students who were keen on learning or improving their language skills – and didn't they have the time of their lives?

Mary admired this cultural trait in Nora, but in her backhanded complimentary style she had often claimed that Nora had not quite achieved the proper *blas* (language finesse of a native speaker). Mary would often jokingly condemn Nora with faint praise by stating with a straight face in front of a group of their amused friends, 'Sure, you murder the Irish language!'

Nora constantly tried to acquire this *blas*. Ironically, or so it seemed to her, she was surrounded by more Irish speakers here in Portland than in her own native area of Ireland. She regaled these older women with tales of Rosmuc, and they especially loved for her to repeat and embellish them. Nora told about being one of the brighter students in her school class, but said she had always been shy around figures of authority. Once when a *cigire* (an Irish language inspector) had come to visit her school near Loughrea, Nora's teacher signaled for her to answer a basic question that had been posed by the official visitor. She froze, of course, much to the chagrin of her teacher and even more to her own embarrassment.

When the *cigire* eventually left the classroom, Nora's disappointed teacher turned to her and mused, 'She stared and still her wonder grew, that one small head could carry all she knew!'

Even though Nora didn't understand this completely, she instinctively knew that it was definitely not meant as a compliment. She had let her teacher and her classmates down, and she carried this disappointment with her over these many miles and many years since they had first stung her.

The story that the older women seemed to like best, however, was of the time in Rosmuc at a local *céili* (folk dance) when an old bachelor farmer there had approached Nora in the hope of a dance with this charming young newcomer. Even though he was probably fifty years or more her senior, Nora had given him this dance and two more before the night was over. She seemed to realize that, as with so many other bachelor farmers in the west of Ireland, these *céilis* were likely to offer them their only social contact in the week, especially with females. His broad smile and the tipping of his cap at the end of the evening were all the thanks that Nora required. Catta and Mary called Nora their "holy innocent," although they both admitted that they might have done the same thing themselves at that tender age.

This caused Catta to proclaim, "Often the best dancers are not the best lookers!"

Nora's mother, although primarily an English speaker, had encouraged her children in Irish cultural activities, especially language and dancing. She had passed along to Nora the famous Irish dictum, '*Is fear Gaeilge bhriste nár Béarla chliste i mbéal Gael* (I prefer broken Irish to clever English from the mouth of an Irish person).'

Nora now continued by telling this small but willing audience of two more about her mother and how she despised people who "put on airs," people who pretended to be more important or wealthier than they really were. She now recited from one of her mother's favorite poems which began,

> *Oh, woman of three cows, a grá, don't let your tongue so rattle;*
> *Don't be haughty, don't be stiff, because you may have cattle.*

These ladies seemed to have a saying or a proverb for almost every occasion. After plenty of biscuits and two more lovely cups of strong tea, and the equally refreshing conversation for which Catta Bhreathnach was well known, Mary and

Nora took their leave, with regrets that they could not stay longer, and proceeded uptown towards the Convent of Our Lady of Mercy on Free Street in the very heart of the city.

On the way, as the day was still frigid, they stopped at a local Irish-owned grocery near the corner of Middle and Plum Streets. Its front window had recently been smashed. The hooligans, as it turned out, were second-generation Irish, or "narrow backs" as Coley called them. They had mistaken the old Gaelic script for "*Groceire*" and the proprietor's name, also in old Irish script, for words in Hebrew. These "corner boys" had done their part, or so they viewed it, to help rid what they called "their city" of an influx of unwanted "foreigners" or "aliens."

The fathers of these boys, Irish speakers themselves, should have been doubly disappointed by the actions of their sons. According to the dejected grocer, however, one of the boys was sternly admonished by his father only for not being able to properly distinguish between Gaelic and Hebrew! Apparently, this father was neither concerned with the vandalism nor with the narrow-minded bigotry of his son.

"What kind of children are we raising?" the grocer sadly asked Mary.

"*Mac an t-athair* (Like the father)," was Mary's succinct response.

Nora, remembering a well-known *seánfhocal* (old saying) from her days in Rosmuc, added appropriately, "*Aithníonn ciaróg – ciaróg eile* (one beetle knows another)."

Nora thought afterwards of how this was similar to other sayings in English, such as 'Birds of a feather flock together' or, relating to the similarities between parents and children, 'The apple doesn't fall far from the tree.' Sayings like these are remembered, regardless of the language, or so it seemed to her, because of the truths they illustrate.

Along that line, Nora mused to Mary, "Every group fears for the future seeing the shortcomings of the younger generation."

The ladies continued their journey up Free Street which was made all the more difficult by the wind that had shifted since the morning and was now blowing directly out of the brighter but colder western sky and directly into their faces. The Convent of Our Lady of Mercy at 100 Free Street offered warmth and solace. Mary had attempted to visit the Convent before the birth of each of her children and this was her mission on this day. She had been able to do this with only the one exception of the troubled birth of poor William, who had died shortly after his delivery. With this exception, and now with young Michael's weakened leg, or "bad knee" as the older Irish women insisted on calling it, all of Mary's other children had been born healthy.

So on this day, and in the presence of a distinctly Irish order of religious women, Mary now prayed for the health of her new child who was regularly kicking up a storm in her womb. She also prayed yet again for a cure for Míchilín's leg that had been troubling him so much lately, despite Mamie's best efforts and loving care. As she prayed, Mary also acknowledged with humble gratitude how much she had here in Portland for which to give thanks.

The Sisters of Mercy had been founded in Dublin in the 1831 just before the potato famine. Their mission was to assist the poor, especially with their specific needs concerning health and education. Most of the Sisters in Portland were of Irish or Irish-American background, and they had a strong presence in this city. In addition to working with the poor and infirm, they ran Saint Joseph's Home Chapel at 120 Walton Street near Stevens Avenue. Since the Folans had moved to Portland, several of the daughters of Coley's longshore co-workers had joined the Sisters, and this was, of course, a great source of pride for their families.

One could often hear prayers at the Convent spoken in a form of such pure Irish that it would have been indistinguishable from anything spoken throughout Connemara itself. This, too, was a comfort to Mary. She had learned her prayers first in Irish, and they still contained a cadence and a familiarity that would never leave her. Nora also had learned most of these common prayers in Irish while studying in the Gaeltacht village of Rosmuc, and she too loved the simplicity of them.

Unlike some of the younger Irish Americans in Portland, Nora had remained very Catholic in both thought and deed. Once, when reflecting on this to a friend who sometimes questioned both her parents and her priest, Nora proclaimed with characteristic loyalty and steadfastness, 'I will always remain true to my Catholic faith, *le cúnamh Dé* (God willing), even if the priests and other holy men are sometimes a disappointment.'

Regularly a priest from either the Cathedral or Saint Dominic's would attend to the sisters at the Convent for Confession or for Mass. One of the younger sisters had once asked why a religious woman, like her Superior, could not take the confession of her sisters. But she was quickly admonished by an irate priest for questioning the traditions of the Church. Although Nora saw herself as a "good Catholic," she also often wondered about the limited role of women in the Church. Nora had even heard Mary state on more than one occasion, 'I can think of many women who would make excellent priests!'

Although they usually agreed on such matters, especially regarding the role of women, they rarely spoke of these things publicly as they feared being ridiculed, or worse, especially by the more traditional men in their own families. Once, when Nora had spoken quietly to a good friend in favor of a fuller role for women within the Church, her young companion had asked in all innocence, 'Nora, are you becoming a Protestant?'

Here, however, in this quiet and safe place, surrounded entirely by women, they both had always felt secure and empowered, and well loved. Refreshed, warmed, and now content at having carried out this important maternal tradition, Mary let Nora know that it was time to be heading back home. Perhaps they might take a slightly different route back. It could offer them the opportunity for maybe one last short visit and perhaps yet another most welcome cup of tea. Mary had often stated, 'There could never be such a thing as too much tea.'

Bundling up now with their shawls snuggly wrapped around their necks and shoulders, but this time, fortunately, with the wind at their backs, this duo now set their sights on returning home – eventually.

Chapter 11

Never Be Dull Again

"We had champagne that night, but we'd real pain next morning..."
– from *The Charlady's Ball*, Harry O'Donovan, early 20th c.

When Johnny had arrived home for dinner that day, Bridgie informed him that all the dinner was gone. This was technically true, except for the two portions that had been set aside for Mary and Nora. The rest, of course, had been splattered over the kitchen wall! So she offered to re-heat some leftovers from last night's supper, which was just fine by him. She liked the eldest Folan boy, but he had failed to notice the attention and had never reciprocated in any meaningful way. His sister, Mamie, could clearly see this. Mamie thought that perhaps it would just be a matter of time before Johnny "copped on," as she put it.

Johnny and Dara had gone back to their respective homes for dinner. This was after their exciting mid-morning near-rendezvous with the past and possible future leader of the Democratic Party, William Jennings Bryan, at the home of Portland's own Thomas Brackett Reed. The boys were bursting with the news of this serendipitous meeting. But both of their mothers seemed to have more pressing concerns on their minds than some gifted speaker from Nebraska, wherever that was on God's good green earth!

By tradition, these mothers normally would be responsible for seeing that dinner would be served to their gaggle of hungry children. On most weekdays, they would then struggle to get their scholars back to school on time without earning demerits for tardiness.

However, on this day, those chores had been fulfilled by Mary's helper, young Brígid Cronin. There was no sign of her younger school-aged children when Mary returned home, and young Bridgie was busy scrubbing the kitchen blinds and walls for some unknown reason. Mary and her companion, Nora Ward, had only recently returned home from their brisk sojourn around the east end, and by then they were already contemplating yet another round of visitations. Mary, however, always had time for her Johnny. But how could these over-worked mothers ever be expected to find time for the discussion of mere politics?

"And who let you into the Reed's kitchen in the first place," Mary had sternly quizzed Johnny. "And, what gave you the right to be eavesdropping on a private conversation between two men of substance and means such as these?"

Although he wasn't exactly sure what she meant by "substance and means," he could guess that Mary was not overly pleased with his morning antics.

Conscious of protecting the reputation of their friend, Delia Walsh, Johnny boldly replied, "Well, ma, I suppose we had as much right as anyone to be in that kitchen. If those politicians didn't want us to hear their conversation they should've closed the pass-through. Was that our fault? And besides, what politician doesn't want to be heard?"

"Nothing good comes from ill-gotten gain," Mary had insisted to her cheeky boy!

"And since when did you become a lawyer, ma? Where did you ever hear the likes of 'ill-gotten gain' before?"

"Well, let me just tell you where, Mr. Man. Mrs. Connolly's son has passed the bar, whatever that means, and she told me that he once said those words to her. This was my first opportunity to use them meself. It seems to me to be just good common sense even though it may be all wrapped up in fancy words by lawyers and other professional men just to make it seem like they know more than the rest of us – just good old common sense. That's my opinion anyway, me bold boy, for what it's worth… You may take it or leave it, even if you didn't ask for it."

"Well, ma, you're the best mind in this house, I don't mind admitting. You must have come from a long line of Brehon lawyers back in Ireland!" Johnny was hoping that this conversation would distract Mary from the obvious fact that he had not attended school this morning.

Mary had smiled broadly and her consternation regarding her son's questionable antics quickly faded. Compliments like these were a rare commodity in the Folan household, but her first-born was usually the source of them when they appeared at all. There's always a special connection between a mother and her first-born child, and Johnny was the acknowledged scholar of the family, up to this point at least, so far as Mary was concerned. There were others in the pipeline, of course, and didn't everyone in the home and even well beyond already know that Mamie could hold her own in any verbal sparring with her father?

Mary Folan had a penchant for picking up English sayings. Some of these came from the Bible and some from Shakespeare or other such famous secular writers. Even though she still could not read, and even if she wasn't always sure of their precise meaning, Mary loved the sound of words and loved hearing and saying them. She had memorized countless similar sayings in Irish, so why wouldn't she also be well attuned now in her newly-adopted language? Mary had been pleasantly surprised to find that English had as rich a treasure of folklore and wise sayings as did her native Irish. *Seánfhocals*, she called them.

People usually believe that their own native language and customs are superior, which is only natural. But unlike her husband, Mary was open to new things, new sounds, and new ways. She fervently wished that this trait would carry over to her children. She wanted them to love and preserve Irish customs and language while also being open to the best of American culture and traditions. Her Johnny already shared his mother's verbal curiosity and skill.

Often these sayings were devoid of any real meaning and were spoken purely in fun. Mary had once paraphrased such a playful piece by the Scottish poet, Robbie Burns, who somehow managed to sneak in a reference to the famous English writer, Ben Jonson:

O, leave my room, you stable groom
And let bold Jonson by.
You may pass like any ass
Between the broom and I.

Whatever did such nonsense words mean? Who knew? But it was both clever and funny, Johnny thought, and he loved to see his mother smile broadly as she uttered these witty pieces. Her memory for verse was, like Johnny's, almost a steel trap.

'Where on earth did she ever get these?' he had often asked his Daide, but Coley would only shrug his shoulders and laugh with the rest of them whenever Mary recited. Another of Johnny's favorites from his mother's collection of verses was also pure doggerel:

It was midnight on the ocean, not a streetcar was in sight,
The sun was shining brightly, and it rained all day and night.
'We are lost,' the Captain shouted as he staggered from the bridge.
'No, no,' cried the First Mate, 'for here comes Coley Ridge.'

Dara Loftus had also experienced a dismissive reception back at his home that same noontime when his mother succinctly and sarcastically asked him what the value of politics could possibly be to her.

She had inquired of Dara, "What did you hear from those grandees up on Deering Street that will serve to put a leg of lamb on our table, or better still a bin-full of coal in our hamper? And as for their opinions on anything, as I've always tried to tell you – consider the source!"

Dara never knew exactly how to deal with these rejoinders. In fact, he often vacillated between thinking of his mother as either a pure genius or as just a simple and unsophisticated woman.

Johnny, however, never had any such ambivalence about his mother. He suspected that the same was also true of Mrs. Loftus. How could these poor women simultaneously stretch a few longshore dollars, keep their large and growing families well-fed and warm, and keep their own sanity all at the same time?

Neither boy openly admitted this hidden admiration for their mothers, of course. They were boys, after all! They both figured that these disparate and demanding tasks were by nature what all mothers were supposed to deal with anyway!

If mothers had any luck at all in this earthly vale of tears, they would live long enough for their children to catch up to this reality – most mothers are miracle workers, plain and simple. This truth sometimes seemed to dawn on children only when they were eventually forced to set up housekeeping on their own, and thus begin the task of raising their own families with all the attendant challenges. All mothers enjoy watching this revelation occur.

"Do you think we'll find wives for ourselves that are like our own moms?" Johnny was once asked by his best friend.

"Of course, and how could it be otherwise… but don't ever admit that to your ma or to mine – as if they don't already know!"

~ ~ ~

Finally, back out on Fore Street after dinner, Dara and Johnny were joined yet again by the bold Francis Feeney. He had given them the slip that morning in order to sneak in a visit with a girl he was starting to get sweet on. Frank was a bit older and more street-wise. He had always seemed more familiar with the ways of the world. He now wanted to report to his chums about his latest amorous rendezvous, but possibly out of innocence in the field of romance they were more keenly interested in talking about something they felt they had some knowledge of, politics – so they compromised and did neither. Frank had a mischievous streak in him, and it could hardly have come as a surprise when he came up with a scheme that excited both of the others.

"Let's see what's up in 'The Bight,' ye boyos!"

"The Bight" was located near the base of Munjoy Hill. It was Portland's true melting pot containing most of the city's small Negro population and two of their churches. It also housed Portland's current red-light district and everyone knew it. Years earlier this distinction had fallen upon Sebastopol, closer to their homes and near the corner of Franklin and Middle Streets, but that area of late seemed to be cleaning itself up with a number of small businesses, several of them Jewish-owned, moving outward from the downtown district and further along Middle Street, especially near the corners of Vine, Deer, and Chatham. There were small restaurants, laundries, and even a tiny synagogue to accommodate the rapidly growing number of Orthodox Jewish immigrants now settling in Portland's east end. Rabbi Sprince also lived in this neighborhood on Hampshire Street near the corner of Newbury.

If there was nothing going on in any other part of their small and slow-moving town, they could surely find some entertainment in "The Bight" – it had never yet failed them. Loggers from central and northern Maine, teamsters from Massachusetts, and merchant seamen from the seven seas often converged on this small run-down district just above Portland's waterfront. They were all looking for the same thing – excitement. There one could find Irish and Yankee alike, people of any and all extraction and those in between, and every imaginable social class, all lumped together in "The Bight." The mixture was never completely calm, and at times things could be downright dangerous, and this added to its allure.

These Irish boys swore that they never would be dull again! These words were becoming something of a theme for these three, and Frank, for one, was determined to be true to this goal. The younger ones saw Frank as an inspiration, always stretching the boundaries of propriety as he had done earlier that morning. Although both the Folan and the Loftus parents had warned their sons about spending too much time with him, Frank seemed alright to Johnny and Dara – not bad, merely curious.

But Frank Feeney was certainly not content with the limitations that either the city of Portland or his traditional Catholic family life had attempted to place on him. 'I'll burst these bonds one day!' he had often boasted to his chums.

They instinctively knew, somehow, that this wasn't simply brave talk on his part. There are some who fit in with structure and order, but clearly Frank was not one of them. He seemed to be cut from a different cloth altogether. 'Life's meant to be lived,' he regularly proclaimed, and this seemed to be his personal creed and motto.

Johnny and Dara could enjoy this excitement vicariously, always aware that they might be drawn in and find themselves over their heads if they weren't careful. It would be a balancing act, but a thrilling one for these younger two who were more than willing to take the risk. There is always an air of invincibility among the young.

~ ~ ~

Kitty Costigan was a fascination to most of the men of Portland. The "boyos," as these three were called by Coleman, were certainly no exception. Johnny Folan, Dara Loftus, and Frank Feeney were back in action and now together again for the afternoon – a pack of Irish wolfhounds, three hounds of valor on the prowl – but was Portland ready for them?

"Let's see if Kitty Costigan's up to her usual shenanigans," Frank shouted as the pack gleefully set off to the east along Fore Street and thence to the corner of Mountfort and into the notorious "Bight."

All there seemed to be quiet as Frank knocked on Kitty's door. Had they possibly already missed out on the excitement?

"Here we go again," Dara quietly intoned to Johnny, his expectant partner in crime.

Kitty appeared at the door in her signature silky gown trimmed with faux-fur.

"Well, if it isn't our Lord and Savior!" exclaimed Kitty as she viewed Frank along with his two pals, "and his two devoted apostles!"

She cordially bade them to enter her establishment. It was a ramshackle brick building that appeared to be coming apart at the seams and one that had certainly seen its best days long in the past. Kitty always greeted Frank in this unique way because his longish dark hair and rugged good looks struck her as how a young Jesus might have appeared. Frank always took her salutation as a supreme compliment, but as Mrs. Loftus would often say, 'Consider the source.'

"Nothing going today, boys? It's as quiet today as a nun's fart at vespers! Come in and warm yourselves by the stove. Someone, at least, should get some good from the heat, especially considering the fierce conditions we're sufferin' from outside. I have to heat this damned drafty place regardless. Are youse mitchin' from school again, ye scoundrels?"

Kitty seemed to have an expression for all occasions. Most of them were quite graphic and often irreverent, but all of them seemed original. She, like the building that housed her "business," was also well past her prime. But, when she smiled, one could still see the beauty that had formerly occupied the lines of her sad face. This beauty had once attracted men from all parts of Portland, and indeed the entire state of Maine, to this city's premiere den of iniquity. She was both a Madame and a procurer of illicit liquor. She could provide all manner of forbidden fruits for her lonely and randy customers, many of whom were passing through Portland on their way to other routine and lonely jobs in other routine destinations. At best, Kitty was a way-station for these lonely men.

But to these boys, and to most other Portlanders, she was much more than that. Kitty Costigan had long ago earned for herself that revered and honored appellation respectfully bestowed upon only a very select few – she was a character!

"Time has a way of catching up on us all," she complained philosophically as she looked at herself in a cracked and dim hand mirror while attempting to adjust her long and somewhat unkempt braided hair. "I don't have nearly the clientele that I had only a few years ago. This time of the year I'm glad for any wee bit of company at all to help me pass the time of day."

Life was no bed of roses for her now. Frank had once told the boys that Kitty's wayward son, Walter, was entirely unpredictable and had occasionally physically harmed his mother. Growing up in such a challenging and unusual environment, despite Kitty's best efforts to shield him, but with no knowledge of who his father might be or even if his mother herself knew that detail, all seemed to have had a predictably harmful effect on this obviously troubled young man.

While Kitty seemed to be able to transcend the lowly nature of her work, Walter openly wore this burden on his sleeve. Not surprisingly, he had been teased relentlessly at school about his mother's profession, before dropping out, never to return again, at the tender age of twelve. By now, he had a brooding nature and, as with his mother, was often out of control when disguised with drink. Today, thankfully, he was not at home and Kitty herself was mostly sober. These two things were in the boys' favor, so they could now comfortably remain.

Johnny had met Kitty Costigan on a few occasions, usually with Frank, but everyone in Portland seemed to have an opinion of her, regardless of whether they had met her or not. Most were not flattering and some were downright hostile. Johnny had once overheard an older female friend of his mother refer to Kitty in a most derogatory fashion describing an older woman who was attempting to appear younger, 'She's pure mutton dressed as lamb!'

A few, especially those within the various ladies auxiliaries or the Legion of Mary, had even suggested to the authorities that Kitty should be run out of town because of what they called her "low moral character."

Kitty had spent more than one evening as a guest of the city in the Monroe Street "Hotel," more formally known as the City Jail, but usually only long enough to sleep it off. Even the policemen liked her. The beat Sergeant had often referred to her as "the heart of the roll," a well-known Irish term of endearment. They seemed to understand that Kitty was only trying to get by and scratch out a living, albeit in an unconventional manner. She had at one time or another entertained some of Portland's finest. She was a pure jokester and hellishly comical – at least when partially sober. Kitty was gifted with colorful phrases like, 'Well boys, I had champagne last night but real pain this morning!'

Johnny only knew what he knew, and in his book he reckoned her to be a gentle and caring soul, with a highly entertaining personality. Ironically, her playful Irish traits and mannerisms reminded him of his own mother, though he would never share that insight with anyone in his family for fear of being discovered and thoroughly admonished. Johnny knew that simply being in Kitty's presence, let alone inside her brothel, would have been enough to be judged guilty by association. On more than one occasion Kitty and her clients had been "read out from the altar" at the Cathedral for their unorthodox and immoral behavior.

One of the younger priests, possibly only in his late twenties, however, had been known to visit Kitty on several occasions. Frank seemed to accept this unorthodox behavior on the part of the priest as being a part of his "mission" as he called it. But Johnny wondered if the priest, not that much older than himself, was possibly as intrigued by Kitty's unique style and manners as he was. When a very proper woman of their parish had once publicly rebuked this priest, whom she had seen leaving Kitty's establishment late one evening, he quickly defended himself by explaining to her, 'We all sin and fall short of the glory of God.'

Then, according to someone who witnessed the rebuke, the old wag instantly pointed her finger and retorted to the priest with stinging effect, 'But exactly whose sins are you referring to, Father?'

This day, however, Kitty was in a most jocular and talkative frame of mind and truly happy to have company. She addressed most of her attention to Frank as the oldest. But she was also solicitous to both Johnny and Dara, plying them with tea and her own soda bread served with lashings of freshly made butter. Her stories were what many in the parish might consider to be bawdy and crude, but Johnny noticed that in the telling of these titillating tales Kitty was neither mean-spirited nor judgmental of those who had frequented her establishment. Indeed, the stories were almost all highly comical, especially when she talked about certain unnamed customers whose reputations would have been besmirched and probably ruined had they ever been exposed.

Johnny was particularly intrigued by the sight of a framed needle-point that was prominently displayed over the worn-out piano in Kitty's living room. It featured a quote by Henry David Thoreau, and with letters large enough for anyone to read the message, even at a distance, "The mass of men live lives of quiet desperation."

It seemed to give the place a bit of class, and to Johnny it seemed humorously appropriate. In all of Kitty's grand tales her clients remained strictly anonymous. She described them only by their title, occupation, or place of origin – "the teamster from Leominster," or "the lumberjack from Rangeley," or "the sailor from Portugal," or "the minister from…" Well, she wouldn't even divulge that detail to further ensure his protection. 'We all have our own codes of behavior!' she maintained.

Much of the humor in these bawdy tales revolved around her customers' peculiar requests, needs, or stated desires. The stories were peppered with an endless stream of colorful and graphic phrases such as, 'I never before saw the like of that, as the Bishop said to the chorus girl!'

Their time with Kitty passed quickly. It seemed to the boys that there was never even an awkward pause. Her stories, although sometimes quite graphic, took account of the tender age of her audience that day, and this also greatly impressed Johnny. He never felt out of place or even embarrassed in the slightest. He wondered to himself what there was about a person's character that most appealed to him, and he concluded that kindness and humor were both very high on his personal list of desirable traits. Kitty Costigan clearly displayed both of these traits in spades. She recited several earthy poems and sang to the boys little nonsense party pieces, such as:

Oh there was ham, and spam,
and beer by the buckets and imported jam.
Such a divil of a schlam as you never saw before,
as they all sat down.

Dara earnestly tried several times to repeat this, but somehow he could never remember the entire ditty, so he shortened it in his own fashion, and sang out, "There was beer by the buckets and buckets by the dram on board of the *Buckeye Boo*.' And whenever she or Dara or any of them would finish such a ditty, the boys and Kitty would all gleefully shout out in unison, 'as they all sat down.''

Later that afternoon, Walter returned home and he looked disapprovingly at this young pack of three obviously non-paying guests. They collectively determined that it might finally be the right time to take their leave.

Her son gruffly snorted as he made his way to his own room in the rear of the building, "Jesus Christ, four o'clock in the afternoon and not a single whore satisfied yet!"

Johnny had often heard an even more profane version of that saying from one of Coley's workmates, but somehow it seemed far more sinister and accusatory coming from the mouth of this surly pup. Surely this boy would present a distinct challenge to Johnny's mother's contention that all conceptions are immaculate. What chance did this young man have, Johnny pondered to himself, given his pedigree, or lack of same? Walter had experienced great difficulties during his few precious years of schooling, and even now he seemed to have no regular friends.

On more than one occasion he had allegedly attempted to escort one of Kitty's younger "girls of the night" back to her own home in hopes of gaining her favor for free. One poor girl had resisted his advances on her very own doorstep. Her irate father had chased Kitty's son more than half-way back to "The Bight" before finally being outrun by the younger man. Walter had justified his dangerous behavior to Kitty by pompously proclaiming in all sincerity, 'Sure doesn't the young bitch work for us anyway?'

Now as Walter approached the end of the hallway just outside his room, he again turned and faced the boys directly. He glared at them and pointedly asked, "When will ye all be leavin' boys?"

In most Irish homes this could be taken as a form of polite greeting, representing only an attempt to ascertain how much more time there would be to entertain. But on this occasion his motives were absolutely clear and somewhat sinister. He wanted them out of "his" house, and the sooner the better!

After he loudly slammed his door, Kitty sadly turned to the worried boys and uttered words that were somewhat familiar to Johnny, although he couldn't presently remember their source, "How sharper than a serpent's tooth is the tongue of an ungrateful child."

Kitty seemed genuinely sorry to see the boys depart, but she understood. She addressed them all by name, kissed them all on their foreheads, and then waved good-bye from her front window before slowly going back to again observe her image in the fractured ancient hand-held mirror. But that mirror did not lie, and neither could it erase the pain now deeply etched on her face.

"I think I learned more anatomy and biology this afternoon than in a full term at Portland High School," Dara playfully ventured, to break the silence.

"And surely even a few things about human nature?" Frank pointedly added.

Johnny next contributed his own thoughts on the afternoon as he offered his more serious opinion on that day's events. "There are many folks in this town who have nothing good to say about Kitty Costigan. I venture we've all heard those things many times ourselves. But today we spent our afternoon with a lovely lady, in my humble opinion. And when she kissed us as we were about to leave, I felt the same way as when my ma would do the same just as tenderly whenever we would leave our home for school as young children. Frank, I didn't exactly know what to expect when you suggested that we go to 'The Bight,' but now I'm glad that we came."

They all nodded in agreement. They were back on the cold streets of Portland, but now each of them was warmed externally by Kitty's rickety old stove and internally by an afternoon of good conversation and even better companionship from one of Portland's undoubted characters.

Frank concluded, and he seemed to be speaking for them all when he saluted her, "God bless you, Kitty, and all your kind!"

Chapter 12

In the Land of the Blind

"In the land of the blind, the one-eyed man is king."

– Erasmus

Replenished, rested, refreshed, reinvigorated, and ready for whatever life might next present, Mary and Nora bundled themselves against the cold and quietly exited the tranquility of the Convent of Our Lady of Mercy. The day had become dimly sunny but still cold even for Maine. A steady wind was blowing from the west, but thankfully no sign of snow on the horizon.

"Not laden with humdidy," declared Mary to Nora, mimicking the Yankee speech pattern that she was trying to master. She had thus described clouds that seemed not to promise an increase of humidity or the imminent arrival of precipitation.

"Not laden with much of anything a'tall," responded Nora, who didn't fully understand Mary's meaning but still displayed her characteristically agreeable style.

The observant pair noticed a small group of well-dressed Portland citizens about to enter the Jefferson Theater on the corner of Free and Oak Streets, just two doors up from the Convent. The theater had opened four years earlier and was one of Portland's largest indoor spaces with a seating capacity of 1,600. These citizens appeared to be mostly Yankees, but Mary noticed something unusual and asked of Nora,

"Isn't that the Italian family that just moved uptown from Deer Street?"

Nora acknowledged the truth of this and added, "They are some of the newer Italians in town who now worship at the Seaman's Bethel, unlike most of their Catholic neighbors."

There were many choices for church in Portland, even for Catholics. In Mary's part of Ireland the only religious choice was whether to go to Mass in Carna at one end of the parish or in Kilkieran at the other. That choice was usually made based on which priest one preferred or, more commonly, what friends you wanted to visit on any given Sunday.

"Isn't that Fred Dow, the newspaper man?" Nora asked.

Nora was rapidly getting her bearings in Portland, and she tried to be up on the goings on about town. "I heard him speak once," Nora added. "His father was Neal Dow who fought in the Civil War and was once the Mayor of Portland, if I'm not mistaken. He was called 'The Napoleon of Temperance' and only died a couple of years ago. The family has a beautiful brick house up near Bramhall Hill, in the west end of town."

"What are all of them up to, I wonder?" inquired Mary before answering her own question by having Nora read aloud from the poster on the Jefferson Theater marquee: "W.C.T.U. Lecture and Reading Today on the Topic, 'Why Women Sin!'" They had seen a similar billboard in their earlier sojourn down by the Grand Trunk Railroad. But now it was clear that the lecture was about alcohol. This now caused Mary to state her opinion, "Women rarely sin by themselves. I think a lecture on 'Why MEN Sin!' would draw a much larger crowd, and I'll bet the women in the audience would know as much on the topic as the lecturer!"

Although Nora did not know the exact meaning of those four specific letters, she ventured, "I own it has something to do with the drink. The Dows are big into that – stopping it, I mean. I think that Miss Cornelia Dow is the president of the W.C.T.U. and the headquarters are just around the corner from here on Oak Street. Fred Dow's father, Neal, the one I just mentioned, and even though he was a Quaker, back in 1855 ordered out the Portland militia to control a large crowd that had gathered outside of City Hall. The crowd believed that the mayor was storing rum in the basement there while not allowing the people like us to buy it. Many of our kind were there in the crowd, I've heard, and it was called the 'Portland Rum Riot.' I think a man was shot and killed that day and several others wounded."

"It sounds to me like Mr. Dow was a bit too enthusiastic about saving peoples' souls, even for a Quaker, and especially if someone had to die because of it," Mary interjected in the commonsensical style for which she was famous. "The whole story kind of seems like nonsense to me, sort of like fighting to stay out of a war, or swearing to be more holy!"

"This meeting's about prohibition, I'd guess," Nora went on to say. "They want to make rum and whiskey and other kinds of alcohol available only to their class as some kind of medicine, or so I've heard, while keeping the cheaper booze out of the hands of the regular people, like us."

"Like us?" Mary inquired with a feigned look of distress. "Well, not like you and me, of course, but like the longshoremen and the common laborers – you know what I mean, like our kind of people. They've got prohibition here in Portland, for all the good it's doing, and they want to spread it to the whole state of Maine, and beyond."

Nora was proud to be able to share these bits of knowledge with Mary. This represented the kind of information that she had gained from reading the local newspaper and then by talking with other friends about what she had read.

"No wonder then that Dow's the only man in this crowd of women," noted Mary who in stating the obvious made it seem like a unique discovery. "I can surely understand why women would be against alcohol – what good has it ever done you or me? But the trick will be getting our men on board – now that would be quite a tall order. Coley and his gang look for any excuse to drop in to McGlinchys, or McCarthys, or Mulkerns, or Feeneys, or any number of the other public houses close to the waterfront. Thank God Coley's on the wagon, for the moment at least. He promised me sincerely that he would change his ways for good this time, especially after that last horrible bout of drinking. I didn't see any wages for several weeks and had to borrow from my family and friends just to keep the home intact. He spent many nights down at the Monroe Street Jail then, and I'm sorry to say he had lots of company from his fellow longshoremen. Yes, I can certainly sympathize with these women."

As the small group was about to enter the Jefferson, Nora boldly proclaimed, "They'd be a lot more likely to succeed if they had the likes of you and me on board, I'd venture."

"It's true for you, but not likely in this lifetime, dear," sighed an amused Mary.

Nora followed Mary down Oak and over to Pleasant Street. They shortly arrived at Gorham's Corner, so-named after Rufus Gorham who once had a grocery there many years earlier. It was the heart of the west end Irish community many of whose residents had come from *Cois Fharraige*, the region stretching west from Galway City along the north shore of Galway Bay. Their Irish speech patterns and intonations were nearly the same as Mary's.

Despite this similarity, Mary and her good friend, Barbara Feeney (née

Curran) from Danforth Street, loved to debate about where the purest form of Gaelic was spoken in Ireland. It was generally acknowledged locally that a good friend of theirs had recently won that particular debate. This friend, a Joyce, supported by young Dan Lagerstrom, had declared sanctimoniously and with full assurance, 'Sure the best Irish is spoken neither in *Cois Fharraige* nor in south Connemara, I'm here to tell you, but rather around Recess in the Twelve Pins where my people are from. Didn't Saint Patrick himself visit us a only few years back? And sure didn't he bless the rest of Ireland from that very spot? And he never ventured any further south than Recess, I can tell you that – why would he need to? It's true for you!'

Barbara Feeney, called Abby or Babe by her family, was from Kilroe West, just west of Spiddal in *Cois Fharraige*. Since the family moved back from Cape Elizabeth, her husband, John Augustine Feeney from nearby *Tuar Beag*, young Frank's father, was a "grocer" in Gorham's Corner. It was a grocery in name only. Most of its profits came from the sale of illegal alcohol from the back of the shop, not at all an uncommon practice in prohibitionist Portland at that time – especially when the Democrats were in control.

The McGlinchy family from the north of Ireland had made a substantial fortune in Portland from the manufacture and sale of spirits. The fines they had to periodically pay in the courts hardly seemed to put a dent in their successful business ventures. The often comical reports in the local newspapers of their frequent cases in court made for required reading in the Irish neighborhoods. They were survivors. Abby's husband, John A. Feeney, also made a good enough living on a much smaller scale in the neighborhood as a grocer, publican, counselor, small-time local banker, and amateur politician.

The Feeneys had only recently returned back to Portland after a few years of leisurely living in the nearby coastal town of Cape Elizabeth where they had a wonderful vegetable garden and a breathtaking view of the Atlantic over the beaches of nearby Scarborough. Barbara had often claimed that the coast of Cape Elizabeth was just like that of her native *Cois Fharraige*.

Some said that the Feeneys had moved out to Cape Elizabeth a few years earlier in order to stay one step ahead of law enforcement, but Mary thought that it was Barbara who had prompted the move, a "return to nature," as she had often said. There they could be close to the big city but still experience all of the rustic pleasures almost like being back in Spiddal or Kilroe West in Ireland.

Mary signaled Nora that there was enough time for a quick visit to the Feeneys who now lived at 48 Danforth Street, just down from Maple. She had not been able to visit with Barbara since her recent return to Portland.

"Is your mother at home; is your father working?" Mary questioned the young boy who answered the knock on the door. John Martin Feeney, then nearing six years of age, was full of local wisdom even at this tender age. John was blessed with a full shock of dark hair and an abundance of natural curiosity for the world about him. In that regard he was much like his older brother, Francis, one of Johnny Folan's mates. John Feeney would be a handful for his teachers when he would soon be going to grammar school – he could hardly 'keep his horses in control.'

"My mother is surely at home, and who's asking," young John asked officiously, always trying to act older than his actual age.

Mary chuckled, "Just tell your Máma that it's Mary from Mynish."

"You mean Mweenish, don't you?" young John interjected, thus showing off his knowledge of Irish geography and giving the alternative English pronunciation for this quintessentially Gaelic place name, *Muigh-Inis.*

"You're right, surely, John. Are you five years of age yet?"

"Not at all," John replied confidently, almost defiantly. "Sure won't I be six tomorrow? Did you bring me something for my birthday?" he now asked boldly yet somewhat innocently. "Máma says that I might get something from each of my brothers and sisters tomorrow. It's a tradition in Ireland for the *cuidín,* and that's me! I'll be in school next year, God willing."

As John left to retrieve his mother from the kitchen, Mary exclaimed, "He's too cute by half! They're all such sponges at that age, soaking up everything they hear. That boy's destined for great things, I'd venture, like his older brother, Frankie. And it would be only the right thing for his father to take him over to Ireland some day on one of his trips back home – that would surely open the boy's eyes to the wider world. I wonder if this younger generation will find our Portland to be too small for their curious natures."

Abby entered with a full-faced smile. She warmly embraced her treasured old friend and exclaimed, "Ah, Mary dear, I haven't seen you for months and months. How are ye getting on, and how's himself? Is Coley working?"

"He is, surely, Babe," as Mary preferred to call her friend. "This is my good companion from Loughrea…"

"This would be Nora Ward, I'd venture? *Dia dhuit, a Nora.*"

"*Dia's Mhuire dhuit, a Bhaib,*" Nora replied in her best Rosmuc Irish. She would be relieved if the saints' naming contest didn't proceed any further as she would surely lose that contest with these *Cois Fharraige* and south Connemara women with their enormous store of local saints, such as Macdara, of which Nora had but scant knowledge. "But how did you know my name? We've never before met."

Abby Feeney, Mary Folan, and all the good Galway women of Portland had always made it their job to know such things. "Ah, sure, Norín dear, who else would you be? 'Tis good to live in a place where you are known by your given name. *Tá fáilte romhat anseo* (You're welcome here)."

Abby, although only slightly older than Mary, was already gray-haired, even though her skin and face continued to seem quite young. In appearance she and Mary could have been sisters, or cousins at least. Taking account of the small geographical distance between their two families in Galway, and even closer here in Portland, these two were certainly kindred spirits.

They had first met at the Portland home of Catta Bhreathnach several years earlier. Catta often hosted young, single, newly-arrived Irish girls from Galway, especially if they had no family already living here. Catta gave them a place to feel safe and secure until they could get their feet firmly underneath them. There was always plenty of singing and recitation in her home, almost all in Irish. Social gatherings, such as these hosted by Catta, served to help re-create a familiar setting for these girls now living in Portland.

At their very first meeting, Mary and Babe had each chosen the same old Gaelic song to perform, *Amhrán Rós a Mhíl* (Song of Rossaveal). They performed this lengthy song of longing for Ireland entirely from memory and in perfect tandem. Each of them shared a verse with the other, and between the two of them they impressively came up with several verses that even Catta Bhreathnach and the best Irish speakers in the crowd had not yet heard. This initial joint recitation instantly sealed their friendship. Even though they each had been burdened by the endless obligations of a growing family, they always cherished whatever small bits of time they might find to be in each other's company.

"I'm so pleased that you've moved back into town, Babe dear. I know you were only a short distance away in Cape Elizabeth, but sometimes that seemed to me like the other end of the world from my Munjoy Hill. Are ye and John Augustine happy to be back?"

"I do miss my lovely view of the ocean, Mary, I must confess. But my best friends are all around me here, and surely it's a joy to have old Saint Dominic's just up Danforth Street. It was a burden for the entire family to travel on most Sundays to Mass. And there weren't many of our people out that way, as I'm sure you know. Sure I never heard so much as a single word of Irish spoken there. As beautiful as it was, I often felt quite lonesome at times. I did add to my family while we were living there, as I'm sure you heard, but with the passing of my newborn it seemed to me like the right time to come back home to Portland. It appears that my young John who greeted you at the door will now continue to be the *cuidín, le cúnamh Dé* (God willing)."

"Who knows?" interjected Mary in a teasing fashion. "Sure didn't the Bishop at the Cathedral recently say, 'With every new child comes a new blessing'? So miracles can happen..."

"Well, I'm sure Bishop Healy knows well what he's talking about on the subject of miracles, but I'm feeling well blessed with my many miracles as it is," Babe asserted boldly. She then added, while looking directly at Mary's belly, as if to take the focus off herself and place it squarely back on Mary, "But I can see that a new blessing will soon be delivered to the Folans!"

"Right you are, Babe, any day now, I'd say. I'm starting to get those all-too-familiar signs. Had my poor William survived, this one would be number ten – double digits. 'Double digits,' I like the sound of that. Perhaps that should be the given name for this one, be it male or female. Sure we've already covered all the family names and haven't we also nearly run out of most other good Galway names? But don't get me started on the saints' names – I'm exhausted enough as it is!"

"Well, thank God at least for the work alongshore, that's all I can say," Babe then earnestly declared. "What would you and Coley, or us, or half of Portland for that matter, be doing if it weren't for the blessing of those jobs?"

Mary was forced to ponder the obvious truth of Babe's assertion. For un-skilled and largely illiterate Irishmen from Connemara and other parts of Ireland who were now living in Portland there were precious few alternatives to the hard manual labor of dock work or construction unless, of course, one could open a "grocery" and sell other libations on the side. Making it in Portland legitimately was a constant struggle, and that was the truth of it entirely.

This was why, for the Folans as for many of the Portland Irish, there was a tendency not to judge those who were forced by circumstances, often beyond their control, simply to survive on the margins of what the Yankees called "propriety." 'Judge not, lest you be judged,' and 'Cast not the first stone' – these were biblical admonitions that always seemed to ring true to Mary. It might even be possible to defend the antics of the likes of a Kitty Costigan or others from "The Bight" with the simple understanding that 'There but for fortune...'

Mary now quickly came back to the present, and asked of her host, "Any news from home, Babe?"

"*Diabhail scéal; scéal ar bith*! (Devil the story; no story at all!)" This was Babe's standard answer to this familiar question. But in truth it did seem that there was precious little to report from Ireland these days. "I'd rather have the constant rain and the dark skies over there than this permanent deep freeze that we get here from December through Saint Patrick's Day. Sure, at home the spring comes in at *Imbolg* (meaning "in the belly"). And the days certainly do lengthen back in Galway after Saint Bridget's Day."

Imbolg is the Celtic fertility festival on the first day of February, known in the Christian calendar as Saint Bridget's Day, signifying the beginning of spring and the arrival of new farm animals.

This assertion and the mention of Saint Bridget prompted Mary to begin a familiar recitation in Irish, "*Anois teacht an Earraigh, béidh an lá a'dul cun sinneadh; agus tar éis na Feile Bhríde, ardoigh mé mó sheoil...* (And now with the coming of spring as the days lengthen, and after the Feast of Bridget I will raise my sail...)."

And, as was their wont since they had first met each other, whatever one would start a recitation in Irish the other would finish. And so Abby now completed the verse, "*Ó chúr mé in mó ceann é, ní stoppaigh mé choiche, go sheassamh mé síos i'lá Conte Maigh-o.* (Once I put it in my head, I would not stop for an instant, until I was seated in the middle of County Mayo.)"

Nora also knew this oft-recited bit from Raftery, the poem known as *Cill Eadáin* (from Kileadan, County Mayo), but it would have seemed impolite and out of place for her, or indeed anyone, to interrupt the joint recitation of these two kindred spirits. Really they were pure *anam chairde* (soul mates) to be sure. It was a classic poem of hope and home, of the joy at the ending of winter and the coming of the new season filled with the possibility of growth and opportunity. Instead of a simple townland in County Mayo, precious as it must have been to the poet, each of these three women would have mentally inserted their own place of birth in County Galway and the source of their dreams. For Nora, it would be Cill Chríost; for Babe, Kilroe West; and for Mary, her beloved Mynish – each to her own, but all for Ireland.

For Nora, poems and songs seemed to do just that – they expressed individual and specific longings but also common dreams and aspirations. And though the place names or personal names may change, these hopes and dreams of such poetic verse seem to remain constant and nearly universal by their very nature. Nora believed that people everywhere seem to share these same emotions.

By now Abby's eldest daughter, Mary Agnes, had scalded the pot and the tea was ready for pouring. She joined in with this group of women, along with young John who always observed, learned, mimicked, and, of course, refused to be ignored.

Tea, for Abby and for the Irish, was a constant companion. It seemed to join souls together in warmth, comfort, and friendship. Although it was nearly a universal libation and originated from the furthest corners of the globe, "Irish tea" at home and here in Portland was highly desired. Most teas were now packaged and sold by British concerns, but that truth had never kept anyone here or in Ireland from thinking or saying what one in this group now uttered for them all, "Sure, there's nothing can take the place of a good cup of Irish tea!"

The stories and anecdotes that flew between these two older Galway women fascinated and enthralled Nora. They were "gifted with gab," as the saying goes, and most of it was either humorous or insightful, or both, and so it seemed to Mary's young companion. Abby told the story of a woman in the Saint Dominic's parish who had thirteen children. This, according to her story, had caused one of them to ask her, 'Máma, how did you come to have thirteen children?'

"Well," she innocently responded, "When your Daide would come to bed at night, he'd often turn to me and say, 'Are we going to sleep, or what?' And I'd usually reply, 'What?'"

The woman further embellished this same story by maintaining that her old flat had such slanted floors that her husband often ended up on her side of the bed.

This story seemed to be a local version of the stork bringing a new child or of the well-known 'birds and bees.'

Young John Feeney gazed at this collection of women all giggling like teenagers and, although oblivious to the meaning of their humor, laughed along with them at all the appropriate moments, feigning an understanding of their humor.

Eventually, however, young John took a final handful of biscuits and proceeded to leave the room, but not before firmly reminding them all, "Don't forget about my birthday tomorrow!"

After John's departure, Abby added to the merriment by reporting that this same overly blessed woman from the Saint Dominic's parish had once been asked by Father Robert F. Lee, 'Do you love all your children equally?'

"Do I love them all? Sure, Father, I hardly know the half of them!" This was a well-known story and used often by other mothers on occasion including Mary at least once herself.

After more personal and quiet private conversation between Abby and Mary, it eventually came time to take their leave of the Feeneys and head from the west end of Portland back toward the more familiar terrain in the east. It had been a very long walk for a very pregnant lady. Before Abby kissed each of them good-bye, she gave Mary a bit of very welcome news that had been rumored and anticipated.

"I'm trying to convince my John to move east up to Munjoy Hill where we already have many friends. He and all of us could be a little more removed there from his all-consuming business ventures. And then, of course, there's the blessed Atlantic. I never again want to be too far away from seeing the ocean in all of its many moods, as I often was able to do back in Spiddal and also over in Cape Elizabeth. But I believe that the view of the ocean from the top of Munjoy Hill is one of the most spectacular I've ever seen anywhere!"

"Well, I'll not argue with that," Mary agreed. "This is grand news entirely, Babe. There'll be a fine welcome for you and yours, you can count on that – and I'll be leading the band!"

As the two vagabonds walked east along Danforth Street toward Gorham's Corner, Mary recited the names of several of the families that occupied these humble rentals. She knew many of them well even though this was not her own parish, but others she knew by reputation only. The names were so familiar that both women could be forgiven for thinking that they were back in Galway. "Flaherty, Donovan, Delaney, Walsh, Barrett, Clancy, Hanley, O'Brien, McBrady, Norton, O'Connor, Ridge, McCarthy, Joyce, Costello, Sullivan, Lee, and Conley."

These names often reminded her of Calvary Cemetery over in South Portland where one tomb after another was inscribed with a familiar and clearly recognizable Galway surname.

"Sure we have our names on our mailboxes here," Mary philosophized, "then on our stones over in Calvary; so good luck to us all with the small amount of time that we might have in between! And though Portland may not have been our place of birth, Nora, it's our home now – for better or worse!"

"I feel the same way, Mary. An uncle of mine once said to me, 'If they'd build a bridge back to Ireland, I'd take it.' But it was easy for him to say, knowing full well that no such bridge could ever be built. I'm not sure he'd recognize his own townland any more in any case – sure aren't most of his closest friends already dead or now living over here themselves? Yes, Mary, this ice-box is our home now. We'll just have to hope that it all will thaw out sometime soon, or at least in time to celebrate the Fourth of July!"

Leaving Gorham's Corner behind them, it was now but a straight shot home by way of Fore Street. Portland is a compact and highly walkable city, defined by the Atlantic Ocean on three of its four sides. Thankfully the wind was still out of the west and it continued to blow icy cold, but at least now it was at their backs.

This caused Nora to parody a familiar old Irish prayer by joking, "Well, the wind is surely at our backs now, so I wonder if the road will now rise up to meet us?"

"Not unexpectedly or too suddenly, I pray," Mary teased.

They both glanced up Center Street toward the Fraternity House located over at 75 Spring Street. Incorporated in 1871, it had served over the past five years as a "settlement house" by helping new immigrant families adjust to life in Portland. This section of town that they now ambled through had been Portland's original jagged waterfront before the construction in the mid-1850s of Commercial Street which ran parallel to Fore Street but one block to the south and east, in many places literally touching the edge of the harbor. It had been built on filled land,

and its perimeter was clearly defined by the huge New England granite blocks that were laid on top of each other to re-configure the contour of the city and give ample space for its many waterfront piers. Commercial Street now bustled with numerous warehouses and commercial businesses, both large and small. But Fore Street was left to define itself – this was a chore that would constantly reoccur.

Without slowing or stopping, they passed by John A. Feeney's saloon, several shops and small businesses, and numerous private residences mostly in brick-fronted buildings designed and built after the Great Portland Fire of 1866. That tragic event had destroyed most of this area and almost half of the entire city. It was the nation's worst single conflagration up to that date. Just past Market Street was the Seaman's Reading Room at 368 Fore Street, and next to that they passed 374 Fore Street, the meeting hall of the Portland Longshoremen's Benevolent Society – Coley's beloved PLSBS.

Coley himself would be there in just a few short hours. He had mentioned to Mary that very morning that there was an important issue concerning waterfront work rules that needed to be discussed and voted on this very evening. Uncharacteristically, he told his wife that he planned to speak at the meeting on this critical topic. This had prompted Mary to state, 'Well, it must be important indeed if you will be speaking.'

Coley had responded in all seriousness to his wife, 'These work rules are the only things that we can control ourselves. If we lose them, we lose the heart and soul of our union, and the twenty years of sweat and labor that we've put into making the PLSBS what it is today. Yes, I'd say that it's important.'

Working their way further eastward toward the base of Munjoy Hill, Mary and Nora were reminded that this Fore Street neighborhood seemed always to be in a state of transition. The waterfront and the bottom of Munjoy Hill had traditionally been the two areas where most newcomers would settle in Portland, long enough at least to feel the lay of the land and start to raise their families. Like the Folans, many would remain here. They preferred its familiarity to the comfort or prestige of areas on the outskirts of the inner city. Some, however, would move on once they had achieved some degree of stability. Mary often had asked Coley what these more "successful" families had gained by leaving their friends behind. They were leaving someplace familiar, but it seemed to Mary that they might be going from someplace to no place.

A clear indication of this constant transition along Fore Street could be witnessed by noting the names on some of its various residences or places of business. Although the Irish continued to represent the largest ethnic group in the city ever since the mid-nineteenth century, Italians, Poles, Jews, and others from southern and eastern Europe, were now crowding into this same neighborhood. Russian Orthodox families rented flats or ran small shops here.

Nora now recited, to the best of her ability, some of these unfamiliar names that she observed. "Lidback, Levi, Sulkowitch, Goldblatt, Goldman, Silochovski, Bernstein, Abrahamson, Dulitysky, Younuns, Rabinoff, Cohen, and Rubin." Now getting closer to Mary's home, Nora continued reading other similar names, "Gold, Berenson, Blumenthall, Punsky, Goldberg, and Kavalevsky."

The Folan's own home at 244 Fore Street on the corner of Franklin Street was shared by Joseph Flaherty and Simon Cohen. When Coley had once remarked to Mary about these ethnic changes, apparently showing some concern, Mary replied disarmingly, 'Well, Coley, we have Cohens in Galway, too, only over there they tend to spell it Coen – a small change over so many miles, dear!'

Their own Mamie had often interacted with Jewish friends and peddlers such as Philip Levinsky who lived up on Larch Street. This was on "Munjew Hill" as some of the older Irish now meanly referred to it. One recent summer afternoon while playing with a group of her Irish chums on the corner of India and Congress, Mamie noticed that some of her pals were pestering Mr. Levinsky and making it difficult for him to carry on with his work. According to Mamie's version of the story, out of exasperation Levinsky eventually shouted out in their general direction, 'You wild Irish...' But before he could get out the last word, Mamie quickly interjected her own more serene word, 'Rose!'

That exchange had caused all of them to laugh, including the peddler, and it instantly eased the tension. The gang never again bothered Levinsky, and he and Mamie became the best of friends. From that day forward he always called Mamie his "Wild Irish Rose!"

On the northern or western side of Fore Street, Mary and Nora swiftly passed by Vine, Deer, and Chatham Streets, which ran from south to north and ended at Middle. This old neighborhood and these streets had their own wonderful assortment of names, customs, styles, and smells, signifying the diverse places of origin of its residents. Mary and Nora often spoke of the wonderfully varied nature of their new home which was so very different from Galway's unchanging parochial nature. They both saw this diversity as a plus, but this viewpoint was not shared by everyone, even some of their closest Irish friends.

The sky was beginning to darken as it was still mid-winter and they had been out for the better part of the afternoon. They were nearly home. But now there seemed to be something brewing just beyond the Folan's home. Three doors down at 234 Fore Street, just across from the Loftus flat, a small Hebrew Synagogue had recently opened to serve the religious needs of its rapidly growing community here.

The controversy centered on one man – Marcus King – a one-eyed trouble-maker well known locally for his prodigious consumption of alcohol and for the regular abuse he meted out to his unfortunate wife and his three rambunctious sons. Marcus and a small group of fellow unemployed Irish laborers, obviously his loyal camp followers, had apparently surrounded the Rabbi Jacob Feinkstein who lived nearby at 36 Deer Street. The Rabbi was known to often visit this small synagogue and another also located nearby at 79 Rear Middle Street.

Red-faced and clearly agitated, Marcus as usual was *ar measc* (under the influence of alcohol), as the Irish would say, a condition that for him was becoming semi-permanent. His small group of supporters seemed to be in com-plete sympathy, and they were raucously coaxing him on with his protestations directed at the bewildered Rabbi.

"My son has to pay for breaking the windies down at McCarthy's Public House and Grocery. It's your fault, you weasel. How was he to know that the letters on McCarthy's windies weren't Jew words? Sure the *amadán* (fool) doesn't even know the Gaelic, so how was he to know the difference? He should have smashed your windies up here instead of one of our own up on Middle Street. I'll see that he knows better next time. Perhaps, boys, we should give my son a lesson on how a real Irishman can take care of his own neighborhoods, shall we?"

Marcus's followers appeared gleefully ready and even eager to join in the affray, as the odds were clearly in their favor. They were also convinced that their leader's grievances were legitimate. One of them had been softly murmuring a bit of anti-Semitic doggerel, and the others joined in clumsily trying to mimic the Yiddish accent:

"Foutbull, bazebull, svimink in dee tenk;

We got dee mohney

ant dee kesh eez in dee benk – COLUMBIA!"

It was unlikely that any of them had any idea of what Columbia was, or how any of these three sports could possibly be associated with the poor Rabbi. But that mattered little. The entire scene was quickly getting very nasty and Marcus now had the Rabbi in his grips. Mary, without so much as a thought for her own delicate condition, hurried over to them just in the nick of time. Rabbi Feinkstein seemed confused and King was ready to pounce. The Rabbi had passed by Mary's home many times, especially in fine weather, with a polite nod of his head or tip of his black fur hat. They had exchanged but few words as his English was as rudimentary as hers had been when she first arrived twenty years earlier. The Rabbi could speak only basic English, but Mary felt a certain affinity toward him.

Mary stepped forward pleading, "Now, Marcus. Now, boys. *Ouist!* Step back now. One moment, please, Marcus! Now this is Rabbi Feinkstein from just over on Deer Street, and he's a good friend of my Coley and me." This was stated with more than a slight exaggeration. "He belongs here as much as any of us."

"He belongs back where he came from, wherever the hell that might be," roared Marcus, still undeterred and with his stained eye-patch now more than slightly askew.

The patch was displaced enough to reveal a jagged scar from the knife fight just a couple of years earlier that had taken out that one eye. In that skirmish, Marcus had been shouting a string of obscenities at a young Italian boy over on India Street, calling him, among other things, a "Dago," and thus insulting both the boy and his community of onlookers. The fight had been brief. The injuries inflicted were only those on Marcus. There were no legal repercussions as the local police all knew of Marcus and his drunken ravings. But that incident apparently had neither taught Marcus any lessons nor changed his nature in the slightest. Nor had it discouraged him from provoking other altercations, especially when under the influence.

"He comes from Deer Street as I told you already, Marcus," insisted Mary. "And he'll be going back there directly, as soon as you release your grip."

With that she gently yet firmly placed her hand on Marcus's fingers and slowly forced him to release them one by one from the Rabbi's lapel. Feinkstein's emancipation was nearly achieved. For one brief moment the still enraged and inebriated pugilist considered thrashing both the Rabbi and the clearly pregnant but bothersome woman who had intruded unsolicited to his rescue. He thought better of it, however, when two of his supporters reminded him that Mary was Coley's wife, and that Coley had many friends among Portland's longshoremen. Marcus would be more than willing to prove his manhood by taking on a defenseless Rabbi, or even a pregnant woman, if necessary, but not even he would want to incur the wrath of Portland's formidable longshoremen.

"Let him be, for Christ's sake, Marcus," pleaded another of his devotees, having recognized young Nora Ward as a neighbor. This man wanted no trouble back at his home, either – the odds had now surely shifted.

Confused and embarrassed, Marcus reluctantly complied with Mary's request, but he continued to bluster, "Just don't ever let me catch you in my neighborhood again, you gink."

Then, as if to unwittingly complete his embarrassment, Mary publicly reminded Marcus that the Rabbi was much closer to his own neighborhood than was Marcus himself who lived on the other side of Cumberland Street and was, therefore, the true interloper. The chastened vigilantes and their ringleader slowly recessed, most likely to where they could drown their sorrows and proclaim their heroic victory over the intruding infidel.

Rabbi Feinkstein hurried over to Mary and asked, "How can I thenk you?"

"By not letting the likes of Marcus King bother you too much," she replied. "He and his kind are found everywhere, as I'm sure you already know. They're in every group and in every nationality, and even here in Portland among the Irish, unfortunately. Things haven't gone well for them, and they are scared of change and of what tomorrow may bring them in the form of new challenges or threats that they simply can't cope with. Today you were their target, but tomorrow they're just as likely to turn on one of their own. They're more to be pitied than feared, Rabbi."

The confused Rabbi, however, still appeared to be frightened and more than a little discouraged. "It was not only that one man with de patch, but hez whole gang. They was all against me, too, Mrs. Folan."

Mary looked straight at the Rabbi and murmured, "Some people will follow others simply because they move. In the land of the blind, the one-eyed man is King."

The Rabbi didn't seem to get her exact meaning, but Nora did. She was greatly impressed both with Mary's insight and now this wonderful double meaning, to say nothing of the courage that she had just demonstrated. The trouble had been diffused, but both of their hearts were still racing, and not even Mary was as sanguine on the inside as she outwardly appeared.

The two sojourners finally arrived back at the Folan home. Nora was never prouder to have Mary Folan as her friend, companion, and mentor as she was at this moment.

"That Marcus King should have been born an *O'Suilleabhain* (O'Sullivan)," she joked as Mary opened the door to her kitchen. Both chuckled knowing that the Irish word for Sullivan originally meant 'one eye only.'

"*Muise*, right you are, dear," Mary responded. "Sure there's none so blind as thems that will not see."

In the Land of the Blind

Part III ~ Evening

"The Wealth of Nature"

"He is richest who is content with the least,

For contentment is the wealth of nature."

~ Socrates

Chapter 13

Solidarity Forever

"Come March the 17ᵗʰ the winter's back is broke!"

– Popular Irish saying

Coleman's entire family, but especially Mary, was more than happy to see the small but most welcomed gift of coal that had arrived home with their hero. It would mean warmth for at least another few days as Portland was now about to face into the teeth of a Maine February, often the coldest and snowiest month of the year. John Walsh and another longshoreman whom Mary didn't know had accompanied Coley home with the coal. They were both invited to join the Folans for supper, but they both politely declined as was the custom. Mary didn't follow tradition by making the offer yet again, however, as she could see the look of panic on young Bridgie Cronin's face that there was barely enough to feed the large Folan family along with Nora Ward.

Walsh relieved the tension hanging in the air when he jokingly claimed, "I can do better than your famous 'potatoes and point' at my own house!"

That was a standard joke around these parts referring to a poor person's meal. Having only enough money for one leg of lamb or side of beef for a whole month, some poor families would reportedly hang this precious meat from the ceiling to cure, thus preserving it for as long as possible. Over the next several weeks, the meals for these families would consist of boiled potatoes that would then simply be pointed from the end of a fork in the general direction of the hanging meat, thus producing "potatoes and point" – a poor family's substitute for meat and potatoes!

Young Margaret (Peg) didn't always get these jokes; and so, she innocently asked the amused yet disarmed longshoreman, "So what will you be having for your supper tonight, Mr. Walsh?"

When he and the others laughed at this question, and Walsh hadn't yet answered her, Peg persisted in her line of questioning, "And where did all the coal come from, Mr. Walsh?"

A direct question obviously deserved a direct answer. John Walsh looked Peg squarely in the eye and honestly stated, "Well, Peg, to tell you the truth, it just fell from the sky – it was surely a blessing!"

To everyone's relief, Walsh had dodged another bullet and even Peg seemed more than content with this pleasing and logical, if less than completely truthful, answer. Reflecting the generosity she'd learned from her mother, Peg pointed to the steaming bowl of boiled potatoes, still in their jackets, and directed the same invitation toward these two visiting longshoremen that she had often heard at home, "Take all you want – take two!"

As the laughter of the adults again reached a crescendo, young Peg again appeared miffed. Why had her attempt at politeness been received with such levity? Coley noticed Peg's disappointed air, and so he now sat down next to her at the table.

Pointing to the meager portion of food already on her plate, her dad mischievously inquired of her, "Peg, dear, do you want me to start that for you?"

All of the Folan children had fallen for this same trick at one time or another in their youth, but young Peg was built of sterner stuff. To the delight of all present, Peg once again demonstrated why her parents had often claimed that she was 'too cute by half.'

"No, Daide. When you try to help you always take too much!"

"Your Coley is ever the tool, and I can see he's passed that on to his youngest daughter!" exclaimed John Walsh in admiration.

Walsh was a lifelong bachelor whose only constant companion was his dog Major, who was waiting patiently just outside the Folan's front door for his master's return. Walsh greatly admired Coley and the other charter members of the union, and he was never slow to admit this to anyone who might ask. But now he and his other fellow longshoreman did accept the obligatory cup of hot tea offered to them by Bridgie. It would have been impolite to decline that.

Even with lashings of milk poured into it, the tea served in the Folan house was notoriously strong, and this prompted Walsh to mischievously declare, "You could trot a mouse across that tea, Mrs. Folan!"

After their tea and more comical banter, the two prepared to leave and allow the Folans to finish their family meal together in peace. They all knew that John Walsh was a bachelor and seemed to crave this type of social contact – he loved the Folan family and held its patriarch in especially high regard.

Coley handed them their outerwear with a playful, "Here's your hat and what's your hurry!"

Johnny, not to be upstaged in the arena of humor by his Daide, then added, "And don't let the door hit you on the way out!"

Mary smiled when she heard Coley and Johnny's comments because she knew that such repartee was quite standard in most Irish homes in Portland. Those not familiar with its many forms, however, could often mistake this teasing for impoliteness; although in truth it represented exactly the opposite – a true sign of affection.

Now, with only her immediate family at hand, together with Bridgie and Nora Ward, Mary kissed and warmly thanked her lovie for fulfilling his promise to deliver this small but welcomed bit of coal to his family. She had been fearful of what this night and the coming days might bring to them all.

"If we can only get through this bitter next month starting tomorrow, sure we'll have beaten the devil – with the help of Saint Brígid."

Coley was pleased by her positive attention in front of his admiring brood of children. But it was his wont to try to trump any declarative statement of his wife with one of his own.

So now, as expected, Coley instructed them all, "Sure, your mother's right entirely. February is a short and bitter month, indeed, but you'll all recall that it's always followed by March. And so with the help of Saint Patrick we all know that come March the 17th the winter's back is broke!"

Coley's claim was thus fully established, and Mary's female Saint Brígid had been relegated into a slightly diminished position, trumped by Coley's Saint Patrick, truly a manly man and Ireland's own patron saint. Thus, Mary had been lovingly and gently upstaged by her grinning and self-delighted husband. And didn't the children love these playful moments?

With the exception of young Peg's innocent questioning of John Walsh, there was never so much as a second thought given to the origin of the "bonus" coal or the propriety of procuring fuel in such a dubious manner. This particular batch was anthracite, the highest quality and hottest burning variety of coal. Heat was no mere luxury but a very real necessity. And besides, a "reasonable" amount of pilfering or poaching had always been considered the prerogative of the poor since time immemorial. This was especially true among longshoremen everywhere.

Mary was by now comfortably seated. She felt somewhat guilty to be complaining about a little nausea and an aching back, and so she said nothing. She realized that these feelings probably stemmed from her carefree day of rambling around Portland. Her spirits, however, had been greatly buoyed by her visits to the Convent of Our Lady of Mercy and especially to the homes of two of her best friends, Catta Bhreathnach and Babe Feeney. And now she was thrilled by the sight of the much-coveted coal.

It was little wonder that she finally needed a break as she had spent much of the late morning and afternoon with young Nora Ward. Fortunately, Mary had the help of young Brígid Cronin during the day. Her own Mamie had joined Bridgie after returning from work in preparing supper for ten, eleven counting Nora, plus several hungry longshore half-boarders. In addition, they both attempted to keep Margaret and Michael from murdering each other. Mary's present job, after all, involved carrying the weight of her nearly full-term baby, and that was surely a sufficient challenge on its own. It would be Mamie who served Coleman his favorite meal of stewed lamb generously ladled over boiled potato. Perhaps he liked this meal so much because of his nickname – "The Lamb of God."

There were two family theories as to how Coley had earned this nickname. One was that he was an openly religious man who had periodically uttered the phrase "The Lamb of God (*Agnus Dei*)" from the Catholic liturgy. Sometimes, however, this phrase came out at inappropriate times such as when Coleman was a little *ar meisc*, as the Irish would say, or "under the weather." This description, or another such as "disguised with drink," was how the local Irish referred to someone with too much drink taken – perhaps these were attempts to soften a painful reality. A second and simpler theory was that Coleman's soft gray goatee, like that of a young lamb, had earned him his affectionate moniker. Mary supported this more benign theory.

Whenever Coleman eventually would pass, this nickname would pass on to Johnny and by extension also to the entire Folan family over many generations. Almost all Portland longshoremen had nicknames in order to keep separate the ubiquitous surnames such as Folan, Connolly, Gorham, Mulkern, Joyce, and Flaherty, especially on the payroll roster. This was a tradition that had started in Ireland and now flourished in the New World.

Often fellow workers would know a person only by their nickname, never learning their proper Christian name, or in some instances even the family surname, at least until that person's obituary appeared in the newspapers. The checkers and payroll clerks always needed an index of nicknames in order to make sure that the correct longshoreman was being properly credited for his hours of work.

After the main meal, Bridgie offered the Folans a small portion of apple tart that she had brought over from her mother. This treat was provided as a help to Mary during such a stressful time. That's what neighbors did.

Coleman teased Bridgie concerning the freshness of this sweet by slyly claiming, "Sure I'd wager that this tart has been around in your house since Hector was a pup!"

Coley's facility with the English language had surely improved over these past twenty years, but, as with Mary, he was best at memorizing notable phrases and sayings such as this, even if sometimes used inappropriately.

Once again, not to be outdone by his Daide, especially around young Bridgie to whom he now shot a playful flirting glance, Johnny added, "...or at least since Christ was a carpenter!"

Mary mildly scolded her eldest for wrongly using the Lord's name in front of the children, but his father quickly came to the boy's rescue as he put a comical exclamation point onto what had been a lovely meal.

Coley boasted to them all, in a fashion and phrase to which the children had all become accustomed, "Thank God for this small portion of food. Sure many's the hungry man would call this a meal!"

After supper, Coley washed his coal-smudged face a second time and then trimmed his goatee – a daily ritual. Mary had tried religiously to have Coley do his grooming before the meal, but he would usually counter her protests by claiming that he was simply too hungry and that he needed the additional strength from the food. Coley would often disarmingly add, 'Washing will always be done in its own good time, my lovie, so not to worry.'

On this evening, Coley put on his only suit of clothes, complete with a watch and chain, which together with the nickname "Lamb," were the only two personal mementos that he could pass on to Johnny at the end of his days. Therefore, this keepsake was important to Coley. He had no other such physical memories or attachments from his own father who had died long ago in Galway. When this particular watch was offered to him long ago by a peddler in Portland, at what he insisted was a much-reduced price, Coley quickly purchased it though the family budget was already stretched. It was one of Coley's very few extravagances. He had displayed it with pride ever since, especially when going to Sunday Mass. Seeing her husband wear this watch and chain had always caused Mary to grin because as she had often remarked, 'Time was never of less importance to any human being on this good earth than to my own dear husband.'

Coleman now kissed Mary calling her his "lovie" – the younger children always giggled when he said this to their mother, but the older ones found it quite endearing.

"I'll be home, my dearest, shortly after the end of our union meeting that's starting at eight o'clock. I'll not be late, not on this night at least."

He would not have gone out at all, considering Mary's condition, except that this particular union meeting promised to be a critical one. There would be an important vote on the issue of overtime pay for forced work during the noon lunch hour, a subject of special interest to Coleman and the older longshoremen. Working conditions, or work rules as they were called, were as crucial to their union as was the wage structure itself. These rules were agreed upon and set locally, port by port, and thereafter adhered to ferociously. This was a matter of pride, and it represented what those who were more knowledgeable about the workers' movement in America were then calling union solidarity.

All the children loved to see their father dressed up. It was indeed a rare treat to see him thus attired on a day other than Sunday. Coleman was not a boastful man, but he certainly had his pride. He would often repeat, with a very clear sense of affirmation, the names of the three institutions to which he felt most loyally affiliated. Mary and the children had often heard Coleman definitively declare, as if by rote memory, 'I'm a member of the Catholic Church, the Ancient Order of Hibernians, and the longshoremen's union, PLSBS.'

Coley proceeded quickly through the dark and frigid streets to the PLSBS union hall at 374 Fore Street, less than a five-minute walk from his home. The meeting usually commenced fifteen minutes past the official 8:00 p.m. start, better known as "Irish time," with the reading of the minutes of the last meeting and a report of the Sick Committee. Although there were more than 800 dues-paying members currently in the union, there were usually not more than 100 members present at any of these weekly meetings, unless new officers were being elected or there was a crucial issue being discussed as was the case on this evening. On this night, for a reason that soon became clear, the attendance was less than 50 members.

Union Vice President John Brown chaired this meeting due to the absence of President P.J. Higgins who had been ill for much of the past month. Seven men, including President Higgins, were entitled to receive the $5.00 weekly sick benefit. Another member, one John E. McPherson who had been hospitalized in Pennsylvania, was forwarded the maximum ten-week allotment of $50.00. Next, a letter was read from the Portland Brotherhood of Carpenters. This correspondence was prompted by the fact that the Society had just given its endorsement to the newly created Longshore Carpenters Union one week earlier.

As he slowly surveyed the faces of those now gathered in the hall, Coleman saw many of the friends with whom he had worked over these past twenty years. As a charter member of the union, he was much respected by his fellow workers. This evening many of the younger members, as expected, had alternatively chosen to attend the Democratic Party gathering at the Portland City Hall, thus allowing for the smaller than expected attendance.

Since receiving his citizenship papers, thanks mainly to the assistance of a local Democratic ward captain, Coleman had always voted Democrat, as did nearly all of his fellow Portland longshoremen. But like most of them, he did not truly understand much about the inner workings of politics, even at the local level. However, he did grasp the concept of self-interest.

The Democratic Party had often served to counter the vicious nativism that periodically manifested itself in Maine politics, especially in the rural parts of the state which had long been bastions of the Republican Party. The Democrats, by contrast, had warmly welcomed Irish immigrants into their ranks. This greatly benefited both the Party and the immigrants as their numbers swelled, especially after the Irish famines of the mid-nineteenth century and again with other recurring crop failures and subsequent new waves of immigration in the early 1880s and thereafter. In Atlantic coastal cities like Portland, the Democratic Party also attempted to ease the ritual of gaining citizenship by trying to keep literacy and other voting tests to a minimum. 'Thank God," Coleman had often declared, "I have me shitizen papers!'

Many of the younger and better educated Irish in Portland were now becoming political precinct leaders, especially in Wards 2, 3, and 4, which were closest to the waterfront where most of the Irish lived. Although there were already several aldermen with obviously Irish surnames, Portland's Irish had so far been unable to win the biggest political prize of all, that of mayor. Coleman had often dreamed of this lofty goal, and occasionally he had even stated this hope publicly. 'Maybe with the passage of time even this might be possible. Sure, I firmly believe that we'll elect one of our own as mayor here in Portland, even if it takes 100 years or longer!'

What Coleman clearly understood and felt in his bones was the role played by his union in its struggles with the shipping agents and their stevedores over the past twenty years. Compared to these daily bread and butter issues, national Democratic politics often seemed distant and abstract, almost as distant as the ongoing British war against the Boers in southern Africa reported in daily news headlines. To one of the young longshoremen, who once was reading aloud from the local newspaper about international affairs, Coley had sincerely queried, 'Sure, how's that going to put food on my Mary's table, one way or the other?'

Union "pork chop" issues, as they were called, were much clearer to Coley and the other senior workers. The impact of these work rules on the Portland dock workers and their families were much more immediate and tangible – these things, Coley firmly believed, were the issues most worth fighting for.

As anticipated, that evening under old business the longshoremen dealt with the controversial proposal from the Montreal shipping firm of Mills and McMasters. This firm's local stevedores had demanded that any payment for forced labor through the meal hour should be at the rate of time and one-half rather than the current provision of double-time pay. During periods such as these, when the wages per hour had remained static, these local working conditions and work rules could be defended or even improved upon, thus serving to preserve and en-hance the overall quality of work alongshore. This double pay provision for work during the meal hour had also recently been put into effect at the much larger nearby port of Boston. Thus, much more than local pride was at stake.

"We can't be fallin' behind them ginks in Boston," Joe Loftus had complained to his friend, and if even Joe was becoming politicized, Coley mused to himself, maybe they actually had a chance to win on this issue after all!

At the previous week's meeting, union members had been bitterly divided on this question. John Brown, the acting president, was a feisty Cornamona man from the mountainous area of north-central County Galway. He would often alienate the younger longshoremen and those from other parts of Galway by his abrupt manner. This had occurred at the previous meeting when many of the younger *Cois Fharraige* longshoremen from the southern coastal region of Galway had voted, "unwisely," in Brown's strongly stated opinion, against a ruling of the chairman. Some of these younger members had the temerity to suggest that the PLSBS should strive to become what they called "reasonable" in their dealings with the shipping firms! That set off fireworks!

Predictably, Coleman saw this issue from an entirely different perspective. For the past twenty years he had missed his meal hour all too frequently due to excessive work demands, especially during the busy winter season. He consistently voiced his heart-felt opinion that, 'If the shipping agents want my labor so badly, they should be made to pay for it.'

Coleman had strongly supported the present double-time rule at the last meeting. He now again forcefully argued that this would restrain the stevedores from mandating this overtime work quite so frequently. Coleman believed that the personality or the speaking style of the chairman, or indeed any of the other personal or parochial squabbles among Irishmen from different geographical regions, should never be allowed to affect his working conditions or the union's work rules. One of the more politically astute younger longshoremen called these minor squabbles "counter-irritants." He convincingly argued that these only served to confuse the longshoremen and to take their focus off the more crucial issues at hand.

Coley had no history of speaking at union meetings. He clearly was not a public speaker and had admitted to his friends that he would lose his courage in front of a crowd. But tonight was going to be an exception. Coleman Folan would be speaking tonight from the heart. If his fellow longshoremen recognized this, he believed, it might even affect the outcome of the vote. As he stood and faced his co-workers, a newly emboldened Coleman now implored them to consider several issues.

"How often do you think the shipping agents or the local stevedores go without their lunch breaks? If they promise to give up their right to lunch, I'll give up mine – as long as they pay us the same amount that they're earning for sitting on their duffs there in their warm and comfortable offices. Fair is fair. I need my lunch break as much as the next man and I mean to get it. Or I will damn well be provided for whenever I don't!"

Coley sat down well pleased that his point of view had been clearly, if only briefly, delivered. Many in the hall were nodding in agreement, however the debate still appeared to be evenly balanced. But then a newly-initiated young longshoreman with the unusual name of Dan Lagerstrom raised his hand asking for recognition to speak. Young Dan was a Waters (*O'Tuarisc* in Irish) on his mother's side. According to rumor, he was equally fluent in speaking both Norwegian and Irish! This was unique for someone like him who was of the second generation. No one in the hall yet knew his politics, but it soon became abundantly clear that Dan knew his stuff.

Lagerstrom spoke with authority concerning the fairly-recently passed papal encyclical of Pope Leo XIII known as *Rerum Novarum* (*Of New Things*). The encyclical spoke of something called "social justice," Dan claimed, and he proceeded to detail some of its provisions without the aid of notes of any kind. The Portland longshoremen had never heard the likes of this before. The Church, he stated, held that it was proper to lessen, "the misery and wretchedness pressing so unjustly on the majority of the working class." Dan further stated that it upheld the right of "the working man and the employer to make free agreements."

Lagerstrom confidently concluded with words from the Pope that directly addressed the issue at hand and that now rang true to everyone listening attentively in the hall. "If through necessity or fear of a worse evil the workman accepts harder conditions because an employer or contractor will afford him no better, he is made the victim of force and injustice."

This kind of presentation was both new and exciting. Those assembled in the union hall then burst into spontaneous applause, as much for Dan's graceful speaking style and passion as for the content of his speech – social justice, and from their own Church no less! When the vote was taken shortly after Lagerstrom's forceful presentation, the motion by John Brown that the "rule made on meal hour remain as recorded," was easily carried. The communication from Mills and McMasters was returned with notification that the double-time provision would remain in effect.

All were surprised at the relative ease with which this motion had passed in the final analysis. Coley wondered if the absence of the younger longshoremen, many of whom were more prone to accommodate rather than confront the bosses, had significantly affected the vote. Some of his older friends now told Coley that, in addition to young Lagerstrom's intelligent speech, Coley's own emotional and heartfelt defense of the work rule, although much shorter and more personal, had swayed their vote and was, in fact, the tipping point for several of them.

It had been assumed by these more senior longshoremen that the stevedores would either relent, thus allowing this provision to remain in effect, or that alternatively a strike or some other type of work action might be necessary to counter any arbitrary change on the part of Mills and McMasters. At moments like these the PLSBS was cognizant of pushing for as much as they could conceivably get without openly jeopardizing their very jobs. They were, after all, only one local union and were not affiliated with any of the other larger labor groups within the city or state, or of the International Longshoremen's Association all along the Atlantic coast.

The general mood in the Society Hall after this vote was openly celebratory. The feeling of the longshore rank and file seemed to be similar to that of a newly inspired and animated Joe Loftus who once again openly declared, "If it's good enough for them ginks in Boston, it's good enough for Portland!"

Before concluding the meeting, there was a discussion about how long a gang boss should wait for any gang member arriving late for work. This action stemmed from an inflammatory complaint by one of the newer union members who had earlier stated that 'everyone should pull his own weight.'

No action was taken on this matter. This pleased Coley because he was as guilty as any of occasional tardiness. Heaven knows that it was increasingly difficult for him to keep up with the pace of the youngsters after twenty long and demanding years of working on the coal docks. He for one never liked to be rushed, especially during his meal hour. Within Coley's gang it was understood that one would always cover for any fellow member who was either late or otherwise "under the weather."

He now whispered to Joe, "Would any of these bold younger union members, do you suppose, provide cover for either of us if needed?"

Under new business, Malachy Mulkerrin surprisingly brought up a controversial issue concerning a "colored man" whom he had seen working somewhere along the docks during the previous week. Mulkerrin said that he had reported this to the gang boss who was thereafter seen talking with the walking boss. Several members proceeded to remind the chairman of the provision in the original Bylaws of the PLSBS, enforced since 1881, which stated, 'No colored man shall be a member of this Union.'

One of the older members remembered a similar incident going way back to the year 1883, when a "colored man" named Green was also witnessed working the docks for the Allan Line. Back then, as this older member recalled, it was explained by a company official that Green was "an old and faithful employee" of the Allan Line in Boston. The official had promised the PLSBS that his company had "no intention whatever of introducing this class of labor" into Portland, nor was he aware of any "other man of the above description in his employment."

"Wouldn't you know," Coley quietly whispered to his friend Joe. "Just as we were almost home free and out of here early tonight, some *amadán* (fool) like Malachy would have to bring up something strange like this. We could be here till Easter!"

Just as this issue was heating up, the chairman recognized the walking boss, Bartley Jennings. Jennings reported that he had investigated Mulkerrin's complaint only to discover that the "colored man" about whom Bartley had reported was, in fact, a dark-skinned Italian who was simply repairing a storage shed used by the Italian freight handlers. This seemed to settle the matter until the obviously frustrated and annoyed Mulkerrin then loudly interjected, "So what's the difference between a Dago and a colored man?"

Some members laughed at this, as Mulkerrin was usually not taken seriously and was notorious for stirring the pot without reason. He was not currently a member of any regular work gang as he had often appeared at the shape-ups too late, too drunk, or otherwise not in any condition to work. Malachy was, however, well liked alongshore despite all of these weaknesses, most likely because the issue of the abuse of alcohol hit close to home for many of the Irish families in Portland.

For most of the union members on this particular evening, however, this current issue was deemed to be settled. But not for Malachy! He refused to follow the ruling of the chairman that he "cease and desist." Following a series of profanity-laced invectives hurled in the general direction of the none too pleased chairman, he was fined in the amount of $1.00 – twice.

Coley sympathetically admitted to Joe, "Malachy can hardly afford one dollar, let alone two…"

But then someone, overhearing Coley's comment, interrupted by giving his opinion, "Malachy always seems to come up with more than enough dollars for his booze!"

Joe Loftus, who had not heard the last comment concerning Malachy, turned to Coley and added, "Well, that's $2.00 Malachy won't be contributing to the McGlinchy family fortune tonight!"

A motion was then made, seconded, and passed to adjourn immediately – this motion being made by Seán McAuliffe as this was his well-known designated role at all regular meetings of the Society.

This had been a crucial meeting for Coley who often worried about the future of his union and his role in it as one of the longest serving full-time members. Although he was not on the winning side of all debates and votes within the PLSBS, Coley was always impressed by the workings of union democracy. Although it can be slow and cumbersome, often frustratingly so, debate and voting seemed to ultimately get most things right. As someone had once told Coley, 'Democracy is the worst possible political system, except for all of the alternatives!'

The PLSBS was now enjoying steady work from November until April with nearly 800 members on-loading huge quantities of Canadian grain and off-loading ton after ton of precious coal mainly from Hampton Roads, Virginia, for local use. But Coley was left to wonder, what of the future? What if there's another financial panic like that of the early 1890s? What if any of the all-important imports or exports were ever to dry up? What if coal was ever replaced by some other commodity to warm the homes of Portlanders? What if the grain somehow disappeared? What if...?

These were matters over which neither Coley nor his follow longshoremen had any degree of control, even though they were greatly concerned. They were mere laborers. It seemed that the solution to these large issues was in the hands of powerful people who had no knowledge of the workers themselves. Their decisions could impact these workers' lives in many unforeseen ways. But union work rules were another kettle of fish altogether. And on this evening, at least, attired in his Sunday best with his all-important watch and chain on full display, Coley had proudly done his small part. It was not in his character to be vocal in public, but it seemed to have made a difference.

As Coley left the union hall, now surrounded by his fellow longshoremen, there was a spring in his step. The chronic pain in his shoulder from shoveling coal all that day had somehow disappeared. He was content with his efforts. He now smiled to himself as he recalled one of his wife's favorite axioms, 'Count that day lost whose low-descending sun views from thy hand no worthy object done.'

Meanwhile, several of the older longshoremen from the west end had asked young Dan Lagerstrom to accompany them to one of their favorite hang-outs on Center Street, just above Cobb's Court, that was run by Thomas J. O'Neil. Most longshoremen, especially those with long memories, would tip their caps reverently when passing Cobb's Court out of respect for the family of Patrick Guiney who had been so badly disfigured from fighting in the Civil War. His poor family had never fully recovered from this horrific loss. Patrick Guiney had been their darling boy, but he had come home sadly as one of that war's many tragic casualties.

At O'Neil's, the longshoremen complimented Dan on his skillful defense of their work rules, with one of them boasting to O'Neil, "Dan's got the English!"

Another then comically chimed in, "And the Irish and Norwegian, too!"

Lagerstrom, although normally quite shy and reserved, was apparently enjoying his new-found popularity. He had instantly become a local hero, and when a pint was placed before him the public house quieted as all present eagerly waited to hear his toast.

Dan confidently raised his pint glass and happily declared, to the contented amusement of all present, "The first of the day – and sorely needed!"

Chapter 14

Every Child is a Blessing

"I didn't think this night would be much!"

– Common expression of Jack Ward
of Ballacurra, Kilchriost, County Galway

Bridgie Cronin and Mamie Folan had the kitchen well in hand. Mamie smiled to think that her mother had been bold enough, even at fully nine months, to spend the greater part of the morning and afternoon traipsing outside of the house in this bitter cold. She knew that Mary was a social person and needed her contact with others of her own age.

The half-boarders could certainly be quite an additional chore, and so Bridgie's help in the kitchen and with the young ones was all the more welcomed by the Folans. Feeding them their dinners at noon-time had provided Mary with a small amount of additional income for the household. This money was badly needed, especially whenever Coley was not fully employed. Longshore work was "casual" or seasonal by its very nature, and therefore his work was as irregular as was his income. Additionally, and even more troubling, there were Coley's increasingly frequent periods of excessive drinking during which his wages would dry up entirely.

Other longshore families had augmented their incomes by "taking in laundry" or in many other creative ways, but Mary preferred having partial boarders. Mamie called this additional pittance her mother's "egg money." But Mary had her own unique name for it, her "CBC kitty," short for corned-beef and cabbage! It was remarkable how the Folan family diet was entirely income dependent. The amount and quality of the meat they consumed would decline noticeably whenever funds from Coley's longshore work either diminished or disappeared. This connection was apparent to all, even the children, but they all made do with whatever was provided to them without even so much as a whisper of complaint. That would have been considered very bad form.

Shortly after supper and around the time of Coley's departure for his union meeting, Mary suggested to Nora that they should proceed directly upstairs to her bedroom. Mary was by now beginning to worry that perhaps she had overdone it. She comically remarked to Nora, repeating Nora's own father's colorful way of describing any time that was unexpectedly full of activity, "I didn't think this day would be much!"

Mary had been trying to take things a bit easier over the past several weeks as she was by now full term – she looked it and she felt it. All of her babies had more or less come on schedule, at least up until now. She informed Nora that she was beginning to experience those all too familiar sensations just before her time was at hand. In fact, although she had sensed the baby kicking for nearly three months, Mary had been experiencing small contractions for much of the afternoon. Because she was enjoying the visitations so much, however, she had kept that news to herself.

Mary then reminded Nora that she was not as young as when she had given birth to the previous nine: John, Mary, William, Thomas, Joseph, Agnes, Kitty, Margaret and Michael. With all the "gallivanting around," as she called it, Mary's back and legs now ached. She was thirty-five years old and painfully aware that she was not the young colleen who had arrived in Portland twenty years earlier. As if to punctuate this reality, the new child now gave out a monstrous kick that caused Mary to inhale deeply and sigh,

"Maybe this one would like to play for Galway, Nora. I feel a bit like I just finished playing a full match myself!"

"Sure what would the likes of you know about playing a match, Mary? I've never heard you talk about sport before – is it hurling or football you're speaking of?"

"Football, dear, of course, and what else? We'll leave the hurling to youse heathens with your tiny little sticks from over in East Galway!"

When others in Portland brought up East Galway, Nora was never sure of their intent, but with Mary it was always playful. This sporting comment put a smile on both their faces as neither of them knew much about sport in any case.

"Well, at least we didn't have 'potatoes and point' tonight, Nora. I'm pleased you stayed to have your supper with us."

Nora knew well the meaning of "potatoes and point." It represented a kind of gallows humor. For many Irish, including the Folans at certain times, simply feeding one's own family was an altogether too real challenge.

Because of that reality, Nora had at first politely declined the offer of supper that evening, according to Irish custom, but had then swiftly reversed herself by boldly stating, "There's not much good in a piece of meat hanging from the rafters, Mary, but tonight I can smell the lamb stewing on the stove, and wouldn't I be quite the fool not to accept your hospitality this evening. I'm not one of the Lambs myself, but I sure enough love the smell and taste of it. It's not the same as at home where the poor creatures are always out sporting and playing on the green hills all year round. Faith, these snow-covered hills in Portland are not as fair as those of Galway. But here the meat is tasty enough, and just like in Galway it's sure to be full of bones."

Mary was more than ready for this comparison. She responded with one of her classic Irish sayings, in this case equally applicable to either Maine or Ireland, "When you buy meat you buy bone, and when you buy land you buy stone!"

Mary's bits of wisdom had always warmed Nora's spirits. "Where on earth did you pick up all of these sayings, Mary, and how did you come to have as many sayings in English as in Irish?"

Mary smiled a knowing smile, but she left Nora's question unanswered.

It was surely a wise decision for Mary to finally be in her own bed. Not long after Johnny was on his way to the Portland City Hall and Coley had left for his union meeting, Mary's water broke! Nora, who was usually a calm and collected presence, suddenly was transformed into a bundle of nervous energy.

"Jesus, Mary, and Joseph – this is all my fault, Mary. I kept you out much too long today."

Mary smiled and tried to calm and reassure her young friend by gently reminding her that there were surely other reasons why she was in this situation.

"Not to worry, Nora dear. I own that Coleman had much more to do with my present condition than you, lovie."

"But what should I do now? Other than my one daughter, I've never helped deliver a baby before, only lambs, *laonta* (calves) and bonnives (piglets) back at home. But there my Dada knew exactly what to do. Whatever am I to do now?" Nora asked plaintively.

"Well, you can start by calming yourself, Nora dear. All's in God's good hands now and all will be well with this new one, too, I'm sure."

"*Le cúnamh Dé* (God willing)," Nora quickly interjected, lest any harm should come to the mother or child before God's protection could be formally invoked.

It was Nora's well known habit to utter this phrase, or the equally common English, "Please God," as was equally used by many with Connemara roots – even though Nora was herself from East Galway, the *créatúr* (poor creature). Some in Portland had lately taken to calling Nora "*le cúnamh*" because of this religious habit. More often, however, Mary's older friends harmlessly chided Nora concerning her roots. They would frequently say things like, 'Sure, how would she be knowin' anything about that, the *créatúr* – sure isn't she from East Galway?'

By this time, Mary was edging her body over the side of her bed. It was an all too familiar position for her to help ease the pressure on her back and later in the delivery process. Of course, Mary was right on time again, just as she had predicted.

She steadied herself and asked aloud, but in a manner of speaking directly to herself, "Hasn't it only been two years and a month since I was here on this same bed, in this same room, and in this same awkward position giving birth to my Michael? Don't fret yourself, Nora dear, we'll have plenty of help and plenty of time. My water breaking is only the beginning of the fun.

"Now be a good girl and go fetch Monica the midwife. She already knew that I might be needin' her tonight. And ask young Bridgie to finish with the cleaning in the kitchen now that all have been fed. Sure the children, especially the boys, are more than able for the eatin' but terribly slow to offer any help with the cleanin'. That's men for you all over – great at the start but lackin' at the finish! And now, Nora dear, please send my Mamie up to me – she's helped me deliver two already and has a steady hand, thank God. Don't worry, I'll be fine with my Mamie here…"

"*Le cunamh Dé*," intoned Nora again hastily as she vaulted down the stairs to deliver those messages. She was quickly out the door on her mission of delivery, forgetting even to take along her own woolen shawl to help fend off the cold which she hardly even noticed.

Nora returned in a matter of minutes with Monica Lydon, the midwife, in tow. Monica immediately went to work, first checking Mary's dilation and next asking Mamie to gather warm water, soap, and plenty of newspapers and towels. Monica had performed this needed service hundreds of times back in Ireland and now here in Portland, including all but one of Mary's nine deliveries. Ironically, she had only missed the birth and the subsequent early death of poor William as she was giving birth herself at precisely the same time.

"Well, *a Mháire, a stór* (Mary, my treasure)," exclaimed Monica, "you're at it again, I see, and as always regular as clockwork!"

Monica noted the irony, or perhaps the appropriateness, of a birth on the very last day of the Celtic winter season, *Samhain*, which runs from November through January. This new baby would likely arrive mere hours or even minutes before the beginning of *Imbolg* – springtime in Ireland running from the first of February through the end of April.

Monica also loved puns, playful words, and comical phrases as much as did Mary, and thus, she now hastened to add, "You'll not be *imbolg* (meaning literally "in the belly") for the start of *Imbolg*!" Monica had thus skillfully used macaronic verse, a clever mixture of Irish and English, to great effect. She seemed pleased with herself.

"No, Monica, faith this one wants to be in the world tonight. Perhaps then the two of us can welcome spring together tomorrow morning."

"*Le cúnamh Dé*," Nora again interjected with ever-widening eyes, then sincerely declaring for all to hear, "If there was ever a time to meekly ask for God's intervention and protective hand, surely it is now!"

"Not to worry, dear," assured Monica. "Our Mary and I have been through this ordeal nine times already and she's proven to be a real trooper. Sure, don't you wonder if I'm needed here a'tall?"

"Oh," shrieked Nora who thought that the midwife might be serious about leaving it all in her untrained hands, "I really do think that we need you here tonight, Monica!"

All of this playful banter caused Mary to laugh outloud; at least she tried to in between what had by now become rapid-fire and intense contractions.

"You're all squawking about me like troubled hens. Sure amn't I the one that's doing all the work here?"

This sincere protest caused them all to laugh, eventually including even Nora herself. But Mary's laughter soon changed to a pained groan as her cramps returned with even more frequency. Now they were coming about every two to three minutes apart. These belly aches had started late that same afternoon, but at first they were not terribly intense and Mary wanted nothing to interfere with her pleasant visitations. Mary knew instinctively and by experience, however, that both the frequency and the intensity of these contractions would now rapidly increase. She knew that her time to deliver was at hand, and so she now urged Nora and Mamie to be prepared to help Monica in whatever way was needed.

Monica placed her experienced hands on Mary's belly to monitor this tightening of the womb. The two of them were by now a well-calibrated team. When the "bloody show" appeared, a mixture of blood, mucous, and other bodily fluids giving off a strange but earthy smell, Nora was visibly troubled. She imagined that something had surely gone terribly wrong. But the two old hands knew that this simply meant that the child was now ready to make its appearance at any given moment.

Mamie had allowed the younger children, Agnes, Kitty, Peg, and even young Míchilín, to hover outside the doorway earlier. She knew that this would help to dispel the fear and mystery of childbirth and also assure them that their mother was indeed alright, despite the troubling noises emanating from her bedroom.

But with the increasing contractions, it was clearly time for them to depart. Mamie put the Folan children in the care of young Bridgie Cronin whose tricky job it now was to attempt to put them all to bed. Mamie was needed here where she would be of greater help to both Monica and her own mother on this night, as she had been all along in the care of Peg and Michael.

"*An bhfuil sibh réidh, a Mháire agus a Mháire óg*? (Are you both ready, Mary and young Mary?)," asked Monica.

Nora performed the important role of clasping Mary's hands during the last of her most intense labor pains, now coming only a few seconds apart. Nora was squeezing as tightly as was her older friend – sympathetic labor pains, it seemed, now being expressed through the joined hands of these two *anam chairde* (soul friends). It gave Mary a new meaning to a beautiful and rarely used ancient Irish phrase of endearment which she now uttered to her well-loved companion, '*Táim buoich go cas mé lamh lea*t (I'm happy to have met you, or, literally, I'm pleased that I clasped hands with you).'

When the actual moment of birth finally arrived, it appeared to Nora to be over before it had even started. She looked incredulously at Monica with wide eyes as if to ask, 'Is that it?' For Mary's part, the intense labor was now over and there emerged from her a huge sigh of relief amidst her near total exhaustion.

"*Tá sé críochnaithe!* (It is finished!),*" she moaned, consciously using the same last words as those uttered by her Lord and Savior when on the Cross.

Well, not quite so soon. There was still much work to do, although Mary's part was now largely complete. Nora lovingly wiped the perspiration from Mary's brow and continued to gently squeeze her friend's hands, as if her very own labor pains were now also diminishing. Monica and Mamie proceeded to tie off the umbilical cord in two places and cut the cord between these two ties which caused a small amount of blood to gush forth.

Now after nine long months, mother and child were finally separated – they were simultaneously independent and yet still totally dependent, integral parts of each other's lives. For the next many years there would be a gentle and predictable dance of true separation between them. The separation process would be gradual and totally necessary. Sadly, this also would occur altogether too quickly for both mother and child.

"It's a girl again this time," Monica now declared to her dear friend.

Mary first gazed over at her eldest daughter and her namesake. With equal affection she then turned her attention over to her newborn daughter. She pondered on the fact that these sisters were some fourteen years apart in age. The baby would be at Mary's breast over the next many months, but she knew that all too soon she, too, would be as grown up and as independent as was her eldest daughter now.

~ ~ ~

Mamie was already challenging her father's parental prerogatives. She had recently brought a young man, a Presbyterian as luck would have it, into their home in order to meet her parents. Mary instantly recognized the boy's good character, but Coleman seemed only to be aware of the religious label – Protestant! Somehow he was not able to see beyond that. He later sternly lectured Mamie that this was one of the reasons why he wanted his children, especially his daughters, to go to the parochial and not the public schools, if only they could have afforded the additional cost.

At that critical moment, Coley instructed Mamie directly, forcefully, and preemptively given that she was only fourteen, that she could never marry a Protestant and still be his daughter. Mary had been shocked to hear her husband state this in such unequivocal terms, but she knew with a wife's clarity that once uttered this prohibition could never be retracted. It would be the gospel in their home.

This, Mary knew, was Coleman's nature – and "what cannot be cured must be endured!" But what was not yet fully revealed was the content and character of Mamie's own nature. How would she, their first-born daughter, deal with such an absolute decree? The answer to this was yet to be determined!

~ ~ ~

"Only fourteen years separate my two daughters," Mary murmured, again almost as if speaking only to herself, "and yet they somehow seem worlds apart!"

By now Monica had completed bathing and drying the infant's face. The rest could wait until later. Her early priority as a midwife was to get the mother and child together again for their mutual benefit. The child would need to suckle, to "latch on" as she put it, and thus to begin the process of building up its lungs and its breathing capacity while at the same time gaining both sustenance and protection from its mother's colostrum and later milk. Mary would also benefit in many ways from the breast feeding. It linked the two of them together by nature and also, according to Monica, might help Mary to continue her contractions and thus expel the remaining placenta, or after-birth. This same routine had already been followed successfully by these two time and again.

This new child was added to the physical store of Mary's earthly possessions – her mother's *dudín* (dudeen, stump or clay pipe); a simple but sturdy white china tea mug; and her beloved reverse painting. Her family store was already well stocked with nine happy and healthy children. If it is true, as the old Irish saying goes, that "contentment is wealth," then Mary Folan was indeed a rich woman.

"A girl? Thanks be to God," intoned the relieved mother. "Faith and don't I have a name chosen for her already then – it will be Helen, after my childhood friend from Mynish, *Éibhlín Ní Laoi* (Helen Lee). If only she can be half as kind and gentle as her namesake, we'll all be blessed with a pure treasure."

"Helen Folan?" exclaimed Mamie. "That seems like an unusual name. It almost sounds to me more like a Yankee name!"

"Well, there's Lee's in your family in Ireland, and Helen is a grand old Irish name, Mamie," Monica informed her. "It's in ancient verse and song from Ireland's distant past. Helen, or Eileen, or Evelyn, or Ellen, or Éibhlín, sure they're all one in the same. And didn't even the ancient Greeks fight over Helen of Troy; she was so beautiful and revered? More importantly didn't an ancient Irish *file* (poet) write lovely verse about the 'flower of the hazel glade, *Eileen a'rún*'? It's one of Ireland's oldest songs."

"Sure the pedigree may be nice, and thank you for saying that," Mary agreed with Monica. "But this young child, like all of my young ones, will have to make her own mark and way in the world."

"It's true for you," agreed Monica. "But she will still have a wonderful name to live up to. And every time you call out to her sure you'll think of your Mynish friend and all of your carefree young days together in Ireland. And won't that be a comfort to you? Who knows, the way things are changing and the miles seem to be shrinking, perhaps one day these two Helens might even meet!"

It was at this moment that a quiet knock was heard at the bedroom door. Bridgie had come to ask if she could bring the curious and restless children back in to see their mother one last time, as they had resisted all her attempts to calm and quiet them. Mary smiled and consented. So now, much past their usual bed-time, they were all taking their turn at viewing Helen, the new *cuidín*. The older children, Tom, Joe, Agnes, and Kitty, first ran instinctively over to their mother, while the younger ones were more keene on viewing this new potential rival who was then being cradled in Monica's arms.

"She's not beautiful!" boldly insisted Peg. "Bridgie said that all newborn babies are beautiful, but she's not – she's nothing but wrinkles!"

Monica hoped that Mary had not heard Peg's jealous dismissal of her new sister, but Mary had indeed heard. She heard and saw everything – sure didn't Mary and all mothers have eyes in the back of their heads? At least that's what the Folan children had often been told, and they firmly believed it to be true, with plenty of evidence to support this notion.

"No bother, Monica. Faith, Peg has strong notions and a ready opinion on just about everything! What she thinks, she says! I don't know how we'll ever marry her off with such high and mighty standards – could we ever find someone who would ever please that one? It's sure to be an almighty challenge for us all."

Young Michael said little, but he eventually reached out to grab his newborn sister. He obviously wished to have someone closer to his own age to play with. Peg was his constant companion, but it wasn't always fun for him as she usually insisted on getting her own way. Now, at least, Michael might have other options. He might finally have someone to boss around. He might have a fighting chance with this tiny new one.

After several short minutes of maternal reassurances and these new sibling introductions, Monica firmly announced that it was finally time for them all to let little Helen partake in her first real nourishment. Peg, worrying that she had earlier eaten the last of the lamb stew herself, uncharacteristically owned up to what she feared might have been a mighty transgression.

But Mary gently calmed her daughter's pained conscience by lovingly assuring her, "W*hist*, child. I'm sure Helen doesn't care for lamb tonight. And hasn't she already put in her order for the very same first meal that you all preferred, her own mother's milk – and fortunately for us all we now have plenty of that on tap."

Monica, Bridgie, and the older Folan children laughed, which only left Peg to wonder if she was still in serious trouble or, hopefully, off the hook. Smiles all around eventually convinced her of the latter and that all was indeed well.

"Come, children," said Monica, "and say your evening prayers now around your mother's bed."

They all complied. In unison, the Folan children made the sign of the cross and repeated in perfectly fluid Irish the words known to them almost since birth, "*In ainm an Athair, 's a Mhic, 's an Spoiread Naoimh, Amen* (In the name of the Father, and the Son, and the Holy Ghost, Amen)."

Still in near unison they repeated the words of the Hail Mary three times. All participated, with even with young Michael enthusiastically mouthing the words, as best as he was able. He often unintentionally created nonsensical words or phrases. But he always gave special emphasis to the "Amen" at the end of each verse, both as punctuation and as an outward affirmation that he knew where he was in the program. Peg got most of the words right because she would be starting catechism classes soon and her older sister Agnes, her "pal" as Peg called her, had already been coaching her. Peg had to be careful, however, never to mimic the irreverent version of this prayer that she had occasionally heard her brother Tom secretly proclaim, 'Hail Mary full of grace, Holy Cross is in second place…'

Although Peg wasn't entirely certain what a "Holy Cross" was, she knew instinctively to keep this version to herself whenever her parents or other adults were present. She had once innocently asked her father about this revised, but certainly not standard, version of the prayer and what it meant. Coley had not responded to Peg but had at once gently boxed Tom's ears while silently pointing a stern finger at the young boy's face. Children can be observant, however, and don't think for a moment that Peg hadn't noticed the slight grin on her Daide's own face even while he was administering this half-hearted admonishment. She figured that this, too, was just another lesson that she would only fully understand in God's own good time. Wasn't Peg after all, as she had often reminded the rest of the family, her father's "clever little girl?"

Bridgie was situated closest to Míchilín this evening during the prayers. After they were all finished, she sheepishly reported to Mary concerning her youngest son's unique name for the Supreme Being. Bridgie had clearly heard Michael intone, just as he had at other earlier occasions during the recitation of the Lord's Prayer, 'Our Father, which are in Heaven, Harold be thy name...'

"*Béarla bhriste agus Gaeilge chliste* (Broken English and clever Irish)," Monica joked, turning an old Gaelic axiom on its head. "And who is this Harold anyways, when he's at home? Hard enough, I suppose, for children to learn their prayers properly in one language, let alone in two!"

As with most of the Galway families in Portland, these parents were absolutely fluent in Irish but only slowly becoming more proficient in English. Mary Folan was better than most as she was determined to master this new language in all of its intricacies. The oldest children of these families, those already attending school, quickly exceeded their parents in this newly-acquired skill, as in most other scholarly disciplines such as math and science. Most Portland Irish parents attempted to keep the Irish language alive at home, at least for their older children, but the allure of English had always proven to be too strong. English was the language of the streets, of the schools, of business, and even of their own Church.

This latter fact was true despite the reality that many of the parishioners at the Cathedral in the east end where the Folans worshipped, and also most of those at Saint Dominic's in the west end, were either from Connemara or *Cois Fharraige*. Both of these regions were thoroughly located within *Gaeltacht* areas. Some of the younger priests in Portland, despite their obviously Irish surnames, could speak hardly a word of their ancestral language. '*Is mór an trua é* (It's a great pity),' Coleman would often say concerning this sad fact.

Mary now brought the children close to her and sweetly whispered to them all, "*Oíche mhaith, mo leanbh* (good night, children)."

They all responded to their mother in unison as they had been taught, and with a *blas* (perfect pitch) that would have impressed even the most critical Gaelic-speaker from the west of Ireland, "*Oíche mhaith, a Mhamaí, agus Dia leat* (Good night, Mommy, and God be with you)."

"Polly Veer, Polly Veer," immediately cried young Míchilín who was now in hopes that Johnny would help to put them all to bed by reciting one of his favorite Longfellow poems, *The Midnight Ride of Paul Revere.*

Johnny was now anxious to join his friend, Dara, at Portland City Hall. So, he quickly helped Bridgie corral the children after they had kissed their mother and their newborn sister good-night. They then respectfully said "*Dia leat* (God be with you)" to Monica.

As they each filed out of her bedroom, Mary uttered a familiar prayer be-seeching the aid of Saint Joseph to protect her family and herself in their repose:

> *O, Saint Joseph, I never weary of contemplating you, and Jesus asleep in your arms; I dare not approach while he reposes near your heart. Press him in my name and kiss his fine head and ask him to return the kiss when I draw my dying breath. Amen.*

With the children finally on the road to sleep, the conversation briefly turned serious between these two solid friends with Mary declaring to Monica that she felt lucky and blessed that nine out of her ten children had now been born healthy and had survived. Only William had died in infancy and young Míchilín now had some kind of serious health problem. The words of the Irish founder of the Sisters of Mercy, Catherine McAuley, had always been a great solace to Mary, especially when McAuley had written, 'We must not be discouraged at our imperfections.'

In Mary's eyes all of her children, even her young Michael, were perfect and indeed every conception was a miracle. Monica agreed with Mary on this, know-ing all too well from bitter experience that in Portland as in Ireland many an Irish household had lost at least one child. In some cases, these families had lost several children even before they had reached the age of two. Monica was also concerned about her friend's ability to provide for such a large and growing family.

Thus she now worried aloud, "Also, Mary, there's the question of money.

Coley is working as hard as he's able to, and heaven knows you're doing your part, and more. But how will you afford to feed and clothe this young one, together with all the others? Young Michael seems to be having more and more trouble with his leg, and the doctors fear that it could be something permanent as I've been told – surely you've thought about this, Mary?"

"About little else recently, Monica. But, Bishop Healy said at Mass just a few weeks ago that 'with every new child comes a new blessing.'"

Mary had stated this unthinkingly, as if by rote, while blankly looking straight ahead. But eventually she frowned, and that gave Monica her opening to proclaim, "The Bishop never went through childbirth himself, Mary dear!"

Mary added innocently, "Sure, what could any bishop or priest know about having children, even if these men are the 'apples of God's eyes'?" Immediately after saying this, she blushed slightly at having uncharacteristically criticized one of the leaders of her Church.

"Mary, surely you didn't mean to say that?" implored Nora who was now quite surprised at hearing these two older Irish women saying things that seemed to be critical of the Church and its priests. In her world this simply was not done. Also it seemed to be quite out of character for Mary.

"Well, perhaps I didn't mean to criticize the Bishop or the Church," explained Mary in an attempt to placate her troubled young friend. She then attempted to answer the concerns of both of these women by citing and slightly changing an American axiom of which she had become very fond, substituting the word "wealth" for "love." Mary temporarily silenced her friends by affirming, "Wealth comes as birth does – knowing its own time." While Monica and Nora both stopped to consider the meaning of what their friend had just taught them, Mary quickly added in her own defense, "But what I said before was true, was it not, Nora? I hope you can forgive me, and I'm sure that God already has…"

"*Le cúnamh Dé,*" sighed a somewhat relieved Nora Ward.

Chapter 15

The Great Commoner

"Tara is grass, and behold how Troy lieth low-
And even the English, perchance their hour will come!"

– Gaelic poem by Eoghan Rua ÓSúilleabháin
Translated by Patrick Pearse

"We swore that we never would be dull again…" When did these words that represented the boys' motivational slogan ever ring more true? Especially, Johnny mused, on this particular day when the month, the year, the decade, and even the century itself were all in a state of flux. Johnny pondered upon this inspiring thought as he and his best friend, Dara Loftus, passed through the large and boisterous crowd of frenzied Democrats now surrounding Portland's City Hall.

"We'll certainly never be dull again after tonight," Johnny stated matter-of-factly to his wide-eyed pal. "Have you ever in your life seen or heard a crowd like this? Portland will never be the same again either, I'm sure of it. What a way to see out the last year of the nineteenth century, my boy!"

"What are you talking about, bucko?" Dara quizzed Johnny as he put forth his counter-theory about date and time. "Sure aren't we already in the very first month of the twentieth century? At least that what my calendar says."

Indeed, perhaps they were both right. After all, what did the year 1900 truly represent? Was it the alpha or the omega? Was it a beginning or an end, or was it a transitional year? Learned people seemed to disagree on this very point, so how could these two boys in Portland, Maine, be expected to definitively settle such a conundrum as this? These two teens had been neighbors, school mates, and chums nearly since their births some sixteen years earlier, and since then they had debated nearly anything and everything, large or small. One large question that they never seemed able to satisfactorily resolve was Dara's perplexing philosophical query, 'How many angels can dance on the head of a pin?'

Dara was quite confident that he had his pal trapped when he first posed this puzzle a year or so earlier, but Johnny had cleverly sidestepped the trap by sarcastically replying, 'None at all. Sure everyone knows that the holy fathers of the Church don't look kindly upon dancing at all, so couldn't you just imagine their dismay if it was an angel who was up to no good by dancing, or especially a whole pack of them? In any case, Father Draine stated clearly that there must always be room for the Holy Ghost between any two people dancing! So you'll have to add that additional element into your equation, my boy! You hadn't considered that angle had you, Dara dear?'

Johnny again had the high ground in this exchange. He had long ago internalized some advice, ironically from Dara's father, Joe Loftus, when he had warned Johnny, 'Never accept the premise of a Jesuit – for once they have you captured in their net, logic they call it, it's almost like a spider's web, and neither you nor anyone can ever logically escape. So try to avoid this trap at all costs!'

And so he had. But here he was now using Joe Loftus's own advice to free him from a rhetorical trap that Dara Loftus had carefully laid for him! In that moment Johnny's clever retort took the wind out of Dara's sails, but Dara's record of scoring rhetorical points on Johnny was probably even over time. They both loved to spar verbally, as did their entire families. But should anyone else, like their older friend Frank Feeney, ever try to nudge into these rhetorical contests, the two verbal combatants would often join forces to slay the intruder. And this would happen regardless of the age or social position of the unsuspecting interloper.

"Did you ever...? Did you ever think you'd see a crowd of this size in our quiet little town?" Johnny asked. "And to think it's all for a Democrat – even with us living in a rock-ribbed Republican city and state! These are strange times we're living in, surely."

This last comment prompted Dara to offer his carefully considered opinion on the state of Portland, Maine, politics. And so now he stated the contrarian political observation that times had indeed changed.

"Well, maybe Portland and possibly even Maine is not as solidly Republican as the Yankees seem to think, at least not these days. Portland and many of the larger cities are certainly far different from the rest of the state. Sure didn't 'The Great Commoner' himself choose a man from Bath to be his Vice Presidential running-mate last time around? If Arthur Sewall could have been second in command for the entire nation, then maybe some other Democrat from Maine will also have a chance in the future. Anyways, aren't you tired of always hearing about Hannibal Hamlin, or James Gillespie Blaine, or Joshua L. Chamberlain, or even our own Thomas Brackett Reed? Sure the one thing they have in common is that they're all Republicans. I'd say it's time for some local Democrat to make his own mark in politics. Maybe even someone like Councilman Joseph E.F. Connolly. I'm told that his people are from our very same parish back home, or so my Daide told me, and also that he's already passed the bar exam to practice law anywhere in the entire state of Maine."

Johnny was impressed by his friend's argument and nodded in full agreement. He was now well aware that Dara must have been musing over these issues for some time.

Dara's reference to the common origin of their families along the west coast of County Galway was a common occurrence between these two. They were both very proud of their Irish roots and openly boasted of this among their closest friends, although they'd never own up to any sense of Irish pride at home or in front of their parents – what self-respecting teen would ever do such a foolish thing?

As far as their parents were concerned, their dads especially, these boys and their friends were nothing more than American-born "corner boys" or "narrow backs," as the foreign-born first generation often referred to the native-born second generation. In their parents' minds, you had to be born in Ireland to be truly Irish. On this, as with so many other issues, these children regularly disagreed with their elders, albeit usually quietly and always respectfully.

"Jesus, Mary, and Joseph," Johnny blurted out, sounding just like his father in his intonation, "it's only half past seven o'clock and the streets are packed already! The show doesn't even start until eight. I see the doors are opening down on the Myrtle Street entrance – let's chance our luck over there."

These two, of course, had already seen and heard "The Prophet from the Plains" earlier that day at the home of Thomas Brackett Reed, eavesdropping on a private conversation between these two giants of American politics. Few of their kind had indeed ever been so privileged. What had impressed both of them was the startling degree of agreement between William Jennings Bryan and Reed on several important topics.

These men had both been potential candidates for president from their respective parties, but they were from distinctively different geographical origins and social backgrounds. On the issues of imperialism, expansion, and the present American war in the Philippines, however, they had seemed almost joined at the hip! This had come as a shock to the boys, and yet it was pleasing to them both.

Maybe politicians of different stripes could find common ground after all on the important issues of the day – if only they could get past the partisan political nets that held them back, to say nothing of their own stubborn pride.

The crowd was arriving by foot, in electric streetcars or trolleys, and by any available means of transport. Looking at the noticeably working-class style of dress of the majority of the crowd, Dara said to Johnny, "I'd say the bulk of them came by Shank's mare," a much-used local expression meaning "hoofing it" or, more simply, walking.

They had been gathering since well before seven o'clock. All of Portland must have turned out, together with a good bit of the rest of the state of Maine. To their great surprise, the boys then spotted the elegant white-haired presence of the former Governor, Joshua L. Chamberlain. He was one of the great heroes of the Battle of Gettysburg and had commanded the 20th Maine Regiment in its crucial defense of the strategic redoubt at Little Round Top, thus saving the day for the Union. At Appomattox Court House he was given the honor by Ulysses S. Grant of receiving the formal surrender of the Confederate troops, a task he performed with grace and benevolence.

After the Civil War, and due to his overwhelming popularity, Chamberlain had been elected as Governor of Maine to four successive one-year terms. After leaving politics, he served for twelve years as president of Bowdoin College, his alma mater. He had recently moved to Portland from Brunswick. Here, in his dotage and poor health, Chamberlain had taken up the post of Surveyor at the Custom House, seen by many as a sort of generous old-age pension. He was currently lodging at the stately Falmouth Hotel, at least until he could find a suitable home to his liking. A staunch lifelong Republican, Chamberlain nevertheless attracted a sizable crowd of admirers from this largely Democratic gathering. Greatness often seems to overcome mere partisan labels.

What a scene this was! The boys were much more adept at squeezing through tight places than were the larger and more polite adults. They easily made their way to the open doors of the City Hall and swiftly traversed the polished marble hallway and over to the stunning large stairway leading up to the first balcony, their preferred seating place. Johnny led the way with Dara close on his heels. They spotted two empty seats on the far left side of the balcony in the very front row and quickly laid claim to them. They were thus in place as the hall was filling quickly from bottom to top. The first balcony had an elevated sight line. Additionally, it afforded the boys a wonderful proximity to the stage from which Bryan, their hero, would soon be speaking.

"This is the tops!" Dara shouted to make himself heard over the din of both the crowd and the music of the American Cadet Band then playing on the stage for all they were worth. "It doesn't get any better than this," he exclaimed, "even though we had ringside seats at Reed's house earlier today!"

"And to think," interjected Johnny, "that only yesterday you were complaining about what a quiet and dull little town we lived in, especially in the winter! What's your opinion now?"

"What do you think, Johnny? When have you ever before seen anything like this in our little old port city? You tell me and I'll admit I was wrong, but I doubt that you can…"

"I'm only too happy to concede your point, Dara. You're completely right this time – this is the tops! I can't remember ever having so much fun in the middle of the week. Who would have expected waking up this morning that we'd have such a day?"

The boys talked and shouted and gawked. They tried to spot any of their mates in the audience, but it appeared to be an older crowd mainly consisting of young adult working men, many still clad in their work gear. Youngsters like themselves were in a distinct minority.

Johnny added, "Well, Dara, we might be in the minority age-wise, but look at all those caps and overalls – if there's one longshoreman in this crowd there must be a thousand. I recognize a lot of them from the work gangs that our dads have been in. Sure, I'm starting to wonder now if my Da will have a quorum at the union meeting tonight. At supper, he seemed to be pre-occupied with some important question that was to be debated and voted on. I hope he's not left high and dry for an audience in competition with 'the Prophet from Weeping Water, Nebraska!' But how on earth could my Da and yours ever choose a simple union meeting over something as thrilling as this?"

The American Cadet Band had already gone through most of the well-known American marches, including all the Sousa pieces. The boys knew them by heart and especially liked "Stars and Stripes Forever" that Sousa had written only four years earlier but which was already considered to be the standard American march. But when the Cadets struck up their next piece, launching boldly into "The

Wearin' of the Green," you'd have thought that Saint Patrick himself had drifted down from heaven and taken up the conductor's baton and was now leading this band of mortals. The sound of the cheers lifted to the rafters, and in this huge and beautiful auditorium that was some ways up!

> *Oh and Paddy dear and did you hear the news that's going round?*
> *The shamrock is forbid by law to grow on Irish ground.*
> *Saint Patrick's Day no more we'll keep, his color can't be seen,*
> *For there's a cruel law against the wearin' of the green.*

Yes, indeed, it did seem that all the Paddies had, in fact, heard the news! And now they were responding with the greatest possible enthusiasm. It appeared that the entire assemblage knew all the words, as did the boys. Many were now singing these words in unison, with more energy than musical precision, however, along with the Cadets' shining and triumphant instruments. The crowd displayed the same verve usually reserved only for the most patriotic of American anthems.

"Perhaps," Johnny proclaimed proudly, "this is our new national anthem for this one night, at least!"

The Cadet Band played only the first two verses of this Irish favorite. The crowd was not satisfied, however, and it continued to sing, *a capella*, until the conductor finally relented and joined back in with the instruments blazing away, and with even more emphasis and joy than before. He, too, knew how to read his audience – especially this crowd on this particular night.

> *And if the color we must wear is England's cruel red,*
> *Then let it e're remind us of the blood that we have shed...*

Precisely at eight o'clock, a delegation consisting mainly of local Irish politicians made its way to the stage. They were proudly led by Councilman Joseph E.F. Connolly, the master of ceremonies for the evening. Connolly was accompanied by fellow Councilman F.F. Driscoll and Democratic City Committee member Bartley J. Curran. This all-Hibernian delegation now escorted the first speaker, Congressman John J. Lentz of Ohio, onto the stage to thunderous applause. It didn't matter that few in the crowd had ever heard of this Midwesterner, for wasn't he a Democrat after all?

Wasn't that the only credential that truly mattered on this particular evening? Had not Lentz travelled all the way to Maine in the very middle of winter along with William Jennings Bryan? This was all that the crowd needed to know about him, and he was boisterously cheered while warmly returning his gratitude to the appreciative crowd. This was something Johnny had once heard described as a "mutual admiration society." The crowd loved the speaker and he returned their love. Lentz was now finally in place. Once order was restored the night's festivities were about to commence – what a time to be alive!

It took several minutes for those assembled to fully calm themselves before allowing Representative Lentz to begin his formal remarks. But he had this audience in his pocket from the very first moment with his playfully sarcastic salutation which he did not deliver until absolute silence had been achieved.

"I'd been told that there were very few Democrats in Maine…"

The amused speaker could hardly continue as this brief opening remark called out a visceral response from the audience. They had been told, instructed really, throughout their adult lives that they lived in a Yankee and Republican stronghold, but now they were loudly howling in mock protest to let the seemingly innocent and widely-grinning speaker know that he had clearly been misinformed!

Congressman Lentz next remarked upon the overwhelming reception given to his travelling party at the Union Station, at the Falmouth Hotel where they would be staying, and finally at the admission-by-ticket-only banquet currently going on in another part of the Portland City Hall. In that large room, more than 400 Maine Democrats were dining with "Colonel" Bryan, as he was sometimes ceremoniously called, with an additional 800 or so in the gallery. At this first mention of the name of the "Great Commoner," the overflow crowd in the auditorium again erupted with heartfelt emotion.

Johnny turned to Dara and had to shout to be heard over the din, "We've both heard of Daniel O'Connell and his 'monster meetings' back in Ireland, but they could hardly have been as loud as this gathering tonight."

Representative Lentz was an excellent orator. Although maybe not up to the highest standards of "The Liberator," as O'Connell was dubbed for helping to gain Catholic Emancipation in Ireland back in 1829, Lentz was gifted enough to make Johnny wonder if the Democrats had made a mistake in not saving him for last. There was more to come, however. Lentz then spoke earnestly concerning accountability and of the need for openness in government.

"Good governments are like good men, their record an open book; bad governments, like bad men, have much to conceal."

The crowd was in complete accord with their speaker, most nodding their heads vigorously in support. Lentz criticized the foreign policy of the present administration, specifically naming President William McKinley and his trusted advisor Mark Hanna. At each mention, Lentz's snarling citation of either of these names elicited boos and cat-calls from the partisan and enlivened assembly.

"Let us be honest with ourselves and with the world. If our real purpose in the Philippines is to carry home as the spoils of war their cheap labor and their cheap commodities, let us be manly enough to say so. If our real purpose is to use the Philippines as a fulcrum upon which to rest our crowbar and pry up the commerce of the Orient, let us have the courage to say so, and not with hypocrisy and cant add to the sacrilege that has already disgraced nearly every generation of humanity by pretending that we are doing God's service."

The crowd was attentive and responsive to his every point, even if they didn't all understand the precise meaning of each word or phrase. Lentz next referenced past imperial nations.

"In our effort to imitate and pattern after Europe, let us not forget that the empire of the Romans came to naught, and let us not forget that the Mohammedan advanced from province to empire with sword and fire and yet came to naught. Spain, in all her pomp and in all her wealth, weakened herself, destroyed herself, when she became vainglorious, and today we see Great Britain in her decline."

Lentz's latest rhetorical flourish reminded Johnny of an ancient Irish verse which he had memorized and that now seemed to reflect precisely this same message. As with much well-loved verse, this also seemed timeless in its universal truthfulness.

So now, Johnny softly intoned it almost to himself:

The world hath conquered, the wind hath scattered like dust
Alexander, Caesar, and all that shared their sway:
Tara is grass, and behold how Troy lieth low-
And even the English, perchance their hour will come!

It was at this very point, just as Lentz advanced from ancient Rome to address Britain's current problems that the intensity of the crowd, which was already at a fever pitch, seemed to completely boil over. Dara and Johnny were not least among them in the ecstasy that seemed to shake the City Hall building to its very foundation.

"If any other evidence is necessary to show her decline, it is sufficient to remind you that while Great Britain has boasted for hundreds of years that she is the proud mistress of the seas, yet we have seen her for many weeks with battering rams and Krupp guns so weak and impotent as to be able to break even so much as a window in the humblest little homes in the land of the Boers."

The almost hysterical reaction to this reference to England as the "proud mistress of the seas" – apparently unable to advance into the Transvaal of South Africa – had forced Lentz to smile. He then briefly suspended his speech while seeming to reflect on the effect that these carefully chosen and pointedly pugnacious words were having on his audience. His timing was flawless. Lentz clearly knew that he had the crowd in the palm of his hand. He was not about to let them slip through.

Evidently, Representative Lentz had read this audience properly, as witnessed by his next reference to Ireland, directly and satirically, in the style of Jonathan Swift's *Modest Proposal*. The gifted speaker suggested that the McKinley administration in Washington, D.C., might want to consider offering England twenty million pounds (Sterling) for the purchase of Ireland so that it could be used as a "coaling station" on our way to commercial domination of Great Britain and all of Europe itself!

Sensing the strong pro-Hibernian and anti-British nature of this crowd on this particular night, Lentz then tantalizingly concluded with his hope that, "Some day Old Glory may be the emblem of 'peace on earth and good will to men,' and that Great Britain may yet become a republic, and that an Irishman may be elected her president!!"

The howls, cat-calls, and hosannas rang to the very heavens. It was just before nine o'clock and the next speaker, former Governor John P. Altgeld of Illinois, a hero of the American labor movement, had already entered the hall but had wisely deferred while Lentz was still in full rhetorical flight. Chairman Connolly eventually introduced Altgeld, who picked up almost seamlessly where Lentz had left off.

He expounded upon what he called two contrasting forms of government, "That by oppression of the governed and that by the consent of the governed…"

From there, Governor Altgeld continued his attack on the McKinley administration, claiming that they were mainly serving their own political and financial interests in the Philippines, and elsewhere. In a remark clearly designed to highlight a Portland connection, Altgeld then added, "Even Thomas B. Reed became disgusted with the present administration and called it a 'syndicate administration.'"

Many Democrats in the auditorium loudly applauded this positive comment about the recently retired Republican House Speaker, probably for the first time in their lives. This was indeed a day of firsts. The boys, however, applauded even more loudly since by now they sensed that they had a certain window into Reed's very soul, so to speak, to say nothing of his famously biting sarcasm. The former Speaker of the U.S. House, it was widely reported, had once totally disarmed a fellow Congressman with the sharp barb, 'That man never opened his mouth without detracting from the sum of human knowledge.'

Reed's sarcasm seemed almost Irish to these boys who had both been weaned on this verbal skill. Before the applause had completely died down, Dara leaned over and whispered sincerely into the ear of his friend, "I wish Reed had been born a Democrat!"

The greatest and loudest cheer of the night, however, was reserved for the arrival in the hall at 10:15 p.m. of the man they had all come to hear – the great orator from the plains, William Jennings Bryan. He strode to the stage like a conquering hero, accompanied by the Cadet Band's stirring, if somewhat presumptuous, rendition of "Hail to the Chief."

Bryan's rhetoric matched his reputation and the crowd was never disappointed. He chose to speak on three specific and inter-connected themes: the gold standard, trusts and monopolies, and finally the dangers and threats of imperialism. Concerning the gold standard, Bryan followed the lead of Representative Lentz when he asked the audience to consider that Great Britain had suffered financial and other "reverses" in its attempts to "conquer a few Boers in South Africa."

He then proceeded to ask his audience to consider logically, "What then will become of your gold standard if England ever gets into a real war with a nation of her size?"

As the raucous applause for this line was starting to die down, someone in the back of the audience loudly and provocatively shouted out, "Let them try on

Ireland for size!"

That Hibernian challenge elicited a roar of approval from the partisan and nationalistic crowd and a broad smile from the speaker.

On the issue of monopoly, the Nebraskan singled out Mark Hanna for particular criticism and then made a claim that, "The Republican Party has no disposition to try to control the Trust evil."

But Bryan's fiercest and most pointed remarks concerned the present American military misadventure in the Philippines. He asserted that McKinley and his cronies had trampled on the Declaration of Independence itself and even on the spirit of the founder of their own party, Abraham Lincoln, who had often claimed that this sacred document was the foundation of our Republic.

Here again the speaker was on solid ground and essentially in agreement with former Speaker Reed. Bryan echoed Lentz's earlier comments, and Reed's own published statements on the threats of imperialism. He then issued a warning to the crowd. "No nation ever went into the empire business that it did not fail and fall into decay. This has been the history of the whole world and it will always be so…. The Democratic Party stands for the erection of another republic in the Orient. The Republican Party stands for the erection of an empire here, and a despotism in the Orient."

Bryan concluded his speech with a predictably religious flourish, for which he was already universally renowned. With the crowd now entirely on its feet, he shared his sincere and firm belief.

"If the Republican Party was to prevail, scripture will be reversed and instead of the mortal putting on immortality, the immortal shall put on mortality and it shall then die!"

Before any of those assembled realized what was happening, the golden-tongued orator acknowledged them one last time, gracefully waved his hand to the crowd, and departed the stage. A tremendous surge of humanity pushed to the front of the building in a vain attempt to touch the hand of their hero, whether he be mortal or immortal – but alas their efforts were all for naught. William Jennings Bryan had been with them, he had lifted their spirits to new heights, but now he was all too suddenly gone. The enormous crowd was alone with its tumultuous cheers!

"Always leave them wanting more, I've been told," Dara quipped when he saw what had just transpired from the relative tranquility of their comfortable first balcony perch.

"What more could any one man have offered us?" Johnny asked. And he then opined on the significance of this evening, "These three speakers have given us the facts and have plainly laid out their points of view, but now it falls to the likes of us and all those in this building tonight to move things forward from here. Bryan proposes but it's up to the common working people to dispose, it seems to me. That's what a democracy is about. I wish the women could vote, because I know of at least two mothers here in Portland who would cast their ballot for Bryan. In any democracy like ours, the will of the people is unpredictable, but it will always prevail whether we agree with it or not. We'll now just have to wait for ten more months to find out what the will of the people of America actually is! I only wish that the entire state of Maine could have been here with us tonight to hear Bryan's words. But, at least, Dara, weren't we the lucky ones? What a time to be alive!"

Chapter 16

A Labor of Love

"Ligfeach an taoide tuile ort a' breathnú uirthi."

(One would let the tide come in while looking at it.)

– West of Ireland Gaelic saying

"She's the lucky one. Her mother's last, and a baby girl – plenty of everything to go around!" Mary's midwife, Monica Lydon, exclaimed. They shared many things in common, including having a bit of wisdom that usually rang true for every occasion.

"But," Mary now quizzed her friend, "how can you be so sure that Helen will indeed be my last?"

Monica demurred, but somehow Mary doubted whether this time Monica's wisdom was entirely on target.

After spending nearly the entire day with her older companion, and even assisting in her own small way with the birth of Mary's tenth child, Nora Ward now took her leave to finally return home. She gave her heartfelt blessings to all there, but especially to both the mother and newborn child. In the fashion so typical of Nora, she optimistically proclaimed, "I venture you'll both sleep well this evening, *le cúnamh Dé*."

It was now approaching eleven o'clock. Despite the very late hour, Mary's curious children had only recently retired to their own bedrooms after being allowed a second final brief visit with their mother. This had been permitted primarily to assure them that all was well, but it also gave them yet another opportunity to view the baby. Bridgie had stayed on much later than usual to assist in putting the younger children to bed, although most were still awake.

It had been a long day for Bridgie too, but now she had the help of Johnny, who had just returned home from his own political odyssey that day. It had ended with the thrilling rally at City Hall. Johnny could see that there had been at least as much excitement in his own home on this same evening since the birth that he had witnessed, at a safe distance, nearly four hours earlier.

The children liked to tease Bridgie, or Birdie as the young ones called her, insisting that their eldest brother had eyes for her. This always caused her to blush, for Johnny was surely a very handsome young man who at the age of sixteen was less than one year older than she. And although Johnny may not have revealed any obvious romantic interest in her, Bridgie certainly had eyes for him!

Bridgie Cronin hadn't grown up knowing Johnny all that well, as she had attended parochial schools while Johnny was the product of the Portland public school system. But soon, perhaps, Johnny would start to take notice of girls, and according to Mamie at least, Bridgie was certainly a "good looker."

Her father, Dan Cronin, owned a small grocery just east of the corner of Fore and India Streets near the Thomas Laughlin Company. From around the back of this shop Dan would often sell "split," a mixture of alcohol and water, either by the pint or half-pint. Johnny clearly admired Dan Cronin's gumption. He had more than once stated to friends that he, too, would someday like to own a small business like that of the Cronins.

~ ~ ~

The children still had a hard time going to sleep, and their questions to young Bridgie were coming a mile a minute. Each of the children was trying to ascertain what the birth of this new sibling would mean for them specifically. When Peg was told that she would no longer be the youngest daughter, a role that she had studiously milked for all it was worth, she was predictably miffed.

As was her style, Peg showed her displeasure mightily, and that had caused Bridgie to issue a warning to her, "What a puss! You'd better be careful, Peg, lest that sour look becomes frozen on your face!"

But when Míchilín was informed that he would no longer be the youngest child, he promptly burst into tears and plaintively shrieked, "Me still want to be the baby!"

All the others laughed heartily at his juvenile protest, even Peg, causing Michael to place his hands over his face and eyes so that if he couldn't see them, they clearly couldn't see him either. He often hid in this manner, especially whenever Peg was pestering him.

A nighttime story was traditional in the Folan home, usually provided by their mother. Johnny fondly remembered most of these stories, legends, parables, and riddles that his mother had lovingly shared with him while growing up. Mary had also often asked her first-born puzzling and taxing questions. 'What would you do in this case? How would you solve this problem? What would be the most fair outcome in this situation…?'

Johnny now realized that this was Mary's way of imparting to her children the difference between right and wrong, always combined with a sense of responsibility. Most importantly, this helped each of these children to develop the ability to think for themselves. Johnny greatly respected his mother for this wonderful gift. He now wanted to give the same to his younger siblings, as well as to any children that he might have some day.

When the children were finally all in bed, all eyes and ears, including Bridgie's, were firmly fixed on their eldest brother. When Míchilín again pleaded, "Tell me a story," Bridgie jokingly repeated a funny jingle that she had once heard from Nora.

"Tell me a story, tell me a story, tell me a story and then I'll go to bed. Tell me about the birds and bees. How do you make a chicken sneeze? Tell me a story and then I'll go to bed!"

They all laughed, especially when Peg queried in all seriousness, "How do you make a chicken sneeze?"

Johnny proceeded to deliver Míchilín's choice of a poem, which the youngest always called "Polly Veer." It started, "Listen my children and you shall hear of the midnight ride of Paul Revere…"

After just a few of the many verses of that epic poem, all that was ever needed to please Míchilín, Johnny progressed to one of his own Longfellow favorites, and this one seemed highly appropriate given their present circumstances.

> *Between the dark and the daylight,*
> *when the light is beginning to low'r,*
> *Comes a pause in the day's occupation*
> *that is known as the Children's Hour.*

As Johnny recited all of these lines from memory, Bridgie marveled at his grasp of these verses. He spoke with perfect cadence and with all the appropriate emotion and style. She could be happy, she was dreamily thinking, with someone like Johnny Folan.

As he continued, Bridgie wondered why she had not been taught these lovely

Longfellow poems in her parochial schooling, or why these were primarily only taught in the public schools. Longfellow was, after all, "America's Poet of the Heart" and a native of their own city, for heaven sake. That alone should surely qualify him for more attention, even from the nuns.

Johnny had learned several other poems by heart, including *The Wreck of the Hesperus, The Lighthouse, The Psalm of Life,* and Bridgie's very favorite, *My Lost Youth.* The latter was Longfellow's beautiful and moving tribute to his own place of birth, and also theirs, Portland, Maine:

> *Often I think of the beautiful town that is seated by the sea.*
> *Often in thought go up and down the pleasant streets of that dear old town*
> *And my youth comes back to me.*

Bridgie, to her delight, had heard Johnny recite *My Lost Youth* many times. She even had on one occasion boldly voiced her opinion that the phrase "seated by the sea" might someday make a wonderful title for a book about Portland. But the only Longfellow poem ever taught by the nuns was *The Psalm of Life,* along with its thoughtful and reverential lines, such as, "Dust thou art to dust returneth was not spoken of the soul," and its even more evocative image, "Footprints in the sands of time."

Johnny wasn't taught Latin, and Bridgie wasn't taught much poetry. It was a mystery to them both why the schools of Portland, parochial and public alike, couldn't simply decide what was best for all of the children! Johnny was now finally about to conclude *The Children's Hour*:

> *And there I will keep you forever, yes, forever and a day,*
> *Till the walls shall crumble in ruin, and moulder in dust away!*

The youngest were already sound asleep. Even though the older ones were still trying to pay strict attention, Tom, Joe, and Agnes each had heavy eyelids. Bridgie, long after the conclusion of this last poem, realized that her own eyes were fixed squarely on Johnny. Tonight there would be no need to tell Irish ghost stories, such as *Hockamocka,* or any of the legends of ancient mythical Irish heroes such as Fionn MacCumhail or Cú Chulainn, better known to the youngest Folans as "Phil McCool" and "The Most Man." Even these mythical heroes needed their sleep this night.

And so it was that Johnny now put a postscript on this day for all of his siblings, those still barely conscious and those who long ago had drifted off to some peaceful dreamland. He now softly sang for them all, and also for Bridgie, the well-known words that Coley had taught each of them in turn. It was the Folans' favorite song of longing for Ireland and the pining of aging parents for their emigrant children:

I'm a long way from home, and my thoughts ever roam
To old Ireland far over the sea.
And my heart it is there, where the skies are so fair,
And old Ireland is calling to me.
There's a bright gleaming light guiding me home tonight
Down the long road of white cobblestone.
Down the road that leads back to that tumble-down shack,
To that tumble-down shack in Athlone.

~ ~ ~

In another part of the house, Monica was in the process of reminding Mary about the many important items that she already knew only too well.

"The breast is the ticket for Helen tonight, Mary dear, and for the months to come. Who can tell what good will come to her from her mother's milk? I've heard that some Yankee women on the Western Promenade hire our own young Irish mothers to suckle their children for them – can you imagine the likes of that? Imagine not wanting to cradle and comfort and feed and protect your own holy innocents! Maybe that's why so many mothers today don't have proper control over their own children when they grow older – sure the bond was never properly set when they were infants. 'Raise up a child in the way he should grow,' as the Holy Book says. It doesn't seem to mention anything about letting someone else do it for you!"

Mary wondered from where that particular sermon had originated. Monica, in addition to her substantial skills as a midwife, was also locally regarded as a kind of inspirational counselor who imparted gems of wisdom along with the skilled touch of her trained and helping hands.

Monica then added, "And never forget, Mary, it seems that the breast is also your best protection against having another child too soon. You've been delivering regularly every two years or so since I've known you, and young Helen is no exception to that. Most midwives, including myself, believe that feeding by the breast might give your body a signal that your attention is needed elsewhere for the baby you already have and that you're not yet ready for another anytime too soon. It's no guarantee, I know, but somehow it seems to work after a fashion. And you've already done more than your part to grow this family and this city, I'd say!"

"What about poor Míchilín?" Mary inquired. "He's mostly weaned but he does still come to me occasionally at night even on his weakened leg."

"Ah, the *créatúr*, that'll have to stop now that Helen's here, I'm afraid. She'll be enough of a burden for you, and sure Michael will be alright now that you have him off to a good start. I'll feel better about him as soon as his leg strengthens, and, please God, that will be soon. Is Mamie still giving him the treatment that the doctor suggested, with alcohol wipes and the nightly rubbing with warm oil?"

"She is, faith, and Míchilín seems to thrive on the attention – but there doesn't seem to be much of a change with his poor leg…"

"Perhaps then another visit to the doctor is called for, Mary. Ask Coley or Johnny if they'll take him, or even young Bridgie – she's almost a member of your family by now. And remember, with Helen you'll be eating now for two! You've got to keep up your health and your own energy or you'll be no good to anyone, least of all Helen."

The loving midwife was imparting centuries old wisdom as well as lessons learned by Monica through her many years of experience. It was now being given to one who had already experienced childbirth ten times over, even as young Helen hungrily and noisily sucked and slurped at her mother's breast. As often as she had experienced this sensation, it never seemed to grow old for Mary.

As she gazed down at her Helen, Mary joyfully uttered a phrase in Irish for which the Joyce's back on *Inis Bearacháin* would later become locally famous, "*Ligfeach an taoide tuile ort a' breathnú uirthi* (One would let the tide come in while looking at it.)"

After they both paused to reflect on the beauty of that lovely image, Mary continued, knowing that her friend was soon about to depart, "Thanks, Monica dear. You've been a great comfort to me, as ever. I'm grateful for your being here with me on this night yet again. I'll bring something over to you as soon as we get straightened out and get a little money saved, please God. I'm alright now, and

Mamie will stay with me until my Coley comes back home from his union meeting – he promised me that he'd be right along as soon as it ended."

"Do you think he knows that he has another child waiting at home, Mary?"

"Not yet, but he will soon enough, the *creatur…*"

Monica departed, but only after giving Mary and young Helen a blessing and the warm smile of a true friend. Whatever would Mary do without Monica? She had been such a comfort. Mary knew that in Portland the trend was shifting toward having your children born at the Maine General Hospital, but that seemed so foreign and strange to her and to most other longshore wives, especially with a midwife like Monica available to help with home births. What would the folks back in Galway have to say about this fancy modern notion of going into a hospital for something as natural as giving birth? For another important consideration, it was simply more affordable to have children at home. Maybe the women on the Western or Eastern Promenades didn't need to consider this, but cost was always front and center in Mary's mind – it simply had to be.

~ ~ ~

Johnny had walked Bridgie most of the way to her home, something that was now happening more frequently. He then returned to his home and was finally alone with his mother and young Helen. It had been an eventful day for them all, to say the least. When Mary asked about his afternoon at school, Johnny artfully changed the subject. But Mary, always one for pushing as much education onto her children as their young minds could absorb, recited for him a short phrase from the beginning of an ancient Gaelic poem, *"Aoibhin beatha an scolaire* (Sweet is the scholar's life)."

Although he felt somewhat guilty for again mitching from Portland High School, on reflection he was quite sure that he wouldn't have given up his experiences this day for anything school could have offered. And unless the infamous "mothers' network" of Portland would reveal any of his secret undertakings, Mary would be none the wiser. Yet, being Irish, some guilt would always be there, if only at the margins. Johnny gave Mary and Helen his blessings, leaving them in the care of his sister Mamie until Coley would finally return. Johnny then proceeded to his own bed where he fell soundly asleep almost before his head hit the pillow. Sweet, indeed, was the life of this scholar.

Mary thought to herself that she'd better ask Johnny or Mamie to register

Helen's birth at City Hall as soon as possible. She could never recall if she had ever registered young Michael since there was so much going on at the time of his birth. It was probably too late for that now, she reasoned, but sure what would be the harm? Anyone would just have to look at him to see that he was born – that was just pure common sense! Paperwork, official documents, legal statements, these were all the stuff of confusion to Mary, and even more to Coleman. The only official document Coleman proudly acknowledged was his proof of citizenship – his "shitizen papers," as he called them. Now American citizenship was indeed something to boast of, as he often had publicly done.

"Daide will be home soon, Máma," said Mamie in an attempt to reassure her mother and, perhaps, also herself. "His meetings usually last only a couple of hours and it started at eight o'clock. I know he'll be home with you soon." Mamie then repeated this last sentence, but more plaintively the second time.

Mary declared to her eldest daughter that she was now quite alright and implored her to get some rest herself. Mamie dutifully bade her mother good night, asking her to call out if she needed anything as she would not be able to sleep until she knew that Coley had returned. Mamie had often locked horns with her father, this was true, but she was nothing less than a pure godsend to her overworked mother.

It was by this time well past eleven o'clock, but Mary had confidence in her Coley – she always had and she always would.

Chapter 17

Homeward Bound

"The dreams of the first generation are lived by the second!"

– Kate Moira Ryan from *Leaving Queens*

As the longshore union meeting broke up, several of the joyous members had headed west. One small group was celebrating with their new hero, Dan Lagerstrom, at Thomas J. O'Neil's small place on Center Street while most of the others traipsed downtown toward James McGlinchy's saloon at 236 Federal Street. The Mc-Glinchys were well known in Portland for their involvement in semi-permanent shenanigans concerning their legal and illegal trade in liquor.

For a time, McGlinchy had a famous brewery on Munjoy Hill at the corner of Waterville and Fore. This was said to be one of the last buildings used exclusively as a brewery in Maine since they had been banned by strict local prohibition ordinances passed by Neal Dow, and the Women's Christian Temperance Union. This family with roots in County Londonderry, Ireland, also ran several public houses scattered throughout the city. Longshore patrons regaled themselves by reading stories in the local press that reported on the McGlinchy's legal predicaments and their adept methods of avoiding business closure entirely. Sometimes the family would get off on a technicality, but more often when found guilty they would simply pay the fine and move on – it was "just another cost of doing business," as the senior partner would say!

In past years, Coleman would have joined these longshoremen at McGlinchy's or John A. Feeney's in Gorham's Corner, or at any number of saloons then dotting the west and east end landscapes of the city. He had often imbibed heavily, but today he reasoned that he had transferred enough of his meager wealth to the well-off McGlinchy family. Less than a year earlier, Coleman had been sternly reprimanded by his union officials for multiple bouts of excessive drinking. They claimed that his actions could put other members of his work gang at a disadvantage and possibly in danger. This reprimand remained a source of deep embarrassment to Coleman. Only recently, and at the heartfelt urging of Mary, he had again taken "the pledge" to refrain entirely from consuming alcohol.

Coleman Folan, of course, was not the only longshoreman actively trying to control his desire for the drink. At this very time there were at least nine temperance societies in Portland. The Catholic Temperance Cadets and also the Father Mathew Total Abstinence Pioneers were both popular among Irish Catholics, as was the Sons of Temperance #95 that met on Fridays at 439 Congress Street. This building was well known in the Portland Irish community as it also housed the offices of other familiar organizations including the Irish-American Relief Association and the Portland Longshoremen's Benevolent Association (Society). How long Coley's current sobriety would last this time, allowing him to stay "on the wagon," remained to be seen. But for tonight, at least, he would once again try his best to stand by his promise to Mary.

Coley and two of his friends, including Joe Loftus, walked up Exchange Street all the way to Congress. They were not in a mood to let this evening end quite yet. At the Portland City Hall, just across from this corner, they could see many carriages and dozens of people milling about. There was also loud applause emanating from the large auditorium. It was a reminder that William Jennings Bryan was in town and possibly even addressing the crowd at that very moment.

Coley looked over to Joe Loftus and asked, "I wonder how many of our young longshoremen are in there. Do you think that any of them have heard the results of the voting from our meeting yet? Won't they be surprised? I wonder if your Dara and my Johnny are in there with the crowd. I wouldn't be at all surprised at that! Good for them – I might have even gone myself but for our meeting. Good for them. They're both good boys."

Joe agreed and stated, "Youth isn't always wasted on the young, Coley!"

Whether or not Coley's last assertion about attending this meeting was true would be difficult to say because he was only tangentially interested in national politics. But he definitely knew the significance and the real consequences of victory of one major party over the other – some doors would open and others would close. This, he believed, is the nature of politics, and as his old longshore friend, John Brennan, had often declared, 'Elections have consequences!'

On this night, at least, he'd leave the political burden resting firmly on the shoulders of the younger generation. Coley figured that he'd done his fair share of politicking for one day. The pair then gratefully put their backs to the cold westerly wind and strolled eastward toward India Street and Munjoy Hill. Just past City Hall, and on the opposite side of the street, was Lincoln Park, formerly Phoenix Park.

Passing by the park, Joe turned to Coley and instructed his friend, "That was created as a fire-stop after most of Portland burned to the ground just after the War between the States. It was the worst fire in the country up until then, or so I've been told. That's why the phoenix is on the city's flag, because that bird also arose from the ashes, just like Portland had to on more than one occasion."

Coley nodded, as he enjoyed these bits of history and wisdom imparted by Joe Loftus who was often quite silent in public but usually very vocal around Coley.

Coley then stated the obvious when he thoughtfully added, "Well, there will be no street urchins playing in the water fountain tonight, Joe, unless they have their ice skates strapped firmly on!"

When next passing by the Cathedral of the Immaculate Conception, Joe asked, "Don't you think it's peculiar that many of Portland's largest Protestant churches face directly onto Congress Street, or some other major street, but that our own Cathedral sadly faces onto little ol' Cumberland Street with only its arse end toward Congress?"

This fact was true also of Portland's oldest Catholic Church, Saint Dominic's in the west end, which was originally built in 1833 but now faced onto Gray Street and away from the more prominent State Street. The Cathedral, built after the Great Fire of 1866, was only the second Catholic Church in Portland. Some of their best Irish friends had suggested that this orientation away from Congress Street was an indication of the prejudice against Catholics in Portland. This prejudice was quite evident when St. Dominic's was constructed, clearly against the wishes of many Yankee citizens and land owners at that time. It had continued into the pre-Civil War nativist decades of the 1840s and 1850s, and remnants of prejudice had not yet completely disappeared.

This idea had never occurred to Coley, and he would have to give it some thought. It was difficult for him to grasp the idea of discrimination here in Portland. For one thing, Coley lived, worked, and prayed among his own people most of the time. For another, no matter how bad things might seem locally, as he had often maintained, 'It could never compare with the treatment that the poor farm laborers with no land had received back in Ireland at the hands of brutal English governments and especially absentee English and even some uncaring and heartless Irish landlords.'

Coley's own region, including counties Galway and Mayo ("God help us"), had taken the brunt of this neglect and misrule. Therefore it was not surprising that so many from the West of Ireland were now living contentedly in Portland, Maine, "the next parish west of Galway."

At the corner of Franklin Street, Joe Loftus appealed to Coley that instead of heading immediately home they might pay a quick visit to McCarthy's Tobacco Shop. McCarthy's on India Street, situated only two doors up from Federal, was a favorite hangout for Portland's east end Irish. Upon entering the shop, you would notice tobacco products on the left and various candies and other confections behind the counter on the right. This section represented the "store" – the legal description of McCarthy's. In the back of this small shop, however, there could be found a fairly large and unadorned room with benches around the exterior walls and a beautifully warm and radiant potbelly stove in the very center. The room was, as most Irish would appropriately describe it, very "homely." Its aroma was a sweet mixture of wood smoke and pipe tobacco.

Prominently displayed on one wall of McCarthy's was a life-size portrait of "The Liberator," Daniel O'Connell, together with a handsomely engraved Christmas card from the Honorable John E. Redmond. Redmond had become the leader of the Irish Parliamentary Party at Westminster following the tragically unexpected early death of the "uncrowned King of Ireland," Charles Stewart Parnell, less than ten years earlier in 1891.

John Redmond, together with Lord Mayor Tallon of Dublin, had recently visited Portland during an American tour for the purpose of raising money, allegedly for a Charles Stewart Parnell monument. This Christmas card had been sent to several of Portland's most "prominent citizens" in gratitude for their financial contributions. Joseph McCarthy was more than a little proud of having received this honor, and he was less than shy about publicly displaying this outward symbol of his intense Irish nationalism. His patrons all seemed to share in McCarthy's pride and in his reverence for "Mother Ireland."

Coley had heard amusing stories of similar *sheebins* (semi-legal saloons) in other larger cities. These were sometimes humorously referred to as 'blind pigs' in an effort to avoid the ubiquitous anti-saloon laws. According to legend, the proprietors of these establishments would simply procure a novelty, such as a blind pig, and charge an admission fee for their customers to see this attraction – simultaneously, of course, offering them "free" drinks for their troubles and for their patronage.

As they gathered around McCarthy's stove, as on this evening, Irish laboring men would regularly entertain themselves by speaking on all sorts of subjects. Depending on the age of the group present, the conversation would be either in Irish or in English, or some fanciful combination of both. Sometimes some of the younger sons of these first-generation Irish longshoremen would venture into McCarthy's. This would enliven the conversation with their novel and often unorthodox opinions on such controversial topics as socialism, religion, women's rights, or especially the ever-popular topic of politics. Coley was never sure what to make of this new generation of "corner boys" with their fancy ideas from books. At the same time, however, he keenly anticipated the day when his sons might join in on such discussions or debates and impress his friends with their own "book learning." That would please him greatly.

Coleman Folan was himself illiterate, both in English and in Irish. He had never been properly schooled in Ireland where illiteracy had been widespread, especially in the west. He had worked longshore steadily nearly from the very moment of his arrival in Portland, and there was little time for the "niceties" of life. Coleman's illiteracy, although no source of pride for him, was at least shared by a good few of the other older longshoremen of his generation. He had once been told that at least one in three of this group could neither read nor write, and so at least he did not stand out for ridicule.

Education was seen by the Portland Irish as the primary vehicle by which to fulfill their working-class dreams of financial and social security. Coley had no thoughts of achieving any such social mobility for himself, as his oft-repeated goal was simply to "hold my own." But he and most of those of his generation held out great hope for their children. Mary had often offered her opinion that, 'Education is a precious commodity.'

Coley had wholeheartedly agreed with his wife, even though he had no idea whatsoever what manner of creature a "commodity" was! With some luck and much hard work, their children might someday realize their parents' dreams. And those dreams would be lived out right here, in Portland.

Joe Loftus now took a long slow gulp from his first pint of beer that day, but only after proclaiming, *"Slainte 'gus saol fada* (Good health and long life)."

At this point an older patron of McCarthy's cheerily added, *"Agus gob fluich* (And a wet beak)!"

It struck Coley as somehow amazing that often the smallest amount of alcohol could loosen the tongue of even the most shy or reticent person.

Seán ÓMaille then burst into the room shouting his typically irreverent salutation, "Feck youse all, and alls that belongs to youse!"

At least there were never any females present in McCarthy's who might be offended by what some called Seán's customary use of "the vernacular!"

In another corner of the room, Texas Mike Gorham, Marcusín Gorham's son, was reciting to a small but amused crowd from a piece of doggerel that he called "The Family Overhead."

> *Well, the father sang, and the mother sang,*
> *And the daughter sang as well,*
> *And the parrot sang, and the whole shebang*
> *Gave out an awful yell.*

Texas Mike was a wonderful story teller, a genuine entertainer, and he usually attracted at least this much of a crowd. Coley loved his harmless nonsensical stories, such as the one Mike now relayed about Old Lady Meagher.

"You know Old Lady Meagher? She was good for one big drunk a year, as soon as the clam season was over. She charged 35 cents for all the fried clams you could eat. She'd shack up in a double three-flatter over on Franklin just above Middle where my Da lived. It was $3, or $6 per week including furnishings and heat, and all the cockroaches went with it!"

After the crowd finished laughing, Mike then predictably ended the story with his usual flourish regarding these unwanted bugs, "And the government used to put out free powder for them bastards – they were big Brewsters!"

There was always so much fun to be had at McCarthy's. Coley asked himself why anyone would ever want to leave this place. The conversation on this night was as varied as was the crowd. Someone brought up the Cunningham family and how they were rising quickly in the construction business, and this caused Joe Loftus to add that Mike Greene also had similar ambitions.

In rapid succession in the various parts of the room one could hear a wide variety of discussions. A few older longshoremen were wondering if the next annual July 4th PLSBS excursion would be held at Sebago Lake or on one of the more local Diamond Islands. Another small group was anticipating Tarbucket Night, a local festivity held on George Washington's birthday, and all the booze that would then be consumed. That caused one member of this group to wonder aloud how many of their fellow longshoremen were residing at this very minute at the "Monroe Street College," as the City Jail was sometimes called, sleeping off a night of excessive drinking.

Coley's late-arriving small group joined in to rhetorically wander through such varied subjects as the recent annexation of the area called "Deering," which would thus greatly increase the size of the city.

Then moving on quickly to another seemingly unrelated subject, someone asked, "Did any of ye see that automobile that Maynard Hanson had in town last July? Does any of ye think that them contraptions will replace the streetcars?"

Most opinions concerning the future of these vehicles appeared to be to the contrary. The general consensus of the group was that automobiles were too costly, too noisy, and too smelly, and that there were simply not enough decent roads for them to travel on around Portland, or especially beyond.

"That takes care of that," declared Pat Green, definitively adding as was his usual style, "and the average man can't see much value anyways in them ginks!"

Joe Loftus next brought up the subject of Bishop James Augustine Healy by asking, "Don't it frost you when the Bishop says at the Cathedral, 'Now just one more thing…'? Christ, you know then that he'll keep us all there for at least another hour!"

Bishop Healy was generally well thought of now in Portland. But he had earlier angered many of the city's workers with his strong denunciations of the Knights of Labor (KOL) and specifically its powerful leader, Terence V. Powderly, the Irish former mayor of Scranton, Pennsylvania.

Joe wanted to know what the Bishop had against the Knights or against labor unions in general, and so he asked the group, "After all, aren't unions just for the average working man? And didn't young Dan Lagerstrom give a mighty account tonight of the proper role of the Catholic Church in defending the workers against the bosses?"

"Tell me this, and tell me no more," Phil Conley, who was not a longshoreman, chimed in, "and who is this Dan Lagerstrom anyways?"

At that point Macdara Jennings, one of the most respected of the older longshoremen, spoke up. He was locally regarded as a pure *seanchí* (Irish story teller) from Rossaveal at the western edge of *Cois Fharraige*.

Jennings then instructed the entire gathering. "Young Dan has been to my house a number of times. He's a very fine lad and has great Irish on him. I once asked him what part of Connemara he came from, and do you know what he told me? He says to me that he wasn't from Ireland at all, but from Bay Ridge in New York City! It was there that his father taught him to speak Norwegian and his strong-willed mother insisted that he should learn Irish, too. And he surely has the *blas*, let me tell you. He's the only one that ever fooled me with his perfect learned Irish, and that's saying something. He can remember all the lines of the stories about Fionn Mac-Cumhaill and Gol MacMorna!"

That was one of the strongest endorsements by a native-born Irishman of any second-generation Irish American ever heard at McCarthy's, or anywhere else in this town for that matter. But on this night the more serious conversation next turned to the perennial topic of money, and at first it focused on John Mulkern.

Mulkern owned a small saloon down at 27 India Street. He had recently taken a trip back to Ireland with his wife and his two eldest children. The older men felt that John had been unwise to waste his money in this way. They thought he was only showing off, or "show-boating," as they called it. They wondered aloud why he hadn't put all of this extra money into his business, or to buy a house, something that he could later leave to his wife and children when he died.

John Mulkern had a colorful way of speaking. And as a saloon keeper, he offered bits of his own philosophy about life, even when unsolicited. Regarding making a difficult choice in life, he often said, 'Turn your back whenever you arrive at the crossroads.' In other words, don't look back. But he was also realistic about the rigors and challenges that this new world offered to the Irish, and all immigrants. He regularly stated, 'It's a great country, if you don't weaken.'

This theme of sacrificing for the next generation was quite common, not only among the Irish but with all the immigrant groups in Portland. This country may not have fulfilled the promise of gold in the streets, but newcomers could often find limited amounts of wealth by working on its docks, canals, or building sites. Wealth often eluded these new arrivals, but it would be a different story for their children and grandchildren. The dreams of these first-generation immigrants would be lived by the second generation!

Only a select few of the older longshoremen had been able to arrange a mortgage on a house. "Triple-deckers" or "three-flatters," as these buildings were called in Portland, were particularly desirable but even more difficult to acquire. Coleman had once estimated that as many as ninety-five percent of his fellow longshoremen were renters and likely to remain so. This was irksome to him. It also explained why so many had to live so closely to the docks, as these two neighborhoods offered the only places where they could afford the cheaper rents and still be within walking distance to their place of work.

The few longshoremen who were exceptions to this rule, even though they were admired, were simultaneously envied. In some cases they were even resented and called the "cute ones," simply because they were clever with their money. It was further remarked that they seemed to play their cards too closely to their chest. Some of the younger men argued against the wisdom of tying up all of one's money by buying a home.

Many of the older laborers agreed and seemed to believe that the money could be better invested by buying a saloon or a small grocery store – similar to what John Mulkern, or Dan Cronin, or Joe McCarthy, or John Feeney had already done. This might allow their children to stay in school a little bit longer. Others even dreamed of sending their brightest child off to business school or even to college, or maybe to the seminary if they could qualify.

Coley now turned and confided to Joe, "Sure there must be many smart ways of investing your extra money. I only wish that I had some, even some tiny amount for my Mary left over at the end of any work week. If the rich seem to be smarter than us, Joe, I'd say that's probably because they have the power and the money to do what you and I can only dream of doing – it only makes them look smart. With a little bit of extra money, Joe, we could be dangerous!"

But all of this thinking and talking seemed like a faraway dream that would remain quite out of reach at least for the present. Maybe Johnny or another of the Folan children would be able to use their own native intelligence to fulfill such dreams – don't parents always want their children to complete their own hopes and unfinished business?

It was about this same time that glancing over at the far corner of the small room Coley heard someone calling for "quietness" and then heard the soft voice of a recent arrival in Portland who had come from somewhere between Spiddal and Furbo, or so he thought. This man, one Seán ÓCoistealbha (Costello), was starting to sing in the *seán nós* (old style) a beautiful piece from the very birth-place of Coley's wife Mary. What she would have given to hear this haunting song of longing for home and to be again among friends and family. Coley thought that the song captured this universal desire of all Irish immigrants in

Portland, and beyond – and possibly even of all immigrants everywhere. The singer had the perfect *blas* or intonation, and because the young man who was sitting next to him did not have enough knowledge of the Irish language, Coley gave him his best instant lyrical translation of this piece now being performed, known as *Amhrán Mhuínse* (The Song of Muighinis, or Mynish):

Dhá mbeinn trí léig i bhfarraige nó ar sléibhte i bhfad ó thír
Gan aoinneach beo i mo ghaobhar ann ach raithneach ghlas is fraoch,
An sneachta á shéideadh anuas orm, is an ghaoith dhá fhuadach díom,
'S mé a bheith ag comhrá le mo Taimín Bán, níorbh fhada liom an oíche.

> Were I three leagues, upon the sea, or in mountains far from land
> and not a single soul for company, save the fern and heather grand,
> Snowflakes falling down on me, and a fierce wind blowing them away,
> But to converse once more, with fair Tommy, a stór,
> These long nights would not delay.

A Mhuire dhílis, céard a dhéanfas mé, tá an geimhreadh seo 'tíocht fuar,
A Mhuire dhílis, céard a dhéanfas an teach seo is a bhfuil ann?
Nach óg, a stór, a d'imigh tú, le linn na huaire breá,
Le linn don chuach bheith ag seinm ceoil, gach duilliúr glas ag fás.

> Oh Blessed Mary, what will I do this winter it is coming cold,
> O Mary what have you in store for me for this home and all in its fold?
> 'Tis young of age I leave you, to keen at the very best of times,
> When leaves on trees are turning green and the cuckoo's tune he chimes.

Má bhíonn mo chlann sa mbaile a'am an oíche a bhfaighidh mé bás,
Ó tórróidh siad go groíúil mé trí oíche is trí lá;
Beidh píopaí deasa cailce a'am agus ceaigeannaí is iad lán,
Beidh triúr ban óg ó shléibhte ann le mé a chaoineadh os cionn cláir.

> If my clan were in the neighbourhood on the night I passed away,
> They would surely keen me as they should by dark nights and by day;
> With tobacco pipes they'd wake me and with jugs and kegs salute me,
> There will be three young women from the mountains,
> There to keen for me on the boards.

Is gearraí amach mo chónra dhom as fiorscoth geal na gclár,
Má tá Seán Ó hEidhin i Muínis bíodh sé déanta ón a láimh;
Bíodh mo chaipín is mo ribín inti istigh, iad go ridheas ar mo cheann,
Tabharfadh Paidín Mór go Muínis mé nó is garbh a bhéas an lá.

    And hew a coffin fine for me from the very best of pine
    And if Seán Ó hEidhin is in Muighinis let it be cut from his own hand;
    My cap and nice bright ribbon, fix upon my head so grand,
    And big Pat would take me to Muighinis regardless of the sea.

Gabháil siar thar Inse Gaine dhom bíodh an bhratach insa gcrann,
Ná cuir' i Leitir Caladh mé mar ní ann atá mo dhream;
Ach tugaí siar go Muínis mé, 'n áit a gcaoinfear mé go hard,
Beidh soilse ar na dúmhchannaí - ní bheidh uaigneas orm ann.

    And sailing west by Inse Ghaineamh and let the sails be hanging high,
    Don't bury me in Leitir Caladh for none of my kin there lie;
    Take me to fair Muighinis, where they'll keen me good and loud,
    The sandunnes bright with bonfires – I'll be back amongst my crowd.

The room had, for the first time that evening, become perfectly still. There were even more than a few tough old men with watery eyes, and not just because the Irish are known to be a sentimental people, but because this rendition had temporarily transported them back to a place they longed for over the many miles and, in most cases, many years. Even Dara was greatly moved by what he heard from Coley, and in that instant he wished that his father, Joe, had been more insistent on teaching him the language of his people.

~ ~ ~

Shortly after 11:00 p.m. a few of those younger longshoremen who had attended the William Jennings Bryan address at the City Hall drifted into McCarthy's. Soon thereafter, the conversation shifted from mere money to politics – the real gold standard. Dara Loftus, Joe's eldest son and Johnny Folan's best friend, was among them. He had been to the rally and now arrived flush with enthusiasm and stories. Johnny had opted to return home to look after his mother, but young Dara was far too excited to even think about going home or going to bed.

All other conversations at McCarthy's now ceased as Dara reported to the attentive crowd that a U.S. Representative by the name of John J. Lentz of Ohio as well as the ex-Governor of Illinois, John P. Altgeld, had joined Bryan on this trip to Portland. Young Loftus told the group his thoughts about the speeches, and they were interested in his opinions, especially his proud father, Joe.

Dara had heard that the toastmaster of the banquet, the Honorable Frederick Plaisted of Auburn, in a preliminary speech, had labeled the McKinley government a "syndicate administration." Plaisted further claimed that even Portland's own Republican former U.S. Representative, Thomas Brackett Reed, had come to the same conclusion and had further become disgusted with McKinley over expansionism and specifically getting the United States bogged down in the far-off Philippines.

Another older longshoreman, John Brennan, who was also present at the rally, was the same age as Coleman. But unlike many of his contemporaries, Brennan had always been interested in politics. He supported Dara and told all present at McCarthy's about the explosive applause which had greeted the sarcastic reference by Representative Lentz to the Boer War in southern Africa, especially when he called England the "proud mistress of the seas" that could not advance one step into the Transvaal!

Brennan then enthusiastically proclaimed, "I'm more than surprised to learn that you did not hear the explosive noise from the City Hall all the way up here at the foot of Munjoy Hill!"

Brennan, while on his way over to McCarthy's, had secured an early edition of the next day's newspaper which supported young Loftus and his take on these points. The *Eastern Argus* reported that Lentz's comment, "Called out such wild and enthusiastic signs of the strong sympathies of the partisan audience for the Boers that Mr. Lentz was forced to pause in his remarks and smile at the effect of his own words."

What the paper seemed to miss, but what Representative Lentz apparently had anticipated, because all good speakers must truly know their audience, was that this crowd consisted mainly of Irish Democrats. Therefore, it clearly was not so much pro-Boer as it was decidedly and thoroughly anti-English! Anything that called attention to any form of British inadequacy or ineptitude was bound to win unqualified support from this partisan crowd, as it apparently had. The crowd now gathered at McCarthy's on this evening heartily cheered even at the second-hand telling of this highly emotional episode. It was the next best thing to being there themselves, and far better than simply reading about it in the newspapers!

Coleman usually did not participate in political conversation. In fact, he had hardly heard a word that any of them were now saying. He was still focused on the previous topic concerning home ownership. He was fully aware that he would never be a property owner himself. Too much had already happened this day that needed sorting out and adequate time for reflection.

Coley tried to visualize what his friend, John Mulkern, must have seen during his brief family visit back to Connemara. What he would give for such a chance! Coley had often dreamed of seeing Ireland again someday, and he agreed with a fellow longshoreman who once fervently declared, 'If anyone would ever build a bridge back to Ireland, I would take it!' even though he also knew that this was just an unrealistic and a romantic dream.

Young Dara Loftus spotted Coley in this serious and somber mood and innocently offered him a glass of "near beer" to toast his successful part in the union meeting earlier that evening. Coley, still only half-focused, accepted and instinctively took a big gulp. Immediately, however, he came back to his senses and thought of Mary and of his pledge to her, and to himself. He thanked Dara, but firmly put the half empty glass down on the bar – this was something entirely uncommon for Coley.

With the exception of this one small and inadvertent slip, Coley had stayed, and would continue to stay, on the wagon for this night at least. The taste of beer now in his mouth, however, was both familiar and enticing. He knew that the drink would always remain a very real temptation, one that he would have to defeat one day, or actually minute by minute. It was now clearly time for Coley to take his leave.

As he walked the short distance from McCarthy's to his rented flat on the corner of Fore and Franklin Streets, he was accompanied by young Dara Loftus.

Still focused on the issue raised earlier at McCarthy's, Coley inquired of Dara, "Do you think that any of my children would ever be clever or rich enough to own their own homes here?"

Certainly with so many mouths to feed and small bodies to clothe, Coley's income from longshore work was already stretched well beyond its limits. This had forced his two eldest into the job market much sooner than he, and especially his Mary, had wanted. The added income was needed especially in the slack summer months when the union provided far fewer jobs and there was no compensation or benefits. This forced Coley and many others to try to find manual labor jobs elsewhere on Portland's building sites or along its roadways. But that was the summer, and this was the winter, and although the Irish had an optimistic expression, '*Tiocaidh an Samhramh* (Summer will come),' in reality the summer now seemed a very long way off.

Dara had no ready answer for what he had perceived to be merely a rhetorical question. The two men now paused near the corner of India and Fore to relieve themselves. As the steady stream of warm yellow liquid left their bodies, a trail of pungent steam seemed to follow it up from the ground where it froze almost immediately upon contact.

Dara playfully quipped to his best friend's father, "Beer is a drink you can never buy – you can only rent it!"

It had been a long and a busy day. Coley was thoroughly exhausted and also characteristically late. But he was now much later than usual for a work night. It seemed to Coley that he had travelled many miles since leaving his home for work, some eighteen hours earlier. It had truly been an odyssey – complete with many obstacles, temptations, challenges, victories, and unforeseen adventures.

He bade his young friend good-night and thought that Joe Loftus must indeed be very proud of his son, just as Coley surely was of Johnny and all of his children. As he approached his home the sight of several dimly-lighted rooms surprised him, as he had been anticipating only a pre-midnight darkness. Then the realization slowly started to dawn on him. There was a quiet sound inside as he climbed the few steps.

Before Coley could put his key into the latch, his eldest daughter, Mamie, quietly opened the door for him with a completely unexpected greeting, "Congratulations, Dada, you now have another daughter!"

Several random thoughts raced through Coley's brain in rapid succession at that very instant. A few weeks prior to this day Coleman had repeated to Mary the words recited in the Cathedral by Bishop James Augustine Healy who had preached to his congregation, 'With every new child comes a new blessing.'

But Mary had surprised even herself when she immediately responded to her somewhat astonished husband, 'I wish I knew as little about having children as the Bishop does!'

So now, Coley was about to be faced with a new reality. These confusing thoughts penetrated the very depths of his being. He felt as if he was shouting them out, although he now only barely muttered them, inaudible even to his nearby daughter, "Where will the money come from to feed another hungry mouth? How much longer can I continue to work sixty hours a week through the winter without entirely destroying this tired body of mine? What about the lack of income during the slack summer season alongshore? What would happen if I 'fell off the wagon' again and went on one of my drinking binges for weeks or even months this time?"

Mamie allowed her father the time and space needed to ponder and verbalize these things, as Coley had often muttered to himself whenever confused or over-whelmed. Now Mamie gratefully took the opportunity to proceed to her own bed. The Folan's large and growing family lived on the very edge of poverty, and Coley was right to be concerned. Clearly, Mary was frightened, too. Neither of them could envision any practical alternatives open to support their family. But now Coley lifted his head as he knew that he must face the present like a father and a husband.

Mother and child were resting quietly in the bed upstairs. Little Michael, no longer the *cuidín*, had already been unceremoniously relegated to another room and forced to share a bed with his rival and next-oldest, the bold Margaret who was self-described as her father's "clever daughter." Mary had never really expected her husband to be there for the birth. He had yet to witness the actual birth of any of their ten children – few men ever did!

Mary sighed upon seeing her tardy husband, but she was surely relieved to have him safe and sober at home, whether late or not. She had been wondering to herself if this scene might be repeated yet again in only another couple of years? Every new child a blessing... but hadn't the Folans' blessings enough already?

It had been a busy and demanding day for all concerned. The day had been unusual only for the sheer number of various activities crammed into this one twenty-four hour period. As lamps were finally blown out around the flat, sleep came swiftly to those who needed it most, and now this was particularly needed by Coley. Mary would be at the beck and call of young Helen throughout this entire night and during the many nights to come.

Likewise, Coleman would be at the beck and call of the Portland stevedores. They needed their coal off-loaded by the longshoremen as quickly as possible in order for them, and especially for the large shipping companies that they represented here in Portland, to make a profit. They were in business to make a profit, not to cater to Coleman's needs or those of any of the longshore labor force. He would be waking again in less than six hours. The morning would come all too quickly and force him to test the strength of his back once again against yet another uncaring and unyielding shipload of coal.

Coleman had often remarked upon the irony of his shoveling coal by the ton on a daily basis while his family scrimped and saved to simply preserve their small store of this precious commodity. It was less an irony and more a painful truth, especially now as all of Maine was in the firm grip of yet another mid-winter deep freeze. His friend and fellow coal heaver, Joe Loftus, had once quipped, 'Coal, coal everywhere, but not a lump to burn!'

When Coley repeated that creative line to Johnny, his son had responded that Joe was clever and skilled with words, but that he must have heard that particular line from a fellow ancient mariner. Although Coley smiled, Johnny knew that his Da had not grasped his meaning and that Coley probably believed that Joe had created that impressive sentence out of the clear blue. Johnny made no effort to correct his father. He was coming to the conclusion that learning is a gift, but one that should never be used as a weapon, especially against those such as Coley Folan or Joe Loftus who were largely unarmed. Johnny Folan was always sensitive to this truth, and Mary was there to remind him if necessary.

Today had been the last day of January in the year 1900. It was again turning much colder and windier outside. The loose single panes of glass in the windows of Coley and Mary's bedroom rattled noisily in this icy blast. It was turning colder inside, too, as the coal fire was slowly becoming merely dim embers. Despite Coley's recent pilfering of a few days' worth of precious anthracite, there was never enough to adequately heat their drafty flat, and certainly not enough to waste on heat during the dark evening hours when he and his family would be asleep. The family would have to wait until morning for Mary to re-stoke the life-sustaining fire in the kitchen stove and send them off on their daily missions.

Coleman Folan knew by harsh experience that the new day would bring more of the same. As his head hit the pillow, he continued to worry about how much longer his forty-one year old body could withstand the severe demands of longshore work or the other very real challenges of yet another long and difficult Maine winter. He wondered all of this and more as he quickly drifted off to a much-needed sleep.

What would the foghorn at Portland Head Light soon be telling him about the coming new day? Would the mysteriously swirling arctic sea smoke be forming again and moving like little cat's feet over Portland's inner harbor? Would he be able to pass by McGlinchy's, or Feeney's, or McCarthy's again tomorrow? He anticipated that after work some longshore buddy would innocently tempt him to celebrate together the birth of his new daughter.

Before retiring for the night, Coley had swished away with cold water the lingering taste of beer from his mouth, but the memory of it endured. Had Mary noticed the smell? She surely had a nose for alcohol. He wondered about these and many other things, some of greater and some of lesser importance, as he swiftly drifted off to the relative peace and protection of his dreams – as all the while the sea smoke was encompassing Portland Harbor.

Chapter 18

Between the Dark and the Daylight

"The location may change, but not the Source; nor is it ever exhausted."

– from the *I Ching*

Mother and child were finally alone. The bonding, nourishment, and settling in would now proceed outside of the womb – two separate human beings but connected still by so many tethers. What stronger tie is there in life than that between a mother and child?

The house had stayed quiet for nearly a half-hour since Mamie's departure from her mother's bedroom with some of the gas lights intentionally left burning downstairs. When Mary finally heard the sound of the latch quietly slipping in the front door, she took notice of the muffled conversation between Coley and her daughter. Mamie had been waiting silently in the kitchen for her father's return. Mamie could now fully relax and finally head off to bed. She, too, would be leaving for work in only a few short hours.

Mary would instinctively know within moments exactly what condition her husband was in according to the sound, speed, and the sure-footedness with which her Coley climbed the stairs. Tonight, thanks be to God, his steps sounded steady, crisp, and sure.

Mary was quietly exultant, and she triumphantly proclaimed to her tiny audience of one, "Our Coley is home, Helen dear, so prepare to meet your Daide!" And then to herself Mary softly declared, "Oh, Coleman my dear, how much I love you – in spite of yourself!"

Shortly before midnight, Coley had steadily and swiftly climbed the stairs up to his lovie. He first checked to see that Mary was alright, kissing her gently on the forehead and whispering some personal message for her ears alone. He then gently cradled his newborn daughter in his strong arms and asked by what name she would be known. After being informed that her name would be Helen, Coley turned to his young child and quipped, "So this is the face that will force her loving father to load a thousand more ships!"

What on earth Coley had meant by this strange comment was a mystery to Mary. But Coley often made similar references that she alternatively took to be either brilliant or entirely nonsense – they often seemed to be both at the same time.

He was always saying these fancy words and sentences that certainly appeared to be intelligent, but many times they were equally as perplexing to Mary as to others. Mary instinctively knew that her husband was an intelligent man even though he could neither read nor write. Just like her, Coley loved the spoken word, and even more he loved the precious and complex ideas and thoughts that language could convey.

He said as much once to Johnny, 'Language is a weapon, son, and the person who controls language has the power. That is why the ancient Irish would never intentionally anger or mistreat the *fili* (poets), because they feared that the poets might write disapprovingly about them in verse – and that would last forever. You can say what you will, but they have the power!'

Johnny, who like his mother was quite gifted with words, had once asked his friend Dara Loftus, 'How could someone who is technically illiterate come up with gems of wisdom like what my father does regularly?'

Johnny often wondered about his Daide. He loved and admired him, but there were many times that he just didn't know exactly what to make of Coley. Had he adjusted to life in America, or should he have stayed on the coast of south Connemara? Then, at moments like that, Coley would often cause his adoring children to laugh by saying some intentionally foolish thing to lessen the solemnity of the moment, lest he be taken too seriously. He would pompously entertain his children with complex sentences in English that he had memorized, such as, 'I will intoxicate you all with the exuberance of my vocabulary!'

The children roared their approval of a man who was clearly showing off, "show-boating," and loving every moment of it. Before the laughter had died down, Coley would strike again pointing to Tom or Joe's face and delivering another gem, 'Your proboscis is the outstanding feature of your physiognomy!'

At times like these, Johnny would look at his father in pure amazement. He once asked his bewildered yet equally amused mother, 'What scholar stayed up all night to come up with that chestnut of a sentence, and what on earth do you suppose it means at all in the real world?'

Coley clearly relished these moments. Mary also basked in his reflective glory. His large brood of children looked up to their father in deep respect, especially Johnny, who was the acknowledged scholar of the family.

~ ~ ~

After a precious few moments alone with Helen, Coley gently placed the newborn back into her mother's arms, slipped quietly out of his "go-to-meeting" clothes that were used only for special occasions, neatly folded them, and finally put them away until next Sunday. Hours earlier, he had placed his regular work clothes at the foot of the bed to be ready for him to slip back into early the next morning. Longshoremen always wore the same work clothes all through the work week, with their wives struggling to clean them on Sunday in order to send their husbands off to a clean start again every Monday morning.

Coley promptly slid over to his side of the bed and was now facing away from Mary and Helen. In only a matter of minutes, he was fast asleep. Mary looked at her dear husband, incredulously and perhaps a bit enviously and gently mouthed an old Irish blessing that some had even used as an epitaph, "*Slan agus beannacht le buaireadh an t-saoil* (Goodbye and farewell to the worries of the world)!"

Within a few minutes of falling asleep, as Mary knew well from years of harsh experience, Coley's heavy snoring would commence. Helen would have to learn on her very first night in this cold, cruel world how to deal with Coley's "foghorn," as Mary labeled it, just as she and all the other newborns, all ten now in number, had learned to accommodate it before. The three of them were now alone, and the exhausted mother of the family and woman of the house could finally take her well-deserved rest.

Mary thought of all the ways that she might find fault with her husband for the many things done, or undone, both that evening and over the nearly twenty years since they had been married. Many questions now actively danced in her troubled mind.

Was Coley even aware that she was likely to deliver his tenth child on this evening? Had he not promised to return home immediately after his union meeting? Where had he gone, and why? Had she detected even the faintest smell of alcohol on his breath this evening? Had Coley, or any man for that matter, any idea whatsoever of the ordeal that a woman goes through in childbirth, even with the able assistance of a skilled midwife such as Monica Lydon? Would he now or in the future be able to show anything more than merely a passing interest in this newest daughter, Helen?

But just as quickly these thoughts were replaced by competing ones. The children adored their father, despite his many idiosyncrasies. That was enough for Mary, for she thoroughly loved him too – if only he could now tone down that blasted foghorn of his! Of course, the snoring was not Mary's major concern about her husband, nor was it his habit of telling tall tales, or even his penchant for using words that he did not understand himself – it was the damned drink!

Like so many of his fellow longshoremen, especially other Galwegians now living in Portland, Coley had a fondness for the whiskey, or *uisce beatha* (the water of life) as he called it. It seemed to Mary that it should more honestly be called the "water of death." Coley never disputed her grave concern about the drink, for he knew only too well the consequences of whiskey for his family and for himself.

When Coley was "on the wagon" and sober, he was among the most prominent and respected of longshoremen in Portland. He was greatly admired by all fellow members of the PLSBS, of which he was currently one of the select few remaining charter members. After all, wasn't his "X," his mark, on the original charter? This was simultaneously a symbol of great pride and of great shame for Coley.

'If only I could have written my name properly for all to see,' he often complained to Mary, as he had painstakingly learned to do in the twenty years since the Society's incorporation. Coley had once requested of the union president permission to finally affix his actual signature to the original charter, but this request was denied as the charter was deemed to be an "historic document."

'How elegant,' he had once wistfully murmured to Mary, 'the name "Coleman Folan" would have looked on that framed charter, but I suppose my 'X' will simply have to do. That's who I was when I signed it – I was just the 'X' man!'

When Coley was drinking, however, he was another person altogether. It seemed to his long-suffering wife that there were two Coleman Folans, both inhabiting the same body. Mary supposed this was why local people referred to drunkenness as being "disguised by drink." She knew better than anyone the consequences of his "falling off the wagon." He could be gone for several days, or even weeks at a time. When he would finally return home, his appearance, his smell, and ultimately his shame were almost too much for her to bear. She loved him so very deeply, as did all of his children, but these episodes were becoming all too frequent and that deeply frightened Mary and the entire family, Coley included. Mary in deep despair had once asked her friend Monica Lydon, 'How could such a wonderful and loving husband and father do this to his wife and family?'

Of course, there would be absolutely no money coming into the family's coffers from the union during these drinking binges – they certainly were not considered eligible for sick pay as excessive drinking was seen purely as a personal failing. Mary would have to rely on what little she had put aside, together with the generosity of friends, just to muddle through these trying times. When needed, Johnny had sometimes "loaned" his mother what little he had saved. He had attempted to squirrel away small bits of money from his various part-time jobs in hope of starting his own business one day. He knew full well that he was unlikely to see these "loans" ever again.

"Tonight, Helen dear, your Da has come home sober – that's his first gift to you, and a godsend to your mother."

Some of the Irish called alcohol the "Devil's curse." But Mary had her own response to this suggestion, 'What did the Irish ever do to the poor Divil to deserve such a curse as this?'

Nora Ward once told Mary that she thought it was not so much a weakness, or even a curse, but that it was more like an illness, much the same as poor Míchilín's withered leg. But that didn't seem to ring true, and most of Mary's friends saw it as a flaw in Coley's character, one that only he could correct if he would simply put his mind to it.

Mary was not quite sure exactly what to think about its cause. But what she was absolutely sure of was its consequences. She clearly knew how much her husband's drinking hurt them all, her and their children alike, but probably most of all her dear Coley. When he would finally return home after a drunken episode, Coley would often cry openly and promise his wife faithfully that he'd never do this to her again. But this was the same promise that he had made and sincerely meant to keep, and yet broken, so many, many times before!

The snoring had by now reached a prodigious level of intensity. This seemed a minor inconvenience to Mary, however, compared to the hollow sound of silence whenever Coley was not there in bed next to her. This was especially true during these desolate winter nights which brought both cold and an early and eerie darkness to the streets of Portland. The cold stillness made Portland's streets seem even meaner and more deadly, especially to any poor soul with no home or shelter.

'Where does my Coley spend these lonely nights when off the wagon?' she had asked herself repeatedly in those troubling days? But her husband could not answer for himself. She later learned that many in this condition would avail of the accommodations at the Monroe Street City Jail. On any given night easily a half-dozen or so longshoremen might be found taking temporary shelter there, the vast majority having drunk themselves silly. 'Sure they're harmless!' the beat patrolman was often heard to proclaim. He had said that once directly to Mary, but only once. She had responded by asking, 'But what would you know of the real harm that this causes to their wives and their families?'

Mary, and other similarly afflicted longshore wives, surely knew better than he did that the harm of excessive drinking was as real to the family as to the drunk. That patrolman never made this particular comment again!

Mary now nursed tiny Helen while trying to sleep herself, and she pondered the question of how these sad and confusing memories of their father might play out later in the lives and characters of their children, or even of their grandchildren should they be lucky enough to have them.

Mary now softly questioned herself, "What if this 'Irish curse' is passed on to subsequent generations? Actions do have consequences, so what if any of our beloved children would be forced to carry this same burden? What if they and their families would have to suffer these same nightmares in the future? Who has the worst of it, Coley or his family? When will this ever cease? When will our pain be sufficient? When will the nightmare end?"

Coley was, of course, deep into his own dream world by now. He was deep in the arms of sleep and indeed far from the troubles of this world. Ironically, he looked almost as innocent as little Helen who was now resting comfortably between them in Mary's arms. She, too, was oblivious to everything – she was the true innocent. Mary considered her belief that infants are the only ones that are beyond the cares of the world, but she also knew that even this would not last forever.

Mary's thoughts turned, as they always did with the arrival of any new child, to her third child, poor William, who had survived barely a few weeks. Although he only had a brief time on this earth, William was thought of and spoken of as much a part of the family as any of the others, the survivors. That was how it would always be if Mary had her way and, of course, she usually did. Mary offered a short prayer to William's spirit and an invocation to the powers that be to give Helen a much longer and healthier life than that given to her unfortunate brother. At times like these, she would often think of her own father, William, who was the namesake of her deceased son.

This was Mary's time – "Between the dark and the daylight!" Johnny had often repeated this opening line from Longfellow's *The Children's Hour*, but Mary thought that she understood this at least as well as the poet himself. These all too brief moments between putting her family and her husband to sleep and then waking with Coley and *na leanbh* (the children) early the next morning – this was indeed Mary's time and hers alone! These, she mused, should be called "The Mothers' Hours," these fleeting moments for all mothers to think, to plan, to reminisce, to pray, and to dream. These fleeting moments between the dark and the daylight were among the very few precious things that belonged to Mary and to her alone.

How Mary cherished this time each evening! The day's work was done and the fading coals were still warm in the stove. This was quite unlike the early morning hours, especially at this dreary time of the year when she would have to rise in the dark to stoke the fire and re-warm the kitchen. Mary's kitchen was usually the only truly warm room in their flat. During these precious hours, the house remained quiet, with the notable exception of Coley's rasping foghorn. What a gift was this quietness! Mary had once revealed her thoughts regarding quietness to Johnny. 'Peace and quiet are God's gifts for completing the day's chores.'

Johnny had responded to his mother's belief by once again quoting his poetic hero, Longfellow, who had beautifully put words to this same sentiment in another of his poems, "Each morning sees some task begin, each evening sees it close."

Johnny loved his poetry, and he was able to memorize it quite easily. But Mary loved it best of all. It had become her favorite device for learning the new language of English. Longfellow had reportedly given his opinion that music was the universal language, and he may have been correct in believing this, but to Mary poetry seemed like God's way of communicating to mere earthly mortals like herself.

Now these were the treasured moments when Mary could repeat old stories, legends, and ancient verse that she had learned back in Ireland, as well as to review the new sayings from here in America. These represented simple and meaningful verse – a select few words that could say a great deal. She fondly recalled a favorite children's poem that Nora loved by William Allingham of Donegal:

> *Four ducks on a pond, a grass-bank beyond,*
> *A blue sky of spring, white clouds on the wing;*
> *What a little thing to remember for years –*
> *To remember with tears!*

That was the entire poem! Why did Mary also cry a few tears each time she had recited this to herself? Did it remind her of home or growing up back in Ireland, or of her beloved William, or of happy times with her youthful friend *Éibhlín Ní Laoí* (Eileen Lee) on Mynish? Or did it simply represent the innocence of childhood when life seemed so easy and carefree? She had once stated her opinion to Johnny, 'If God ever were to come back to earth, it would not be as a carpenter or a shepherd, and certainly not as a powerful soldier or world leader, but rather as a poet such as Longfellow, or Allingham, or even the blind Raftery who could see so clearly.'

As one thought will often lead to another, this now brought to mind yet another favorite verse from her childhood. Mary used these minutes and hours before sleep descended upon her to recite from memory. Thus she hoped to fore-stall losing her wonderful store of poems, songs, *seanfhocals* (wise sayings), and heroic verses from ancient Ireland, most of these in the Irish language. Now, with Helen content and finally resting comfortably, she had another set of ears to whisper to and with whom to share these verses. Up until this night, this had been young Míchilín's privilege.

Mary recalled that when she would shortly again awake early the next morning, it would be the first day of spring (February 1 or *Imbolg*) in the Celtic calendar. An appropriate verse of *Antaine ÓRaifteiri's* (O'Raftery's) poem *Cill Aodáin* (Kileadan) now flooded back into her mind:

> *Anois teacht an Earraigh*   Now with the coming of springtime
> *beidh an lá dúl chun shíneadh,*   The days will grow longer,
> *'s tar éis na Féile Bríde*   And after Saint Bridget's day
> *ardóigh mé mo sheol.*   My sail I will raise.
> *O chúr mé i' mo ceann é*   Once I put my mind to it
> *ní stopfaidh me choíche*   I never will linger
> *Go seasfaidh mé síos*   Till I find myself back
> *i lár Chondae Mhaigh Eo.*   In the County Mayo.

Yes, Mary recalled, here in Portland she was by now into the first few minutes of Saint Bridget's Day (February 1), which also marked the traditional coming of springtime – in Ireland, at least. She had always wondered why spring came so much earlier there than here in America. Wasn't it true, as she had once been told, that Ireland was much further north than Maine? So why should the spring be so late over here? Somehow, it just never seemed fair. She loved the four seasons with all of their stunning changes, but the winters in Maine seemed to go on end-lessly and the spring, when it finally did come, was far too brief a respite between the extremes of winter's cold and summer's heat. How she cherished the long gentle green springtime of Ireland. Mary suffered from both of these seasonal extremes, but, as with most of the Irish in Portland, it was the summer's heat and humidity that often seemed the most challenging. The heat of summer, however, was far from being Mary's most immediate concern at the moment.

Mary had convinced herself that Helen was enjoying the soothing cadence of the recitation of these poems. Her child was now sleeping soundly. Spring was a pleasant albeit distant dream for Mary just now as Maine was about to enter what was normally the snowiest and coldest month of the year. Not even the most opti-mistic Yankee would be so bold as to welcome spring on the first day of Febru-ary. Here in Maine, not even the spring equinox on March 21 was any guarantee of warmth or greenery, or even the faintest scent of life for that matter.

Locals called March the "mud season," a time when roads and fields became nearly impassable. In rural areas, fields would thaw during the daytime only to freeze again each night, deeply and thoroughly, thus pushing back the planting season well into May, and often much further. What would any Irish farmer have thought of this bad fortune?

Back in Callowfeenish and Mynish, *Imbolg* harkened to the season when the sheep and cattle would become impregnated, thus ensuring the farmers a steady supply of wool, leather, milk, and meat for the coming year. Maine had its Arctic current, which was bitterly cold for most of the year, but all of Ireland, as has been noted, was washed by the Gulf Stream – a miracle of nature that gave this North Atlantic island its verdant hues and green grass for the farm animals all twelve months of the year.

Mary weighed the advantage of the brilliant blue skies of the New World against the more moderate temperatures, albeit often accompanied by cloud-filled skies, of the Old. It was a wash, she ultimately decided – but better to be washed by the Gulf Stream than this blasted Arctic current. If only she could have the best of both worlds!

Mary pondered these things in her heart, even as her breathing was becoming slower and deeper. She considered the extremes of Maine versus the temperate nature of Ireland. Was it true, she now asked herself, of the people, too? She admitted that she loved the golden and multi-colored Maine autumn with its stunning "Indian summer" – one last gift from nature before it delivered a bitter slap to everyone's face. Right now, however, on the last day of January in the year 1900, the answer for her was an easy one – Mary would take an early Irish spring over a Maine midwinter any day of the week!

During the long months of winter, her rising for work always occurred well before dawn. Often during these lonely hours before the dawn, one large question rattled in Mary's mind – had she done the right thing in leaving Ireland and her family and friends behind? She was familiar with these same sentiments from an evocative Ulster emigration song, one verse of which concluded that it was primarily for financial security that many left the land of their birth. "But to live poor I could not endure, as others of my station; To Amerikay I sailed away, and left this Irish nation…"

Was that the true reason after all? Had Mary, like the Ulster emigrant in this song and countless millions of others, left Ireland purely for the prospect of an easier existence on the other side? "Amerikay" had not been any land of milk and honey, either for Mary or for Coley, or for most of their other dear friends either. But few here would ever admit that truth to their concerned and loving families back in the Old Country. "Amerikay," however, was indeed a land of opportunity as had been promised, but it could also be a land of cruel and bitter challenges and deep disappointments.

The settled Yankee community in Portland was only too happy to have the Irish and other immigrants do their manual labor in times of prosperity, like Coley's work of shoveling coal, or the digging of the Cumberland and Oxford Canal linking Casco Bay to interior Maine all the way to the top of Long Lake. It was this back-breaking work that was offered to them – "skull-dragging" work as the longshoremen called it. Mary, like many other young single women from Galway, had started here as a domestic worker in the home of a wealthy family near Portland's Western Promenade. There was certainly no gold paving the streets of Portland, but here opportunity abounded, at least for those willing to work for it.

Mary's experience as a domestic worker had taught her several valuable lessons, and she often remembered them during this time of her waking sleep. Perhaps most importantly, it had facilitated Mary's use of the English language. That happened not necessarily through interchanges with the family members themselves, for those were few and far between, but rather by communicating in English with the Irish domestics who had been longer in this country. This experience reinforced in Mary's mind a lesson that she had learned long ago in Galway – never assume either the best or the worst about someone until you know them well and can judge them on their own terms.

Mary's first laboring experience had been just as unpleasant as her second experience had been rewarding. Barely off the boat, and only two weeks in the country, Mary had found a friend from Carna who worked at a large hotel in Portland's downtown area and who spoke to her about a possible job. A Mr. Kilmartin did much of the hiring for the large and elegant Falmouth Hotel, often giving a leg-up to Irish "cousins" or friends of friends. At Kilmartin's recommendation, Mary had applied for a job at the home of the hotel owner. His family home was just one street back from the Western Promenade in the most elegant residential section of town.

Mary had heard that most domestics were given a half-day off on Thursdays and Sundays when most of them would walk the Eastern or the Western Promenade, or Prom as they called it, in the hope of meeting others from back home. There might be the occasion to see an Irish boy from her own parish. Then, as she was approaching the ripe old age of twenty, Mary thought that she might include herself in this romantic-sounding promenade!

Dan Lagerstrom had been recently collecting stories from many of these older

Irish immigrants. They spoke colorfully, even in what was for them a second language, and he hoped one day to have a store of these interviews, enough to document the presence of these otherwise forgotten people. One had recently vividly described these promenades to young Dan. 'They were here from Galway to Connemara, Mayo and Corrnamona... you wouldn't hear anything after Mass on Sunday but Irish, up and down the sidewalk. The Munjoy Hill people going west and the St. Dominic's people going east on the other side, before dinner going in to get a bottle of beer if they could. It was a shebeen in our Hall that sold it.'

Mary had once protested to Nora, 'Why don't we women have someone like young Lagerstrom to collect our stories, too? Don't we have something to say? Don't we women hold up half of the households – and all of the babies?'

Young Galway women in Portland, including Mary when she was first here, were employed to do cleaning, washing, ironing, cooking, and the minding of others' children. But on Thursday and Sunday afternoons they, too, could enjoy these far too brief moments of freedom for themselves. Another much older Irish woman, who was unknown to Mary because she hailed from the tiny coastal townland of Cleggan, even further west from Clifden, had once recited to Dan a piece of verse composed here in Portland. Even though it was half in Irish and half in English and only one simple verse added to a much longer familiar Irish refrain, it did represent a cry of freedom and pure joy typified by these highly-anticipated afternoon jaunts. It joyously proclaimed,

Oró mhíle grá, siar aniar Congress Street and back the Promenade!
(O, a thousand loves, to and from the west
along Congress Street and back the Promenade!)"

This Cleggan woman was quite taken by Dan and his marvelous gift for the language. As with anyone that he interviewed, Dan imparted respect and a keen interest in whatever they had to share. Uniformly, they could hardly believe that he was not himself a native speaker. The woman from Cleggan had paid him the supreme compliment for his old style of speaking when she proclaimed, *'Tá blas agus dath ar a chuid cainte.* (His speech is clear and colorful.)'

~ ~ ~

Mary's eyes were finally beginning to feel quite heavy now. But her reminiscing continued concerning a conflict that she had first encountered working for the wealthy family on the Western Promenade. Ironically, it was not so much dealing with the Yankee family itself, but with one of her fellow Irish domestics. There were often one or two such workers who had been in Portland the longest time and who had taken on the manners and graces of their employers. Mary had heard this referred to as "civilities and amenities." It almost seemed as if they were pretending to be Yankees themselves by mimicking their employers in style and accent, as well as in attitude.

One of these Irish Anglophiles, Dervla Rynne from Galway City, had called young Mary a "country bumpkin." But Mary declined to respond, not knowing exactly what these words meant. She therefore tried to weigh whether it was a criticism or a compliment. But later that day when this same woman who was from Spiddal – as luck would have it, in front of the other domestics – referred to Mary as "a common *spailpín* (seasonal farm laborer)." Mary got her drift instantly this time and immediately gave out to her in beautiful but highly colloquial Gaelic – a language that the clergy surely did not know! When she was finished, Mary punctuated her tirade by referring to this pretentious woman as an "*óinseach* (a foolish woman)." The baffled domestic, who by now had lost most of her Irish language, had not understood most of Mary's heated diatribe. However, she did know the meaning of the last overly-emphasized word. Dervla then immediately, and spitefully, reported Mary, the new hire, to the matron.

Mary was dismissed on the spot, without wages as she recalled, after a little less than two weeks on the job. She would sometimes see this same Anglophile "pretender," as she called Dervla, on the streets of Portland. Dervla was still working at the same low-level job as a domestic in the very same house some twenty years on. Mary initially would stare daggers at her, even though eventually she actually felt somewhat sorry for this lonely woman all the same. The woman had neither married nor even had a steady male companion, so far as Mary or anyone else in Portland knew. No children – that would be her penance! *Is mór an trua é* (More's the pity)!

Coleman, however, was not as forgiving as was his wife. For years, whenever he saw this unfortunate lady after Mass on a Sunday, or walking the promenade on a Thursday afternoon, he would often mutter, audibly to those in his presence, 'And there's our own little Dervla Rynne, all dressed up in her only decent outfit, still putting on airs. Sure, she's pure mutton dressed as lamb!'

Mary hardly ever dwelt on the negative. She always preferred to recall the happier memories of her second job as a domestic. She now wistfully reminisced on her pleasant days working at the Falmouth Hotel, Portland's largest and finest, which was the source of employment for many female Irish. She was constantly among friends. She shared many a good time and a good laugh there at the Falmouth, in both languages. It was also there that Mary's familiarity with English blossomed. In addition, the natural wit she was been born with re-emerged. Mary was finding her way in America, but her own kind nature remained intact.

Mary often sadly reflected that language could be a barrier for both the poor newcomer as well as for the more privileged natives of Portland – it hindered both in their ability to understand each other. She had never been a shrinking violet and knew that she was gifted with memory along with intelligence and wit. But how does one demonstrate these gifts in a new and complex tongue? Whose language is the privileged one? At these times in the late evening, thinking only to herself, Mary was constantly amused by the realization that her Yankee "superiors" often made no sense even in their own single native language while she, albeit sometimes haltingly, could come up with gems of wisdom in two!

Mary, naturally, preferred to speak her native Gaelic whenever possible, especially among her own crowd. More than anything she seemed to enjoy the bits of doggerel or nonsense pieces that she had heard in the twenty years since her arrival in Portland. Usually these were told by Irish tongues quite unfamiliar with American traditions or English idioms. She smiled now as she recalled how Mike O'Tuarisc had once confidently proclaimed, 'I think Thanksgiving is on a Thursday this year. Well, that's my story and I'm sticking to it!'

Mike was well known for strongly stating his opinions about anything dealing with Ireland, usually punctuating these beliefs with, ''Tis the truth – I read it in the Bible!'

Patsy Connolly had once complained to Mike about his verbosity. Patsy told him, 'The day you stop talkin' you'll be dead for four days!'

Nora Ward was Mary's source for several of these amusing lines, many coming from her own family both here in Portland and back in Ireland. Her father Jack had plenty of sayings like, if dealing with someone in a hurry, 'The man who made time made plenty of it…'

Mary now grinned as she recalled even more expressions attributed to Jack. In answer to the innocent question, 'What are you looking at?' he would often reply,

'Can't a cat look at the Queen?' Or, regarding any boastful woman, he would proclaim, 'She thinks her geese are swans!' Describing another of his daughters, Nora's younger sister, Jack would claim, 'Her face is her fortune,' and then add that she had 'a winning smile and a coaxing eye!'

Even though Jack was not a native Irish speaker, coming from near Loughrea in East Galway, he would sometimes spice up his sentences with an occasional Irish word. If someone voluntarily offered to give him something, for instance, he might respond, 'You're very *flaithiúil* (generous) today.'

Another of Nora's sisters, one who was married to a Burke from Derrynane, frequently would say dismissively, 'You're no good, and neither was your father before you!' Or to her children, if they were acting improperly, she would dismissively shout, 'You're not allowed!' This sister's husband, Nora informed Mary, often began most sentences with, 'Tell me this and tell me no more...' or the more familiar short salutation, quite common in Ireland, 'Come here to me now...'

These were wonderful phrases, Mary thought, and she hoped that she would never forget them, which is why she repeated them to herself almost nightly. With the exception of young Dan Lagerstrom, few if any of the younger generation seemed interested in capturing these stories or unique phrases for the future. Mary thought that was a great pity and had once grumbled to Nora, 'How will anyone in the future even know that we were here?'

~ ~ ~

By now, Mary was feeling the profound need for sleep. It had, after all, been quite a day for the entire Folan clan. Nine children to care for tomorrow instead of merely eight – and she was still of child-bearing age!

"Good God in Heaven!" she mouthed to herself as she considered that prospect, while being careful not to waken Helen. That was a frightening thought for this woman who just one day earlier had felt stretched to the very limit just to keep her existing household fed, clothed, and warmed.

Mary knew that Coley had similar concerns, especially since she had given up her job at the Falmouth Hotel shortly after Joe was born. Ever since, Coley had become the sole bread-winner for this large and growing family, with the small exception of what little Mamie could bring in, or even any smaller amounts from Johnny. Up to this point, however, this reality had not prevented Coley from enjoying connubial bliss with his still attractive and healthy wife. 'What's a man supposed to do?' he had only recently asked Mary.

They were both aware of the Church's official and firm pronouncement on this question. They could both repeat the official ruling word for word, almost like part of a Catechism for married adults, 'Each and every marital act must of necessity retain its intrinsic relationship to the procreation of human life.'

Neither Mary nor Coley, of course, knew exactly what each of those fancy words meant, as this was exactly the kind of English that threw them both for a loop. But they clearly got the gist of it, and Coley seemed to thoroughly understand this familial obligation. Therefore, and predictably, a new child had arrived for the Folans every two years on average since the day of their marriage. The Folans would qualify, without question, as good Catholics!

Young Helen was sleeping blissfully under her warm blanket. She would sleep in the bed between her parents for these first few months – Mary saw this as a form of "natural" contraception which was certainly more than welcome. She whispered, as she grinned to herself, "Surely, the Church fathers could have no objection to that!"

Johnny had been born nine months to the day from their marriage, and the other children all had arrived as if on cue. Mary intoned plaintively to herself, "Have I not already done my part? Amn't I already a good Catholic mother?"

The naming of the children had always been Mary's prerogative. Coley seemed more than willing to defer, although he had insisted that the first-born female should carry her mother's name, Mary. He had never seemed inclined, however, to name any of his sons "Coleman" after himself and that seemed odd to Mary. That honor might have to wait, Mary mused, for another generation. She had complied willingly and gratefully in the naming of their first daughter, although she insisted on adding Magdalene as her middle name, thus giving her daughter a unique and pious nomenclature – she would be called Mary Magdalene.

As any parent knows, no matter what name you give to your child, the child will eventually determine what it will be called. This daughter had decided in her early years that she would be known simply as Mamie, and so it was to be – a determined shift from the sacred to the secular! Young Margaret, who always insisted on being called Peg, also seemed quite headstrong even at the tender age of four. When Mary had recently asked Peg, 'What are you doing, dear?' Peg had truthfully answered her mother, 'I don't know, Mama. I'll tell you after I'm finished!'

Closer and closer to sleep, Mary now sang softly to Helen from one of the most ancient of Irish songs. It was written about another Helen, or perhaps Eileen, *Éibhlín*, or Aileen, but one who lived years ago in fourteenth century Ireland:

> *I know a valley fair, Aileen aroon. I know a cottage there, Aileen aroon.*
> *Far in that valley's shade I know a gentle maid,*
> *Flower of the hazel glade, Aileen aroon!*

But Mary's favorite line from this lovely song was its powerful and provocatively insightful final verse:

> *Youth must with time decay, Aileen aroon.*
> *Beauty must fade away, Aileen aroon.*
> *Castles are sacked in war, chieftains are scattered far,*
> *Truth is a fixed star, Aileen aroon!*

Yes, Mary dreamed, truth is a fixed star – there are indeed truths in life that are fixed and eternal. The love of a mother for her child, and the hope that all mothers have for their children's futures, and those of their children's children – these are certainly fixed and eternal truths! Mary had often wisely counseled her children, 'Never love anything that can't love you back.' And that kind of wisdom would surely come back as a source of strength in their later lives.

Also eternal is a mother's striving to provide a good life for her entire family, at least while they are all still together. What would Helen's life bring to her in the way of opportunity, chances of marriage, and children of her own? Would this new twentieth century be any more kind to humanity than the one now ending? Would castles still be sacked in war? What would Helen's life be like in America compared to the lives of her many cousins still in Mynish, Callowfeenish, Carna or other townlands of Connemara and along the glorious coastal plains of *Cois Fharraige*? These and other questions she pondered sleepily.

As Mary's eyes were now drooping and sleep beckoned appealingly to her, a lovely vision of the hills and mountains of Connemara, the stately Twelve Pins with their frosty white caps in winter, and the visions in her mind's eye of the silvery-shining hills framing the Irish coast came flooding back to her with pure joy – it was a joy that was almost pain.

These *aislings* (perfect dreams or visions) had warmed Mary on a nightly basis. *Bán chnoic Éireann, oh* (The fair hills of Ireland, oh). Were these visions real, or just dreams?

> *I will make my journey, if life and health but stand,*
> *Unto that pleasant country, that fresh and fragrant strand,*
> *And leave your boasted braveries, you wealth and high command,*
> *For the fair hills of holy Ireland. Uileacan dubh O!*

All this seemed so real to Mary as darkness was fading to sleep, now only a merciful few hours before the dawning of a new day.

"Is glas iad no cnoic i bhfad uainn (Faraway hills are green)," she whispered almost silently so as not to disturb the pleasant sleep of Helen, or that of her loving husband, or the beautiful images from the deepest recesses of her mind where memory alone resides.

These images were fainter now, coming and going, gently and intermittently.

The hills of Portland, Munjoy in the east and Bramhall in the west, were now thoroughly snow-covered and would remain so for months to come. The lambs on Ireland's green hills might sport and play, both in summer and winter alike, but here in America Coley and Mary's nine young lambs likewise had hills on which to romp and play, even though they were now encrusted with ice and snow. Snow was general all over Maine, from its mile-high peak of Katahdin to its craggy and rocky coastline at Acadia and even at nearby Portland Head.

Surely all here had earned a rest from their labors. Coley's snoring had miraculously abated. Maybe he was too tired even for that added effort. Helen's breathing was soft and regular, and reassuring. Mary was being warmed by the physical presence of her newborn nestled close to her, and also by the comforting thought of her dear husband who was surely also dreaming by now on the far side of their bed of their beloved Ireland. Was ever a woman so warmed and so well-loved?

Pleasant thoughts of Ireland were fading now, but they were never completely gone. The Chinese saying was surely true, as Mary believed it to be. 'The location may change, but not the Source; nor is it ever exhausted.'

But exhaustion had captured Mary's body and now, finally, her mind as well.

It could no longer hold onto any further thoughts or images. All was fading into utter darkness and nothingness.

The far-away hills seemed further and further away.
Further and further away and even more far away still. Far away...

Glossary of Irish Words and Phrases

(in order of appearance)

Calibhfuinse – Callowfeenish

Cois Fharraige – Beside the Sea (coastal Galway)

Tír na n-Óir – Country of Gold (America)

Iorras Aithneach – a peninsula in western Galway including Carna and Kilkerran

Talamh gan cios o'n bhliain seo amach – Land without taxes from this year out

Inis Bearacháin – a small island off the coast of Lettermore

amadáin – fools

Ní Chualáin – daughter of Folan

Dia dhuit ar maidín, a Mháire – God be with you this morning, Mary

Fionn MacCumhaill, Diamaid agus Grainne – legendary Irish heroes

Daide – Father

Muighinis – Mynish or Mweenish

Buíochas le Día – Thanks be to God

cuidín – cudeen, the "little portion" or the baby of the family

le cúnamh Dé – God willing or Please God

creatúr bocht – poor creature

Dia dhuit – God with you (traditional greeting, single person)

Gaeltacht – Irish or Gaelic-speaking area

Dia's Mhuire dhuit – God and the Virgin Mary be with you (response)

a chuid – meaning my little portion (term of endearment)

Mac an t-athair – Son of, or just like the father

Tar eis La Féile Bhríde – After Saint Brígid's Day, on February 1st

céili – Irish dance party with live music

cailín – colleen, female

creatúr – whiskey

uisce beatha – the water of life, also whiskey

poitín – moonshine

Tá Gaeilge go leor ag na buachailli bó – The cowboys speak good Irish

seanchi – story teller, local historian

Ná bach leis – Don't bother with it

is cuma – it's equal, no problem

Táimse i mo codhladh, 's ná duise mé – I'm sleeping, don't waken me

Meiriceánach Dána – Bold American

Suigh síos a Mháire – Sit down, Mary

mo leanbh – my children

Gaeilige bhriste – broken (unclear) Irish

Is fear Gaeilige bhriste nár Bearla chliste i mbéal Gael

   – I prefer broken Irish to clever English from the mouth of an Irish person

An glór neamhspleách – A true independent or the independent voice

An bhfuil aon chance ort, no an bhfuil tú squarailte cheanna?

   – Is there any chance with you, or are you already squared off (taken)?

Philipín bocht – poor little Philip

blas – perfect accent, literally means taste

a stoirín – my treasure (term of endearment)

púncán's – Yankee's

leabharlann – library

Aithníonn ciaróg – ciaróg eile – One beetle attracts another

girlín – slang for little girl

gliomaigh – lobsters

fir chomh maith le na athair – men as good as their fathers

dún do chlób – shut your mouth (your trap)

maith go leor – literally good enough; slang for being drunk

ar meisce – drunk

Míle grá le m'anam í is gear go mbeidh sí mór

   – A thousand loves of my soul, it's not long before she'll be grown *zPeigín Leitir Móir* – Peggy of Lettermore (well-known song)

báinín – the thick, lanolin-saturated, woolen flannel material for weaving sweaters

Níl fhíos agam, a Mháire – knowledge is not on me, or I don't know, Mary

craicailte – cracked, or crazy

oinseachaí – foolish women

Breathnach – Walsh or Welch

aithníonn – recognition

buachaillín bán – fair-haired boy, term of endearment

Briseann an dúchas tré suile an cáit – literally, culture breaks out through a cat's eye; what is bred in the bone will emerge

Gaeilgoirí – Irish language learners or enthusiasts

blas – language finesse of a native speaker

cigire – an Irish language inspector

groceire – grocery

seánfhocal – old saying or proverb

Tá failte romhat anseo – You're welcome here

Amhrán Rós a Mhíl – Song of Rossaveal

Diabhail scéal; scéal ar bith! – Devil the story; no story at all

Imbolg – meaning "in the belly"; Celtic first day of spring (February 1st); Christianized to Feast of Saint Brigid signifying rebirth

Anois teacht an Earraigh, béidh an lá a'dul cun sinneadh; agus tar éis na Feile Bhríde, ardoigh mé mó sheoil…

– And now with the coming of spring as the days lengthen, and after the Feast of Bridget I will raise my sail…

Ó chúr mé in mó ceann é, ní stoppaigh mé choiche, go sheassamh mé síos i'lá Conte Maigho.

– Once I put it in my head, I would not stop for an instant, until I was seated in the middle of the County Mayo.

Cill Eadáin – Raftery's poem, Kileadan, about County Mayo

anam chairde – soul friends or mates

Ouist! – Stop!

muise – indeed

laonta – calves and bonnives – piglets

An bhfuil sibh réidh, a Mháire agus a Mháire óg?
  – Are you both ready, Mary and young Mary?

Táim buoich go cas mé lamh leat – I'm happy to have met you; literally, I'm pleased that I clasped hands with you

Tá sé criochnaithe! – It is finished!

dudín – a dudeen or clay pipe

file – an Irish poet

Eíbhlín a'rún – Eileen aroon, ancient traditional song

In ainm an Athair, 's a Mhic, 's an Spoiread Naoimh, Amen – In the name of the Father, and the Son, and the Holy Ghost (Holy Spirit), Amen

Is mór an trua é – It's a great pity

Oíche mhaith, a Mhamaí, agus Dia leat
  – Good night, Mommy, and God be with you

Ligfeach an taoide tuile ort a' breathnú uirthi – One would let the tide come in while looking at it (or her)

Aoibhin beatha an scolaire – Sweet is the scholar's life

sheebíns – semi-legal saloons or drinking parlors

Slainte 'gus saol fada – Good health and long life

Agus gob fluich – And a wet beak (an answer to the toast above)

Tiocaidh an Samhramh – Summer will come

fílí – poets

Slan agus beannacht le buaireadh an t-saoil
  – Goodbye and farewell to the worries of the world

Tá blas agus dath ar a chuid cainte. – His speech is clear and colorful.

spailpín – seasonal farm laborer

flaithiúil – generous

aislings – perfect dreams or visions

Bán chnoic Éireann, oh – The fair hills of Ireland, oh
Is glas iad no cnoic i bhfad uainn – Faraway hills are green

Acknowledgements

First and foremost, to my *anam cara*, Becky Hitchcock, who makes my life sweeter and my every day brighter.

To Michael Lyons and Mary Anne Hildreth of Tower Publishing who took on this task, but especially to Mary Anne who made editing seem like a joy and the complex appear simple.

To those who offered their words of praise for the book, including Gov. Joe Brennan, Secretary of Labor Marty Walsh, Máirtín Ó Catháin, Morgan Callan Rogers, Dr. Ed Rielly, Brian Frykenberg, and Irish Consul Laoise Moore.

Appreciation to those who read and gently critiqued earlier versions of this novel, including Becky Hitchcock, Ellen Murphy, and, in particular, for the careful reading by Catharine Moser, both for her trained eye and her warm heart. Also to Charles Todorich, who in addition helpfully pointed me in the direction of the publisher.

To Rebecca Blaesing, for her thoughtful and creative work on the design of the book's cover. And especially to Holly Ready, for her kind permission to use her beautiful original artwork for the book's cover – this was not the first time that Holly aided me in this most generous way.

Seán Ó Coistealbha, for his evocative translation of the Irish *seán nós* piece, *Amhrán Mhuinse*.

Bob Greene, for his insight into the lives of the early Black community of Portland, and especially for his thoughts concerning Portland's early Abyssinian Church.

Mary Concannon of Norwood, MA, for her ever generous help with Irish words and phrases (any errors therein are my own alone).

And finally, to my colleagues and friends at both Saint Joseph's College of Maine, where I spent thirty-six happy and productive years; and to all those at the Maine Irish Heritage Center who have honored me and have always supported my work over these many years. *Go raibh míle maith agaibh.*

Author Biography

Michael C. Connolly is a life-long resident of Portland's Munjoy Hill. His experiences growing up in what was one of the city's main ethnic, predominantly Irish and Italian, working-class neighborhoods greatly shaped his thinking and have had a continuing influence on his writing. He was encouraged by his parents to be the first in his family to graduate from high school, let alone college.

He earned his B.A. in Social Sciences at Florida Southern College (1973), his M.A. in Modern Irish History at University College Dublin (1977), and finally his PhD in American Immigration History at Boston College (1988). Beginning in 1984 he taught for 36 years in the Department of History and Political Science at Saint Joseph's College of Maine. Mike retired in May 2020 and now holds the honorary title of Professor Emeritus.

His research has focused on Irish and Irish-American history and the labor movement in Ireland and America. In 2004, the University of Maine Press published his edited collection of essays, *They Change Their Sky: The Irish in Maine*. Along with Dr. Kevin Stoehr of Boston University, he co-edited another collection of essays, *John Ford in Focus: Essays on the Filmmaker's Life and Work* published by McFarland in 2006. In 2010, the University Press of Florida published the book largely based on his Boston College dissertation, *Seated by the Sea: The Maritime History of Portland, Maine, and Its Irish Longshoremen*. In the summer of 2016 he completed a documentary film, *Building Bridges: Connections between Maine's Governor Joseph Brennan and Senator George Mitchell*.

In October of 2016, Mike was honored by receiving the Claddagh Award by the Maine Irish Heritage Center in recognition of his long-time promotion of Irish history and culture in Maine. During each of three previous sabbatical leaves from Saint Joseph's College, he was pleased to offer three history courses for the Semester at Sea program on its around-the-world voyages in Spring 2004, Spring 2011, and Fall 2017, and he is scheduled to sail again in Spring 2023 along with his life partner and *anam* cara, Becky Hitchcock. He still resides on his beloved Munjoy Hill.